An Excerpt:

There was a fifteen minute break between classes. Since the two buildings were right next to each other, that was plenty of time for me to browse EYEnet. My primary question regarded the old man's warning that I'd fail the scan. I focused on the blog from my friend in high school—the one whose sister failed.

According to Galina's posts, she'd been afraid of failure early on, and on the day of the Health Scan, she'd made another post reiterating the same fear. She'd been having hallucinations that liquids would shape themselves from images in her thoughts, and she was sure she had theophrenia.

It'd been almost a year since Galina left, but I wasn't sure how long the recovery effort lasted. I checked the last active day she was on her account. There was nothing since the day of her scan.

I checked other blogs, searching for any references to fear of failure. One girl thought she could fly. Another guy swore he could read his professor's mind. All signs of advanced delusions, and in each case, they didn't return.

Three years passed. Five. Nothing.

A chill ran through me. The old man said to try controlling vines and grass. That was crazy. Impossible. And yet . . . I'd felt that stem move. I'd *seen* it move.

My phone chimed a one-minute warning before class. Students stirred and finished their conversations, and I stared at the small screen of my phone. Only one person, out of the entirety of blogs I'd found, had ever come back.

STEPHANIE AND ISAAC FLINT

DISTANT
HORIZON

INFINITAS PUBLISHING

Connect with the Authors

Blog: http://sbibb.wordpress.com
Facebook: https://www.facebook.com/infinitaspublishing/

Visit our website to subscribe to our newsletter!
http://www.infinitaspublishing.com
https://distanthorizonbooks.wordpress.com/

Copyright 2016 by Stephanie Flint and Isaac Flint
Formatting and cover design by Stephanie Flint
Cover art stock images from Dreamstime and Depositphotos
Edited by Liz Ellis

ISBN: 1539128024
ISBN-13: 978-1539128021

CHAPTER
ONE

The first time I flushed adominogen, the oblong capsule tumbled from my hand and bounced off the bathroom sink, once, twice, then fell into the toilet with a finalizing *plop*.

Gone.

I waited all day for someone to ask why I didn't report accidentally losing my pill. But no one did, and I didn't have any of the hallucinations that the health officials said I would have if I didn't take it. Instead, the world around me felt so much more . . . alive. My attention improved, not that it was bad to begin with, and I could think clearly. Be more efficient.

After that, I stopped taking the pill. I graduated high school and started my first year of college—no sign of any hallucinations or crazy delusions that come with being infected by theophrenia. But when our hall advisor announced that the annual Health Scan would take place in two days, I panicked.

I needed three things to graduate: excellent grades, as many efficiency points as possible, and to pass the scan. It wasn't often someone failed, but it did happen. One of my friends in high school had a sister who failed—Galina. She took the scan at the clinic downtown, and Special Forces escorted her away, all while assuring everything would be fine.

I didn't want to end up like her, so right after the announcement, I took the pill. It was like throwing a clear, plastic tarp over my world. I felt like an unbalanced gyroscope and I spent half the day in the bathroom, sick to my stomach. But I couldn't go to the doctor for the symptoms. Not taking the pill was an international offense.

The next day—today—I shuffled around a bathroom stall, fighting to extract an orange pill bottle from my backpack. For the love of efficiency—the stupid thing had dropped between my textbooks. I shoved the books aside, snagged the bottle, and tucked a pill into my palm. I didn't need it skittering across the floor where someone might notice.

My phone beeped and I dropped the pill.

The plop echoed and the toilet flushed automatically. The pill swirled to its watery demise. The toilet gurgled, and the water rippled in the bowl.

Well, I *had* considered taking the pill, but that wasn't happening now. I stared at the toilet a moment longer, then hoisted my backpack onto my shoulder and froze halfway out the stall door. A woman wearing all black stood between me and the sinks. The red, rising sun half-cog of E-Leadership was stitched across her left shoulder sleeve, and though she wasn't wearing her visor, the sight sent a jolt of terror through me.

Special Forces. If she'd heard the plop . . .

She glanced at the orange pill bottle in my hand and raised an eyebrow. "Everything all right?"

I nodded too quickly. "Yeah—I forgot to go to the bathroom before I left my room."

She scowled. "Aren't you late to your morning meeting?"

I stared at her, my whole body shaking. Of *course* I was late, but I wasn't going to tell her that. I fumbled for something to say, but she shook her head and sighed before I could speak.

"Freshmen," she muttered. "You need to get your act together if you plan to get anywhere in life. You can start by washing your hands."

I rushed to the sink and dropped the pill bottle on the counter.

"The Community is safe," she said.

"The Community is secure," I replied. What was Special Forces doing here?

She crossed her arms in the mirror, her eyes firmly on the pill bottle. "The Community is efficient."

I wasn't sure if I remembered to say, "It is our duty," before I snatched the bottle from the sink and dashed out. The hall blurred around me and my sneakers thumped the tile as I sprinted from the bathroom. I stuffed the bottle into my backpack. Maybe Ivan would be late to the morning meeting. Just for once, he could be late. Not just me.

Not just —

I flung the glass doors open to the lounge, skidding as the roomful of students stopped listening to the morning announcements to give me a curious stare. Lance gave me an accusatory "where were you?" glare while Sam — college gossip — cocked her head, interested in my evident demise. Because, of course, Ivan wasn't late.

No one said a word. The heater rattled softly as it blew air through the vents along the windows. The words "Safety, Security, and Efficiency" framed the smooth stone wall behind Ivan, while a lone screen hanging near the windows flashed silent reminders. "Take the pill! Theophrenia kills!" and "Are you seeing something strange? Save a life — get your Health Scan today!"

Ivan cleared his throat. He was tall and slender, dressed in the crisp gray uniform of a hall advisor. At twenty, he was only a couple years older than me, but he was prepping for E-Leadership. *Not* the guy I wanted to mess with, especially after being late to all but one of my classes yesterday. He waited as I slid into the only empty chair and pulled my backpack into my lap. The books settled unevenly, but their closeness offered some comfort.

Ivan made a notation on his tablet. "You're late. I'll have to deduct efficiency points from your record." He looked up at me and his forehead wrinkled with concern. "Everything all right?"

"I'm fine!" I clutched my backpack, speaking too fast to sound innocent. "I was just worried about the Health Scan and didn't get any sleep. I had a nightmare that I failed and security was chasing me."

The monitor near the windows flashed to a mug shot of a man with dark circles under his eyes. Underneath, the subtitles ran a story I'd read a hundred times. The man had killed his family because he didn't take the Health Scan and theophrenia made him think he could control fire. We'd all been forced to watch a documentary of the old news coverage as kids, and some images just *didn't* go away. I shuddered. The man had burned his family alive. That's what the plague—theophrenia—could do. Make a person go crazy. See things that weren't there. Hear voices or act on terrible impulses. My father's parents had died during the plague years. What had they seen? Anything?

What if I started seeing things, too?

I clamped my hands around my backpack straps, but Sam giggled, oblivious to my thoughts. She twirled her fingers through her curls. "Don't worry, I'm sure you'll do fine. Besides, you aren't supposed to run *away* from security. They're the ones who help you." She started to lay a sympathetic hand on my shoulder, but withdrew when I glared at her. She'd probably borrowed that gesture from some video of Lady Black, or maybe from reading *How to Behave like a Proper Leader*, a textbook for the one class I'd permanently dropped.

"Sam's right," Ivan agreed. "Security is here to help." He turned his attention to the rest of the students. "As a reminder, tomorrow afternoon is this year's Health Scan. Be on time so that everything runs efficiently." He shot me a warning glare before addressing the rest of the room. "That's all the news I have for today. The Community is safe."

"The Community is secure," we replied automatically. "The Community is efficient. It is our duty."

Dismissed, the other students filed from the lounge and into the hall. I must have been later than I thought. Normally I got to the meetings on time, but after being sick yesterday, I had a hard time getting to sleep last night. I hadn't lied. I really *did* have nightmares of security guards chasing me around campus, pelting me with white adominogen pills and Health Scan fliers. The whole dream sounded ridiculous now, but it had been terrifying while I slept.

I waited for the crowd to pass until my best friend, Lance Mechnikov, came up beside me. He waited until we were behind everyone else, then lowered his voice so that I was the only one who could hear him. "You know, Jen, I heard of a guy who got stuck working road crew because he was absent too often."

"I'm feeling better, okay?" I forced a smile, though I was still jittery from my encounter with the Special Forces agent. "Let's get food."

Lance patted my shoulder. "Sure. We can talk after breakfast."

The bright blue LEDs in the downstairs cafeteria glinted off the polished stone walls, making them shine. Though most pre-Community buildings had been burned to prevent further spread of the plague, I understood why E-Leadership made the effort to keep this one. The craftsmanship was amazing; the seams where the stones had been placed were hardly visible. I'd only noticed because I'd found a tiny bit of ivy creeping from a crack in the corner of the building where I liked to study.

We dropped our backpacks at a nearby table and took our place in line. The smell of egg burritos, complete with tangy salsa, wafted through the cafeteria. Apple juice drizzled into the glasses of students who were already ahead of us. If it wasn't for the Health Scan tomorrow and already being late to the first meeting, this day would almost be normal.

"Jenna! Lance!"

Tim, a sandy-haired guy, pushed his way through the breakfast crowd, a backpack hanging loosely over one shoulder. He fished a tablet from his pocket, breathless. "Did you hear? They're doing the Health Scan—"

"Yeah, we've heard." I accepted my plate from the server. It was warm from sitting beside the heating elements. "Ivan told us yesterday."

Tim paused, then followed us to our usual table. "You already knew?"

"She worried herself sick." Lance twisted his lips and glanced at me, but it wasn't my fault I'd gotten sick. Not exactly.

"What are *you* worried about?" Tim protested. "I'm the one whose pills have been missing for a week!"

Lance held up his fingers. "Four days. You lost your pills four days ago."

"*Almost* a week! What happens if the scan doesn't register that I've been taking them? What if I fail? What if —"

"They would've given you replacement pills if it was that big a deal," Lance said. "Think about it."

"But how do I *know*? My grandmother died in the plague. What if I'm a carrier?" He scooted into a chair at our table.

Lance and I exchanged glances. Neither of our parents wanted to talk about our grandparents. Few did. Theophrenia had wiped out half the world's population. Who wanted to remember that?

I shifted uncomfortably. If the disease was still out there, even in the slightest, I might carry it and accidentally infect others.

"Your parents were fine." Lance nudged Tim with his plate. "You've only been off the pills for a week. Like Miss Worry-wart over here" —he glared at me— "you'll pass."

Tim scowled, then scuttled toward the breakfast line with his tablet. I poked my fork at my burrito, but I'd lost my appetite. The other students around the room chatted as if the Health Scan wasn't a big deal. But why would they worry? They took the pills.

"Lance—" I looked up hesitantly. "Have you heard anything from Galina?"

He sighed. "You're really worried about this, aren't you?"

"Well *duh*. We need the scan to graduate."

"You take the pills, right? You'll be fine." He smiled. "Galina was an odd case."

"Did she come back?"

His smile faltered. "I'm not sure. You were closer to her than I was."

My chest constricted. How long was the treatment supposed to take? If theophrenia was supposed to be dead—or dormant, at least—how did Galina fail? Had her failure been a precautionary measure?

I glanced around the room. A Special Forces agent sat at a table near the wall. Security guards I was used to. But Special Forces? I'd never seen any agents on campus before. It felt like a sign of impending doom.

The agent paused from his breakfast and looked up, as if he realized he was being watched, and I quickly returned my attention to my burrito.

A moment later, Tim returned to the chair beside me and sat his plate on the table. He twisted his fingers in the chain of the light bulb efficiency charm around his neck, opened his mouth to speak, then paused. "So, Jenna . . . Do you think you might be able to talk to Sam for me and see if she's going to community service tomorrow evening?" He talked so fast that his words muddled and I almost didn't catch what he said. "If I could get a date, it would take my mind off the pills." He smiled, his blue eyes wide and hopeful.

"I'm not really that good at talking to her," I said hesitantly.

"Please? I'd owe you a huge favor."

I glanced to where Sam sat with her group. They giggled and pointed to her phone. She was probably showing them a picture of her mangy cat, Little Beastie, the photograph I'd seen enough times in biology class to recognize the blur of pixels from a distance.

She flipped a blond curl over her shoulder, laughing a little too loudly, then whispered something to one of the girls, who nodded vigorously. She pocketed her phone and headed our direction.

Tim's eyes went wide. "*Well?*"

"Sure," I mumbled. "I'll see what I can do."

Sam joined us beside the table, her hands clasped behind her back as she cozied up to Lance. She had tucked her yellow shirt into her pale blue slacks to reveal more of her form than usual, as if she were trying to look like a member of E-Leadership. "I'm going to community service at the gardens tomorrow," she said. "Do you have a partner yet?"

Lance's cheeks flushed red. "Jenna, we're still good for tomorrow, right?"

I gave Sam as big a smile as I could muster. Beside me, Tim's eyes widened. "Of course," I replied, then looked toward Sam. "But Tim doesn't have a partner."

Sam gave Lance a baleful pout. "Uh, sure." She flashed a halfhearted smile at Tim. "I'll see you then." She waved and returned to her friends, who all patted her back and said their disappointed apologies.

"*Thank you,*" Lance mouthed. Tim punched the air, gleeful in our unplanned success, and I suspected he would be posting this to his EYEnet account later. At least it would give him something to distract his mind.

If only I had a good distraction, too.

Tim might not have taken the pills for a week, but I hadn't taken them for six months.

CHAPTER
TWO

Brisk October air snapped against my cheeks. Gray clouds obscured an even grayer sky, casting a dull shadow across the courtyard and the stone buildings, which loomed overhead with their tall domes and steep, towering columns.

I always admired the imposing structures because they had survived the plague. So many things hadn't. But these bits of history I could touch with my fingertips: statues worn smooth with time, their copper turned green from rain, and best of all, the ivy that snuck through the cracks of a time-ravaged campus.

Lance and I were headed for our first morning class when a low, steady drone rumbled overhead. Lance yanked my sleeve. "Look!"

A well-decorated airship peeked through the heavy clouds. Brass, gold, and bronze ornamental railing adorned its gondola and complimented the high, arched windows. Elegant frames decorated the rotors with artistic flourishes. The symbol on its side was the Lady of the Cog: a crimson half-cog rising like a sun, embellished with the silhouette of a lady perched across the spoke-like rays.

My breath caught in my throat. The only people who used the Lady of the Cog belonged to International E-Leadership—the highest-ranking officials of the Community. Maybe Lady Winters was paying us a visit. She was one of the few leaders actually worth the speeches she gave. As

Head of Efficiency, she made sure the Health Scans were thorough and that our international laboratories advanced. Maybe she was coming to tell us that she had made an advance against the plague, and I wouldn't have to worry about the Health Scan anymore.

"That's Commander Rick's airship!" Lance grinned, his cheeks rosy from the wind.

I raised an eyebrow. "The commander?"

"Maybe he's coming to visit. Let's get to class — we might find out more there!" He dragged me down the sidewalk through the early crowd. Once inside, we took our seats in the second row. The first row was already filled — apparently in similar anticipation.

Professor Dragomirov smiled at everyone's enthusiasm and put an image of the seventy-year-old commander on the giant touch screen at the front of the classroom. The chatter quieted as she spread her hands along the wrinkles in her uniform and puffed out her chest with pride.

"Tomorrow, Commander Rick is delivering a speech to our university regarding the upcoming Health Scan. Be advised, I will assign extra efficiency points to those who can secure an interview with the commander and produce a two-page report regarding his efforts in the security and efficiency of our modern society."

More chatter erupted at the news. Lance grinned and nudged my shoulder. "It's your lucky day."

Lucky? If I accidentally let slip that I didn't take the pills around the commander, I would not only be booted out of college, but out of the Community.

"Miss Nickleson?"

I jerked to attention at my name. Professor Dragomirov tapped the screen beside her. On it was an image of a tower with a gleaming set of windows. The whole thing was shaped like an absurdly unsafe letter "F."

I blinked. "Yes?"

"Where was the final rebel base in Australia located when Commander Rick ended the resistance against the Community?"

Two locations popped into my head at the mention of Australia, and I knew Sydney wasn't it.

"The Northern Territory?" I suggested. Hopefully she didn't want the name of the actual town.

The professor smiled, switching the image on the touch screen to reveal a map. "Correct. Located near what used to be Birdum, Australia, the tower and its surrounding city thrived from those who threatened the Community's security."

She went on to repeat the same history lesson we'd heard since primary school: how our founding father, Lord Black, died infiltrating that tower, and how Commander Rick took his place, stomped out the Oriental Alliance and the remaining rebellions, declared world peace, and became the living embodiment of the Community and its virtues.

Nice resume, if I hadn't heard it a dozen times before. I would've preferred that we spent our class learning something *new*, like who developed the treatment for theophrenia. I glanced at my book, then at the professor. She was paying more attention to her lecture than to the rest of the class, so I flipped to the back of the book, searching the index for "t" until I found theophrenia listed with a dozen page numbers.

I already knew that the first known treatment for theophrenia came shortly after EYEnet's formation and that once the Community was established in 2027, the treatment was made routine. Occasional outbreaks of the disease—like the one that killed my grandparents—were common. While most of the book had information I'd read before, it added that Lady Bridget Winters had a hand in creating the most recent treatment—the one which effectively contained the threat in 2065.

A few pages later, I found the answer to my question. Apparently, Lady Winters' predecessor, Dr. Sanders, had developed adominogen with funding from international E-Leadership—the original founders of EYEnet. The book went on to discuss the Community's rise across the globe, but offered little else regarding the treatment.

I frowned and rested my cheek against my knuckles. Theophrenia was supposed to be dormant, but the book said the plague was only contained. That explained how Galina failed the scan. But most diseases only needed a single vaccination to offer a lifetime of immunity, so why did we take the pills on a daily basis? Did the pills have to be adjusted for various strains of the disease?

I flipped to the next passage, only half-listening as Professor Dragomirov went on about Commander Rick's military prowess. It was thanks to his leadership that theophrenia was contained five years after he took power. He understood how people with theophrenia thought, and he personally assembled the best teams to seek out the last rebel hideouts. Despite my grandparents' preference not to talk about their past, I'd managed to weasel a few pre-Community stories from them. Their tales about those who were infected mostly ended in chaos and destruction. The infected were paranoid and hard to catch. Crazy. They thought they could command the elements, and often took extreme measures to try manifesting their beliefs. They'd light themselves on fire, leap from tall buildings to prove they could fly . . .

I closed the book as the professor wrapped up her lecture. There was nothing about why we took the pill daily. The book was only a history book, and all it told me was the same lesson I'd heard since my year four teacher explained that E-Leadership created peace in the world, and that we should all be thankful the days of the plague were over.

"Come on, Jenna — this is perfect. You need the points; I get a good name in, and if the commander remembers me when I graduate, he might recommend me to international Special Forces!" With a smooth swipe of his hand, Lance pushed the straggling strands of his brown hair from his eyes and then brushed his shirt free of wrinkles. I took a step back, eyeing him cautiously. Lance stood straighter, more proper than before.

"Well, what do you think?" he asked. "Think I'll make a good impression?"

"You look . . . nice," I said halfheartedly. "I'm sure he'll consider you." Lance beamed. "Awesome!"

"Yeah, awesome," I mumbled. I shouldered my backpack uneasily as Lance headed for his security class. He could probably get into a regional team and be charged with the wonderful task of protecting gossipy leaders, but regional agents were stationed all over the world. If he got recruited, I might never see him again.

I hunched my shoulders and hurried to calculus. I could almost swear the agents wandering around campus were watching me. Throughout class, when I *should* have been focusing on logarithms, all I could think about was the agents' dark visors, their stern postures, and how they were tasked with protecting the Community against all kinds of threats, including theophrenia.

I pictured the agents escorting Galina into the back of the van. What if I never saw her again? What if she couldn't be cured?

Needless to say, I bombed the calc test.

I returned to my dorm room, dejected, and switched my materials to the *Basics of Agronomy and Horticulture*. At least this was a class I enjoyed. When I lived at my parents' house, I spent what free time I had in the backyard or the community garden cultivating herbs and vegetables. Whenever I was worried about how I'd do on my core graduation tests, gardening was the most efficient way for me to relax.

I trailed my fingers through the leaves of the potted spider plant on my desk. If only plants could understand people. Plants wouldn't tell anyone about not taking the pills, or failing a computer class, or —

The stem of a spiderette wrapped around my finger and wriggled beneath my palm. I yelped and yanked my hand away.

The plant just *moved*.

Not only that, but spiderette stems were stiff, not malleable like a vine. They shouldn't be able to wrap around my finger even if plants *could* move of their own accord.

I stared at the plant, but it seemed the same as before. Just a normal stem in a normal pot.

I swallowed hard. I could *not* be hallucinating. Not this close to the Health Scan. I grabbed my bag and stuffed the books inside, then rushed out the door. I was stressed and needed lunch; that was all.

Downstairs, the spicy aroma of sloppy joes mingled with the antiseptic stench of cleaning supplies used in the cafeteria. My stomach churned. Bad idea coming to the cafeteria. Really bad idea. I should've just taken the pill and been done with it. Maybe I would've gotten accustomed to the lack of focus. I could still go back and take the pill. Maybe—

I stopped short at the lunch table.

"You okay?" Lance stabbed his fork into a half-eaten sandwich. "You're pale. Maybe you should see the nurse."

"No!" I gripped the loose ends of my backpack tight. Lance gave me a puzzled look. I shut my mouth, then set my backpack in its proper place under the chair. "It's just . . . I failed the calc test."

He cocked his head with a knowing grin. "Sure you did—you won't have the results until after the Health Scan. You know, you're starting to sound like Tim." His smirk turned into an amused smile. "Want me to get you a plate?"

"Go ahead," I said, and he left me alone at the table. I traced the spot where the stem had wrapped around my finger. My blood pounded in my ears, mingling with the messy roar of the cafeteria. The stress of the upcoming scan was getting to me—bad. Hallucinations were the first sign of theophrenia. If someone had theophrenia, they'd have hallucinations and delusions of grandeur, and eventually, they'd die. But theophrenia was supposed to be a thing of the past. Contained.

"Jenna?" An elbow brushed my shoulder and I jumped. Tim stood beside me, holding a plate of steamed broccoli. "Are you okay?"

Not really, no. But I couldn't tell him the real reason I was worried. "I bombed the calc test," I said.

Tim cringed and took his seat. "Ouch." He stirred his fork through the broccoli, wrinkling his nose and making a face. But I'd never seen him put something back if it was good for him, and he took a bite. "Lance said you can make up yesterday's points."

"Maybe, if I get an audience."

Tim pulled his tablet from his pocket and sat it beside the plate, then flipped through the screens with a swipe of his finger. He showed me a photograph of the commander next to his transport ship. "Do you think he'll autograph this for me?"

I nodded weakly. I never did understand autographs, though most E-Leadership members were happy to give them. Lady Winters never signed them, though, and when Master Matoska made a rare appearance, he only did so if the signing was on his schedule.

A plate of food slid in front of me. "I got you extra broccoli," Lance said.

Warmth flooded my chest. Unlike Tim, I actually liked broccoli—and Lance knew me well.

I smiled. "Thanks."

ॐ

After lunch, I excused myself early to slip outside. I had a few minutes before the next meeting, plenty of time for a walk to clear my head. The sun stole through the clouds in the courtyard and lent warmth to the chilly afternoon. Students swarmed the flagpole at the center of campus, waving tablets and books in the fresh air.

A tell-tale safari hat rode across the crowd and my breath caught in my throat. Unlike Lady Black, who often used her revealing outfits to stand out from the rest of us, Commander Rick did not flaunt his "attractiveness." He always went for regal attire—except for that safari hat he always wore—and his word was absolutely, positively *good*. If he said he would do something, we could bet our efficiency points he'd do it—not that betting was in any way efficient.

I took a step back, my chest tight. I wasn't ready to ask the commander questions. What if I got the interview, but they had to do the scan first?

I turned to take the long way around campus, but nearly collided with a confident woman as she passed me on the sidewalk. She nimbly stepped aside, then glanced at me, surprised. Wisps of dark hair tickled her face, and her green eyes were complimented by the antique, diamond and brass pendant she wore on her chest, the same kind of pendant members of international E-Leadership wore.

"Lady Black?" I stared at her, dumbfounded. She had to have been cold. Her dress was impractical—it twisted and shimmered in a harsh gust of wind, and her skin was pale where the silky black dress revealed far more of her chest than normal citizens would ever show. She opened her mouth to speak, but I skittered away before any words could be exchanged.

I didn't check to see if anyone had seen us before I ducked into the closest building. Once inside, I pressed my hands against the stone wall and caught my breath. Too close. What if I'd said something about the pills in a moment of panic? I half expected an agent to come waltzing through the glass doors and ask why I hadn't reported my earlier hallucination.

I took a deep breath, ignoring the puzzled stares of passing students. Though I couldn't shake the feeling that someone was watching, no agent came to question me. I waited for my nerves to calm, and then headed back to the dorms for the afternoon meeting.

CHAPTER
THREE

After the incident with Lady Black, I had this constant, nagging feeling that *someone* stood right behind me, watching me. Stalking me. If I really did have the plague, then I could only guess that this was the onset of a delusion that I was somehow important enough to warrant special attention. Or maybe I was just paranoid; the Health Scan *was* less than twenty-four hours away.

My bedroom door rattled and I looked up from my biology book. Faint, golden light traced my desk, highlighting the leaves of my plant and trailing along the edge of my bookcase. As I stared at it, the doorknob rattled again, followed by a new, chinking sound of metal. I scooted from my chair and checked the door's peephole, but no one was there.

Maybe the air pressure was playing with the hinges. I opened the door and stuck my head into the hall. A couple students passed by, but they'd been too far back to even touch the door.

I sighed. I wasn't getting any studying done here anyway, so I grabbed my coat from my bed and headed downstairs with my biology book. An agent nodded to me on my way out. I forced a smile before scurrying around the corner of the building.

Golden light seeped through the clouds, highlighting the tops of trees. Sidewalk lamps flickered on, each a pale, cold blue against the evening sky. The harsh wind carried the warm smell of soup from the cafeteria across campus.

I pulled my jacket tight and went straight to my usual reading spot. A tiny bit of ivy clung to the wall, out of sight from maintenance, and I tickled its leaves. Such a cute plant. I nestled onto the stone bench nearby, then set my book in my lap and tried to absorb myself in my studies.

The sky was nearly dark when an elderly man cleared his throat, interrupting my train of thought. I glanced up from the book. "Can I help you?"

"Would you mind if I shared the bench with you?" he asked.

There was plenty of room, though why he'd want to sit *here*, I wasn't sure. Given the sharp business attire and his trim, salt-and-pepper beard, he probably belonged to the business class of E-Leadership. Maybe he was here to speak in a lecture. His face was tired, and he leaned against a simple cane, so I scooted over. "I don't think I've seen you around here before," I noted.

"I'm just visiting."

I frowned. He didn't elaborate, so I tried again to focus on my book. Just as the chapter started to get interesting, the old man suddenly made a motion as if to tug at his hair. "Plan on joining E-Leadership?"

Hair? E-leadership? It took me a moment to realize that he was referring to my hair being dyed in the same manner as a few E-Leadership members. "Oh, no — I accidentally over-bleached it."

If "accidentally" meant purposely forgetting to look at the clock before starting the process . . . then yes, accidentally. It didn't look half-bad, and it wasn't one of the same natural colors that everyone else had. I'd cut my hair too short intentionally, just below my chin, and last I checked, my hair looked near-white. The style wasn't *technically* regulation — I'd gotten a firm reprimanding from Ivan to go to a hair dresser next time — but it wasn't so bad as to merit a deduction of efficiency points, either.

The old man rested against his cane, casting a wayward look to the end of the alley. "Good," he murmured. "It's hard to join E-Leadership if you fail the scan."

I shifted uncomfortably. "Why would I fail the scan?"

He touched the bit of ivy growing from the wall and I recoiled. The ivy shivered under his hand, shaking as much as I was. I stared at it, shocked.

A worried smile crossed the old man's face. "You've been hallucinating, haven't you?"

I shook my head, trying to get the words out of my throat so I could deny the accusation, but they wouldn't come.

"Don't worry, Jenna. I see it, too. But your hesitance makes you look guilty." He lowered his hand from the vine. "You need to speak faster. Otherwise you'll be caught."

I closed my book slowly. The chill of the stone seeped into my legs. How did he know my name? I needed to get out of here, but if he knew I didn't take the pill, he might tell security —

"You don't recognize me, do you?" He clasped his hands overtop his cane. "I know we've never met, but your father could have at least kept a picture of me."

A gust of wind swept though the alley and rustled my jacket. "What do my parents have to do with this?"

"I'm your grandfather," he replied matter-of-factly.

"Impossible." I scooted to the edge of the bench. There were agents all over this campus. All I had to do was scream and they'd come running.

Or *I* could run. I was good at running.

"Please let me continue," he urged, and an overwhelming desire to listen flooded through me. His voice rose in a hurried pitch. "You're in danger. You have to trust me. If you don't—"

"Trust you? Are you kidding? I don't *have* to trust anyone!" I pointed to his cane. "For all I know, you've got a sword in there!"

The man's eyes darkened. "It would be foolish of me to come unarmed." His free hand pushed back his jacket, revealing a pistol at his side. My jaw dropped.

"Jenna, listen to me. I'm not going to hurt you." He reached his hand for me but I staggered off the bench. "What you saw wasn't a hallucination. Theophrenia is a lie to conceal various powers. You're a plant elemental. You can control plant growth. Because of that, you won't pass the Health Scan."

"Plants?" I whispered. Voices shouted in the distance.

"Listen . . ." He stood quickly, pausing as he glanced toward the voices. "Walk with me."

I clutched my book to my chest and stood nervously. "Where to?"

"Just walk." He motioned the opposite direction of the voices. I followed, and he drew closer. He kept his head low, yet managed to retain his confident posture, as if we were just talking. "Try controlling a vine or grass. Just try it. See what happens."

"What's supposed to happen?" I asked. "I can't mentally control plants. That's impossible."

"Not impossible. Not when you're a plant elemental."

We came to the end of the building and I faltered. The old man had led me behind the dormitory to the side with few windows and only the basic security lights. Unlike the main path, this alley was already dark.

I stopped walking, and the old man turned to look at me. "Jenna, please. We don't have much time."

In the distance, boots thumped against the cobblestone path. My heart pounded in my ears. I edged backward. "I'd rather stay in public."

A female voice sounded behind the old man. "Pops, we've got to go."

I spun, trying to see the source, but the alley was empty except for me, the shadowy space between buildings, and the old man.

"Please—" he begged, grabbing my arm. His fingers dug into my skin. "Come with me. I may not have another chance to help you." For a strange, surreal moment, he disappeared, and so did I. Looking down, I couldn't see my hands or my book. I felt his hand grip my arm, but he wasn't there.

I yanked my arm away, then swung my book where the old man's ribs should've been. The book hit *something,* but the grunt that sounded was female and the old man reappeared.

"A textbook? *Really?*" the female voice protested.

Two security guards rounded the corner as I stumbled back, swinging my book in case whoever I hit was still around. The old man spotted the guards, his eyes wide. He stretched his hand toward me. "Jenna, come on!"

He seemed so determined. I needed to hear him out. I needed—

A bullet cracked the air. Red liquid bloomed on the upper arm of his jacket, and the female voice cursed. The guards turned, searching for the source of the voice, but the alley was still empty of anyone except for the old man and me—

It finally dawned on me that the old man was bleeding. I rarely saw blood, except when someone injured themselves during track. It was mesmerizing in a horrible way. The old man clutched his arm and hunched to the ground. He muttered a curse word I hadn't heard since Dad dropped a desk from the living room onto his toe.

The guard, one of Lance's professors, cocked his gun for a second shot. "You are under arrest."

A few students gathered at the end of the alley to watch the commotion. I slipped between the old man and the guards. What if he really was my grandfather? He looked familiar.

"Who is he?" I asked.

"Keep back." The guard motioned to the pistol at the old man's side. "This man is dangerous."

I eyed the blood on the old man's arm. He gritted his teeth, his free hand pressed against the wound. Goosebumps rose on my neck. Despite that moment where I couldn't see myself, and the creepy alley, something about his insistence and determination to talk made me want to know *why.* "Where are you taking him?" I asked.

"The coolers. Stand aside while we handle this."

I ran my fingers along the little dents in the textbook's smooth surface. "He said I'm in danger."

The guard raised his chin. "Probably has dementia, too."

Considering how the old man had talked to me, they'd probably execute him on charges of delusions of grandeur. He was too old to be worth the time for treatment.

One guard moved toward the old man while the other came and stood beside me. "You need to come with us for questioning," he told me.

"Wait—what?" I stared at him, horrified. "But I didn't do anything!"

The guard's eyes narrowed and he clamped his hand around my wrist. "You were talking to an unidentified man who shouldn't be on campus. Anything you know about him may prove useful to our investigation."

The old man didn't struggle despite the indignant look he gave the guards as they retrieved something from his pocket and then jabbed a needle into his arm. A moment later, the old man slumped, his eyelids fluttering as he struggled to stay awake.

The guard hefted him up, muttering, "*the Community is safe.*" The second guard turned to me. "Now, Miss Nickleson, I have a few questions I need answered."

"That won't be necessary," a lilting voice interrupted, "though your concern is appreciated."

The old man's eyes widened in horror. "Jenna, she'll trick you! Her power is persuasion. Her power—" He trailed off as he lost to whatever they'd drugged him with.

Lady Black stood behind the guard, her hand resting on his shoulder. Her dress fluttered softly, and the diamond pendant she wore dangled from her neck, glinting in the overhead lights like some oversized identity charm.

What was she doing here?

The guard straightened quickly, his eyes wide. "But, my lady, protocol says—"

"Special Forces has information on this man. He was stalking Miss Nickleson. Now that you have him in custody, he is no longer a threat." She smiled. "Have faith in our system. The Community is safe."

The guard's grip lessened on my arm, then relaxed altogether. "Of course, my lady," he murmured, dazed. "Of course the Community is safe."

"The Community is secure. Why don't you aide your partner with the suspect?" she suggested. "A pair of agents will be along shortly to assist you."

He nodded feverishly, and together the guards braced the old man on their shoulders and dragged him along the path toward the outer road.

I turned to Lady Black. "What did he mean, your power is persuasion?"

"Theophrenia, dear. He's delusional."

"Jenna!" Lance pushed through the crowd and joined me at my side. "Are you all right? What happened?"

I blinked, noticing the huge size of the crowd for the first time. Sam stood between two large, brawny guys. She giddily pointed to her phone as it replayed the evening's event, but the guys looked more in shock than excited. Amidst the crowd, Commander Rick stroked his chin, watching me like I was some sort of prey. The sapphire and brass pendant around his neck sparkled in the bright lights along the building. A silvery pistol gleamed at his side.

The guards might make the Community safe, but . . . "The old man said I was in danger and would fail the Health Scan," I accused the commander. "What did he mean?"

"Relax," Lady Black crooned, brushing my cheek with her gloved hand. "You'll do fine."

As much as I wanted to pull away from her touch, I closed my eyes. She was *safe*. I wanted her to stay with me, to protect me from the old man and theophrenia. Her touch was comforting and secure . . .

"Trust me," she whispered.

I smiled and swayed, dizzy with warmth. Of course I trusted her. She was an international leader. Why *wouldn't* I trust her?

Ivan shooed the other students from the scene. "Thank you, my lady. Commander. The Community is safe." He looked to me. "Why don't you go inside? You'll feel better in the morning."

I murmured affirmation. Lady Black kissed my forehead and stroked her hand through my hair. "Yes, Miss Nickleson. Come along. Perhaps I could keep you company until your nerves have settled?"

My cheeks warmed, but Commander Rick cleared his throat. The lady pouted at him, then whispered goodnight and returned to the path beside him. Together they disappeared into a cluster of Special Forces agents who walked them through the courtyard.

A sullen cold settled over me, dull and hazy from the loss of . . . well . . . I wasn't quite sure.

Lance lifted my chin. "You look tired. Why don't I get you back to your room?"

I shook my head. My nerves tingled, frazzled. For all the leaders' fancy clothes and proper manners, they were like history professors who said the same thing over and over again.

What had the old man said about Lady Black? Persuasion?

I pressed my hands against the cold stone at the edge of the building and watched until the leaders were out of sight.

"Odd," Lance murmured. "That guard shouldn't have let you go."

I glowered at him. "Thanks for the vote of confidence."

"But it's true! He should've had you tested for theophrenia, both you and the old man."

I frowned. Lance was right. It didn't matter that an international leader had given me clearance, the test was protocol. So why hadn't the guards followed it?

Cool blue efficiency lights lit the now-empty path, but those lights didn't eliminate the feeling that I was being left in the dark.

"Come on, Jen," Lance urged softly. He guided me past the onlookers and the maintenance man who had arrived to clean away the blood. The reminder of tonight's incident would be gone by morning.

Very *efficient*.

I crossed my arms. "That old man was trying to talk to me. Warn me about something."

"He was delusional."

"Why come to me then? What made me so special?"

"I don't know. You might be able to find out more tomorrow." Lance pushed me through the glass doors and up the stairs.

"Why couldn't they have told me tonight?"

"It's a security thing."

"So is checking me for theophrenia."

Lance groaned. "I'll see you at tomorrow morning's meeting, okay, Jen?" He stopped in front of my room and nudged my shoulder. "Don't worry too much. I'm next door."

I sighed. "Your sword isn't going to help."

"Why not? I've been practicing. Got to make up for everyone else using guns."

"Think there might be a reason for that?" I glared at him, but couldn't hold back an appreciative smirk. "Guns are more efficient."

"Yeah." He squeezed my hand and poked my cheek. "But it got you to smile." He winked, then disappeared into the adjacent room.

I snorted. Some help *he* was. The conversation just reminded me of all the agents crawling around campus.

I shut the door behind me and dropped my biology book into my backpack, then crawled under the cold sheets. I'd heard of agents using the occasional odd weapon—a sword, a crossbow, a mace—I'd even seen one agent who carried a whip. But most of them used rifles. More efficient, really.

But Lance had his sword that he practiced with in his room, and it was mostly by accident that I knew it was sharpened. One of those little rules we knew the other broke.

I paused. How many agents normally attended the Health Scan?

Two international leaders?

The old man?

I frowned, staring at the sliver of ceiling that was visible in the window's light, then slid out of bed and flipped the light switch. A new, white flower blossomed on the spiderette of my potted plant, but it shouldn't have been blooming; it was night.

I lifted the thin stem and laced it around my finger, careful not to break it. "He said I was a plant elemental," I murmured. But, for the love of the Community, I had no clue what that *meant*. I closed my eyes, picturing the plant moving like it did before lunch.

The stem snaked across my wrist. I gasped and jerked my hand away. People with theophrenia thought they could do strange things, like the guy who thought he could control fire. Doctors even said that people could share in their delusions. But the old man had seen the plant move *before* I said anything.

He knew too much to be some random guy.

I opened my phone, searched through EYEnet for the family database, and then checked the Nickleson family tree.

There I was: Jenna Nickleson, with plain photographs of my parents above me. Mom's parents were both living, and they had their familiar pictures under her profile.

But Dad's parents —

Dr. Nickolai Nickleson; 2006-2051;
Cause of Death: Theophrenia

For all that the old man was considerably older than the picture in the database, the similarities were striking. Dark brown eyes. Same facial structure — and I'd gotten a good look when I'd spoken with him in the alley. If it weren't for being dead, the old man could easily have been my grandfather.

I flopped on my bed and stared at the ceiling. The day's events raced through my mind: the moment I couldn't see myself, the gunshot, Lady Black's weird ability to persuade the guards, the moving plants . . .

There was only one logical explanation.

I had theophrenia.

CHAPTER
FOUR

A little after six in the morning, I pressed my nose to the cold window of my room. Stars twinkled in the navy sky. Special Forces agents strolled across campus, their dark uniforms briefly illuminated by the pale sidewalk lamps before blending again with the gloom.

Since security hadn't scanned anyone who'd come close to the old man, and since the Health Scan was tonight, I doubted it'd matter if I went about my day as usual. Maybe the hallucinations were just stress, not the plague.

Then again, my plant still had its new bloom.

I closed the blinds and hoisted my backpack over my shoulder. Hopefully I was wrong about all this. I headed to the lounge for the morning meeting and Lance gave me a promising thumbs-up as I took my seat. I'd actually arrived on time; Ivan entered the lounge a few seconds after.

"Good morning." He jumped into his seat and folded his legs underneath him. Funny how he could be so relaxed with the Health Scan tonight. It was like he was going for Lady Black's style.

"Last night's security issue has been resolved," he said, though everyone already knew. I'd checked EYEnet before I flushed the pill. The blogs were covered with speculation, although there was no footage. I'd been hoping to compare pictures, but even Sam's blog hadn't yielded any useful clips, and I *knew* she'd been recording the spectacle.

"Jenna?"

The whole room was silent, waiting for a response to a question I hadn't even heard. Ivan narrowed his eyes, like he was supposed to be watching me closer than usual.

He probably was.

"What was the best and worst of your day yesterday?" he repeated.

I fiddled with the wooden arm of the chair and traced the spots where the pale, faux leather had been nailed to the frame. "The worst was that they wouldn't give me any straight answers. I want to know why the old man was stalking me. He said I was in danger, and that I would fail the scan, and I want to know why he thinks that."

"Jenna, he was delusional." Ivan paused, hesitant. "Would you like to talk in private?"

"Actually, I'd like to speak with the old man if you can arrange a visit."

Ivan frowned. "That would be unwise. He isn't safe."

I glared at him. What wasn't "safe" was that Lady Black hadn't scanned me right after the incident. "I go to history class and it's the same story about how Commander Rick is the perfect world leader and how he brought world peace and safety. But if the Community is safe, why can't I speak to the guy?"

"To protect you, and keep the Community safe," Ivan reiterated softly. "Here—I'll assign you a pass to the counselor. You've had a traumatic experience."

I gritted my teeth. There it was again . . . that "wasn't safe" bit. If I couldn't arrange a meeting with the old man, I'd never learn what he was going to say about the Health Scan—especially if he was convicted before I had a chance to talk with him. And what if the old man *was* my grandfather? I couldn't dismiss the idea that I might have two living grandfathers, instead of just one. What could I learn from him? What could he tell me about the days before the plague?

My phone vibrated. According to Ivan's EYEnote, I was to miss the first half of programming class in order to make a special trip to the counselor. I might have skipped the appointment, but defying an advisor's orders would get me suspended, and I wanted at least *some* chance of returning after I failed the scan.

At breakfast, Lance plucked a napkin from the napkin holder between us. "Are you *trying* to lose efficiency points? You already lost your chance to talk with Commander Rick, and if you're not careful, everyone's going to think you're crazy."

"I'm not crazy! It's just . . . stress. The Health Scan is in a few hours, and I want to know what I'm getting into. I might be infected."

Lance shook his head, smiling. "You'll be fine. Just try not to argue with your superiors, okay?"

"It wasn't an argument."

"What wasn't an argument?" Tim slipped into the seat between us and fiddled with the light bulb charm on his necklace. "What'd I miss?"

"Jenna had an argument with the advisor."

"You argued with Ivan?"

"Relax," I muttered. "It was more of a disagreement than an argument."

Tim stared at me expectantly, but I kept my mouth shut. What I'd say was not what Mr. Perfect Citizen wanted to hear, so I let Lance explain the morning's incident.

"Maybe she really does need to see the counselor," Tim said, then shrunk under my glare.

"Maybe." Lance glanced at me. "But I can only imagine what it'd feel like to have a dead grandparent suddenly show up alive and well. If I were you, I'd arrange a visit directly through security."

That was it! Ivan might not be able to arrange a visit, but *I* could. Then I could talk to the old man and get my answers.

"Then again . . ." Lance frowned. "He'll probably be dead by the time the form goes through. The criminal justice department is efficient. The paperwork . . . not so much. Dad's been arguing for a more efficient filing system ever since he got into office."

"You're *so* optimistic." I rested my cheek against my hand, brooding.

"I'd go to the counselor," Tim said. "If it keeps the Community safe, it's a good thing." He tried to look me in the eyes, but I dropped my gaze.

"Sure, the Community's safe. Except when I'm trying to get answers from the delusional guy who might be my grandfather. The guards didn't even ask me any questions. Lady Black just waltzed in and told them 'everything is fine.' How is a counselor supposed to help me with *that*?"

"It'll be okay," Tim assured me. "The counselors can explain Lady Black's reasons better than we can. Studies show that ninety-eight percent of counselors are efficient at their job."

"What happens to the other two percent?"

Tim blinked, stunned. "Well . . . they're inefficient. They're demoted."

I snorted. Tim had been to the counselor once or twice. Once, he nearly flunked a test and the stress pushed him into drawing all sorts of conclusions about what might be wrong with the education system. Turned out the professor had accidentally assigned the wrong EYEtest to the class, and was later demoted to an office assistant at a different university. I hadn't heard from her since.

"Come on—let's get food," Lance suggested. "Might make you feel better."

I wasn't really hungry, but I humored him and took my place in line.

He nudged my shoulder. "Cheer up. Even if we fail, they'll just send us someplace to cure us. They've got the tech. You're the science major, you should know that."

"Plant biology, not pharmaceuticals. I've got no idea how the pill actually works. Do you?"

"Well . . . no." He twisted his lips and frowned, and I rested on my case through the remainder of our breakfast period.

The counselor's waiting room was painted pale yellow. Several brochures sat in a metal rack on the receptionist's desk. She confirmed my EYEnote through her tablet, selected two brochures to give me, and then offered me a seat, the firm kind found in doctors' offices.

While waiting, I glanced at the brochures: "What to do if you feel insecure," and "How to overcome stressful situations and deal with frustration." The first brochure was worse than the title made it out to be, with cheesy graphics leading to a happy conclusion of two Community citizens who stood confidently beside a smiling, scantily clad leader. The second was a bit better, as it mentioned special breathing techniques. But the rest of it was dedicated to referring to the advice of the counselor and, like the first brochure, had cheesy stick figure sketches.

A few minutes later, the counselor beckoned me to her office. I tossed the brochures into the recycling bin and followed.

"Please, have a seat." The counselor, Miss Karen, according to the plastic name tag pinned to her shirt, motioned to the chair in front of me. "I understand that you had a scare last night. The incident was managed, but your hall advisor says you're still worried." She clasped her hands in her lap.

"The old man said I'd fail the Health Scan, and the guards wouldn't answer any of my questions."

Miss Karen furrowed her eyebrows like Sam did when one of her friends went on about boy troubles. "Could you explain further?"

I sighed and explained my fears of failing the scan, omitting that I didn't take the pill, then told her a modified version of last night's incident.

"Very few students fail the Health Scan," Miss Karen told me gently. "The only danger came from the stalker." She placed her hands on her knees, still smiling. "You're under a lot of stress from your classwork. It's perfectly normal to feel worried. But the Health Scan is an important step in becoming a safe, efficient Community member. You needn't be afraid."

"It'd help if I knew the worst that could happen. What happens if I fail?"

She gave me a pitying look. "I'm afraid the health network doesn't share that information. Patient confidentiality."

"You can't tell me anything? Not even about the generic treatment?" Goosebumps rose on my skin. She should have *some* access to the health network.

"Each case is different." She paused. "Have you considered arranging a visit with the gentleman? You would be in a safe, managed environment, and you might be able to ease your fears. If he's delusional, it should be readily obvious in the way he speaks. I'm sure you're familiar with the symptoms."

"He'll be convicted by the time the forms go through," I said quietly. Between Ivan's refusal to help me arrange a visit and Lance's oh-so-optimistic belief that the old man was probably already dead, I wasn't getting anywhere.

She tapped her chin thoughtfully. "Fill out the forms directly at the security center," she suggested. "They should be able to process the information faster there."

I sat upright. "Really?"

"Certainly. In the meantime, these will help you relax." She smiled and retrieved an orange tube from the cabinet, then tipped the tube and dropped a pill into her hand. After a pause, she added a second one.

I tensed. "I don't need a pill."

"The pills will help," she insisted. "I'll let your advisor know you've had them. He'll watch for side effects. Do you want a glass of water?"

"No, thanks. I'll take them in the lobby." I closed my fingers around the capsules. They felt cold and slick, like adominogen. Only these pills wouldn't make me sick; they'd put me in happy-land. I wouldn't care whether or not my might-be grandfather was executed before I got my answers.

"The Community is safe," the counselor said.

"The Community is secure." I stepped outside before she could say anything else. The bathroom was the next door over and after my personal business was complete, I flushed the capsules. I'd been forced to take these when I took the core graduation test in high school. They'd given everything a cheerful, friendly glow. I'd even flirted with Lance — and decided never to take the offending pills again.

Outside, the chilly air slipped into my jacket. I snapped it shut and huddled near the archway of the history and technology buildings. The pale Community flag cracked hard in the wind, and high above, a tiny, oblong airship reminded me of the leaders' presence.

Across the courtyard, the guard who shot the old man stepped outside the security training building, straightened the cuff on his collar, and nodded politely toward me before heading the opposite direction.

He acted as if nothing had happened. As if everything was fine. As if he hadn't cut me off from the one person who seemed to know anything about the Health Scan.

I hunkered behind the archway and searched out the local security center on my phone. I found instructions to get a taxi, but the Community intentionally put their prisons outside populated areas, and I'd need more than one class period to get there and back. There was no way I could contact the old man before I failed the scan, and then I wouldn't have a chance to arrange the visit.

Shivering, I slipped into the eerily silent hall of the technology building. Faint snippets of lectures and conversations drifted from the classrooms. I stopped at the door farthest down the corridor and attempted to turn the metal lever, but I already knew it'd be locked. So much for returning unannounced.

I knocked, and a young professor pushed the door open. "Do you have a pass?" She arched a stern eyebrow. I half expected her to deduct efficiency points right then, but when I showed her my phone with the message Ivan gave me, she let me enter.

The room was dark as usual. Glowing blue screens highlighted the students' intent faces. I took my seat. The soft tapping of keys continued. I started the program we'd been working on last class period, but a small gray box with a programming quiz popped up onscreen.

I groaned. I'd completely forgotten we were supposed to have a quiz, and because I was late, and everyone else had finished their quizzes, I'd have to take an inevitably harder version to avoid the potential for cheating.

I already had a low score in this class, a pitiful "B," as it was.

"You have a commendable skill with computers, Mister Zaytsev," the professor said, jarring me from my thoughts. She hunched over Tim's bright screen, her face illuminated in harsh blue shadow. Students crowded around the two of them and pushed into each other to see what Tim had done this time.

I paused. Tim had hacked computers before. The last time I did Tim a favor by asking a girl out for him, he hacked her EYEblog account to see if she liked him. Turned out she had no interest, and Tim turned his attention elsewhere.

Maybe he could hack the health network and find out what happened to the people who failed the scan. My next class was Advanced Biology, and I hoped to get an answer from the professor. But if that didn't work, I might not need to visit the old man to understand his warning.

I returned to the timed quiz, but the numbers on my screen jumbled into a maze of prison walls and coding, and my pitiful "B" became an unacceptable "C" as I flunked the quiz.

There was a fifteen minute break between classes. Since the two buildings were right next to each other, that was plenty of time for me to browse EYEnet. My primary question regarded the old man's warning that I would fail the scan. I focused on the blog from my friend in high school—the one whose sister failed.

According to Galina's posts, she'd been afraid of failure early on, and on the day of the Health Scan, she'd made another post reiterating the same fear. She'd been having hallucinations that liquids would shape themselves from images in her thoughts, and she was sure she had theophrenia.

It'd been almost a year since Galina left, but I wasn't sure how long the recovery effort lasted. I checked the last active day she was on her account. There was nothing since the day of her scan.

I checked other blogs, searching for any references to fear of failure. One girl thought she could fly. Another guy swore he could read his professor's mind. All signs of advanced delusions, and in each case, they didn't return.

Three years passed. Five. Nothing.

A chill ran through me. The old man said to try controlling vines and grass. That was crazy. Impossible. And yet . . . I'd felt that stem move. I'd *seen* it move.

My phone chimed a one-minute warning before class. Students stirred and finished their conversations, and I stared at the small screen of my phone. Only one person, out of the entirety of blogs I'd found, had ever come back. He'd undergone some kind of minor surgery and was free to go.

I slipped the phone into my pocket and nervously shouldered my bag, then mingled with the rest of the students who were headed inside. I settled into a second-row desk in the center of the biology room, welcomed by the aroma of fresh soil and the sting of formaldehyde. I took a deep breath, removed my book from its bag, and then set it beside the pens, pencils, and the notebook that would be filled by the end of semester—assuming I was still here.

The professor, a balding, middle-aged man in a pale green uniform, took his place at the front and powered on the touch screen. Several minutes later, after the blue loading bar finally vanished, *The Origins of the Health Scan* flickered onscreen. Given that the history department got all the funds and the fastest tech, and *still* didn't tell us anything interesting, the technology in the biology department was due for an upgrade.

I sank in my chair. Of course, with Commander Rick visiting, it made sense that he'd put funds into something that would fuel his ego. Why couldn't Lady Winters have been the one to visit? Wasn't training future generations to combat theophrenia more important?

The professor cleared his throat and announced that, due to the events of the day, we'd be taking time to examine theophrenia and how science prevented the global extinction of humankind. He went over the basics of bacteria and viruses and explained that we would cover them in-depth next month, then moved on to how adominogen had successfully immunized a majority of the population.

I raised my hand and he paused mid-speech. "Yes, Miss Nickleson?"

"If the majority of the population is immunized, why do we still take the pill? What does it do?"

His head bobbed in what might've been an approving nod. "Good, good. Bacteria, if not properly eradicated, mutates. Such mutations are stronger, livelier, and often more deadly to the host—us. While the majority of theophrenia was eradicated, and indeed, many of us developed a natural immunity, some people may still contract variations of this disease. Some are harmless, while others are considerably more dangerous."

"That's why we take the pill," I suggested, scribbling the note.

"Yes." He smiled, tapping the touch screen for emphasis. The different squiggles of bacteria zoomed in to twice their previous size.

"So what does the pill *do*?"

The professor clicked a button on his remote, advancing a couple slides beyond the current presentation. "The human body naturally has the genetics to prevent theophrenia from taking hold. However, the gene responsible is not always active. Adominogen activates that gene."

I wrinkled my nose. "What happens if someone doesn't take the pill?"

"Theophrenia can infect them. The Health Scan" —he pointed to the presentation— "scans the body to ensure that a full-fledged immunity has been achieved. If so, the patient is free to stop taking adominogen. If not, the person in question must undergo treatment to ensure the safety and efficiency of the Community as a whole."

I clenched the rubber grip of my pen, accidentally drawing a long streak across my notes. I hadn't been taking the pill. That's how I got theophrenia. The immunity hadn't had time to develop.

"What's the treatment?" I asked, trying to keep my voice steady.

He smiled. "The treatment ensures that all bacteria is removed, and it creates an immunity."

"But what *is* it?" I rotated the pen between my fingers. "How long does it take?"

The professor's cheeks creased with wrinkles as he frowned. "Depends on the person. A simple surgical procedure often does the trick."

No. That wasn't right. If it was, why did only one of the twenty-something relevant blogs I checked mention that? Why hadn't the others ever responded?

"And the treatment itself?" I asked. "How does surgery treat bacteria?"

"I am not sure of the exact details," he said gently. "But rest assured, it is efficient. Now, if there are no more questions, we shall proceed." He returned to the lecture, leaving me with half-written notes.

For all the efficiency seals in this place, I felt like a cold draft had seeped into the room and centered on my desk. Maybe I wasn't asking the right questions. Maybe the textbook would have answers.

But the book, like the professor, was vague. "The treatment keeps the Community safe," was all it said. There was nothing about how the treatment worked.

I closed the book's cover, numb. I needed someone to confide in, but I couldn't talk to the officials. I'd be thrown in the coolers, no chance of coming back. But I had to tell *someone*.

I closed my eyes and took a deep breath. Lance was my best friend, and with his help, I might be able to convince Tim to hack the health network and get my answers.

I was doomed to fail the scan, but at least I could know what I was getting into.

CHAPTER
FIVE

The moment class let out, I rushed from the room, dodging students and making a break for the open courtyard. The two domed towers framing my dorm threatened the dark gray sky and loomed over the crowd of students next to the security building.

"Lance!" I called. I spotted him at the center of the sidewalk. He stepped to the edge of the path and scanned the crowd for me. I waved my hand in the air, and his chin rose in acknowledgement.

If I was wrong about trusting him, I'd be sitting in the coolers beside the old man.

"We need to talk." I pulled Lance to the cross-section on the path, where fewer students would bump into us. They were already clearing out, disappearing into their respective dormitories for lunch.

Lance frowned. "What's up?"

"You know the pill?" I twisted my fingers, nervous.

"Yeah . . . what about it?"

"We talked about it in biology. The pill—adominogen—creates an immunity to the plague."

Lance eyed me cautiously, and then hoisted his bag on his shoulders. "Your point?"

"I—the pill activates a gene that creates the immunity. That's what the Health Scan checks for. Lance—" Whether he knew it or not, he had a *really* intense gaze. "I don't take the pills." I crossed my arms, rubbing them fiercely. "I haven't taken them for half a year now. I tried to take one two days ago, and it made me sick. That's why I couldn't sleep."

Lance turned away, staring at the high, arched design across the doors of the dorms. A cold chill settled through me. I wished it was just a bit sunnier out so the monstrous stone buildings didn't look so creepy.

He sighed. "The worst that can happen is that you have to go for treatment. It's a delay, but the Community is efficient. I'm sure you can get the botanist job you want." He forced a smile.

"You don't understand. I'm showing symptoms of the plague. You'll be fine, since you've been taking the pill, but I—"

He frowned, his expression somber. "What happens to the people who fail?"

"They don't come back." I pulled the backpack off my shoulders and removed the biology notes, then thrust them into Lance's hands. "I checked the blogs. Galina never came back. I thought maybe it took awhile to treat, so I checked the previous years, but out of everyone who failed, only one ever posted to their blog after the scan."

Lance scanned the notes, tracing his fingers across the long streak I'd accidentally left on the page. "Maybe they're busy."

"For five years? You have the same EYEblog account for life. None of them have been active since the day of their Health Scan. Even my *dad* updates his account once in a while."

Lance winced and handed me the notebook. "Look—I don't know about either of us, okay?"

Wait. Either of us?

I gaped at him. "You're not taking the pill, either?"

Lance shrugged and stuck his hands in his pockets, his thumbs hanging off the edges. "My sword practice gets better when I don't take it. I feel more alive. More connected. I haven't taken it for the past couple months. Didn't think I needed to."

The harsh air stung my throat. He was a security official's son. I'd never thought . . . "I feel like the world's muted whenever I take the pill," I said. "The feeling doesn't go away until I stop taking it again."

Lance put his hands on my shoulders. "You're sure those people didn't come back?"

"Yes."

He glanced at the dorms. The crowd had slowed to the trickle of the occasional student returning from class. "If what you say is true, then we're both at risk. We—"

"What's going on?"

My heart beat double-time. Tim stood behind us, his eyes wide and his cheeks rosy from the cold, one hand looped over his efficiency charm, like always.

"Risk of what?" he asked.

I exchanged looks with Lance, who shrugged casually. "Jenna found out that the pills do some biology thing with genetics that make you immune—"

I waved him off. Leave it to sword-boy to butcher the whole explanation. "People naturally have the genetics to prevent theophrenia from infecting them," I explained. "It's a bacteria. However, the gene that activates that part of the immune system isn't always on. The pill—adominogen—activates that gene until the body is resistant, so someone who hasn't taken the pill is at risk for becoming a carrier—and that's what the Health Scan checks for."

Tim's face paled. "Wait—you think I might be at risk? I haven't taken the pill for the past five days. What if—"

Well, that wasn't quite what I'd meant; Tim would probably be fine, unlike *some* dolt who hadn't taken the pill for half a year, but . . .

"That's what we were worried about," Lance spouted quickly. He rubbed the back of his neck, shifting on his feet as if he was getting ready to start sword practice. "Jenna checked to see what the treatment was, but no one ever came back."

Tim grasped his necklace tighter. "That's impossible. The treatment—"

"One person came back," I corrected. "He underwent some kind of surgical procedure. The other blogs were untouched from the time they took the Health Scan. I looked back as far as five years. No response."

Tim bit at the inside of his cheek, worrying his necklace between his thumb and forefinger. "The Community is safe. Maybe the treatment takes longer for some people."

I shook my head. "Not even the councilor had access to information on the treatment. For all we know, security incinerates the bodies to prevent the plague's spread."

"That *would* be efficient," Lance agreed.

All color drained from Tim's face.

I forced a smile. "If only we had someone who could hack into the health network and find out what happens to the people who fail."

Tim's jaw dropped. "That's illegal!"

Lance shrugged. "Doesn't matter to dead men."

Tim stared at him, horrified.

"So . . ." I let out a slow breath. Tim was the only one I knew who could hack computers, and the only one who thought he had anything to lose if he didn't. "Can you do it? I mean, if you want a chance to go out with Sam later . . ."

"We just want to know you'll be here," Lance said. "Go in, take a look—that's it."

I nodded. "You can use my computer, and if anyone asks, I'll say it was me."

Tim narrowed his eyes. "Like you could hack the network."

I winced. No doubt I had an upcoming "C" in programming. "Can you do it?"

"Well, yes, but—"

Lance pressed his hands against our backs. "Come on; we're attracting attention." A cluster of Sam's friends murmured to each other and pointed our direction.

"Right," I said, and we hurried down the path.

The three of us rushed up the stairs, our sneakers thudding the rubber skid strips on each step. I shed my jacket once we were inside my room, then locked the door, checked that the window was shut, and made sure no one was hiding in the bathroom. I wasn't taking any chances that someone might be spying on us.

Tim took a seat at my computer and cracked his knuckles, then opened one of the applications I'd barely touched. His fingers flew across the keyboard, typing out a string of commands I couldn't even begin to guess.

"What if they actually *do* incinerate people?" I whispered as Lance peeked behind my bookshelf.

"I'm sure we'll be fine," Lance said quickly.

Liar.

I grabbed his arm. "Lance—I've seen plants grab people. The old man said—"

"I'm in." Tim swiveled in my chair and jabbed his thumb at a new screen. "Rerouting the lunch system was harder."

I blinked. "Really?"

"Well, no . . . but I got in, didn't I?"

Lance shot me a warning glare—a hint to not mention my hallucinations around Tim—then leaned over our resident computer expert. He pointed to an icon that said "Receiving." "What's that?"

Tim hardly touched the mouse before another window loaded. This one was different than the clean systems I was familiar with. It consisted of mostly green and black colors, pixilated words and two-bit images. "I don't think they've updated this program since EYEnet was invented."

"No kidding," I muttered. The whole thing looked pre-Community.

Two categories popped up. One said "Shielded," and the other, "Recruited." Tim selected the first one, which sorted into years and names, but not much else. A dead end.

"Go back," Lance said. "What's 'Recruited?' "

Tim typed in a new command and the screen revealed years going back to the time of the plague. Tim clicked on the most recent one. Beside the names were the patient's sex, age, and a strange list of hallucinations.

"Fire and flight are among the most common listings," Tim said.

I tapped his shoulder. "Stop scrolling for a minute." He did, and I ran my finger along the list. "Ice." "Persuasion." "Plants."

"Community," I whispered in disbelief. "The old man said people with theophrenia have powers, and he said Lady Black's power was persuasion. He called me a plant elemental."

"Victims of theophrenia are known for having hallucinations," Tim pointed out. "Maybe this is a list of what they see."

"If that's the case, why does it say 'Ability?' " Lance asked.

I nodded at Lance. "Galina's blog said that she thought she could see patterns in liquid. Tim, look up Galina Maly. Search last year."

A moment later, he found her name listed under the 2075 recruited list. "You're right . . . she's listed with water as her ability."

Lance frowned. "What was she recruited for?"

"I don't know," I whispered.

Lance pointed to a category on the screen labeled "Status." Tim clicked it, revealing another list of names. Beside each was a note: "In progress." "Transformation complete." "Released." "Deceased."

I rubbed my arms, trying to avert the oncoming chill.

Tim found Galina's name again, but she was listed as "Deceased."

Lance laid a hand on my shoulder. "I'm sorry."

I couldn't stop shaking. Tim minimized the program. "We shouldn't be doing this." He looked at me, silently pleading with me to give this up. But I couldn't. Something wasn't right.

"We've gone this far. We can at least find out what's going to happen to us—you," I corrected myself. "What could happen to you. There were other categories. Transformation complete . . . released . . . Where does everyone go?"

Tim bit his lip, typing fast. The windows jumped into a blur of images, but moments later, he had an organized nest of images onscreen.

"Looks like there are several treatment facilities," he said. "There's one here in northern Russia, but it closed twenty-five years ago. Now they take people to the facility in Afghanistan." He frowned. "Afghanistan?"

Lance shifted nervously. "Maybe they don't want the Community to smell like burning flesh."

"*Or* maybe that's where the victims relax until they're cured," I interrupted, trying to dispel the image.

"Relax. Right," Tim muttered. "You've got snow, or you've got sand. Or rocks. There's a lot of rocks, too."

It didn't sound *that* bad to me—the biodiversity would be amazing. But I kept my mouth shut and let the two of them argue out the efficiency of placing a treatment center there, in Mexico, Canada, Egypt . . . There were too many places to count.

I pointed to a little icon that looked like a map. "Can you check that?"

Tim swiveled the chair back to the computer. "Whoa. This thing runs deep."

He flipped to a different image, one that showed the facility from a horizontal perspective. There were five levels, each separated by at least three meters of earth. Most of the facility ran underground, though part of it sprawled across the surface. This particular facility was located somewhere within a mountain range.

"Holding cells, cleansing rooms, tanks, transformation chambers . . . Let's see if I can find out what this refers to." He continued typing. "There we go. Let's try the security cameras." He froze. "Community . . . what *is* that?"

The footage was black and white. A crisp image displayed the details of a small, metallic room, which was bare, save for the *creature* pacing near the walls. It had slender, gangly limbs too long for a normal human torso, and it was naked. It turned its face toward the camera, giving us a clear shot of its feline eyes and pointed ears, and a face that looked almost, but not quite, human.

"Is there anything to say what it is?" Lance asked.

Tim pointed to a little descriptor box in the upper right-hand corner. "Transformation chamber number thirty-two. Beast number four-five-eight-six-zero . . ." He stopped reading after the fifth number, and we stared at the screen, speechless.

He started typing again but the door shook with a heavy thud. The screen went blank without Tim touching the mouse. "Special Forces," a man's voice said. "Open up."

Lance half skidded across the floor, scrambled around the side of my desk, and unlatched the window. He swung his legs over the windowsill and dropped, followed by a distinct rattle of leaves from the bushes below.

Tim stared at the door, his eyes wide.

"Go!" I snapped at Tim, and he darted under the bed. The doorknob rattled again as I slammed the window shut after Lance's drop.

The door swung open, and Lady Black strolled inside.

CHAPTER
SIX

Two agents entered my room before Lady Black shut the door. She gestured gracefully to my computer. "See what you can find," she said. "Miss Nickleson's records don't suggest an aptitude for computers."

Goosebumps prickled my skin. It didn't matter what my records said. The computer's history could prove me guilty. I silently cursed as I remembered the camera at the top of the screen. What if security had been watching us this entire time?

But if they *had* been watching us, why check my computer? Why not arrest me right now?

I waited at the foot of my bed while the man and woman in black uniforms placed themselves between me and my computer. They wore the rising sun cog on their left sleeve and each carried a matte black gun on their hip. Thanks to the visors covering the upper half of their faces, the only way I could tell them apart was the general shape of their bodies and their name tags.

Agent Kirsch—the same agent whom I'd seen in the bathroom yesterday—clicked through my EYEblog account, searching through file after file of personal information. "That's odd," she murmured. "Take a look."

The male agent—Agent Bodrov—leaned over the screen and typed in a new set of commands.

I didn't move. I didn't look at the bed. If Tim made even the slightest sound, we'd be out of the Community before we could recite the pledge, never mind how well we did on the Health Scan or if the computer's history revealed anything.

His records *did* show an aptitude for computers.

I glanced at Lady Black, but her attention was solely on the agents. Bodrov typed at a pace that matched Tim's, his face smooth as stone. "Nothing," he said, surprised. "According to its history, the last time Miss Nickleson used this computer was to check her EYEnet account five hours ago."

The other agent straightened, her hands linked behind her back. "I'd advise having Commander Rick's tech master take a look. This is beyond us."

"Thank you," Lady Black told the agents. "Could we have a little privacy?" Her eyes twinkled under the LED light panels, and the two agents stepped outside. "There now, Miss Nickleson—" She settled onto the edge of my bed and gently patted the place at her side.

A lump formed in my throat. "Yes?"

"You have a delightful room, dear. Have a seat." Lady Black smoothed the covers of the crisp fabric, toying with the hem between her fingers. "Your spider plant adds a nice touch."

I swallowed hard and sat beside her. "My dad gave it to me before I left for college. You know . . . to bring me luck? Not that I've been having much luck lately."

"That's unfortunate. It looks like a lovely plant." She smiled reassuringly, then pointed to my neck. "No charms or anything?"

Heat flushed to my cheeks. Though wearing charms wasn't a law, everyone wore them. Charms were a way of identifying a person's role in the Community. Tim had his light bulb efficiency charm. Lance had a globe charm, for history, and a gun charm, for security.

As for me, I'd never found one that looked appealing. The leaf charms always looked too fake, and the genetic DNA charms didn't interest me.

"I never saw the point," I admitted.

The lady tilted her head, and her long hair framed her face in dark wisps. Funny—in most pictures she had olive skin and bright green eyes. Here, the light made her look exceedingly pale.

"I'll admit, the charms can be redundant." Lady Black played with the pendant on her chest, and her lips quirked into a flirtatious smile. "Given your choice of hairstyle, maybe you'll choose something like this." She lifted the pendant and winked. Then her expression darkened. "However, there is the matter of you hacking the health network."

"What do you mean?" My voice was too high to convince anyone of anything.

She let out a soft breath and took the moment to smooth the wrinkles in her satin dress. When she met my eyes again, my whole body went rigid. She *knew*. That look—

"Please don't lie to me, Miss Nickleson," she said, her voice firm. "Hacking the health network, or any government network, is an international crime. Most sentences end in death."

"What's going to happen to me?" I whispered.

The lady brushed my cheek with the tips of her fingers. After a moment, she tucked a fallen strand of my hair away from my eyes to behind my ear. "Believe me, I don't wish that sentence on anyone as lovely as you." She paused. "You're worried about theophrenia, aren't you?"

I nodded.

"Don't fret, Miss Nickleson. You're not a bad person. Many victims make irrational decisions once they've been infected."

"So I *am* infected?"

"Let's check." Lady Black called Agent Kirsch back in. "Scan her." The agent produced a small, rectangular box with several dials and buttons. "Don't worry," Lady Black told me, "it doesn't hurt."

Of course it wouldn't. I let out my breath, allowing myself to relax. Maybe it was better this way. Lady Black seemed friendlier than the doctors who would normally perform the scan.

Kirsch knelt beside me, raising the scanner from my shoes to my skull, then back again. She stopped when it beeped twice.

"Verdict?" Lady Black laid a gloved hand on my shoulder, but even she looked concerned.

The agent showed her the scanner. "Positive."

My breath caught in my throat. She had just confirmed that I was infected.

Lady Black eyed the screen and nodded. "Thank you."

Agent Kirsch stepped away. The leader clasped my hands in hers. "I'm sorry, Miss Nickleson."

I took a deep breath. "The old man said I was a plant elemental," I said, testing her reaction while the agent packed her scanner away. "I've been having hallucinations of plants . . . growing . . . for me. Faster than plants would normally grow."

Lady Black smiled gently and, for just a moment, I could see where Sam got her sympathetic tendencies. "Hallucinations are different for each victim."

There was that whole list on the screen. Plants, flight, persuasion . . .

"He said your power is persuasion. What did he mean? What's going to happen to me? He said he was my grandfather. I checked my family database. The old man and my grandfather look related. Who is he?"

The lady pursed her lips. She settled my hands on her knee, then leaned into my ear and whispered softly. "Don't worry yourself about the old man. He has theophrenia, and he's had it for a very long time. We've lost him to the plague." She stroked my cheek, searching me with her eyes. "We need to give you a shot to protect you, all right?"

I squirmed at the thought of a needle, but Agent Kirsch situated herself at my side and Lady Black lifted my chin with her forefinger. "The old man needs treatment. He's deluding others and exposing them to disease, just like you've been exposed. You can't deny the hallucinations, can you?"

"No, but still—"

"Come with us, Miss Nickleson. We'll answer your questions." She offered me a smile.

I started. "You will?"

There was movement in the corner of my eye, and then the needle plunged into my arm. I hadn't even seen the agent roll up my sleeve. Hadn't even noticed —

Everything went gray and fuzzy, like I was moving too slow and everyone else was moving too fast. I squinted at the door, trying to clear my vision. My whole body felt weak, like a broken tree branch hanging by fibers.

"Everything will be fine," Lady Black crooned. "But we need to get you someplace more secure than a university campus. The injection will temporarily protect us, but we shouldn't chance any more exposure than necessary. The old man has done enough already." She looped her arm around my shoulders, guiding me toward the door.

"Wait — how does injecting me protect you?" I stumbled away from her and grabbed my backpack from beside the nightstand, then shoved my phone and textbooks inside. Maybe I could study while I was gone.

"We can't risk the bacteria mutating," Lady Black explained. "This way, you don't put anyone else at risk."

That didn't make sense, but it sounded right. And Community, I felt sick. My plant . . . So lifeless. Just a cold, dead . . . living plant.

I tried to puzzle how that worked.

"Don't forget your coat," Lady Black said, handing me the jacket I'd worn earlier. "The day is cold."

Coat. Got it.

The two agents flanked us as Lady Black led me down the hall, one arm around my shoulders, the other helping steady me. Several students stopped on their way back from lunch and stared. None of them approached. They knew I had failed.

"You'll feel better soon enough," Lady Black told me. "These agents will answer your questions, and after I return from this afternoon's speech, I'll do the same."

The whole hall spun like a centrifuge and I staggered on my feet. Lady Black steadied me, her grip firm but gentle. We took the stairs.

Sam nearly bumped into us as we turned the corner. She held her books to her chest, curls bouncing as she jumped. "Jenna?" She gaped at me, then at the agents, then at Lady Black. "I—" She ducked her head and quickly retreated, then peeked at me from under her bangs. "I'm sorry. Do you want me to tell Lance?"

My chest clenched tight. She'd swoop in on him the moment I was gone. Or maybe . . . maybe she'd have some pity on me and give him space. Besides, *someone* had to tell him, and I doubted the guards would.

"Thanks," I told her.

The agents lead me through the back door of the dormitory. More agents stood around the patio, their bodies as rigid as the stone walls. An armored van was parked across from us with the rising sun half-cog painted across its side, glinting with a metallic red sheen.

Community . . . They were taking me away, just like when they took Galina.

I turned to Lady Black. "Am I going to be incinerated?"

She gave me a puzzled smile. "No, dear. Where in the Community would you get that idea?" She leaned into my ear. "I know you're disoriented, but you have to go with them. Relax, be strong—"

I could relax. I could be strong.

I stepped into the back of the van. Three cushioned seats lined one side, each with heavy-duty seat belts. On the other side, a long bench was bolted to the frame. Just above the bench were rows of locked, metal boxes that formed an upper compartment.

Agent Kirsch strapped me in place while Bodrov took the driver's seat.

"The security center's about thirty minutes out," Kirsch told me. "I realize we may have intruded on your normal lunch schedule. Can we get you anything? Water? A snack bar?"

My stomach churned, but I nodded. "Thanks."

While the agent retrieved my so-called lunch from the metal compartment, Lady Black knelt beside me. "I promise I'll answer your questions when I return. Try not to worry yourself." She kissed my cheek. My skin tingled at the touch of her lips and I nodded.

She patted my shoulder and disappeared out the back of the van, closing the doors behind her. They locked with a clang and a thud. The agent sat a snack bar in the adjacent seat.

"How are you feeling?" Kirsch asked. She took her place on the bench. "The injection can be a doozy."

"I've had better days."

"Don't worry. The feeling will wear off."

I turned my attention to the front window, which was partially obscured by a metal grid separating the back of the van and the cab. The campus blurred into a lulling scene of spruce and pine as the van started down the road. Stark buildings protruded from the landscape as we passed through the suburb where my parents lived.

All the housing here was made from the same smooth concrete, two and three stories high. Farther down the street, the drab gray and tan colors extended into one-story buildings of commerce: a bank where my dad worked, a diner for the early morning crowd, and a general store with special treats like chocolate candy bars. The closer we got to the edge of town, the faster my heart raced, and I gripped the edge of the seat so tight that I left little nail marks in the faux leather.

No more visits to the bank. No more chocolate bars.

The distant thump of the wheels on the smooth pavement gave way to the van's silence.

Too quiet.

"Why did I get sick from the pill?" I asked, sitting up in my seat.

Kirsch glanced to the front of the van. "It's what happens when you contract theophrenia," she said. "The pill detects neurological damage and causes a minor reaction." She craned her neck toward me, but I couldn't see her face through the visor. "You're *supposed* to go to the doctor. They recognize the symptoms and get you checked out."

Oh.

"So . . . I've been carrying the plague for half a year?"

"It's possible. Why didn't you go to the doctor?"

"I was more efficient without it," I said, closing my hands in my lap. I might never see my parents again. Or Tim. Or Lance . . . Lance and Tim were with me right before I got caught. We were hackers. *That* cleared my head, at least for a moment.

"What's going to happen to me?" I asked sharply.

Kirsch clapped her hands on her knees and sat straighter. "Well, Lady Black wants to speak with you. They'll take you to a treatment facility after that."

"Where are we going now?"

"The prison. We'll wait in the security center until the speech is over. It's easier to contain a possible outbreak there than on campus."

I lowered my eyes and toyed with the wrapper of the snack bar. My attempts to be more efficient had put everyone at risk. But where had I picked up the disease? It wasn't like I ever left St. Petersburg. Someone must have brought it in from one of the other Communities.

"What's the treatment? I asked the councilor and my biology professor, but neither of them knew."

"We try not to go into much detail," Kirsch explained. She motioned to the snack bar. "You need to keep up your strength."

My stomach wasn't as queasy now, so I unpeeled the wrapper and took a bite. It was honey flavored granola and surprisingly calming despite the injection's effect on my stomach. "What *can* you tell me?"

"The treatment depends on how far the bacteria has progressed. Therapy and mental training help combat minor incidents. There's surgery for more advanced cases." She paused, rubbing the tips of her fingers together.

I waited, but when she didn't elaborate, I sat the snack bar back on the seat.

"What are beasts?" I wriggled in my seat, easing the seat belt from cutting into my shoulders.

Her head turned sharply. "What are you talking about?"

Given her reaction, I probably shouldn't have said anything. But I was already going to the treatment facility, so what did it hurt to ask?

"There was a cell with a beast in it. It looked different. Cat-like eyes, pointed ears, a different facial structure. What was it?"

Kirsch frowned. "Where did you see this picture?"

"It was — never mind," I finished, but her shoulders tensed.

"That information is not available to the public. Who showed you that image?"

I shook my head. They already knew I couldn't have hacked the computer, and anything I said might incriminate Lance or Tim. "Something the old man showed me," I lied, turning my attention to my sneakers.

"Don't believe everything he told you," Kirsch warned. "People in the later stages of theophrenia are masters at lying. That's how the plague spread so far in the pre-Community days. Anyway, that 'beast' you saw was probably a photo edited by terrorists."

I stashed my hands in my pockets, my palms sweating. The "picture" I'd seen wasn't a photo, and if the feed had been edited by terrorists, then what was it doing in a government network?

The van slowed and I cringed as my stomach did another somersault. The prison gate loomed over the road. The chain link fence could open for armored vehicles to move in and out, and two guards stood just outside. Both wore stiff gray uniforms. Upon prompting from Bodrov, they opened the gates.

He drove the van around the side of the building, and the engines quieted as he parked. Agent Kirsch released my seat belt. "Come. We'll wait in one of the holding rooms until Lady Black returns."

Cold air gusted in as Bodrov unlatched the doors. I pulled my jacket tighter and shouldered my backpack as I hopped down from the van. The world spun into a jumbled blur of dead grass and gray sky.

"Easy, now," Agent Bodrov said, moving to steady me. "You're feeling the effects of the injection."

My throat constricted. Thick pines created a shadowy forest around the smooth, concrete compound, and I shuddered. The agent looped his arm around my shoulders. "Let's get you inside."

I paused. There was something in the sky. It was small, dark, and quickly approaching. I blinked, trying to clear my vision. It didn't look right. The approach was too direct to be a bird, and it was too oddly shaped. I pointed. "What's that?"

Both agents looked up at the same time, hands reaching for their guns.

Suddenly my breath was punched from me and I stared at the sky from my back. I gasped for air, trying to breathe, and rolled onto my side. A blast of cold, moist air twirled around us. Something large—*human*—flew overhead, and then landed in a crouch with no visible wings or method of transportation. The flying man leveled a gun at the two agents.

"Alec! Behind you!" a voice shouted.

The flying man—Alec—spun and fired at guards approaching from the gate. One of the guards dropped lifeless to the ground, and Alec leapt into the air. He circled once, evading their fire. A dark green and brown suit hugged his skin, complete with shiny plastic plates on his elbows and knees and across his chest.

Bodrov grabbed my arm and yanked me to my feet. "Move!" He pushed me toward a metal door. I stumbled and lost my sense of direction as a young man with short blond hair streaked past us toward a third intruder—a burly man in a dark green jacket. The man snatched Kirsch by the collar of her uniform. "Where's the man you took in yesterday?" he demanded. He slammed her against the wall. The agent rammed her knee into his stomach and the burly man gasped for breath as she twisted around him and latched her arm around his throat. She brought her gun to the back of his head.

The flying man—Alec—dropped from the sky. He bowled into Kirsch, ramming her into the concrete wall. The concrete shuttered, spewing broken chunks. As the burly man picked himself up, the grainy dust cleared, revealing a gaping hole in the side of the prison.

Bodrov let go of my arm and thrust his palm toward the burly man, who went flying as if an invisible force had slammed into his chest. Bodrov cocked his gun.

I couldn't look away.

Not only did the intruders have strange abilities, but Bodrov did, too. I couldn't breathe. I was hallucinating. Delusional. The burly man had dog-like claws for nails. His face was haggard and rough, scarred with thick, pink lines, and his reddish hair was gnarled and knotted past his shoulders. I rarely saw a man's hair so long — the only exceptions were Master Matoska and the occasional leader.

Bodrov leveled his gun at the intruder's head, the visible half of his face twisted in rage. I started to edge away from him when a cold gust nearly knocked me over, encrusting the agent's vest with a thin layer of ice. More ice encased his gun. Behind him, the burly man bolted through the hole.

I had to get out of here. If I could get to the front door —

I turned to find the blond-haired man in the form-fitting, blue-gray suit standing directly behind me. "You're cuter in person," he said, winking. "Name's Chill. Now, let's get you to safety." He grabbed my hand, his fingers cool against my skin, and yanked me toward the outer perimeter of the facility. I dug my heels into the ground, trying to slow us down and get back to the building, but instead, we ran face-first into an invisible wall.

I tripped over my feet, but Chill turned on his heel, ice forming across his fingers.

"Get behind me," he warned.

Bodrov strode toward us, cocking his gun and aiming.

"But — what in the Community is going on?"

"Now!" Chill's determined expression mixed with fear, and he ushered me back. Ice formed around the barrel of the agent's gun. Bodrov tried to break the encasement, and when that didn't work, he simply looked at us and lowered his weapon.

Without warning, Chill's head snapped back. His face was caught in surprise as he collapsed in a crumpled heap on the grass.

What just —

His neck was broken.

Bodrov strode toward me, his gait slow and heavy. He motioned for me to step aside and I moved back. The man was dead. Somehow — somehow the agent had killed him.

The agent pointed his gun at the intruder's body and fired a solitary shot into Chill's skull from less than a meter away. Something warm spattered against my hand. I choked. Moments ago, Chill had been living. Then — his neck snapped?

Bodrov removed the gun from the man's holster and grabbed my upper arm. "Come with me."

I staggered after him. "Who were they? Their abilities . . ." I tasted vomit in my mouth. "Let go of me! You did something — but you're supposed to be Special Forces. How could you —" My words merged into some mixture of Russian and English, and I wasn't even sure those were coherent.

Bodrov sighed, his shoulders slouching before he returned to his usual erect posture. "I think you would be safer if we had you in the coolers. The suspension will keep the disease from progressing."

My whole body threatened to collapse, but Bodrov guided me over the rubble. Just inside the building, Agent Kirsch lay at an odd angle, her body broken from the impact. Nearby, Alec lay with bullet wounds in his back. Dead.

Why was this happening? Was I imagining this?

Bright blue efficiency lights gleamed in the sterile halls. My limbs felt heavy and weak, but Bodrov guided me down hall after cold, gleaming hall, all the way to the coolers.

A couple guards in gray security uniforms hurried past, trading comments through their radios. Goosebumps rose on my skin. I'd made myself a criminal. I'd stopped taking the pill and risked everyone around me. I'd connived Tim into hacking the health network. I'd finally crossed that line between stupid rules and one they'd kill me for. And I'd been wrong. After half a year of not taking the pill, I'd contracted theophrenia. That fact hit me like a punch to the gut.

Bodrov guided me into a small room lined with four tall, cylindrical tubes. Tiny blue LEDs shone from the metal ceiling panels and reflected on the frosted glass.

Before now, the only functioning coolers I'd seen were in the training detention center of the security building. Here, two of the coolers were occupied. One held the burly man with claws, and the other held the old man. They slumped against the glass, frozen in sleep and covered with a thin sheet of frost.

"Your backpack, please."

I gave it to him. He placed it in a locker at the back of the room.

"It'll be here for you once Lady Black gives the okay for your release."

I doubled over, shaking. I didn't dare look at the shining blue tubes any longer than I had to.

"Miss Nickleson—"

Bodrov positioned himself by a computer console at the side of the room and pressed a key. The front panel of a cooler slid up. It hissed and let out a cloud of chilled air.

"I wish the best for you." He tried to give me a smile, but it looked forced. "It won't hurt."

Of course not. I knew how coolers worked. I wouldn't feel anything. I'd just stand there, frozen in sleep, never knowing if I'd wake again.

If I went in, I might never come out.

Horrified, I spun around to face Bodrov. I clutched the crinkly fabric of his sleeves and spread my feet to get better footing on the rubber grate—anything to keep him from putting me in one of those things.

I yipped and flailed as my feet left the floor. An invisible force gently pressed my arms to my sides and pushed me into the tube. I stared at Bodrov. "What are you doing?" Theophrenia. I had theophrenia— The agent retreated from the glass. The door to the cryogenic unit snapped shut. My feet touched the floor again.

"Wait! No!" I pounded my fists on the glass. My palms stung from the useless struggle. Fog rose through the little holes in the floor, obscuring the man outside. The tube was so small. I barely took a step back before my shoulders touched the glass walls. Ice seeped through my clothes.

DISTANT HORIZON

I frantically searched the tube for a sign of escape. Ceiling—metal, with numerous little holes. Floor—same. Wall—cylindrical, translucent, no escape—

The room drifted.

CHAPTER SEVEN

A blue light faded into darkness and the mechanics of a door hissed as it released, letting in a gust of warm air. I collapsed into comforting arms. A heavy coat crinkled under my chin as a familiar, earthy tang drifted to my nose.

"You okay?" a male voice asked. His hands slid under my armpits and lifted me into a comforting position against his shoulder. I grappled at that shoulder to stay upright and shivered.

Lance.

He wrapped his arms around me, fleece jacket pressing against my chest. Warmth, safety . . . I wasn't alone. Not anymore.

I flexed my fingers, and ice crystals cracked into tiny water droplets.

The fight outside . . .

Alec and Agent Kirsch . . .

I blinked, trying to clear my vision of the thick, meaningless shapes around me. The couple pale shapes were probably people in Community attire. Lance I knew from the voice. Tim I could guess by his hunched, nervous stance. A Special Forces agent in a dark outfit stood at the console, and two figures sat beside the door.

I rubbed my eyes, grimacing from the painful light as my vision cleared. My breath caught in my throat.

Despite the fitted black armor, the black-haired woman at the console didn't wear the rising sun cog of Special Forces. For all that she had the poised stance of an agent with her hair pulled back in a regulation-tight ponytail, she wore a pair of sunglasses on top of her head.

Sitting nearest to the door was the burly man in his dark green jacket. He grimaced and popped his back. Beside him, the old man rested his head against the wall, one hand testing the bandage around his wounded arm.

"Why are those guys free?" I asked Lance. My throat was sore from the coolers, and my voice grated against my ears. "How'd you get in?"

He squeezed me tight and rested his cheek against my hair. "We'll get you out, okay? Sam said they took you, and Tim told me about Lady Black."

I pulled away, nearly falling before he caught me. "Get me out? I tested positive for theophrenia. I had all these crazy hallucinations of people flying and shooting ice from their hands. The agents put me in here to—"

Behind Tim, a dead agent lay sprawled on his back, a pool of dark blood seeping from his rib cage. Though his face was obscured by the helmet, I recognized the name tag.

Bodrov.

His blood came from a ragged slash mark, skillfully placed where his vest wouldn't protect him.

Everyone but Lance, with his sword strapped around his waist, had guns.

My vision wavered, and Lance rushed to catch me.

"Jenna? You all right?"

"Of course I'm not all right! That agent was supposed to be protecting me from these people and you—you killed him!"

Lance set his jaw. "I saved you. That agent would have shot us. We need to get you out, and currently, we're wanted."

"Think that might have something to do with being infected with a hallucinogenic plague?" I snapped. Lance had put my safety before the Community. I wasn't sure whether to feel grateful or sick.

"Plague ain't real," the burly man said. "It's a nice little cover-up to hide powers."

"I think they're telling the truth." Tim motioned his tablet to the woman in black body armor. "Inese turned us invisible when Special Forces started chasing us."

"Why were they chasing you?" I demanded. "How did they figure out you were the hacker?"

"They're Special Forces, that's how." Lance rested his hand on the pommel of his sword. "Tim said you were acting funny around Lady Black, so when Sam told me they took you, I figured we should try contacting you. But Special Forces almost got us before we left the meeting, except Inese turned us invisible when we were trying to escape from the hall. She's been helping us since then. She even made sure we used the right code for the coolers."

"Yeah—I didn't want to execute you." Tim laughed nervously, his cheeks red.

My blood drained to my feet. "Execute me?"

"You have to give the kid credit," Inese said, retreating from the console and dropping her sunglasses onto her nose. "He gave the first group of agents the slip by telling their computers we took a different taxi. Not a bad move." She knelt by the old man. "You ready? I've already moved the car, so we should be set."

The old man nodded once, and Inese helped him stand. "What about Chill and Alec?" he asked. His voice was so hoarse that I barely understood him.

Inese lowered her eyes. "They didn't make it."

He glanced at me, evaluating me with a quiet, uneven expression. I shivered. Did everyone here have theophrenia? This couldn't be real. All those strange powers . . .

"Jack, can you move?" the old man asked.

The burly man, Jack, pushed himself from the floor. "Sure—" He grunted. "How're we doin' on time?"

Inese snatched Tim's tablet from his hands. "Commander Rick's van just arrived. Won't be long before security realizes we've cut the external feedback from their cameras. Can you three move all right?"

"I'll help Jenna," Lance said.

I tried to push myself away from him, but he wouldn't let go. I lowered my voice. "What are you doing? Theophrenia causes delusions. These people are putting everyone at risk by not turning themselves in. The agent you killed?" I pointed to the body. "He said theophrenia *can* be treated, if caught soon enough." I gritted my teeth. "I've been *infected.*"

"Jenna—" Lance took my hands, his eyes pleading. "Tim hacked the health network, and I've killed an agent. You didn't take the pills. Those are international violations. The guards have been ordered to kill us on sight."

"But—"

Lance squeezed my hands and looked me square in the eye. "Jen—if we stay here, we're going to die. We have to leave. Please come with us."

For the love of everything secure . . .

They must have caught the disease from me.

"Are you coming or not?" Inese poked her head in from the doorway. "It's clear for the moment, but if Commander Rick catches us, we're done for. Pops will be tortured, and they *will* find the rest of our team. Stay if you want, but don't keep us here."

I opened my mouth to speak, but the old man, Pops, spoke first. "She's coming with us." He pushed himself from the metallic wall. "We can't let them hurt her."

I let out a gasping laugh. "Would someone please tell me what they think is going on?"

Pops sighed. "Theophrenia isn't real. We have proof. Just give us a chance to show you."

I stared at him. There was no pull to believe him. No trust. Nothing like yesterday, when I *wanted* to believe him. Nothing like today, when I wanted to believe Lady Black.

"You said Lady Black has persuasion. What did you mean?"

"Persuasion? It's a power that allows you to influence people."

"What about you? Do you have this so-called persuasion power?"

He inclined his head. "Yes."

He was admitting to it? "You were using it last night," I tested. "To get me to come with you."

"You're from the Community. Your priority is safety. So yes, I was using my power then. I wanted to explain the situation without risking my team members."

I set my jaw. I had no proof that his story was true. But that blond guy, Chill, died trying to protect me. My stomach twisted. What was I supposed to believe? That these powers were *real*? That people were dying because they believed in these abilities?

But I'd seen them, too.

"We've got to move." Inese turned toward the lockers on the back wall, counted softly, then opened the third to last. "This ought to help." She tossed Pops his cane. Next locker, she had my backpack. I shot away from Lance and tried to grab it, but ended up tripping over my own feet. Lance looped his arm around me and I cradled my backpack against my chest.

"I don't trust them," I whispered. I *couldn't* trust them.

Lance squeezed my shoulder. "We don't have a choice. If we stay here, we're dead."

I clenched my fists around my backpack straps and locked eyes with the old man. "We'll come with you. But if you're lying, we'll leave. And we *will* find a way to leave."

Lance let out a sigh of relief and we hobbled into the hall. Rows of blue-tinted light panels in the ceiling made the silvery hall gleam. Boots echoed behind us, and every few steps, one of the lights streaked. I used Lance's shoulder as a crutch while Tim ran ahead with Inese. She vanished before each corner, and then reappeared to give the all clear. No one else seemed to mind, but I jumped each time she disappeared. We finally reached a large exterior door, and Tim furiously tapped the screen on his tablet, trying to guess at the security codes.

"Try this." Inese unzipped a pouch at her side and handed him a mess of wires. Tim's eyes went wide and he linked the tablet to the keypad by the door.

Jack scowled. "Hurry up, will ya? This ain't a homework assignment. You don't have to be exact."

"Actually, I do," Tim murmured. The keypad beeped and the door rumbled open. "Got it!"

"Good job, kid. Now move." Jack shoved Tim through the open door and the rest of us followed. Inese took off running and vanished again while the burly man strode across the lawn.

I shivered. The hairs on the nape of my neck rose, and I turned around. A leader I didn't recognize stood less than a meter behind me. He wore an odd assortment of baubles and trinkets inside a long brown trench coat. Antiques spilled from his pockets. He smirked, altogether too amused.

Lance stopped short and stared right at the leader — or through him, really — and frowned. "What are you looking at?"

"You don't see anyone standing there?" I asked.

The man had unkempt, reddish-brown hair poking up in prickly spikes, but it was matted on his forehead by a pair of glass and leather goggles. He winked, and his bright green eyes glinted in the light.

Lance shook his head. "No."

The leader removed a small, orange pill bottle from one of his pockets, then rattled it near his ear. *The game begins. Let's see how well you fare this time.*

I could've sworn I'd heard that voice in my head. But the man was gone. Vanished. No sign of his existence at all.

"Jenna —" Lance nudged my arm.

"Hurry up!" Jack called. Several guards raced toward us, pistols raised. A sleek, four-door sedan with old, square fenders materialized in front of us. The tinted windows rolled down and Inese stuck her head out the driver's window.

"Coming?"

"Nice car," Tim whispered, his eyes wide.

FLINT

Lance grabbed my hand and yanked me inside as the guards took aim. Tim jumped in after us. Inese started the engine. A bullet tinged off the back of the car and she cursed, but as the guards aimed their second volley, the car lifted into the air. I about lost the snack bar I'd had all those hours ago.

The car was flying.

CHAPTER EIGHT

The car hovered, then rose into the air above the treetops and the pristine lawn. There was no sign of battle. Even the side of the prison had been repaired and —

Tim and Lance disappeared. The car disappeared. *I* disappeared.

I yelped, grabbing for Lance's wrist. I heard him gag and another wave of nausea passed through me. I was invisible, flying, and for the first time in my life — motion sick.

The earth sped beneath us, leaving behind the mountain and suburbs for sea.

Whoever these guys were, they weren't Special Forces or E-Leadership, or anyone I'd ever heard of. These so-called rebels could do whatever they wanted with us and the Community wouldn't be there to help.

I cradled my arms over my stomach. These rebels and their "powers" seemed far too real to be some hallucination. I reached my hand out and hesitantly patted where Lance's knee should've been.

"Jenna?"

"Are we . . . are we flying?" I whispered.

"I think so."

He saw it too. I stared at the ground zipping below us. "So . . . this is real."

"Yeah."

I let out a breath and exhaustion took over. Half an hour later, I woke to a sharp nudge in the ribs.

Hidden in the clouds, a small, pale object grew distinctively in size. It soon became recognizable as a large dirigible hovering between dark, velvety blue thunderheads. Tim let out an excited breath and my jaw dropped at the close-up.

The dirigible looked like one of the original E-Leadership models. Nothing near as fancy as what Commander Rick flew, but massive compared to the car. The whole vessel had been painted with muted colors: gray, blue, and brown, all masking its once imposing framework. A symbol had been spray painted across the side of the metal envelope: a full yellow circle with the upper half of a blue stick figure raising its arms under an upside down "U." Below the rigid, air-filled envelope, a large gondola supported three levels to the airship. Three jet engines were fixed to the back: two on either side and one directly underneath.

I felt Lance lean forward. "That's not Community. Where'd they get it?"

"You see it, too?" I asked.

"Kind of hard to miss a giant airship."

Not a hallucination, then.

Two large, paneled doors slid around the front of the airship's lower decks. The car flew under ornate glass windows, and the whole landing went far smoother than I expected. We set down with a soft *thump* before going visible.

"Everybody out," Inese called.

Lance scooted out and helped me stagger to my feet. "You all right?"

I glared at him. "I tested positive for theophrenia, spent who-knows-how-long in a cooler, and now I'm standing on a rebel airship that may or might not be real. What do you think?"

"I don't know about you, but I think he's going to be really sad if this isn't real." Lance jerked his thumb at Tim, who circled some sort of old, beat-up helicopter on the other side of the corrugated metal room. The rusted contraption consisted of an egg-shaped, brown pod beneath a series of cone-like rotors.

I doubted it could fly.

"Whirligig," Inese said, amused. "Car's more practical, considering how slow this thing is."

No kidding. The whirligig looked like it'd fall apart the moment anyone tried to start it. But Tim's eyes lit up when he poked the lowest rotor and the metal spun freely. I sighed. Give him any sort of tech or a girl's attention—in this case, both—and he'd be happy. Never mind that we might be losing our minds.

A loud clang echoed through the room as the car door slammed shut. Jack spun around and pointed a clawless finger at Pops. "What happened back there?"

I blinked. Hadn't he had claws earlier today?

"Why didn't you tell us the Camaraderie would be there two days early?" Jack demanded.

Two days early? Camaraderie? I edged closer to Lance, who kept his hand tentatively on the pommel of his sword. But none of these people seemed to notice.

Pops leaned against his cane, testing his words before he spoke. "I expected them to show up the day of the scan. Not before."

Jack shook his head, his lips twisted in anger. "You thought wrong. Don't expect me to tell Crush that his brother isn't coming back."

He started up the metal stairs, then froze.

A young, lean man in a gray and black jumpsuit stood at the top of the stairs, his mouth parted in surprise. He had pale blond hair, and he looked a lot like Alec. Jack glanced at Pops. His rage was gone, but not the accusation. "Never mind. I guess I just did." He stormed up the stairs and slammed the inner door behind him.

Crush didn't move from the railing. "Not coming back?"

"Alec and Chill didn't make it," Pops said quietly. "Unfortunately their bodies were removed by the time we escaped."

Crush swallowed hard. "I—excuse me." He turned and pushed through the door. It swung and hit the wall hard enough to echo.

Inese cursed under her breath and chased after him, leaving the rest of us alone in the hangar with Pops. A high-altitude chill seeped through the closing hangar door, and with it, a glimpse of the dark, endless sky.

Goosebumps rose on my skin. I wished the hangar bay door would hurry and close. The airship seemed rickety enough without having the door open. Its inner framework consisted of metal bars and copper plates welded precariously to the original components. A bare wire dangled from an overhead ceiling light, and the rest of the lights offered a florescent purple cast. They weren't even using LEDs here.

E-leadership would never have let this workmanship pass. My mom once had to scrap an idea just because the engine room showed pipes. But these guys didn't seem to care. We were a long way from the ground . . . and the Community. A long way from safety, security, and efficiency.

I shivered. The electric tang of storm and moisture lingered, and everything around here felt too real to be a hallucination. If this was real, then the commander had been lying to us. And if theophrenia's so-called hallucinations were actually powers, then what happened to everyone who failed the treatment?

I glanced at Pops. "So . . . you're Dr. Nickolai Nickleson. My grandfather."

He rubbed his forehead gingerly. "Please, just call me Pops."

I frowned. They weren't treating us like prisoners, but none of us knew how to fly the whirligig or this flying car-thing, which left us uncomfortably at their mercy. They didn't *have* to treat us like prisoners for us to be hostage.

"What are you going to do with us?" My voice sounded too loud in the room's creaking silence. "Are we prisoners?"

Pops shook his head. "No, you are our guests. We aren't going to hurt you."

"But who *are* you?" I asked. "Rebels?"

"We're the Coalition of Freedom. We do what we can to protect people from the Camaraderie. Small acts of sabotage, providing intel to larger organizations . . . things like that."

"Coalition of Freedom?" Lance asked.

Pops nodded. "Let me introduce you to Jim. He's been around since the beginning. He can give you a better idea of what the world's really like."

"So we'll get our answers?"

Pops nodded and motioned us toward the stairs.

I glanced around the hangar. This place shouldn't exist. After the fall of the rebel base in Australia, the rebels were gone. No more attacks. World peace.

Yet here I was, standing on a rebel airship, uncomfortably sure that all of this was far too real.

CHAPTER
NINE

Pops led us into a dark, narrow hall, a far cry from the neatly glowing dorm corridors. What might've gleamed with bright bronze reflections was now a dull, dented bit of metal. Yellow lights ran the length of the ceiling in small round inlets, casting a weird, brownish glow over the area. One of the lights was burnt out, and another was completely missing, the socket bare.

We headed up the second flight of stairs. The elevator we passed had a piece of yellowed paper with a "DO NOT USE" warning taped across it.

"We've been running on minimal repairs," Pops explained. "We have decent funding, but we haven't had a chance to resupply and Crush only has so much time to work. He usually monitors the computers for signs of enemy activity." Pops stopped at a plain bronze door at the top flight of steps. "This is Jim's office. My room is across the hall."

Inside, a dusty world globe sat on the corner of an ornate wood desk obscured by various file folders and papers. Books were piled high, their spines haphazardly stacked like a puzzle game. An ancient, faded rug lay beneath the desk, so worn that its vibrant, geometric shapes and numbers were barely distinguishable. Bookshelves surrounded us from floor to ceiling, organized and decorated with models of antique stealth planes and trinkets. A giant arched window graced the far wall, overlooking the night sky, and two red, plush chairs sat opposite the desk, where a reading lamp blanketed the room in a warm glow.

Lance whistled. "That's a lot of books."

I nodded my agreement. Behind the desk sat a heavyset man with dark brown skin. He wore small, rectangular reading glasses. Despite his age, there was something in the way he sat that made me think he was more resilient than most elders I'd encountered.

"Jim," Pops said, "this is Lance, Tim, and Jenna — my granddaughter." I shifted uneasily.

"Nice to meet you." Jim removed his reading glasses and set them beside his book.

The three of us inclined our heads in an indication of respect to an elder. "The honor is ours," we said. He certainly met the qualifications by Community standards. Come to think of it, I probably should've said the respect to Pops, too, but I'd been too distracted by him trying to kidnap me.

Jim gave us a wry smile. "No need for the formalities; they make me feel old."

"You *are* old." Jack leaned against the doorway, one arm craned over his head. He'd changed into worn jeans that weren't so bloody — though his dark green jacket remained.

"Pops said you were here since the beginning," Tim said. "How old *are* you?"

Jim's eyes sparkled in the reading lamp. "I lived during the pre-Community era, and I was a member of the Super Bureau before the Camaraderie destroyed it."

I glanced between Pops and Jim. "Super Bureau? I'm guessing you have 'powers,' too?"

"Super toughness and telekinesis." The globe on the corner of Jim's desk wavered, then eased upward so that it hung in midair. A model of an old space shuttle floated around it, no strings, nothing touching. "Unfortunately, I got hit by one too many cars and my body got stiff."

Tim's eyes went wide. "You got hit by cars?"

"I could stop cars with my hands, yes." The globe rested itself on the books while the shuttle flew to its place on the bookshelf. "It still hurt. The last one I got hit by paralyzed me from the waist down. Super toughness just made it easier for me to survive encounters with the agents of villains like Lord Black and Sanjorez."

"Lord Black was a noble gentleman, not a . . . villain," Tim protested. He held a model of an old biplane to the light, reflections glancing off the peeling paint and plastic. He frowned and carefully replaced the model on the shelf.

Disapproving wrinkles creased at the corner of Jim's eyes. "Lord Black was the Community's founder, but he was also the founder of the Camaraderie of Evil. He destroyed multiple democratic societies, and because of him, there are precious few superheroes remaining."

Tim scowled. "Pre-Community societies were ineffective, corrupt—"

Lance shushed him. "Camaraderie of Evil? Superheroes?"

I took a seat in one of the chairs. We were going to be here a while.

Behind us, Jack snorted. "Superheroes—like comic books. You've heard of comic books, right? Video games?"

The three of us exchanged glances. We'd played interactive educational activities on EYEnet, but those weren't particularly humorous or fun.

"You've . . . you've *heard* of video games, right?" Jack pushed himself from the doorway and gaped at us.

We shook our heads.

Jack grunted. "Pops, I'm telling you—the Community sucks."

Tim stuffed his hands in his pockets. "The Community is safe, secure, and efficient. It's not . . . bad."

"For those who are not elementals or power users—yes. For those whose genes designate they have powers, the Community is hardly safe," Jim said. "In order to preserve their status, members of the Camaraderie sort power users into three categories: those they shield, those who are loyal enough to join Special Forces, and—"

"My dad never said anything about powers," Lance countered, "and my Mom was Special Forces. He would've said *something*."

"Lance—" I started, and Lance spun around. "Your dad might not have known. Think about the councilor. She didn't know."

"He's the security official for St. Petersburg—how could he not know?"

Jim rested his hands on his stomach. "Depending on their clearance, Special Forces agents are told different stories about how theophrenia works. Some are told powers are a side-effect of theophrenia. Others—including security officials—might never know that the Camaraderie exists behind E-Leadership."

Lance scowled and sat back in his chair.

"Okay—what exactly *is* the Camaraderie?" I asked.

Jim motioned to a bookshelf, and a binder lifted from the lower shelf and floated to his desk. "The Camaraderie is a widespread organization that controls approximately a third of the world's population. It manages the Community and the surrounding territories, but keeps its existence a secret. It consists of four primary council members, whom you know as international E-Leadership, as well as its military and select officials within the Community.

"Before theophrenia, we were unaware of their identities. We thought they were just the founders of EYEnet. Instead, they infiltrated Special Forces, disbanded the Super Bureau, and used EYEnet as a front for their politics. They were backed by Jellyman, whom you know as Lord Black."

"Jellyman?" Lance raised an eyebrow.

"Us 'heroes' got to calling him that for his natural form. He was a shapeshifter whose natural form looked like translucent blue jelly. Figured that out when we took a shield to him and he turned to a pile of goo. But he was also a skilled telepath. He understood politics, and he used that to his advantage."

"EYEnet is helpful," Tim interrupted. "They found the cure for theophrenia and made sure it was available to everyone. They were more efficient than the previous government, so the United States citizens called for a change in power."

"Not quite. Since Lord Black was behind EYEnet, he easily spotted political opposition online and eliminated threats to his rise to power. In addition, his telepathy allowed him to sway voters to his side, and he used shapeshifting to charade as politicians. Between him and the rest of the Camaraderie members, they ousted the Super Bureau and linked our powers to 'theophrenia.' The common person — in fear — bought those lies and gave up their freedom in return for the safety of the Community."

Lance twisted his lips and Tim worried his charm between his fingers. "We're free enough," Tim said. "The Community keeps us safe, we're secure in our careers, and it makes our workflow efficient. That's hardly evil."

"You have choices," Jim agreed. "But those choices are limited."

"He's right." Lance glanced at us from his chair, his chin propped against his knuckles. "We choose from a list they make for us from our test results. Seems like a pretty good way to keep everyone under control."

"But it's efficient!" Tim protested.

"Efficient, yes," Jim said. "However, it limits a person's potential to grow and become something more than a basic drone."

"Sounds like theophrenic delusions of grandeur," Tim grumbled, one hand linked over his light bulb charm.

Jim patted his books. "Theophrenia is not a real disease. Best we can tell, the only 'true' form of theophrenia was a telepathic sleeper seed — a mentally planted suggestion that had to be placed by an elite telepath. Not contagious. However, the seed caused its victim to make irrational claims about their powers or act harmfully against themselves and others, thus making them look like threats. The Camaraderie was afraid that those with powers would turn against them, so they claimed their drug — adominogen — could protect against theophrenia, and they use it to suppress powers. Hence why someone's 'delusion' that they have special abilities goes away while they're taking the pill."

I crossed my arms. "Okay, so what happens to people who fail the scan?"

A quiet hush settled over the room, and Jim and Jack exchanged glances. The eerie silence paved way to the perpetual tick of the airship's heaters.

"They're taken to a transformation facility," Pops said softly.

"Beastie plant," Jack corrected him.

"Wait . . ." I turned to face Jack. "Beasts. You mean with cat-like eyes, pointed ears . . ."

Jack raised an eyebrow. "How'd you know that?"

I pointed at Tim, who blushed. "He found a security feed of one when he hacked the health network."

"What are they?" Lance asked.

"They're subhuman monsters made from people with powers," Pops explained. "When a person fails the scan, they're given the choice to join the commander's army of beasts — though they are not told of the impending transformation — or to join Special Forces, where they learn to use their powers. In some circumstances, they have a shield surgically implanted to block those powers. But the choice is rarely a true one. The Camaraderie employs those with persuasion powers to tip the balance one way or the other, depending on the person's expected loyalty. Very few can resist." He glanced at me. "Had you stayed, you would likely have been transformed into a plant beast."

"Plant beast?" I shuddered. When it came to beasties, I much preferred the image of Sam's mangy fur ball, Little Beastie, tearing up my garden back home than the image of the creature in the security feed.

Jim telekinetically removed another book from the shelf, opened it to a central page, and then floated it to my lap. This book had crisp white pages and sharp, detailed photographs. I stroked my finger along the caption beside the photo. The image had been taken in a jungle, with thick ferns and tall trees spiraling around the frame. It focused on a vaguely humanoid creature. Thick, woody vines wrapped around its hands, twined across its shoulders, and curled around its collarbone. The vines rested loose against its bare chest. The creature — male — was naked, with pale, green-tinted skin and a thicker brow. Like the beast we'd seen in the security feed, this one had cat-like eyes and pointed ears.

The photograph gave me the chills, and I handed the book to Tim. "I don't understand what could cause this kind of deformity."

"A genetic mutation caused by a very specific radiation," Jim said. "You'll have to talk to Pops for the details, though. Radiological genetics are beyond my expertise. Regardless, Community citizens and rebels alike are sent to the transformation facilities, where they undergo a brutal process that strips them of their memories, their will, and their humanity. They are the Camaraderie's foot soldiers."

Lance shifted uncomfortably in his chair. "What does the Camaraderie need an army for? No offense, but I haven't seen anything here that a squad of Community guards couldn't take care of, let alone a good Special Forces team."

Jack smirked. "Ain't us they're worried about."

With a little fishing, Jim retrieved a map from his desk and motioned to a large chunk of Asia. Bright yellow dots were marked across the continent in strategic clusters.

I frowned. "Commander Rick defeated the Oriental Alliance a long time ago. Everything was converted to Community government."

Jack grinned. "That's what he *wishes* happened. In reality, the OA holds their own."

"You say they've got beast armies, and Special Forces has some pretty advanced tech. They should've captured any rogue territory by now," Lance pointed out.

"Well kids, beasties are only so effective against mechs." Jack motioned to Jim's tablet. "You got a picture we can show them?"

"We've seen mechs before," Tim protested.

Jim chuckled and floated a tablet to Lance. "Correct me if I am wrong, but the pictures in your history books were from a few decades ago, correct?" He pointed to the photograph. "That," he said, "is the modern mech. They were developed in the last fifteen years, and they are now in use."

"Whoa," Tim whispered, looking over at the tablet. "Its engine must be really efficient to power something that size."

"Giant death machines and he's going on about efficiency," Jack muttered.

I leaned over the arm of the chair toward them, and Lance got up from his seat to show me. The tablet revealed a gleaming metal contraption that was maybe two stories tall with guns for arms. Smaller creatures were frozen in mid-leap as they clawed at its glass pod. Dirt, mud, and blood coated its metal exterior, and the dent in its side somehow made it look even more threatening.

"Given the amount of 3D rendering the sciences use, that mech could be an image of a prototype that was never actually manufactured," I said. "Until we see one for ourselves, we can't know it exists."

"For crying out loud!" Jack waved his hand at the tablet. "What more evidence do you need?"

I spun in the chair. "You're contradicting everything we've ever known, and you expect us to believe you? Sure, you've proven that powers are real. But that proves nothing about the Community's history. When, exactly, are we going to get to go back? Ever?"

Pops sighed. "Don't worry, Jenna. If you choose to return to the Community, I won't stop you. But I want you to have all the information about what could happen if you do. There is a lot out there that you should know, but we can't tell you everything in one night. Please, bear with us."

"Fine — one more question. Who are the people behind this so-called Camaraderie?"

"Commander Rick leads the council, and he controls their armies using telepathy and beast mastery," Jim said. "Lady Black acts as their diplomat. She uses shapeshifting and persuasion to convince her targets that she has favorable terms. Master Matoska is their primary bounty hunter, and he uses psychic tracking and his skill with crossbows to hunt enemies. Lady Winters is their primary telepath, which she uses in conjunction with memory steal to take the information she wants from the people she interrogates. Together, they rule the Community under the guise of benevolent leaders."

I sat back in the chair. Commander Rick I could understand because of his military prowess. Lady Black I could see because I'd experienced her persuasion firsthand. But I had a hard time picturing Master Matoska as some sort of bounty hunter, though being the head of Conservation and Wildlife did give him the advantage of spending time away from the Community. As for Lady Winters . . . "How does being the Head of Efficiency relate to interrogating people?"

Jack snorted. "Because she's 'efficient' in her methods."

Lance squeezed my shoulder. "Special Forces protects the Community," he whispered, "but what if there's more to protecting the Community than just security? What if Commander Rick and Lady Black really are the villains, and it's our job to stop them?"

I didn't want them to be the bad guys. I wanted world peace and for the Community to be safe. But whether I liked it or not, these rebels didn't seem to have any reason to lie. I thought back to Chill, who had died protecting me.

I glanced at Jack. He stood in the doorway, scratching his chin, which was covered with thin gashes about a fingers width apart. All those faint silvery scars looked like claw marks.

"Have you ever fought a beast?" I asked.

"Well, *yeah*. Why would the Camaraderie send Special Forces when they can send a beastie? Beasties are easy to come by. An agent takes time to train."

I sighed and faced Pops. Exhaustion was setting in from today's events, and I wanted to talk to Lance and Tim in private. "If you don't mind . . . it's been a long day. Where are we going to sleep?"

"And dinner," Lance suggested.

Pops took his cane from the wall. "I'll show you around, and then take you to your quarters so you can rest."

I glanced at Jim. "Thanks for talking with us. The Community is safe," I said automatically.

"Unless you have superpowers," Jim said quietly. He picked his book off the desk, removed the ribbon marker, and resumed reading.

CHAPTER
TEN

"This is the command room," Pops said. Venting fans drowned the airship's hum with a set of perpetual clicks, which were slightly out of time with the blinking blue, green, and yellow lights that flashed across the monitors. The smell of warm plastic mingled with dust. A huge flat screen computer sat front and center, with two smaller screens near the windows. They each streamed data, though one flickered a monochrome yellow. Wires held together by colorful, labeled twist ties were tucked into corners and suspended from the ceiling.

I felt like I'd stepped back half a century.

"Everything's so . . . old," I murmured.

Tim stared in disbelief at all the exposed wires. "Don't you have wireless networks?"

Pops shook his head. "We can't risk the Camaraderie hacking into the ship and getting our coordinates. So everything goes through ethernet cables."

Tim grimaced at the wires, then edged back out the door. "Is it just me, or does this room give anybody else a headache?"

"Just you," Lance said.

Pops snorted, then led us to end of the hall and introduced us to the cafeteria. The room had a sink on one side, a few cabinets, and three small tables crowded together at the center.

My stomach rumbled involuntarily; I hadn't had a decent meal all day.

Lance peered inside the kitchen door. "When's dinner?"

"Whenever you want," Pops said, motioning his cane toward the tiny cafeteria. "We've got rations stored in the cargo hold. Help yourself to anything here."

He led us down the narrow staircase and paused at the second deck to point out the sick bay, public restrooms, countless storage rooms, and what counted for a training room.

"What about that room?" Tim asked, pointing to the one beside the sick bay.

"Used to be a brig," Pops said, "but we use it for storage." Lance took a second glance at the unmarked room as Pops motioned to the stairs. "This way. We can get you settled in."

The lowest floor had a maintenance room at the end of the hall, and a row of several rooms with plain doors and soft yellow light. Pops showed us where everyone else lived, then showed us to our rooms. "Why don't you three take a look around? I have some things I need to attend to." He stepped out and closed the door behind him.

Each of our rooms had basic furnishings and a shared restroom. The showers had warm water, despite the lack of pressure, and my bed was covered in a simple, dark blue sheet.

While Lance and Tim explored my room, I trailed my fingers through the leaves of a small, leafy plant that sat on the corner of my desk. It was different than the one I'd kept at the dorms; this one was some kind of vine. Possibly a heartleaf philodendron?

I frowned, wondering if Ivan would give my spider plant to my parents. The guards would tell them I was a security risk, but whether my parents would hear that I'd died, been sent away, or was a threat, I couldn't say. The guards wouldn't say I'd escaped . . . not after everything that happened. The only thing they could confirm was that I was infected.

Then again, they might not say anything at all.

I shivered. I needed to tell my parents what happened. They might know about Pops.

I shrugged off my backpack and pushed aside two slightly dented textbooks. A small blue light flashed at the bottom of the bag from my buried cell phone reminding me that I had an EYEnote. I flipped the phone open and punched in my parents' number, then noticed the tower indicator.

No signal.

I couldn't call my parents if I tried.

"So we're stuck on an airship with no signal and no way of contacting anyone, with a group of rebels who shouldn't exist," Lance said, pacing in my room. He paused, swiveled on his heel, then stood straight. A single fluorescent light strip glowed from the ceiling, shining off the metallic walls and illuminating his face. "But they have powers, and as far as I can tell, theophrenia isn't real."

"I'm not denying that they have powers," I said, wearily picking at the precooked Salisbury steak I'd found in the freezer for dinner. "What about everything else they said? Beasts and mechs and all that? Shouldn't we have heard something?"

Lance rubbed his hands and sat on the bed. It sagged beneath him, which was surprising considering he was mostly lean muscle. "One of security's tactics for preventing riots is to cover up details that aren't necessary to everyday life. Maybe E-Leadership doesn't talk about powers or beasts because they're trying to prevent mass chaos. Jim is right . . . it makes us easy to control."

Tim glanced at Lance, then me. "For all that I don't think the rebels plan to hurt us, they could be lying. Have you considered that Pops might not be your grandfather?"

"Sure. But if he isn't, why didn't Lady Black say so in the first place?"

"Could be because she was trying to keep you from freaking out," Lance said, "*or* because she's really a super villain trying to use you as bait to capture someone who obviously cared enough to come rescue you."

"Maybe he has some other use for me—I obviously have *some* kind of plant power."

Tim frowned. "You guys keep mentioning this plant power, but I haven't seen it."

I glanced at the potted plant on my desk. It was just *there*. A plant. I closed my eyes, trying to imagine it growing like the other plants did, but nothing happened. I sighed. "If I do have powers, I'm going to have to wait until the injection wears off. I think it's like the pills. Jim did say they block powers."

"I guess you're right," Tim said. "It's just . . . this is all so unbelievable."

"I know it is. But these guys haven't done anything to make me feel threatened. And if what they told us is true, then Chill died trying to protect me from being turned into a beast."

My chest clenched. The Community was safe. Efficient. I liked that. But if the rebels weren't lying to us, then we needed a way to tell the rest of the Community what was going on before anyone else got hurt. "For now, we should find out what these people have planned. Jim seems willing enough to speak with us. Let's find proof of what they're saying, then decide what to do from there."

Tim tugged on his necklace chain. "Do we have an escape plan, in case they're lying?"

"Unless you know how to fly an invisible car or a whirli-whatcha-call-it, not really." I glanced at my signal-less phone.

Tim muttered that he wouldn't mind having a go at the car, and Lance grinned. "Hey, maybe we can save the world from the evil rebels and you can impress Sam with all your awesome adventures." He jabbed Tim playfully.

I sighed as the two of them joked about their low odds of getting a date here. At least they could make light of the situation. I couldn't stop thinking that we had nothing to compare notes with. These rebels could tell us anything, and we'd have no way of checking their sources.

A soft rap echoed behind us and I sat up quickly. Pops stood in the doorway. "Your rooms are ready," he told Lance and Tim. "You're welcome to continue talking, but it has been a long day." He paused. "I'll be in my office if you need me. Good night."

He closed the door behind him.

Lance let out a sigh, then pushed himself from the bed. "He's right; I'm exhausted. Are you going to be okay in here?" He wrapped his fingers nervously around his sword. "I mean—"

"I'll be fine." I pushed my plate aside and plopped on the now-warm bed. "Get some sleep."

"You too, Jen." He nudged Tim. "Coming?"

Tim packed up his tablet and the two of them headed into the hall.

The airship felt colder as I crawled under the covers. The sheets rustled with my every move. I tried to close my eyes, but Chill kept dying in front of me.

I blinked at the reflective ceiling and focused on the soft, foreign hum of the engines.

Tomorrow, I'd see if these rebels were telling the truth.

CHAPTER
ELEVEN

Harsh light flooded through the porthole window at the head of my bed. Morning came bright. I sat up, looking for a clock, but there wasn't one.

I struggled out of bed, limbs dragging, and snagged my phone from my backpack.

10:33

Late!

Frantic, I straightened my clothes and darted outside. I counted the rooms, then pounded on Lance's door. No answer. Tim's door—no answer.

Wait a moment.

I was on an *airship.* Outside the Community. If I needed to get up, someone would have come to get me. As it was, the hall was empty.

I headed upstairs and stopped on the second floor, but only heard the soft tick of the heater rattling through the vents. The doors were shut with no sign of movement on the stairs above or below me, and while I heard the distant clang of repairs in the hangar bay, I doubted anyone would come looking in the next few minutes.

Time to see if these "rebels" were telling the truth.

I glanced at the bland door in the middle of the hall—the one Pops said had been a brig. After another furtive check to see if anyone was coming, I tried the knob. It turned easily, despite the squeak of unoiled hinges. No light shone inside, so I pushed the door further, fully expecting to see functioning coolers or a dungeon cell with chains and shackles.

Instead, I came face-first with a teetering stack of cardboard boxes. They were all labeled in red and black marker with quickly stroked letters that said: "BOOKS." "DVDS." "MISC."

They kept books in a brig? And DVDs? Talk about outdated.

I slipped inside the room and pushed a rubber door stopper in the door.

Farther inside, an old computer covered in thick dust had been positioned beside the door. More boxes were scattered around it and three steel cells towered behind them. I stood on my tippy-toes and peeked inside their peephole windows. Boxes in two, and an empty cell behind the other. It looked like they didn't use this place much after all.

I scratched my head and checked the doors' inner frames. The rebels didn't even have force field technology, if the lack of conduit points suggested anything.

As for the boxes, only a few had been taped over and the closest one with tucked corners sat beside the desktop. The lid gave easily, and once open I found a layer of old books and folders filled with yellowed pages. One book was a few decades old and was filled with text and diagrams. Another had pictures printed with black ink, distant images of strange, mutated creatures racing through jungle and field, and a couple close-ups of a facility somewhere in Central America. The pictures were blurred and indistinct, except one of a creature that looked like it suffered from major burns. The skin around its arms and legs was black and ashy and it lay surrounded by charred foliage.

I ran my finger along the page, skimming for details, then paused at the passage just below the photograph.

> *March, 2021: I finally secured a picture of this poor fellow. Had others, but most were destroyed in the subsequent attacks. I'll*

have to leave the good pics to those with experience. Anyhow, this was a fire beast. Roasted several of my companions before Mendez took him out. From what I can tell, they've got a decent range, so long as they have something to burn.

A throat cleared behind me. I dropped the book and spun around, my heart pounding in my ears. Jack leaned in the doorway, the tattered door stopper between his fingers. "I gotta hand it to you for trying to make sure you didn't get locked in, but it helps to check if the door can be locked from outside." He tossed the door stopper into the corner and crossed his arms over his chest. "Helpful tip—the only doors around here that can't be opened from inside are the three behind ya." He jabbed his thumb at the cell doors, and I couldn't help but notice he didn't have his claws back.

"I wanted to know if Pops was telling the truth."

Jack snorted. "Did you *want* to find something?"

"Of course not! But . . ." I glanced around the musty room. "Why all the boxes?"

He shrugged and scratched his five-o-clock shadow. "Jim's room is full. I keep trying to convince him these things are outdated, but he seems to think these old books might have some little bit of info that'll sink the Camaraderie."

I slipped the book back into its box and tucked the corners how I'd found them. "Where's Lance and Tim?"

"Upstairs." He raised an eyebrow. "Why don't you grab some breakfast, and I'll let Pops know you're awake?"

I raced for the door before it could shut behind him, but he was right. There was no lock on the door. I let out a sigh of relief and hurried up the stairs. Tim's voice echoed down the hall, and I found him and Lance sitting in the kitchen at a table stacked with dirty dishes. An empty scabbard rested against the side of the table.

"Morning, Jenna," Tim said, far too chipper.

I glared at them. "Why didn't you guys wake me up?"

"Pops said to let you sleep." Lance drummed his fingers on the table. "He sent us to Jack instead."

"And you just now had breakfast? I'm surprised you waited that long."

"Actually, I came back for a snack."

"Figures. At least *you* got up on time," I grumbled. "What's for food?"

Lance motioned to the cupboards. "According to Jack, anything you can find. I'd avoid the granola, though. Tastes funny."

"We're on an *airship* with a bunch of *rebels*, whom we don't know much about, and you're complaining about how the granola tastes?"

He held up a polishing rag and grinned. I peered over the table. His sword rested in his lap. For the love of efficiency . . . I rubbed my fingers against my forehead. "Let me guess, you've been cleaning your sword for the past three hours?"

"Two," he corrected, and returned to polishing the blade, careful not to touch the metal with his fingers. "Jack didn't give me the supplies I needed until he woke up, which was about an hour after we talked to Pops. But guess what? They don't care if I carry the sword with me around here! Jack even promised to give me fighting lessons, and he has these katanas —"

"So what about you?" I asked Tim, hoping to avert a long discussion on the craft of various weaponry.

Tim handed me his tablet and twisted his charm necklace between his fingers. "I can't get a connection with EYEnet or their computers since they don't keep a wireless network, but Inese gave me a set of documents detailing how anti-gravity technology works. Their flying car was a Camaraderie prototype, and it has an invisibility generator. I'd thought she was using her powers . . ."

I got it. They each had something of endless fascination, and they'd decided these rebels were trustworthy.

"Have fun with that," I mumbled, returning his tablet. Mom could make sense of the technical details. Me — not so much.

I headed to the kitchen counter, but this place was in as bad a condition as the hangar. One of the cabinet handles dangled by a single screw, and the sink was lined with seeping cracks. The front side of the fridge was covered in black mildew, and a stained, crumpled towel hung haphazardly off the edge of the counter. The cupboard offered a couple boxes of cereal, a box of instant oats and a tall stack of granola bars, while the rest of the shelves were bare, complete with peeling, floral printed paper. One of the boxes had a brand of cereal I didn't recognize, with a photograph on the front that showed a bowl with a variety of brightly colored objects floating in milk. Out of everything here, it looked the most appealing. Cereal chosen, I found an open milk container on the upper shelf of the fridge. The odor wasn't much worse than cafeteria milk, though I guessed it must have been powdered at some point.

After I poured my cereal, I returned to the guys and took a seat. Strange, colorful shapes floated to the top of my bowl and I poked at them with my spoon, letting them bob in the liquid. They didn't look particularly edible.

I took a bite, then nearly spit the stuff out.

Lance frowned. "You all right?"

"Yeah," I mumbled, choking down the offending cereal. "It's *sweet!*"

"Isn't it great?" Lance beamed.

I eyed the bowl suspiciously. Sure, cereal usually had *some* amount of sugar in it, but this was ridiculous. There were *marshmallows* in my cereal. "I'd prefer corn puffs," I grumbled, but ate it anyway. The milk was tainted by traces of color from soggy marshmallows, but at least this was food—even if it should've been dessert.

After I finished breakfast, Pops joined us in the kitchen. "Good to see you're awake," he told me. "Are you feeling all right?"

"More or less." My legs were stiff and I didn't want to go flying around in an invisible car anytime soon, but I didn't feel like I was going to pass out.

"Good to hear. Feel free to talk to me if you have any questions."

He gave us a curt nod and hobbled down the hall. Messy airship aside, Pops reminded me of the dignified E-Leadership officers in the efficiency department with their formal business suits, staunch postures, and general sense that they were in charge.

I rinsed my dishes and put them where I'd found them, then waved to Tim and Lance. "I'm going to see what else I can learn from Jim."

Lance raised his cleaning rag and smiled. "Have fun."

I snorted. He was just happy someone around here shared his interest in swords.

Once at Jim's room I knocked on the partially open door. Jim looked up from his book. "Ah. Thought you might return. How can I help?"

I left the door cracked, forcing myself not to greet him formally. "I was wondering what else you can tell me about the world—if you don't mind."

The elderly man placed a sturdy bookmark between the pages of his book. "What specifically would you like to know?"

"Well—I want to know more about this rebellion. You mentioned the Oriental Alliance. Do you guys work with them?"

"We work with multiple organizations." A stack of books rose from Jim's desk and he slipped a map out from underneath. "While the Oriental Alliance is the largest opposition, there are a few good sized rebellions outside of Asia who undermine the Camaraderie when they can."

"Why fight the Camaraderie at all? If there's no war, no one would need beasts."

The wrinkles on Jim's forehead creased as he frowned. "They would still root out people with powers, and anyone they see as a threat." He paused. "Are you interested in history?"

"Sure, but it's been the same thing since high school. No one talks about pre-Community history, except to mention the riots. If you don't believe me, I can show you my textbook."

"Before the Camaraderie, most 'riots' were peaceful demonstrations. Camaraderie members incited the riots themselves. The violence gave them a purpose to their claims that the general community needed security . . . and gave them a means to their rise in power. However, I would be curious to see your textbook. I am interested to know how it has changed."

I sprang from my seat and accidentally knocked the map off my lap. Someone with pre-Community experience was interested in discussing history? I grinned. "Let me grab it—I'll be right back." Jim chuckled as I scrambled to grab the paper from the faded rug and then rushed out the door.

When I returned after several stairs later, there was a thick, hardback book sitting on my chair. I handed Jim my textbooks, then picked up the one he'd left for me. The cover was printed with a bright painting of young ladies in long white dresses, each carrying a basket of grapes. It was a lot more colorful than the covers on the textbooks we had in the Community.

"That book was written before the Camaraderie took power," Jim said, gesturing to the book in my hands. Each page was ripe with text and illustrations, some familiar and some I'd never seen. My insides fluttered. Not only was this world history, but a pre-plague book was nearly impossible to find. Most of the older books had been burned to prevent further spread of the disease.

"Knowledge is power," Jim continued, "and history is the greatest knowledge one can use. It is a power that the Camaraderie prefers you do not possess. You can borrow that book if you like."

"Really?" I clutched the book to my chest.

"I have an extensive reading list ahead of me." He motioned to the stack of books on his desk. "Why don't you hang onto it, and if you have any questions, feel free to return."

I grinned. "I'll do that."

Jim folded his hands across his stomach and smiled. "It is not often I find someone interested in pre-Community history."

"No idea why." I stepped to his desk, my arms wrapped around the textbook. Even if these stories turned out to be lies, they'd offer insights about these rebels I couldn't even begin to ask directly. "Thank you."

I left his office, still admiring the worn, glossy cover of the hundred-year-old treasure. I had every intention of speaking with him again, and I would definitely add this textbook to my study list.

☙

I spent the next couple hours reading Jim's history book. Then, shortly after lunch, Inese called everyone to the command center. Sunlight streamed through an uneven set of cracked blinds along the giant windows at front. Even Jim's silvery walker glinted in the light, leaving tiny, purple dots in my vision. Golden dust specks danced around the crew and swirled in eddies near the computer fans and vents, and Jack waved a particularly thick cluster of dust from his nose.

"Glad you guys made it," Crush said, nodding to us. Although he looked about Inese's age—early thirties—he had faint traces of a Welsh accent instead of Inese's English Community accent. He handed Pops a rectangular, white device. "It should be calibrated now—hopefully it'll read life signs this time."

"What does it do?" I asked. It looked similar to what Agent Kirsch had.

"The scanner contains a list of different power traits," Pops said. "It reads your genetic radio frequency and matches it with a known set of abilities. If you have powers, you'll have one major power and up to two minor powers."

I raised an eyebrow. "You can tell this by scanning? You don't need any genetic material?"

Pops nodded. "The exact science of radiological genetics was developed by the Camaraderie. Same as a lot of the other tech you see around here. The Community scanners use a code rather than giving the exact details, and whoever administers the scan can use that information to determine whether or not they intend to make the patient a beast or invite them into Special Forces." He gestured to Lance. "Step forward, please."

The team dispersed into a semi-circle as Lance went to stand beside Pops, a spring in his step. Since his mom was Special Forces, and agents tended to have powers, it made sense that she might've passed them on—and why Lance was so excited.

Pops held the scanner just above Lance's skull, then lowered the device to his feet, repeating the procedure until the scanner beeped. "Your main power is linked to motor coordination with a weapon or item," he explained as Lance fidgeted. "It's a subset of enhanced agility. Put simply, a person with a weapons power can use that weapon as if it were an extension of themselves. They inherently have the reflexes necessary to use that particular type of weapon."

"Also known as an extreme weapons skill," Jim said, smiling. "I would bet that your specialty is swords."

I half expected Lance to start swinging his sword around then and there, his face was so bright. He grinned. "I can go with that."

"You also have enhanced speed and portal creation," Pops said.

"Portals?" Lance glanced between Inese and Jack, one hand cradling the grip of his sword.

I frowned. Portals *did* sound intriguing, but we'd just left the biological realm of possibility and jumped into quantum physics. Why couldn't I have been a couple more years into college before this happened? I might've actually understood how this was supposed to work.

"We'll do our best to teach you," Inese said. "Just takes a bit of training."

"All right, Tim, you're next." Pops set about trying to administer the scan, but after multiple swipes of the device, he narrowed his eyes. "It broke again."

Crush took the scanner to a computer desk, where he twisted the knobs and tested the voltage, muttering about how it wasn't even calibrated for binary code or digital images. Everyone waited silently until Crush's face went red.

"What . . . how is this even—" Crush gaped at the scanner, mortified.

Jack glanced over Crush's shoulder and burst out laughing. "Now, there's something ya don't see every day." He patted Inese on the back. "You could catch a cold in that outfit."

She raised an eyebrow at Jack, then gathered with the rest of us around Crush, who hid the face of the device against his chest. "Nothing!" he protested. "It's nothing! Just a glitch!"

Jack chortled and Tim snatched the scanner, giving me a brief glimpse of the black and white image of Inese wearing less than the scantily clad leaders in those cheesy Community brochures.

Pops sighed. "Clear your mind," he told Tim. "I assume you've had a programming class? Picture running a basic program. Focus on the codes."

The image dissipated into a stream of ones and zeros, and Tim's face flushed a deep, crimson pink. He sheepishly returned the scanner to Pops.

Jack grinned and nudged Inese with his elbow, and received a glare in return.

"Come on, now." Pops scoffed and resumed his scan. "We're all adults. *Anyway* . . ." Pops turned his attention to Tim. "You have techno sight, the ability to control and manipulate computer technology with your mind. Your second power is enhanced intelligence. I'll have you spend most of your time here with Crush. He'll help you understand your powers and train you on navigation, if you wish."

Lance elbowed him. "Nice."

Tim nodded, his eyes wide and his cheeks pink. Crush forced a weak smile. I could only imagine how hard it would be on him to train someone new right after his brother died on the previous mission.

"Jenna?" Pops held up the device. "While we know you're a plant elemental, we don't know what other powers you have. Most people have two or three. I have two powers. Your grandmother had three."

"My grandmother?" I hadn't imagined she might be alive.

But it didn't sound like she was.

"Your father also has powers."

"But I thought—"

Pops held up his hand. "He is among those who are shielded. When you weren't taking the pill, did you notice anything different about him?"

I paused, remembering an incident when I'd hugged him last summer. "If I touched him, everything felt dull. Lifeless."

"Skin contact?"

I nodded.

"There's a device, called a Benjamin's Shield, which blocks powers in an individual. That's the surgical operation they perform. But shields block *all* powers, so if a power user comes in direct contact with someone who is shielded, their powers are blocked as well." He folded his hands overtop his cane, his lips forming a thin line under his salt-and-pepper mustache.

"So . . . my dad has powers, too."

"Yes. Shall we proceed?"

I nodded, squared my shoulders, and then stepped under Pops' scanner.

CHAPTER
TWELVE

I jumped as the scanner beeped. The tiniest of a smirk tugged at Jack's lips and I glared at him, earning an even bigger grin.

"You have two powers, like Tim," Pops said. "Plant manipulation and speed."

"Speed?"

He nodded, showing me the screen of the scanner. Plants I understood, given my recent experiences. As for speed, running came naturally, and I enjoyed the sensation of the ground flying beneath my feet. But I'd never equated it to special powers.

Jack grunted. "Two kids with speed? Really?"

"Don't worry, it just means fewer people complaining about my car rides." Inese nudged him in the ribs, and even Crush laughed a little at the glare Jack gave her.

"You and Lance will train with Jack," Pops told me. He fastened the scanning device in a small white case and handed it to Crush, who placed the device among various other gadgets.

"Wait a minute," Jack protested. "Isn't one student enough?"

"You're the best one to train her for plant powers."

"Sure . . . plants are going to flourish wonders for me now that I've got someone to mentor."

"You garden?" I asked. The burly man didn't look like he'd have any inclination toward gardening except for the bit of grit under his claws, which had returned.

Jack snorted. "No. According to the scanner, plants are supposed to flower all pretty-like around me." He waggled his clawed fingers. "But they don't like to cooperate."

Crush hauled the box of gadgets across the room and sat it with a thunk beside a pile of boxes. "At least you get to use *one* of your powers," he said softly. "I rarely get to use either of mine."

"All right, everyone," Pops said. "Back to work. Crush—see what Gwen is up to. Inform her about the latest developments."

"Yes, sir," Crush said, and the rest of the crew filtered through the door while Jack led Lance and I to the opposite end of the airship.

There was a service entry behind the stairs that opened to a large, empty room. Pipes ran to the ceiling from the center of the lower deck and split at odd angles. Stainless steel counters surrounded the thick metal pipes; remnants of what might have once been buffet tables. Holes resembling claw marks punctured the larger pipes, as if Jack had practiced climbing them. A track—which might've been a basic walkway before the rebels claimed it—led around the upper floor. A simple, bronze-coated railing kept us from a steep fall, though the cylindrical rail had been bent out of shape as if something had run into it. The dents looked a lot like the damage Alec did to the prison, and the ceiling was high enough for flying.

About the only things that didn't look dingy were the giant windows set along the farthest wall. Coppery metal panels covered those windows from outside, meant to protect the glass while not in use, and the two doors on either side had caution tape wrapped around their handles. Given the sheer size of the windows and the potential view, ambassadors might've used this ship at some point. But everything else was so bent and rusted that the ship must've been running for a long time.

Jack cocked his head, watching us examine the gym. "Lance, come with me. Jenna, if you've got some kind of plant here, go get it and meet us downstairs."

I left Lance behind and headed to my makeshift room. I grabbed my plant, and by the time I returned to the lower training deck, Lance held a long, sleek sword with a lightly curved blade. Its handle was wrapped in flat trimming. The sword wasn't like the hand-and-a-half he already carried, and he almost tripped over himself to show me.

"Jack's going to teach me how to use two swords at the same time! I know a little, but not enough to actually fight." He grinned, out of breath with excitement.

"Hopefully you'll know enough," Jack said. "Beasties are tough—a pain to deal with. Brutal, but not smart." He tapped his forehead. "The question goes to how smart the beastmaster is. But you won't be training with that." He tossed Lance two polished wooden staves the same length as the sword. From the way Lance caught them, they had some heft. "Start doing exercises or routines, whatever you usually do to warm up."

Lance nodded and stretched his arms to the sky, crossing them behind his head and grabbing his elbows. I hadn't really watched him stretch before, and he exhibited a lot more gracefulness than I'd expected. His movements were smooth, as if he really did have some special knack for all this.

Once Lance finished stretching, Jack grabbed one of the staves and dropped into a crouch. Lance caught on, tracking Jack's footwork as they ran through routines.

"Keep at that," Jack said eventually. He came to me and pointed at the plant. "Don't drop it, okay?" I nodded, still holding Pops' gift. Jack touched his clawed hands to the leaves, which looked miniscule against his large, scarred hands. He gritted his teeth, but none of the leaves so much as twitched. He sighed. "The scanner's wrong about me; I ain't no plant elemental. But let's see what you can do."

"I haven't—"

"Close your eyes."

I closed my eyes, holding the planter and trying not to shiver.

"I'm going to take the plant from you, but keep your eyes closed. Follow the plant."

The heater's draft tickled my nose as the clay planter slipped from my fingers. I felt naked. Jack seemed more like a fighter than a gardener, and likely less patient. His boots thudded against the floor, and I swiveled on my feet, trying to figure out where he stood. I didn't want my back turned to him.

"I don't think this is going to work," I said, pivoting my body. Then I stopped. Someone stood directly in front of me, and I reached for him.

"Normally I'd agree" —Jack's voice came from behind me and I spun around— "but I've seen this sort of thing too many times to doubt it."

The planter sat on the floor, on the opposite side of the circle from Jack—the direction I had been facing when he spoke. There was even a little flower blooming at the end of a vine, which reached out as if to touch me. I stared at it. I thought I'd been following the sound of Jack's movements.

"Are you really that quiet?" I asked, bewildered.

"Powers work on instinct. That's the reason beasties can still use 'em. Work on sensing where the plants are. It'll help if you ever need something to protect yourself. Now make it grow."

"How?" Even if I *could* make it grow, I wasn't sure I wanted to. My powers were making the plant behave oddly. This particular type of vine wasn't even supposed to have flowers.

"No idea." Jack crossed his arms. "I can't make a blade of grass wobble without blowin' on it. Why don't you imagine feeding it or watering it or something? I've heard that helps."

I sat beside the planter and petted the waxy green leaves, then closed my eyes. As strange as the memory from the dorms was, I could almost feel the little spiderette stem wrapping around my finger and refusing to let go. What could I do if I actually tried? I imagined the plant growing, but when I opened my eyes, it just sat there with a single flower hanging off a lonely vine.

"Try again," Jack said, his silhouette looming against the overhead lights. I scuttled a few centimeters away from his leathery boots. Now I could see the hanging lights with their metal frames behind him. They weren't the room's original lights, but in their glow I could imagine sitting in my parents' backyard, the warm sun heating the dewy ground. Pollen flitted through the air, tickling my nose. Mentally, I reached into a small plastic sack and closed my hand around a handful of pellets, then sprinkled the nutrients across the moist dirt. The dirt clung to my finger tips, soft and velvety. Flowers budded around the plant, relishing the warm sunlight.

"How are you doing that?" Lance asked.

"What?" I opened my eyes. Lance had abandoned his exercises to stare at me. I clutched the planter to my chest and looked down at the pot. Two new leaves and a small flower budded at the end of one of the vines.

My idea worked!

"Keep doin' that while I spar with Lance," Jack said. "And try to keep your eyes open. If a beastie's attacking you, you want to know where to dodge."

"Right. If a beastie's attacking." I shivered. Several leaves fanned out from the plant, trying to hide me. These leaves were too small to do much good, but it gave me another idea to distract myself from my new reality.

Over the next half hour I tried convincing the plant to unfurl its leaves and grow new ones. But when the plant actually listened, the tendrils crept along like snails. Then the vines stopped cooperating altogether, and I left the half-bushy plant on the floor in the corner of the room so I could practice fighting on my own.

After a minute of wondering if the vines had grown again, I forced myself to focus on watching Lance and Jack spar. Despite the number of times Lance had to pick himself off the floor, he surprised Jack by blocking the occasional hit. Still, Jack's skill was considerably better. He used minimal movement to strike, whereas Lance swung his whole body into a blow Jack easily fended. I tried copying the patterns myself, but my feet wouldn't cooperate and my arms grew sore after a short ten minutes.

Half an hour later, Jack let up on Lance and brought us together at the top of the stairs. "You've both got super speed, so let's see it in action. Race the track." Jack shoved us against a wall. When he shouted, "Go!" Lance shot off, leaving me perplexed.

No countdown?

"Well, *go*."

I sprang forward, the smooth floor gliding under my feet. Lance fell behind at the corner. The metal walls blended into a distant stream of light, and I knew I could go faster . . .

I skidded around the second corner, nearly landing on my face, but I managed to get my feet back under me in time to keep going. One more corner and I would almost reach Jack. I wouldn't give up. I could get there . . .

I shrieked, only stopping behind Jack because he sprang out of the way. "Watch it, kid, and stand straight. You'll get more air into your lungs that way." Jack patted me on the back. I nodded and gasped for breath. My throat was dry and my muscles ached from the exertion. I forced myself to stand straight.

How fast had I been going?

I turned. Lance was only halfway around the track. How was that even possible?

Before I could figure out the logistics of super speed, Jack handed me a warm bottle of water. The taste was off, but it didn't give a brain freeze like the school's cold fountain water.

When Lance finally made it to us, he stared at me in disbelief. "How'd you *do* that?"

I shrugged, clueless.

"Looks like you could work on your speed," Jack told him. "Or maybe it's like my so-called plant powers. Either way, let's test your portal capabilities."

Lance nodded, doubled over with his hands on his knees as he caught his breath. To his credit, he *had* been working out with Jack for an hour while I daydreamed about my parents' garden. After a moment, he straightened his back and reached his arms overhead. "Okay, what do you want me to do?"

"Create a portal that gets you from here to the end of the gym." Jack leaned over the rail. "Imagine a doorway in front of you, and another one that opens in front of the wall."

I leaned against the railing while Lance squinted and tried to make a portal appear. I caught a brief glimpse of a purple mass several meters away. Then it was gone, a spot of light dancing against my eyes.

"Close, but I wouldn't trust going through it at this point," Jack said.

"Was that—was that a portal?" Lance asked, his eyes wide.

"Yep." Jack nodded. "Try again."

Lance squeezed his eyes shut and I glanced at Jack. His face was marred by rough scars, much like how the dents marred the once majestic room. He was still alive, for all the fighting he'd apparently been through, but Chill wasn't. Alec wasn't.

My heart sank. "What's going to happen to us?"

Jack shifted his weight against the railing. "If you're lucky?"

I nodded.

He sighed. "You won't die. We aren't out to have fun; we're out to stop the Camaraderie from destroying us and our freedom. The only thing *you've* known is the Community. Safety this, efficiency that. It was different when I was a kid. Sure, there were rules, but we did our own thing. Sure, we all knew that the 'war' overseas was nothing more than an excuse for an invasion, but all the riots were in the big cities, not in little rural towns like ours. I didn't come from a great town or a great family, but that didn't matter—until zealous Community lackeys decided to enforce their rules." He scowled. "When their agents came, I ran."

The air felt cold now, even after my sprint. I looked toward Lance to see if he had been listening, but his eyes were closed and his cheeks were scrunched in concentration.

"How old were you?" I asked.

"Fourteen. Old enough to have claws. I refused to take the pill. Whole family did. Later, I joined up with the Coalition. Found out the

Camaraderie was behind the invasions and the riots. Found out they were turning us into beasts." He glanced around the room, quiet. "Used to be more people here, 'til Great White got involved."

"Great White?"

"Great White, Master Matoska, White Bear—same guy."

I paused. "Jim said he was a bounty hunter."

"Yup. Killed a number of my friends. He was among the first of the mercs they recruited to take out the Coalition. He gained fame for his success in hunting the people who escaped the fall of Freedom Tower."

"Freedom Tower—*that's* what you called the rebel hideout?" I stared at him.

Jack shrugged. "Big, hulking tower in the shape of an 'F.' I like to think we should've had a university nearby, so we could've told off the Camaraderie by satellite. Unfortunately, the tower fell a few years after I joined the Coalition."

"If the Camaraderie is so powerful, how come they haven't already caught everyone?"

Jack smirked. "Because not all the Camaraderie leaders agreed with their tactics. Clara—a thief—turned on them and stole us this airship. When they caught her they tortured her, but the whole time she laughed. That image became our symbol." He frowned, accentuating the jagged scars on his cheeks. "That was the one thing I didn't understand when I joined—why the Coalition's symbol was a woman being tortured."

I remembered the strange blue and yellow half person painted on the side of the airship, its arms upraised. "What does it mean?"

"The symbol? Defiant to the end. It was meant to be a lesson from the Camaraderie, but one of our members got ahold of a photo of Clara's last moments. He drew up the symbol in her honor. Now she's forever tortured; forever defiant."

I clamped my hands on the railing, my palms sweating, and glanced at my potted plant. Its leaves wavered in the breeze coming from under the door. "Forever tortured?"

Jack grunted. "If Pops knows what's good for you, he'll take you to South Africa. Get you a place there."

"What if he doesn't?"

Jack grimaced. "Not all of us have gone down smiling."

Chill. Alec . . .

Too numb to speak, I didn't ask him anything else on the subject.

Not long after, a portal appeared to the right of Lance, while another appeared a half meter above the floor beside the cabinets. I edged away from the nearest one, which swirled at my height with dark, opaque purple matter. Jack stepped through and dropped from the other portal, then landed in a crouch. I poked Lance repeatedly on the shoulder until he opened his eyes. The portal vanished, and he blinked when he realized Jack was all the way across the room.

"You did it," Jack called, signaling us with a thumbs-up. Lance grinned as Jack returned to us via the stairs. "Good work. Keep practicing when you get the chance. We'll do this a few times a day until we get a good routine going. Stretch beforehand," he warned Lance, "and stretch afterward. Or you'll be sore — real sore. Same goes for you, Jen. I'll have you practice with us during hand-to-hand combat. Meantime, you need a portable plant. Can't have you fighting beasties with *that*." He jabbed his thumb at my planter, all trace of his earlier concern gone. He looked between the two of us. "Go drop off the plant and swords, and then you're free to do whatever."

I glanced at Lance, and then looked at Jack. "Do you have homework for us?"

"Homework? No-no!" Jack flustered. I shrunk away from him and bumped into Lance, who gripped my shoulders. "You two have no idea what free time is, do you?"

"Well, normally I'd garden," I said. "Or volunteer at the greenhouse."

"I . . ." Lance paused. "When I don't have any assignments, that's when I practice sword fighting. Except, we've already practiced."

"Community folk. Sheesh." Jack scratched the stubble under his chin. "Meet me at my room in ten minutes. I'll wrestle Tim from Crush and introduce you guys to the wonderful world of violent video games." He grinned.

"Video games?" Lance asked, but Jack was already out the door.

CHAPTER
THIRTEEN

"Here we are." Jack gestured to the inside of his room. "Have a seat."

"Where?" I asked. Piles of ancient DVD cases were stacked next to a worn, broken down couch. Open soda cans littered the floor near a large TV, and a chipped dinner plate sat atop one of the DVD stacks. His room was only slightly less outdated than the brig.

He smirked. "Anywhere you can find."

I avoided the scattered papers and twisted aluminum cans, then sat at the center of the couch. Tim squeaked as it sagged underneath him, its springs too broken to fight even his scrawny frame.

Jack punched a button on a boxy machine under the TV. "You guys should like this—it's a superhero game."

The screen changed to a warning and a bold logo, followed by a growing crescendo of music and flashing images. The speakers blared, filling the room with pulsing energy. The music throbbed, faster and heavier than the music I was accustomed to hearing. Whatever this was, it wasn't classical. An unbelievably huge grin crossed Lance's face, and Tim eyed the speakers with caution. I resisted tapping my foot to the beat, waiting to see how it played.

"What exactly *are* superheroes?" I asked. "You mentioned them earlier."

"Right—" Jack squatted beside a mixed pile of books and papers, then tossed us a stack of flimsy booklets.

I passed a handful to Tim, then cautiously took one for myself. *Firelight: Volume 23.*

The cover flaunted a bold woman in a shiny, skin-tight outfit that was a bright mix of orange and red. I flipped through the pages with their numerous images and short bits of dialogue. The woman on the cover, Firelight, fought a man with green, glowing hands. Looking at these costumes, I could see where certain E-Leadership members got their ideas of fashion.

"Superheroes," Jack explained loudly, "are people who have special powers. Kind of like us—'cept we're real. They use their powers to thwart super villains . . ." He pressed a button on his bulky remote. ". . . someone who uses his powers to harm others or cause destruction. Sometimes you have an anti-hero, and you can't tell who the real bad guy is."

After eyeing my comic book, Tim carefully laid his back in the stack and exchanged it for one that had subdued, grungy tones. "So, a superhero tries to save the Community from a super villain, who wants chaos?" he asked.

Jack grunted. "These were written well before the Community. Now forget the books; we've got a game to play." He tossed us each a block of plastic with several buttons and two small, circular thumb sticks.

"What are we supposed to do with these?" I wasn't sure how to hold it.

"Press this button to fire." Jack clicked the right, trigger-like button. "Press this one to use your power." He went on to explain movement and how to change inventory. "Now make your characters." The screen split into four segments, each with a different character. A little experimentation on my part resulted in changing the character's sex, hair, and form-fitted attire, and then revealed a list of weapons: a sword, an oddly shaped club called a baseball bat, a rifle, and two pistols. I chose a sword for my blond-haired, yellow suited lady.

According to Jack, we were supposed to run our tiny characters around the screen, destroying things for points and beating up "bad guys." Jack, of course, killed the villains with ease. As for us, Lance kept hitting the pause button instead of the attack button, resulting in multiple deaths before he figured out what each button did. Meanwhile, I managed to take out a couple bad guys before seeing my character gutted in painful slow motion.

If this is what happened to actual heroes, I wasn't sure I wanted any part of it. I remembered Chill's death all too well.

"Look!" Tim grinned at us, his hands free of the controller. "I can move my guy around just by thinking!"

Jack twisted his lips. "Good for you, kid."

I wasn't sure if he was annoyed or impressed . . . though I couldn't believe Tim's techno sight power let him do that.

Lance grunted as his character died again. "Eh—This game's not really for me. I'm gonna see what else is going on." He nodded politely to Jack before tripping over the wires on his way out.

"You might at least watch the cords," Jack grumbled, leaning over to plug the controller back in. "Did you guys want to keep playing?"

I frowned. Lance only ran away like that if something upset him. "I'll be back in a moment. Go on without me." I hopped over the mess of wires and peered out the door. Lance stood by the stairwell, his back to the wall.

"You all right?"

"Hmm? Yeah, I'm fine."

I squinted, trying to make heads or tails of him. Normally I would have thought he was upset, but right now he seemed more contemplative than anything else.

"What's up?"

He rested his hand on the hilt of his sword and stared at his distorted reflection in the wall. "All this time, I've wanted to go into Special Forces. I wanted to be the best of the best. You know, like my mom."

I leaned against the wall next to him. "Yeah, I know."

He sighed. "Then I end up here, and I like it better. Fewer rules. Fewer regulations. Immediate training on the weapon I want. The video game's not that great, but the comic books are cool. It's like . . . the perfect world."

"Except that these are the people we've been told are a threat."

"Exactly. But the rebels haven't said anything that makes me think they're lying. To be honest, I want to look around for myself. See what I can find without them looking over my shoulder."

I glanced behind me, but there was no sign that anyone was watching us. "If you're curious, check out the brig. It's just upstairs, and it's filled with old books. There's a computer, too. I don't know when they used it last. You could probably sneak in there and take a look around. The door doesn't lock."

He smirked. "I take it you've been snooping?"

"Sort of, but Jack caught me."

He looked me over, then let out a slow breath. "Be careful, okay? They could turn on us without warning."

"I'll keep Jack busy with the games for a little while. Just try not to get caught."

He grinned. "I was training for security. I can run an investigation."

"Sure," I teased, and I couldn't help but smile.

Lance headed upstairs and I returned to the noisy video game.

"Kid all right?" Jack asked, never taking his eyes from the screen. Tim was giving him a run for his money, forcing Jack to dodge a slew of fireball attacks.

"He's just restless," I said quickly.

Jack grunted affirmation, and a weight lifted from my shoulders. He didn't know Lance was planning to look around. I jumped back in the game. It was like self-defense practice, only I didn't feel so bad about the idea of hurting anyone. It was a nice relief from thinking about home. Well . . . what used to be home.

An hour later, Jack turned off the console and shooed us out. I wandered the halls, looking for any sign of Lance, but he did a good job of staying out of sight. On the upper deck, Pops' voice echoed from inside his room. ". . . be careful. I don't want you getting caught between them."

I edged the door open. "Pops?" It felt weird to call him that. Informal.

He lowered his radio momentarily from his lips, then finished what he was saying. "I'll talk to you later, Gwen. Good luck."

I couldn't tell what the voice on the other end said, but Pops put away the radio and smiled. The skin crinkled at the edge of his eyes. "I was wondering when you would stop by. I assume you have questions?"

He motioned to a chair with a simple metal frame and blue, crosshatch-patterned fabric. LED efficiency lights glinted off the metallic walls and lit the picture frames hanging there. One was of a woman in a simple green dress holding the hand of a young boy, and one was of a family picture with my dad, mom, and myself when I was only a couple years old. The final photo was of a charismatic man with his brown hair combed back. His dark eyes resembled my father's, and his hand lay on the shoulder of someone who might've been my grandmother. His other hand rested on the shoulder of a guy my age. But the photo had seen better days. The spot with Pops' name tag had been ripped, and there was a dried blood stain on its tattered corner.

Pops rearranged the materials on his desk, pausing at a small, pixilated picture of me from my freshman year in high school. "It took a lot of work to find you after your father moved."

"The family database isn't password protected. Shouldn't have been that hard to find me," I said carefully.

"I was excommunicated from the Community. Made it harder to keep tabs on your father—and you—once you were born. Unfortunately, Ron failed to see that you were in danger."

I eyed the torn photo and the faded blue and yellow symbol painted on the front of Pops' desk. The woman being tortured.

I averted my eyes from the symbol. "You said the Camaraderie uses a beast army. But forcing a transformation should use more resources, not less. Why spend all the money to produce a pill that blocks powers if only a small percentage of the population is likely to have those powers? It's not efficient."

His lips parted in surprise, but he raised his chin in acknowledgement. "You are correct. But the Camaraderie could not control a population that knows the extent of their lies. They need powers to be a secret. It's how they maintain control."

"They use powers for Special Forces; why not other fields?"

"They do," Pops said softly. "Certain powers don't translate well into beasts, and certain people don't make good soldiers. Yet those people find themselves hired with the assurance that their powers are little more than a side effect of the treatment for theophrenia. They're told to keep it secret, and what they're told varies by what best benefits the Camaraderie."

I frowned. "Seems like a good way to get caught."

"By blocking powers in the general population, they don't have to single anyone out before assessing their personality, and this way, they don't worry about powers upsetting their governing bodies." He rubbed his salt-and-pepper beard thoughtfully. "You said Tim hacked the health network. Imagine fighting hundreds of hackers, all wanting to know their secrets. Some malicious, some merely curious."

He had a point. Besides, if the Camaraderie wanted to blame theophrenia for the disappearances, they couldn't very well take toddlers away from their parents without raising suspicions. They'd have to come up with a decent explanation for a disease that only affected children . . . though that sounded simpler than their current procedure.

"Fine. Where do you fit into all this?" I leaned back in the chair, but it wasn't nearly as comfortable as the one in Jim's room.

"The Camaraderie is too strong to fight directly, so we find alternative methods to subvert its power. We run errands for other rebellions and make minor acts of sabotage. Recently, we've been contacted by a village in Guatemala. Gwen, our ambassador, is negotiating with them now to protect an artifact, which, according to the village, may have the power to let us stop the Camaraderie at its source. While I doubt there's anything truly special about it, the fact that Camaraderie mercenaries are snooping around the area leads me to think it has to be of some importance. Either way, I have a few calls to make before I give Gwen the go-ahead to make the arrangements. Did you have any other questions?"

"Actually, yes. Why doesn't my cell phone have a signal?"

"We jam signals whenever we're near a tower. They would make us an easy target. It's the same reason we don't use wireless networks. Instead, we use radios for long range communication." He held up the radio he'd been using earlier.

"So . . . I won't be able to contact my parents?"

He shook his head. "Your parents use EYEnet and none of us have the hacking skills to break in."

"Tim might."

"The three of you are too close to the Community. For all we know, you could contact security the moment you get a signal."

I sighed. At least he was honest. "I'm going to want to talk to my parents eventually."

"I understand. But right now, for your safety and theirs, we can't risk contact. The Camaraderie will be keeping a close eye on them." He placed his hands in his lap. "I realize this is overwhelming, but I appreciate you coming to talk with me. I want you to feel at home."

"You're right, it is overwhelming," I said softly, "but I don't think I can ever call this place home." I stood to leave. "Regardless, thanks for being honest."

"Of course," he said. "That's what makes us different from the Community."

CHAPTER
FOURTEEN

Fiery orange light poured through the windows of the command room, detailing the arc of the horizon over the glassy sea. Wispy pink clouds floated beneath us like threads of cotton trimmed in gold, and the hum of monitors faded into a distant murmur.

This place was beautiful.

I sighed and returned to watching Tim and Crush battling each other for computer supremacy. Once Crush finally managed to regain control of the main screen and Tim offered to bring him a glass of water, I plopped into the seat next to him. Crush rested both hands against the desk, trying to catch his breath.

"That kid's good," he said, wiping beads of sweat from his cheeks. "How long has he been off the pills?"

"A week, maybe."

"A week?" Crush's eyes went wide. "He really *is* a genius."

I glanced toward the open door. "Pops was the one who wanted to rescue us, wasn't he? Why doesn't he trust us?"

"Would you trust someone you'd just rescued from a society that brainwashes everyone into thinking powers are the result of some hallucinogenic plague?" Crush gave me a curious smile. "Give him time. He just wants to make sure you know all the facts and don't endanger the rest of us while you're learning to use your powers."

"He sure as hell better not endanger the rest of us," Jack muttered behind me. I spun around so fast in the swivel chair that I almost lost my balance. When had he come in? He rapped his knuckles on the metal frame of a nearby monitor, then took a seat at a computer near the window. "He's lost enough men. If one of you decides to go back, you'll face the consequences alone."

My skin crawled. He sure didn't take it easy on Crush.

"They knew going in to rescue you could be a trap, but they decided to go anyway," Crush said softly. I winced, trying to think of something to say, but Tim returned with Crush's water and they went back to their feverish race. A few minutes later, Jack cursed and closed the archival program he'd been searching through. He turned in his chair.

"How's the kid doing?"

"Kind of busy at the moment—" Crush rapidly typed computer commands as new screens popped up faster than the old ones disappeared. Seemed Tim was winning.

Jack grinned. "Suppose the boy gets into your personal files. You gonna put an extra layer of encryption on those 'leader' photos of Inese?"

Inese walked in at that exact moment. She raised an eyebrow, but Jack was too busy paying attention to the screen and Crush, oblivious as the others, was too engrained in his work to even realize he'd been addressed. Inese held a finger to her lips, winked at me, then turned invisible.

I scuttled to the other side of the room. Jack shrieked and yanked at the back of his jacket. Three little ice cubes clunked to the floor. "*Inese!*"

She materialized beside Crush, grinning maliciously. She held an ice cube between her fingers. "What was it about photos you were saying?"

Jack grimaced and readjusted his jacket. "Nothing. I'm sure you and him only ever talk about flying cars in that room of yours."

Tim peered up from the console. "What's going on?"

Crush—now red—scratched the back of his neck. "So . . . you never skipped the pill?"

"No. Not intentionally."

Inese smirked and tossed the ice cube to Jack before returning to the computer she'd initially headed for. Jack palmed the cube, muttering about the "cruel lady" abusing her powers. He left the room, fidgeting with his jacket.

"Kind of wish I had techno sight," Crush murmured, watching Tim type. He smiled. It was one of those genuine smiles that could make anyone feel warm inside, and I smiled back.

Even though he'd lost his brother to save us, he didn't seem to harbor any resentment.

Over the course of the next week, I perused Jim's textbook and learned what I could about the rebels I'd fallen in with. Several times each day, Jack brought us to the training room and made us practice our individual skills, but as far as I could tell, the rebels didn't mean us harm.

Lance and I had already been practicing fighting for a while today. Sweat trickled down my back, the training room's draft chilling my skin. Lance crouched, his feet separated into a T-stance so that one foot was forward while the other was to the side. He swung his staff to my left. I blocked and automatically switched my training staff to defend my right.

Repetitious practice was supposed to help our reflexes in case of an actual fight. I humored Jack's training, but I would've preferred avoiding the fight altogether.

Lance aimed for my feet. I skittered out of reach, attempting a shot at his shoulder. His staff went up, caught my swing, and swiftly disarmed me. My baton rolled down the ever-so-slightly uneven incline of the impromptu gymnasium.

He grinned, wiping sweat from his forehead. He brushed back his hair. "What'cha think so far?"

"About what?" A burst of speed and I caught up with the runaway stick. We might not have had powers in the Community, but they were certainly useful.

Lance gestured to the railing above us. "This place. The Coalition."

"I guess it's not *bad*. But I prefer the Community. The only problem is that they hide the truth about our powers."

Lance smirked and came at me again. I tried blocking the strike, but he switched angles at the last minute. "What about the pill? And the Camaraderie turning people into beasties?"

I winced, rubbing my new bruise. "I'm still not sure I believe that. Superpowers—okay, they've proved that one. But turning people into monsters? You've got to admit, it doesn't make sense biologically."

"Yeah . . . because you know *so* much about biology."

I glared at him.

"And don't forget how boring everything was." He paused, sizing up my movements. "Ready to go faster?"

"Not really."

Lance chuckled and then tossed me another short staff.

Two? What was I supposed to do with two?

I dodged his first attack, but I hadn't counted on Lance's powers being so helpful. He disarmed me in seconds and I fell, landing on my back. Pain radiated from my chest. I grumbled, pushing myself off the floor as Lance hurriedly offered me his hand. He pulled me up, then stared at me longer than usual.

"Lance?" I waved at him. "You okay?"

"Sorry." His lips twisted into a faint smile. He pointed. "You've got a hair in your face. Want to try again?"

I grimaced and brushed away the stray hair. "I'm good, thanks." I wasn't particularly interested in trying again until I could stay upright for longer than five seconds. Time to switch the subject. "I've been reading one of Jim's history books."

Lance wrinkled his nose and grabbed my fallen staff. "Any good?"

"It's not Community."

Lance grinned. "Maybe there's hope for you after all." He elbowed me in the shoulder and I winced. There was a bruise there, too.

"Since when did you become so anti-Community?" I asked.

"Since I found out they wanted to turn me into a monster." He put the training weapons aside and sat on the floor, stretching his fingers to his toes. "Besides, the Community's boring. There's no excitement." He paused. "Do you remember when we used to pick blackberries off the neighbor's bush?"

I nodded. Walking home from school, we used to take the back alley to our parents' houses. One time I noticed a dark blackberry poking out from a broken slat in the fence. The neighbors could've been fined because the fence hadn't been repaired in a timely manner. The berry was ripe, and touching it left a deep purple-red juice stain on my fingertips. Lance had stopped behind me, then popped the berry into his mouth.

"What if someone saw you?" I'd hissed, as much enraged that he'd stolen the berry as I was that he hadn't offered it to me.

He reached his pocket knife into the splintery hole. "I'm doing them a favor." He offered me the sawed-off branch, and on it was a single berry, slightly smaller than the first. "Want it?"

I'd shaken my head. Maybe he could get away with it, being a security official's son, but I couldn't. "No thanks," I said, though blackberries were seasonal and our bush hadn't produced much that year.

The hole in the fence was less noticeable now, and thanks to Lance's work, the neighbors had a little more time to fix it before an inspector noticed. Having uniform appearances meant everything—which was why the backyard was fenced, the front yard neatly mowed, and the house touched up whenever the paint peeled. It prevented jealousy.

We decided then that if we kept the alley free of berries, we were doing them a favor, and as a result, we'd had a summer of blackberries.

"I remember," I said.

"Back then, we were helping them, even though they weren't following all the rules. They didn't deserve to be fined. It's the same here." Lance paused. "As long as we're here, we're in this together, right?" He held out his hand.

"Right," I said, and in one downward shake, my chest clenched. I couldn't go home until I knew the truth. But if the rebels were right, then we could never return. Not with our powers.

Not with Lance's tendency to bend the rules.

Several days after the sparring incident with Lance, Pops caught me in the hall on my way to training. I stopped, halfway up the stairs, as he tapped his cane on the floor for attention. He held two small bundles under his arm. "You aren't easy to keep up with," he said.

I frowned. The airship was too small to avoid anyone.

"I've been around. What do you want?"

"As much as I'd like to keep you safe, you may be needed on the ground. We have too few people otherwise." He offered me the bundles. "I hope these will protect you."

If he wanted a fighter, I wasn't the right person for the job. All he had to do is sit in on one of Jack's sparring sessions to see that. "I haven't agreed to join your rebellion."

"I won't ask you to fight for us," he reassured me. "But you wanted to see the truth for yourself, correct?"

I nodded hesitantly.

"While I will do my best to keep you out of harm's way, there is no guarantee that danger won't find *you*," Pops continued. "My best course of action, then, is to make sure you are able to defend yourself."

I *had* been hounding them for proof. I took the bundles and unwrapped the faded paper, which had been printed with an assortment of pale colors and shapes. A small vine fell from the wrapping. The vine was connected to a long pouch made from white fabric. The pouch contained damp soil and nutrients.

"What's this?" I asked, gingerly twining the tender vine around my index finger. It was kind of cute.

"Armbands." Pops fastened one around my upper arm. His cologne was like what Community leaders wore — far too strong. "Now you can always have a weapon on you."

I wrinkled my nose and tried convincing the vine to grow, but it barely nuzzled my sleeve.

"Perhaps you could imagine the vines like mint, and urge them to grow the way you convinced mint to grow. It's all about convincing the target to do what it already wants to do: in this case, flourish. You used to care for mint in secondary school, didn't you?" He looked at me with a genuinely curious expression across his wrinkled face.

I suppressed a shudder. During my freshman year of high school I'd grown mint on my windowsill. It wasn't in any records; I'd kept it to myself.

Still, I tried imagining the little plastic pot sitting in my window, the one with a couple centimeters of mint poking through the dirt. I'd watered it once a week, on Tuesdays, and checked it each day before the sun rose. One morning I found numerous fragrant, tiny leaves waiting for attention while the original one stood several centimeters tall.

I opened my eyes, and at my command a small vine crept from the root plant. Warmth fluttered through my chest. "That's cool," I said, watching the writhing tendril unfold. Pops handed me the second armband and let me wrap it myself. The thing felt odd, but at the same time, completely natural.

I smiled. "Thanks."

"You're welcome." Pops hobbled up the metal stairs, leaving me with a feeling of unsettled pride. He knew me too well.

I continued to the training room, and Lance nearly collided with me as I entered. He gave my vines a funny look.

"Uh, Jenna?"

"Yeah?"

"You're wearing vines."

I stroked the thin tendrils, twirling them through my fingers, and grinned. "Yep. Personalized weapons."

"Uh-huh." Lance took a second look at the armbands and chuckled.

"We might make a fighter of you yet." He scowled and crossed his arms, giving his best impression of Jack. It wasn't half-bad.

I smirked. "They're plants. I don't think I'm going to be fighting anyone with these."

"I don't know about that. Plants *can* be pretty scary." He leaned against the stair's railing and winced as he found a bruise. "Have you ever heard of a honey locust tree? One of the North American transfer students said those things are nasty. Has thorns this long." He motioned with his hands and grinned. "Or Venus fly traps. Or . . . something poisonous."

"Knapweed, if you're a horse."

"Exactly. So, what can you do with a vine?"

I couldn't hide my smile. This was the Lance I remembered. The guy I'd been friends with for so long. Not reassuring, though, considering we were deciding just how dangerous a *plant* was. I shook my head. "I guess I could strangle people?"

"There ya go. Or maybe you could make grass grow really tall and hide me when I ambush one of those beasties." He patted my back. "Come on. You don't want to be late for training with your new weapons."

"Ambush the beasties? You *want* to fight?" I stared at him. "You're crazy."

But it made sense. I *could* use the vines to defend myself.

While Jack continued training me personally in hand-to-hand combat, I focused on using my new vines instead of conventional weapons. Most of my practice was dodging, rolling, disarming, and generally staying out of the way since I didn't have the strength to parry.

The more I practiced, the better I understood how to use Pops' gift—and what he meant by urging the plant to do what it already wanted. It was all preparation for missions if we decided to stick around, and considering we knew nothing about living in South Africa, practice didn't sound like such a bad idea. Especially if we wanted proof of what the rebels were saying.

In mid-November, Pops began spending most of his time in his office. Though I'd tried to be patient, I had to find some way to contact my parents. They would be worried sick if they'd heard about my disappearance. I rattled the handle of his door, but it was locked. With no success there, I sought out Crush and found him in the command room. Warm air radiated from the constant use of computers and flickering screens.

Crush barely glanced at me before he returned to typing. I positioned myself behind him, catching the vines of my armbands between my fingers as I watched the screen. It showed Guatemala. The map turned into a satellite image before zooming in on dense jungle. Sections of it were blurred out, unreadable.

"What's going on?" I asked.

Crush ran his fingers across his short hair. "We haven't had any contact with Gwen for the past three days. She should have checked in by now."

"Maybe something's blocking her signal. Or maybe she's busy."

He frowned. "We have protocols for missions like this. Something's wrong. We may have to go to ground." He lowered his eyes and took a long breath. "Problem is, we don't have the people to do it. This is the kind of reconnaissance Alec would usually do."

I licked my lips, glancing back to the screen.

I'd always wanted to see a rainforest, and I did want to see the outside world . . . see if what the rebels were saying was real.

"Tell Pops I want to help," I said, "and I'm sure Lance will, too."

Crush turned. "Jenna—"

"I want to see what's out there, and this way we can help you find Gwen."

"You don't have to make up for anything," he said gently. "I don't mean this in a bad way, but you can't take his place. Life doesn't work like that."

I swallowed hard. "I understand."

"Then I'll let Pops know. And Jenna—" He relaxed his shoulders and looked back at the screen. "Thank you. I don't want to lose Gwen, too." He gave me a sad smile and returned to work.

I decided to wait to ask him about my parents. They would already know that I was gone, and it couldn't be much different than the usual deal when someone got theophrenia. Not if the Community was as big into keeping secrets as Pops said.

CHAPTER
FIFTEEN

I sprung out of bed, startled by the *briinninnin* **noise of my alarm** clock, then groaned and flopped back into the covers. The new clock Inese dug out of storage for me started ringing at zero eight hundred. It was now zero eight fifteen. I shut the thing off and straightened my clothes of their persistent wrinkles. Inese lent me a pair of jeans and a t-shirt shortly after I arrived, but they felt so stiff and strange that I only wore them long enough to wash and dry my own clothes in the maintenance room. Besides, Tim and Lance gawked at me whenever I showed up in her outfit, and I didn't like being stared at.

Wrinkles it was.

Outside, Lance's alarm clock buzzed through his doorway, and when I knocked I got a half-Russian complaint about being almost ready. That hadn't changed, at least. I left him there and headed to the kitchen. Tim was already halfway through breakfast. I was surprised he hadn't gotten up earlier.

"Morning." I moved to the stove and wrapped a tortilla shell around the powdered eggs Crush left warming in the skillet.

"Good morning," Tim replied. "How were your dreams?"

Mom once told me that the telling of dreams was supposed to bring everybody together as a whole Community. My dreams hadn't felt like that lately, with Commander Rick looming over me, scowling and saying lies about how the Community was safe, and Lady Black quietly leading me through the dorm halls with everyone gawking.

"All right," I lied.

"I was working on a computer program," Tim explained without my having to ask. "Then I was flying in a large plane, and . . ."

I sighed and ate my burrito, not really listening until Lance came in with his hair dripping water down the back of his neck. He acknowledged us with a "hi," then plopped into a chair, squinting as if he wasn't awake.

"Well?" Tim asked.

It took us both a moment to realize he expected Lance to tell his dreams, too.

"You don't really want to talk about dreams, do you?" I asked.

"Jenna's right," Lance said. "We don't have to, so why worry about it? Anyway, what's for breakfast?"

Not exactly what I'd said, but at least I wouldn't hear about planes and powers again. None of the rebels participated in the telling of dreams. Though I missed the routine I'd had at home before college, dreams weren't one of them. Mom's breakfast was.

Half an hour later, Tim and Lance were arguing over the benefits of a second burrito when Inese swung into the kitchen. She wore full combatant armor, like the day we'd first seen her. "You ready, Jenna? We're going after Gwen."

I blinked. "They found her?" That was good. Once we found Gwen, Pops wouldn't have to worry about his team anymore and I might be able to contact my parents.

Lance glanced at me. "I'll come, too. You might need backup."

Inese nodded. "The more, the merrier. Tim?"

Tim twisted his fingers around the chain of his charm necklace. "I guess I could use the tablet to run analytical programs on any tracks we find." He bit his lip nervously.

I didn't blame him. If it weren't for already telling Crush I'd help, I wasn't so sure I wanted to go. My training was nowhere near ready for a full-fledged mission.

"Good. You've got ten minutes to get to the hangar. Jenna, I want to talk to you privately."

"Privately? Uh—sure."

Inese followed me to my room and waited for me to fasten my armbands. "How well can you control those?"

"Sort of well?" The vines curled at my command, but that was about it.

They *might* react to fear.

Maybe.

Inese extracted a pistol from the holster at her side and offered me the grip. I recoiled. I'd never held a gun before. Guns were for security. "You aim and pull the trigger," she said. "Make sure to release the safety lock before you do."

I stared at it. "I've never—"

"Firing is simple." She stood beside me and showed me the basics: how not to hold the gun, how to release the safety, to shoot with both hands at the largest target, and that pointing a loaded gun at anything I didn't want dead was a bad idea.

"I've got another one in the car," she said when I tried to hand it back. "Besides, Lance has swords, and Crush and I are training Tim with a pistol. Your vines are great and all, but you may need something with a little more . . . oomph."

I felt the weight of the gun in my hand. Its heft made me nervous and insecure. Security had training courses for a reason. What if I shot it wrong?

Inese planted a hand on her hip. "Is the safety lock on?"

I checked it, then nodded. She handed me the holster.

"Good. Let's get going."

For the next hour, Inese flew Tim, Jack, Lance, and myself over the ocean, where blue-green waves crested and fell until we sighted land. We flew over a beach, and a short while later, we finally descended into dense green jungle. Inese landed the invisible car in a small clearing, scattering a flock of scarlet macaws.

The three of us and Jack slid out from the car, and the moment we were outside the car's boundaries, we turned visible. The car lifted away and the wind that startled the birds earlier buffeted against me.

There was plant life everywhere. Sweet-smelling flowers scented the air. Trees towered overhead, growing and reaching for the bright sun. Vines and moss draped from their branches, providing moist shade. Water trickled from a nearby stream. Despite the encroaching heat and warm breeze, the weather wasn't bad.

"Inese isn't coming with us?" Tim asked.

Jack pulled his jacket tight, avoiding the troublesome foliage as he plowed into the jungle. "She'll keep watch from the air in case there's trouble. Always good to have a fast escape. But, just in case any of those mercs are running about, we'll maintain radio silence."

Tim twisted his lips and diverted his attention to his tablet.

That must've been why Inese gave me her pistol. She wouldn't need it—but we might.

"Now," Jack's voice cut through the chirruping frogs and cooing birds, "if we do run into trouble, remember that I'm team commander. If I tell you to run, run. I tell you to fight, fight. I tell you to hide, hide. Otherwise you'll end up dead, captured, or worse."

"Worse?" Tim squeaked, clenching his tablet. I sighed, fingering the snap that held the pistol in place. It'd be easy enough to get to. I just wished I had more training.

"Made into a beastie." Jack tried pushing the jungle vines aside with his clawed hands—with little success. "Way I hear it, the transformation isn't pleasant. It wipes the beastie's memories and humanity. Lets them be controlled by a beastmaster, someone with the power to control animals. And you three would be beasties if Pops hadn't decided to save you. Don't forget that."

While the idea that beasts could be controlled wasn't complete proof that the rebels were telling the truth, if we *did* see a beastmaster controlling those creatures, that cast a decent motive on the Camaraderie for using beasts in the first place. Jim did say the Camaraderie was fighting the

Oriental Alliance. Perhaps beasts didn't question orders. That'd been a problem among soldiers since pre-Community times.

After a long, itchy silence, Jack motioned for Lance to hack the vines from their roots with his sword. I flinched with each stroke, sensing the plant's separation.

"Any idea what happened to Gwen?" I asked, trying to distract myself from the destruction.

"No idea. Inese had a hunch that she was in trouble. Crush tried to contact her, and when he didn't get an answer, Pops decided it was time we started lookin'. " He stroked his stubbly chin, then motioned to me as Lance gave his now-slightly-duller sword a puzzled look. Jack pointed to the tangled mass of vines, roots, and stems. "Huh. The plants are tougher than usual. Jenna, give your powers a shot."

I smirked. The foliage had held up quite well.

I closed my eyes, imagining the plants moving and untwisting from each other. It was unlikely that I'd be much help, but using my powers was better than letting Lance and Jack destroy everything in their path.

Jack chuckled. "There ya go, Jen. Yer practice is payin' off."

Using powers was slow going, even when I tried to focus on using my secondary speed power, but the semblance of a path eventually formed in front of us. Jack grinned, murmuring that he preferred patience over dodging Lance's wild sword strokes.

After half an hour of untwisting vines to make our own path, the trees gave way to an open, well-traveled dirt road, thereby relieving me from my duties. Large insects landed on my exposed skin and bit my neck and fingers, despite the bug repellant we'd sprayed earlier. I slapped one bug, then grimaced at the welt left on my hand.

At least I was wearing long sleeves and pants when I left the Community. But the sleeves were warm, clinging to my skin from humidity. Russia was never this bad. I wiped my forehead of sweat, and Tim gasped for breath.

"How much farther?" he asked.

"Eh. They're around here somewhere." Jack brushed some unfortunate insect's blood stain from his hand and onto his pants. "I'm surprised we haven't seen the locals yet."

"No kidding. We've been out here forev—" Tim squeaked, barely grabbing a tree to steady himself as he tripped.

"You okay?" I asked.

He scrunched his nose. "That log felt squishy. Does everything rot this fast in a jungle?"

Jack turned on his heel and knelt where Tim had stumbled. Seconds later, he kicked a pile of broad leaves aside, and the three of us quickly stepped back. Jack's search had revealed a human body. It was dressed in a plain cotton shirt. Claw marks raked the chest and burn marks scored the corpse.

Trees spun, and I pressed my hand against a nearby branch.

Community . . . I was going to be sick.

"What did *that*?" Lance asked, staring at it with horrified fascination. I swallowed hard, pulling on every memory I ever had in biology class to keep myself focused. The agent Lance killed seemed pleasant in comparison.

Tim closed his fingers around the light bulb charm. "Wild animal?"

I shook my head. "Doesn't account for the burn marks."

The corpse was mutilated. Its face wasn't recognizable, and a swarm of flies buzzed around the maggots that squirmed across its flesh. Bile rose in my throat. "That's not going to happen to us," I murmured forcefully. "It can't."

Tim nodded, pale. Though Lance would've seen the occasional devastated body in his security classes, and I had the advantage of biology, Tim had neither.

"Tim's closer than you think. Beasties got this guy." Jack knelt beside the corpse and pushed it onto its stomach. The bile came back and I scrunched my shoulders. Lance set his jaw; he must've been forcing himself to watch.

"You said this place was clear," Tim yipped.

Jack nodded, somber. "That's what we thought."

This was what a beastie could do? The idea that the beast had been human, a student like me, did not settle well with my stomach. There was nowhere to run out here. If one of those beasties attacked us, I wouldn't know where to go.

I traced the holster of Inese's gun, wishing I had better control over my powers.

Jack clicked his radio. "Inese? We found a dead local. Beastie attack."

The radio crackled. "Yeah—looks like beasties have moved into the area, and there's at least one beastmaster out there."

Jack frowned. "That's what I was afraid of. Be ready for a quick getaway. Jack out." He turned off the radio and straightened his back. "Let's go. Lance, have your sword ready. Tim, your gun. And Jenna—" He flicked the limp vine around my arm. "You've got the whole jungle at your disposal. Focus on the plants and let us know if you feel anything unusual."

I nodded, mute. Even if I didn't know how to shoot the gun, I now appreciated Inese's foresight. I pressed my fingers together, trying not to imagine what could've done such a horrible thing to the corpse in front of us.

Clawed and burned—nothing I knew of made burns like that.

Lance stepped over a second disfigured corpse and I skirted around it. There were three more bodies on the trail, each as mutilated as the first. Jack motioned us deeper into the jungle, and I parted the vines that were in our way. They curled like snakes, slithering off the ground to let us pass. Above, a monkey swung from a branch, hooting when I accidentally disturbed its roost with a stray vine.

Jack led us toward a large, stone structure set on a barely marked trail. "Gwen might've been around here somewhere." He led us through a thick of jungle flora, closer to the towering pyramid. Huge chunks of the stone tower had fractured from the upper portion of the temple and now littered the clearing. A few of the giant pieces were covered with a thick blanket of moss; apparently they had been here a while. The other chunks of stone looked devoid of plant life, their breaks fresh and powdery. A battle must have happened here recently, as evidenced by the discovery of several more bodies; some human, some . . . something else. Tim excused himself from the immediate scene of decay and vomited in the bushes.

This was just like those pictures I'd seen in the brig. The beastie's corpse lay stretched in an unnatural position. Fine hairs stuck at odd angles from its body where dried blood attracted gnats. Almost human, it had sharp teeth and ears that flattened against its head with pointed tips.

Something had eaten its eyes.

This creature was impossible, an abomination, a monster.

A bright blue butterfly landed on its chest. How could something so beautiful live among this?

Something tapped my shoulder and I shrieked. Birds fluttered from the trees, their colorful wings flashing in the dappled light. I gasped, trying to catch my breath.

"That'd be a beastie." Jack gestured to the corpse. "And ya ought to keep quiet. Otherwise the locals'll find *us*." He patted my shoulder and returned to investigating the stone structure.

"Aren't we trying to find *them*?" Tim asked, his voice shaky. "Aren't they allies?"

"Sure, but if there's been an attack recently, they might not ask many questions before defending their territory."

I clenched my teeth, unable to look away from the corpse.

Beasts. This is what the rebels had warned me about. Beasts were real. "Why would they do this?" I couldn't believe anyone would create something so monstrous. It wasn't efficient. It wasn't right. No wonder E-Leadership kept this secret. If people knew this is what happened to those diagnosed with theophrenia — real or not — there would be chaos.

"Hrmm?" Jack turned as he pulled his gnarled, reddish hair into a ponytail and out of his face.

"Why would anyone create this — this *creature*?" A burning fury curled in my throat. Fury that the rebels would lie and say the leaders who created peace could do such a thing, and fury that those same leaders might've actually done the accused.

Jack scowled. "The Camaraderie of Evil calls themselves evil for a reason. Whatever else they might try to hide, they ain't hiding that fact."

No leader would call himself evil. It wasn't natural. But neither was this corpse. A disease couldn't cause this kind of physiological mutation. The cat-like eyes. The pointed ears. The thicker brow and elongated limbs. It couldn't. There had to be something else involved in the transformation.

Lance stepped cautiously around the body, while Jack examined the stone structure. He traced his finger along a jaguar carving that stylistically morphed into a serpent around the temple's base.

I shut my eyes and tried to think of something other than beasts: a blue and green flag with a little gray stick figure family on it. Safety, security, efficiency — stitched into the fabric, beasties lying dead on the ground . . .

I shivered. Something was watching us.

I scanned the trees and the undergrowth, my hairs on end. *I'm just nervous, that's all.*

There was nothing out here but a line of plant growth tracing to a bundle of vines that clustered high in the trees above the temple.

A bead of cold sweat trickled down my back, and I hurried to where Jack inspected the temple's stone blocks. He scratched at the moss and chipped the stone, then inspected the chips between his claws. "Looks like the damage was recent," he murmured, looking up at the top of the temple.

I followed his gaze. The stairway was broken halfway up the temple's side. The whole upper section had crumbled. Broken stone smothered the thick grass, crushing the plants that now lay dying for lack of sunlight. I withdrew my senses, unnerved. I could *feel* the plants dying. Craving light, nourishment —

Life.

Overhead, a bird cawed and rustled through the thick canopy, vanishing into the bright, cloudless sky. I shuddered and glanced over my shoulder, making sure the dead beastie hadn't suddenly returned to life. Beyond the broken stalks and vines, the trees glowed with power. Pulsing and thrumming with uneven energy. Whispering . . .

Maybe being around this many plants so soon after discovering my powers was a bad idea. Or maybe full-immersion was better. Who knew?

I wriggled uncomfortably. I could sense the weight of something pressing into the grass behind the temple. The plants there felt different from the drooping ferns close to me. But they also felt different from the plants being crushed under the weight of the stones. The pattern felt wrong. More organic. I circled around the stone structure. I could see Lance from here, so long as I walked far enough out from the temple's base. Lance knelt at the beastie's corpse, examining it closer and prodding it with a stick.

He had more nerve than I did.

The other side of the temple greeted me with a rotten, horrible stench. I gagged and held my hand over my nose. A pile of bodies both human and beast lay stacked across each other, each mutilated with burn marks or disjointed jaws and heads. Some were strangled from vines wrapped around their throats.

Nutrients for the forest.

The jungle crowded in on me. Too much plant life, too much decay. I shivered. Nutrients for the forest? What was I thinking? Community . . . this place was horrible.

I took a deep breath, and once I was sure my legs weren't going to collapse under me, I staggered forward, trying to get a better idea of what happened. Some bodies had metal spears goring their chests and legs, while others held those bloodied and forgotten spears. Though many of the victims wore green uniforms and camouflaged gear, some had plain clothes.

"Jack? I found more bodies . . ." My voice reached a higher pitch than I knew possible.

Jack sprang over a log, pursued by Lance and Tim. When he saw the pile, he moved forward and pushed the bodies off one another, faster and faster.

Minutes later, he stepped away and let out a heavy breath. "Gwen isn't here."

Relief surged through me and Lance let out a low whistle. If we weren't careful, that would be *us* in the pile. Goosebumps rose on my skin.

Jack brushed his hands of pollen and dirt, then grabbed his radio and spoke into it. "Looks like the locals had a bout with mercs. Not sure who won."

"Any sign of Gwen?" Inese's voice crackled from the speaker.

"No. She's not here. We're heading to the nearest village coordinates to see if they know anything."

"All right. Be careful."

"Careful? That's my middle name. Same goes to you. Jack out."

He grabbed one of the cleaner spears and thrust its shaft at me. "You need a weapon." When I protested that I had a gun, he added, "Something you know how to fight with. Warning—tip's electrified." He pressed a button on the shaft, and the pointed tip crackled. He grounded it against a metal buckle and the corpse danced.

I stepped back. The staff looked long and unwieldy and . . . electrified. And I hardly knew how to fight with it. On the other hand, Lance glared at me with jealousy.

Totally taking the spear.

"Look," Jack continued, "this mission's more dangerous than we thought. Be on your guard at all times—"

"Where's Tim?" Lance asked. We looked around us, silent. No sign of Tim.

My heart skipped a beat. If he got lost, he might suffer the same fate as the corpses in the clearing. Jack must have had the same thought, because he sprang from his crouch and raced to the other side of the temple, only to stop there and scowl. Tim stood beside a battered stone door, scanning the markings with his tablet.

"Unfortunately, that translator doesn't translate ancient hieroglyphs," Jack said.

Tim glanced up. "It doesn't?"

I peered over Tim's shoulder. Recent pictures of the temple covered the tablet's screen, and he switched to a transliteration document filled with partially completed sentences.

Jack gently pushed me aside, then gaped at the tablet. "That's impossible."

"What is?" Tim double-checked the screen. "Everything's right here."

Jack snatched the tablet and traced his claw down the scrollbar. "I'll be damned. It does translate hieroglyphs."

Tim's eyes darted from the screen to Jack.

Lance peered around Jack's shoulder. "Cool."

Jack showed us the half-completed translation. Since the document hadn't been grammatically corrected, the fragments were a conglomeration of verbs and nouns and descriptors, like a set of shuffled grammar cards.

I pushed the tablet back to Jack.

"Using techno sight and super intelligence to translate ancient documents. Crush'll want to see that." Jack took a moment to scout for signs of danger, then checked his own tablet for maps to the nearest village. "Let's keep moving."

Lance prodded at vines with his sword while I nudged them aside with my powers. I was now the most heavily armed of us four — given that I had vines, a gun, an electric spear, *and* the whole jungle at my disposal — but I barely knew how to use any of the weapons in question.

We walked for a solid hour without finding anything, and all of us, except Jack, had half-empty water bottles. "Are we there yet?" Tim complained. He had already shoved the tablet into his pocket and abandoned his attempts at translation. Lance took another swig from his canteen, then woefully shook it. It sloshed, emptier than mine.

"They should be within a mile." Jack said. "We'll find —"

"*¡Manos arriba!*" a rough voice snapped. Seven men in t-shirts pointed rifles and silvery-white spears at us with tips that crackled with electricity. They had golden skin, dark eyes, and dark hair. They'd seen a lot more sun than even Jack had. Tim stared at them . . . canteen shaking in his hands.

"Or they'll find us," Jack muttered. "Hands up."

I swallowed hard and did what he said.

"*¡Tiren sus armas!*" the man at the front demanded. I took a wild guess that he was their leader.

Hopefully a friendly leader.

"Put down your weapons—slowly," Jack said.

My hands shook as I set my spear down on the grass, though there was nothing I could do about the plants around my arms. A local held the tip of his spear mere centimeters from my face. A little spark nearly connected with my nose—deterrent enough from trying to use a gun I couldn't aim.

"We're friends," Jack said carefully. "We're with the Coalition of Freedom—unless you've recently joined the Camaraderie?"

The leader stamped the butt of his spear against the ground, ranting in stilted English. I could barely comprehend his accent . . . and I didn't understand enough Spanish to catch the other bits.

"Where did you get the spear?" The leader's face twisted into a hateful snarl, and he pointed to the spear lying in the dirt. I gulped, willing myself not to step back. Electrified or not, I had no desire to be shish-kebabbed.

Jack kept his voice even. "There was a pile of bodies by a ruined temple. I gave her the spear so she could defend herself from beasties and mercs."

I wanted to clench my hands together to keep them from shaking. This wasn't the Community, where guards were focused on our safety. *We* were the trespassers. There'd be no day in the coolers; no chance of appeal. And they had spears! Who carried spears in this day and age?

Except Lance. Lance didn't count. He'd been fascinated with swords ever since I'd known him.

I kept an eye on the guy in front of me. He narrowed his eyes, checked my arm bands, then murmured something in Spanish to one of his friends. A rifle pointed my direction. *Stupid efficiency*. I was the most heavily armed. They probably thought I actually knew how to use everything. I tried to give them a nervous smile, but neither of them moved their weapons.

"We're looking for a friend—Gwen Vansant," Jack told them. "She had information from one of your villages on the Camaraderie's movements."

The discontented murmur from the men made me wonder if he'd said the wrong thing. "They took her in an attack," the leader said. "We lost several members of our militia."

"I'm sorry," Jack said grimly.

"The Camaraderie showed interest in the temple. They stole *la piedra de los viajeros*. We had asked Gwen to hide it." Then he added something in Spanish, but I didn't catch what.

"I see," Jack said, obviously getting more out of the stilted conversation than I. "A stone. Any idea who took Gwen, and where?"

The leader shrugged. "Mercenaries. Thieves. We wounded them. Trailed them. Quit when we reached the facilities."

"The facilities?" Jack's quietness made me shiver. What were the facilities?

The leader wrinkled his nose. "Yes."

"Can you take us there? If we're going to save Gwen, we've got to get going."

"*Vamos*," the leader called to his men, and they directed their weapons away from us. My "captor" grabbed my spear from the ground and tossed it to me. The weapon landed awkwardly in my hands.

They led us down a narrow trail that was covered in wood chips and surrounded by encroaching walls of green foliage.

"Nothing good'll happen if Gwen is in Camaraderie hands," Jack told us. "We need to find her before they have a chance to interrogate her. Her life-spirit power will give her some ability to hold her own, but not much. Not if they bring in higher-end telepaths."

"Where are we going?" Lance asked.

"One of the Camaraderie's bases."

He didn't say anything further. The silence wracked my nerves until finally, Lance peered over Tim's shoulder. "Any luck with that translation?"

Tim nodded and showed him his progress. "The gist of it says, 'Beware the changing guardian; he who carries the five stones travels time in the circle of stone at the longest day.' Portions of it are missing, though; some of the sentences are incomplete." He scratched his sandy hair.

"Time stones?" Jack shook his head.

"That's what it says. It also says something about 'deities.' What does 'deity' mean?"

Jack blinked and glanced at him over his shoulder. "A deity is one of their gods or goddesses."

Tim tilted his head quizzically.

"The powers that be? Gods? Really high-ranking leaders?" Jack rubbed his forehead in exasperation. "Didn't you study mythology?"

"Mythology isn't practical," Tim said matter-of-factly. He clicked out of his translation document, revealing a background shot of Lady Black perched on the rising sun half-cog, her signature scrawled across the portrait.

Lance smirked and nudged Tim in the ribs. "Neither is having pictures autographed."

"At least I got one." Tim yanked the tablet away defensively.

I groaned. "For the love of the Community . . . you're arguing over an *autograph*!"

Jack frowned. "Practical or not, those beliefs were their way of life. Still is, for some of them. Just like those autographs are part of yours. Anyways, if you see some strange stone lying around the facility, grab it. I think these guys are gonna want it back."

"It also says something about jaguars bringing the stone from the sky," Tim said.

Lance burst out laughing. "Space cats, right?" He turned to Jack. "Don't you have a comic where the bad guys came from Mars?"

Jack waved his hand at the notion and I shook my head. We were heading to an enemy facility and they were jesting about space cats and time travel.

At least we'd die amused.

"*¡Bestias!*" a man shouted, and the nearest locals vanished into the undergrowth.

The macaws stopped chirping and fluttered away in a rainbow of feathers. Jack waved us into a thicket. "Quiet. Don't start fighting unless absolutely necessary. Stay back."

I huddled in the bushes. Waiting . . .

A soft breeze rattled the leaves. Sweat trickled down my back. Heavy, flowery fragrances clogged my nose, threatening to make me sneeze. I had no idea how long I hunched there, brushing the damp soil with my fingers and sensing the nearby plants.

There was no sound but wind. A few of the locals moved forward, their spears low and almost out of sight. An unnatural weight shifted behind me.

My breath caught in my throat. A man crouched in the trees, his white armor glinting in the tiny spot of sunlight peeking through the leaves.

He raised a crossbow and sighted an arrow.

He was aiming at us.

CHAPTER
SIXTEEN

"Jack!" I grabbed his arm and yanked him back. The arrow snapped centimeters from his face and pierced the tree beside him. He cursed, eyes wide.

The man had another arrow notched. Aiming.

I mentally yanked the branch he was standing on. The branch shot forward and the man dropped his crossbow. The man caught the branch and grappled to keep his hold. He shot me a glare, then withdrew a knife from his side, holding the branch with ease.

He jammed the knife into the branch.

My world flared in a blaze of the *plant's* pain as the man calmly dropped several meters from the tree and landed in a crouch. I gaped at him as I nursed my throbbing arm. He should've broken his leg, and my arm *hurt*. It was like he'd stabbed *me* when he stabbed the tree.

The man stood, popped his neck, and then held the knife with its point to the sky. A ruby pendant on his chest sparkled in the sunlight, stark against his white armor.

"Community . . ." I hunched closer to the ground. That pendant . . . "Master Matoska?" Only international leaders wore those pendants, and though Master Matoska rarely made public appearances, I'd seen enough videos of him to recognize his face. The set jaw, the dark, watchful eyes. I'd heard Sam gush about how handsome he was—"*too bad he never makes a public speech,"* she'd said.

With the white body armor and the knife in his hand, I'd argue that he looked far more comfortable out here than on a public stage.

"Run," Jack said coldly. He unsheathed the katana from Lance's side before Lance even realized he'd done so.

Lance gaped at him. "But we're a team. We can take him—"

"No, you can't. Now *run.*" Jack raised the katana and barreled into the forest while Master Matoska waited, toying with the knife in his palm.

I shook my head, feeling dazed and confused.

GROARRR!

I staggered and fell on my behind. I turned my attention to the jungle ahead. The trees spread into bushes, then ascended into a large, grassy clearing. Just past the bushes, several men fought a giant, not-quite-human monstrosity. It towered over the locals, hulking muscles extended beyond human capacity. Blood seeped from a gaping hole near its ribs and stained the tattered remains of its clothes.

The beastie's attacker wove back and forth, leading the beastie's dull eyes. The creature had a thick brow, wiry hair, and its legs and arms were too long for its torso. It hunched, snarling, then swiped a bulging hand at one of the locals.

My whole body trembled. It'd been human once. Now it was hideous.

"Come on!" Lance shouted. "Run!"

Tim was already ahead of us, skirting the outer edge of the clearing and dashing into a thicket of leaves. Lance ran the opposite direction.

"We're supposed to stick together!" I shouted. But they were too far out to hear me.

I followed Lance, since he was closest, and we huddled in the leaves, taking shelter from the fight. A local rushed the monster, but the beast grabbed him by the throat and yanked him from the ground. Bones snapped and his screams fell short.

"We've got to help," Lance said.

I wasn't sure if it was his heart or mine pounding double-time in my ears. The beasts were brutal. No wonder Inese gave me her gun.

Behind us, there was no sign of Jack or Matoska, and I couldn't hear anything more than a mingled mass of screams and shouts. Ahead, more beasties darted through the field, half-loping, half-running. One was lanky and pale. What little clothing it wore was hooked over its bony waist. Crusted blood and clods of dirt plastered its skin. A feline eye stared my direction. The other was swollen shut. Other beasts were bulky and heavily muscled, swinging swords or metal clubs, bashing in the locals' skulls if they got too close. A large glob of water hovered around a beast that stood straighter; more human than the others. The creature lunged at a man and water splashed onto the electric spear. Static traversed the metal shaft. Both man and beast crashed to the ground as electricity coursed over the beastie's water-slick skin.

I couldn't keep my spear steady. This was all so impossible.

A local yelled and jabbed the giant monstrosity in the clearing. The beast brought its fists down, attempting to crush the man. He tumbled and drove his spear into the beast's side, then flicked the switch. The creature roared in pain. It crashed to the ground, and a moment later, the local tugged his spear from its side.

Nearby, a beastie with flames flickering around its blackened, scarred hands sent a plume of fire from its fist. Flames ran across the beast's skull, and its arms were scabbed to the elbows, like a charcoal-covered turtle shell. Back and forth, it slunk through the tall grass before standing on its hind legs, straight as a soldier. Tim fired his pistol from the trees, but his hands shook so badly that his shot fired wild and missed the beast altogether.

I focused on the grass around Tim, urging it to grow, and when that didn't work, I set sight on the bushes beside him. It'd be like a sunflower, maybe, or how trees grew full during summer. I imagined the leaves growing thicker and greener. The branches extended, piece by piece, until new sprouts of green blossomed into large pink flowers.

Tim froze. The beastie sniffed the area, fire licking the palm of its hand.

If I kept using my powers, I'd draw attention to him. So I stopped, waited, and after a second longer, the beast's attention shifted to a local and his rifle. I let out a sigh of relief. Tim glanced my direction and mouthed, "*Thank you.*"

I nodded. I didn't want anybody getting killed, let alone my friends.

The air *whooshed*, drawing my attention back to the clearing. A fireball engulfed one of the locals. I shielded my eyes and took a deep breath, unable to block out his terrified scream. My back felt sweaty and cold. Cold and hot. Too much noise. Too much *pain.*

Without warning, Lance hurtled from the trees' shadows. I clutched my spear, rooted to my spot, too distracted by his battle cry to pay attention to the surrounding battle and anyone who could use my help. Lance plowed into a squat, burly monster with a thick forehead and wild, uncombed hair. It tilted its head, sluggish, its eyes dull, lost . . . then opened fire from its rifle.

"Lance!" I fumbled with my pistol, straining to free the safety lock before firing. The bullet shot into the branch over Lance's head. My shot had been too close. Too poorly aimed. Why couldn't Inese have given me a bit more training before now?

I grabbed my spear and stood, but Lance was already ahead of me. The beast cried out as he stuck his sword into its back. My stomach roiled as the beastie grappled for its fallen gun and clasped it between thick fingers, then swung the gun like a club.

Lance blocked the blow with his sword and staggered at the impact. Panic stabbed me—I concentrated on the grass around the beastie's feet. The grass sprung up like honeysuckles around a fence post, but the creature swatted the grass as if it was nothing more than a pesky mosquito.

Like morning glories on a wooden trellis, I told myself, picturing the gun being flung as far as I could throw it. The long strands of grass flicked the gun half a meter out from the beastie's grasp and I yipped, giddy with success.

The beast froze, and for a split second Lance had the same puzzled expression.

Come on, Lance . . .

He recovered from his surprise, then stabbed his sword into the beastie's chest. I held my breath, waiting to see if he'd killed it. Lance braced himself with one foot on the ground, one foot on the body, and removed his sword.

I cringed. Leaves clustered along my ankles, comforting. We could do this. We could fight the beasties, stay alive, and find Gwen. We'd do it together, just like we'd promised.

More beasts appeared over the hill and charged our diminished team. One had blackened skin, fire lacing its arms and hands, while another beastie, female, raced through the clearing with terrifying speed, lunging to rip out a local's throat with its teeth.

Beasties are tough, Jack had told us, *a pain to deal with, but they're brutal, not smart. The question goes to how smart the beastmaster is.*

The beastmaster!

Blood pounded in my ears as I scanned the horizon, trying to spot the culprit.

There.

At the top of the hill, two human soldiers stood silhouetted against the sun, too straight and proud to be beasts. One kept a sharp eye over the events while the other held an assault rifle. Both were in Special Forces uniform.

The beasties raced past them, uncaring.

I hunkered in the leafy bushes. Of the two men standing on the hill, the one scouting everything was my most likely candidate for beastmaster. He was the one to blame for this; he had to be. I didn't trust my aim with Inese's gun, but several long vines draped in loose coils from the branch above him. I focused on those vines, drowning out the sound of electrical zaps, bullets, and screams.

"Come on," I whispered. "Grow for me."

The vines coiled and tightened, wrapping around the mossy branch until the vine extended downward, revealing a tip that slid toward my target's head. I closed my eyes, imagining the vine coiling around the beastmaster's twitching body. If I killed him, maybe the beasties would stop their attack.

The vine grasped the beastmaster's throat and he snatched at it, screaming wordlessly.

I had to keep my eyes open. I had to see what I was doing. "Keep holding," I whispered, trembling. "You're a strong vine."

The beastmaster's fingers tightened around the vine, trying to tug it free, but my grip was tighter. I curled the vine into a noose, like I'd seen in history books. The sentry next to him fumbled to unhook a knife from his pocket.

Tears gathered at the corners of my eyes.

Don't let go.

Memories of dead locals and the eyeless beastie ran through my head. I squeezed the vine tighter and the beastmaster lifted from the ground, his neck caught. The sentry yanked his knife free and for a simple, horrible moment, I remembered the pain of the knife stabbing into the tree and I withdrew my power.

The vine severed, but the beastmaster struggled and went limp. The sentry stared at his partner. The beasties hesitated. One turned and tackled the sentry. I looked away, staring at my hands. My fingers were covered in moist dirt where I'd dug my nails into the underbrush.

What if he wasn't dead, and he was suffocating? I found the severed vine in my mind and urged thorns to erupt from the vine's cell walls. They found resistance, then hardened in the beastmaster's throat.

If the man wasn't dead earlier, he was now.

I gulped for air and huddled in the bush's embrace, my arms wrapped around my knees. I'd just killed a man. A potentially evil man, but a man nonetheless. This had to be a lie. A horrible, completely unfounded hallucination.

I opened my eyes. It wasn't a hallucination. The beasties still fought each other or ran deeper into the jungle. One leapt over me and disappeared among the trees. I held my breath. The broad leaves rustled and the wind whispered through the ferns as birds returned to their playful calls.

The beasts were gone. So were the locals.

I silently counted the remains. The seven human bodies belonged to the locals who'd been helping us, and the rest belonged to a countless number of beasts.

"Jenna?" a voice called, quiet at first, then louder. "Jenna!" Lance stood at the top of the hill. He paused to wipe his sword in the grass. His shirt and pants were stained with blood. Tim followed behind, frantically looking around him, pistol in hand.

I loosened the vines around my arms. Humid air flooded through my sleeves where the cool leaves had cut the heat, and I tried to wipe away the tear stains from my face. Dirt smeared on the back of my hand and cheeks.

"Jenna!" Lance called, cupping his hands around his mouth.

"I'm here." I wanted to stretch my arms and legs, but I shook too hard to steady myself.

Lance flung himself at me and wrapped me in a bear hug. "I thought you were dead." I coughed, trying to breathe. "When I couldn't find you—" He pulled away and checked me for bruises.

"*I* didn't run into the middle of the battlefield," I reminded him. How could he worry about me? He was the one who'd been out there, trying to kill beasts! A nervous half-laugh choked in my throat. Lance was alive, but the beastmaster was not. I'd ended that man's life on a hunch, on a *guess* he was the one controlling the beasts. What if he had a wife? Children? Surely the wife could support them; the Community would assign her a new partner if it was more efficient. But she might have loved him.

A lump formed in my throat as the mental image of the beastmaster's broken partnership morphed into an image of my parents. What if something terrible like that happened to them? I shook my head quickly, my skin clammy.

Something terrible like that *had* happened. Right now, *I* was the one who was missing. The one they probably thought was dead. How would Mom and Dad feel if they knew I was out here?

My limbs felt heavy as I trudged up the hill. Tim and Lance followed.

The sentry had been dragged halfway across the field by a rampaging beastie, his body in shreds. The other man, the one I'd targeted, was blue in the face, clearly dead.

The sleeve of his uniform revealed a small patch with "Beastmaster" labeled beneath it. I pried the thorns from his neck, wincing as blood seeped from his fresh wounds. The beasts had scattered when I killed him. He must have been coordinating those attacks. Ordering them to kill people. To burn them alive. I clamped my hand around my spear, furious that he could do such a thing.

Lance nudged my shoulder. "You okay?"

"He was controlling them," I said bitterly. "Using them to attack us." I explained what happened. How the beasts stopped fighting and ran once I'd killed him. I'd wanted proof, and this was all the proof I needed. "We need to find Jack."

Lance nodded and wiped sweat from his forehead. He took a swig from his canteen, eyed it, then frowned.

We were getting low on water.

"Let's go," he said, hooking the canteen next to his empty scabbard.

We stuck close to each other as we scouted the area, but there was no sign of Jack or Master Matoska. Just broken tree limbs, trampled berries, and deep ruts in the dirt from their boots. All the signs of a struggle, but no sign of the parties involved.

"Can you contact Inese?" Lance asked Tim.

Tim shook his head. "I don't have a radio. Inese should be able to catch the nearby Camaraderie signals, but she doesn't use wireless."

"What about GNSS?" I asked, thinking of EYEnet's navigational satellites. Surely we could access them, even out here. "Can we get a map of the area?"

"Maybe." He fiddled with his tablet controls. "Nope. That's odd. There's no signal here. There *is* some sort of tech to the north, though. If we follow that transmission, we might find people." He looked up at us, his cheeks flushed from the humidity.

Lance ran a hand through his longish hair. Though all of us could have used a bath, he'd taken the brunt of the physical toll. His hair was a mess of crushed leaves and broken twigs, and he was covered in plant stains, mud, and drying blood. "We should stay here, in case Inese brings the car this way."

"Does she even know this path exists?" I rested my head against the tree, not welcoming another trek through the jungle. I was tired, hungry, and scared. If we didn't find people soon, we'd spend the night here alone, and I didn't know what our chance of survival was with those beasts on the loose.

"If we find people, maybe they can lead us to Gwen," I suggested.

Lance stared at me. "We're not in any condition to stage a rescue."

"If the people are part of the local village, they'll know how to contact Inese. If they're part of the Camaraderie, they can give us their version of the events. I want to know why they would use beasts to maim and kill."

Lance frowned. "We should wait."

"The tech signal is moving away from us." Tim swiped his finger across the tablet. "They're currently about thirty-five minutes north of us, but it won't take them long to get out of reach."

Lance sighed. "Fine. Let's get moving. We'll be on our guard, just in case. And keep an eye out for Inese," he said firmly.

We each took sips from the remainders in our canteens, and then headed the direction Tim indicated.

Forty minutes later, the trees thinned and gave way to tall grass. My feet ached and blistered, and we'd slowed to a sluggish gait. For all that I could use my powers, I was starting to feel like I couldn't sense anything *but* plants. Grass. Trees. Shrubs. Roots. Roots everywhere, crowding the soil . . .

"Where are they?" Lance asked, coming to a halt. He'd sheathed his sword after his arm muscles tensed. "Tim—"

"I don't know!" Tim worried his lip and cast a fearful glance at us. "They should be right here!"

Lance looked over Tim's tablet, his lips twisted in frustration. He grunted. "So what do we do now? There's no telling how far out we are."

I stretched my legs, not daring to sit. "Is there any chance we could send a flare of some kind? Smoke signal? Someone's bound to notice."

"With what?" Lance pulled at his pockets. "I've got a sword and an empty canteen. Admit it—we're lost." He glared at Tim.

"It's not my fault!" Tim protested. "You agreed that this was our best option. We could've stayed back there. Isn't that what your Special Forces training would suggest? Stay in a known area until rescue comes?"

"I'm not Special Forces! I'm not even fully trained in security!" Lance tucked his arms over his chest and wandered several paces away. "Now we're lost."

"It was my fault," I said. "I'm the one who suggested we walk."

"I agreed to it," Lance grumbled.

"We all did," Tim reminded him, his voice meek. "And we're not going to survive if we don't stop fighting."

Lance's shoulders sagged. "Don't split up. That's one of the rules. Have a partner back you, and don't fight with partners. Any disagreements can be settled when you aren't strained and frustrated." He sighed. "Now what?"

The sky above was bright blue, hinting on the first signs of evening though I couldn't see the angle of the sun. No sign of invisible flying cars, either.

Stupid invisibility.

There was movement in the corner of my eye, a flash of light in the grass.

I raised my spear, hesitant. "Is someone there?"

Please be someone, not something. I wasn't sure what kind of predators might try to make a meal of us.

"Behind you!" Lance shouted, drawing his sword.

I spun around. A large form in gleaming metal armor stood up from where he had been crouching in the clearing. The long grass wavered around him. His silvery white armor plates blinded me with spots from the sun, and even his silver half-cape with its green trim fluttered brightly. His ruby pendant glinted.

How in the Community had we missed him? His armor made him look like a silver mirror.

Master Matoska crossed his arms over his chest and smirked. "What are you three doing so far from the Community?"

CHAPTER
SEVENTEEN

Lance raised his sword, aiming to strike Matoska's unprotected head, but the man caught Lance's arm and twisted his wrist. Lance squawked. His sword fell. Without hesitation, Matoska thrust his knee into Lance's stomach. Lance gasped for breath and collapsed on his knees.

Matoska grabbed him by the scruff of his neck and yanked his head back, then held a knife to his exposed throat. He looked at me and let out an exaggerated sigh. "Miss Nickleson—my orders are to take you alive. You. Not them." He gestured to Lance and the general direction Tim was hiding.

"Let him go." I clamped my hand around my spear. I wasn't sure if the tingling in my arms and legs was from adrenaline or from my powers. Everything seemed to move so *slow*.

The man grunted. "You're a rookie plant elemental. I'll bet you don't have a clue how to use that thing, and from my little demonstration earlier, you haven't learned to control how much power you put into your target."

Right. That tree he stabbed.

"What'll it be? You're not calling the shots, kid. Oh—if your buddy over there pulls the trigger, this guy's taking the bullet." Matoska nudged his head toward Lance, and then looked right at Tim. "I suggest you show yourself."

Slowly, Tim stood, his hand tightly grasping the pistol. He looked between me and our assailant, his eyes wide. He lowered the gun.

"Smart boy." Matoska returned his attention to me. "Are you coming?"

I nodded.

"Good." He tapped his finger on an earpiece. "Secure them and move out."

Several men and women in crisp black uniforms stepped out from the trees. A few cleared grass from their pants as they stood. Those closest to us leveled their rifles at our heads.

They'd been waiting the whole time.

Master Matoska shoved Lance toward me. "Don't try anything stupid, all right?"

"No, sir," Lance mumbled, trembling. He rubbed his throat uncomfortably and edged toward me, his eyes burning with unspoken hatred. Tim followed behind us, his head down as if that would protect him if the agents decided to shoot. They led us along another long, weary trail, and none of us spoke. What could we say?

Master Matoska really was a bounty hunter. He was tall, his gait proud but cautious, even though his agents could've easily stopped an ambush without trouble. He kept his hair in a black braid that wrapped over his shoulder, and his metallic armor looked well cared for, despite the pits and dings that covered the plates.

Given the leader's resources, that armor was probably lighter than it looked. Still . . . for all that he strode forward at a gait that quickly tired me, Matoska held his left arm close to his body. A ragged gash in the fabric under his arm revealed the tan skin underneath and a considerable amount of dried blood.

"You're wounded," I murmured. Had Jack done that?

Matoska didn't respond.

"What happened to Jack? Did you kill him?"

Lance and Tim exchanged glances.

"Where are we going?" I demanded. "Why did you attack us?"

Still no answer.

Frustrated, I stormed toward him, my hands clenched on my spear. Next thing I knew, I was face-up on the ground, my head throbbing. The sky and trees and a pair of agents wobbled in and out of each other, like a kaleidoscope.

I blinked and struggled to sit.

Matoska waited until I was upright, then raised a finger, and both Lance and Tim cried out as the agents kicked the back of their knees. They collapsed, and the rest of the agents trained their rifles at my friends' heads.

I reached for my spear, but Matoska planted his boot firmly on the shaft. He knelt beside me and pressed the spear into my hands, leaving his own hand just below the shocky tip. "Go ahead. Press the button."

I stared at him. "What?"

"If I thought any of you were a threat, I would have taken your weapons long before now. So go ahead. Press the button." He looked down the shaft, his eyes unconcerned. "It'll hurt, yes. But it'll hurt them more." He nudged his chin in the direction of Tim and Lance. They quivered, frozen, waiting for my action.

I swallowed hard. I wanted to press that button so bad . . .

"You're the only one I need alive, missy. I can take you by force, and there will be two additional bodies out here for the animals to snack on. Or you can come *quietly*, and your friends may have a chance to live. Which will it be?"

I trembled, still clutching the spear.

He wrapped his other hand around mine, the same one that held the button. He held my gaze, his eyes hard, and didn't let go. Panic welled through me.

"I'll be quiet," I whispered.

"Good." He released his grip and I nearly dropped the spear. "Next time, I'll kill them."

I struggled to stand. Once Matoska had turned his back, I rushed to Lance and Tim. "I'm so sorry," I whispered. "Are you okay?"

Lance grunted, rubbing his legs uncomfortably. Tim edged away from the agents, who'd returned to watching the surrounding jungle. Their expressions were impossible to read under their dark visors.

The thick trees loomed overhead, their vines draped in uncomfortable clusters. The heat was sweltering as the jungle threatened to collapse in on me. Even with every weapon Jack and Inese had given me, I was utterly helpless.

Our trek was shorter than I expected. About ten minutes after the incident that nearly got my friends killed, Master Matoska led us to a paved road. Another fifteen minutes, and we stopped inside the barbed wire fence of their facility. I assumed it was the same one where they'd taken Gwen.

Master Matoska watched as they locked us inside a bare room. The agents took our weapons and Tim's tablet, leaving us with nothing but a conference table and a small refrigerator. "You'll stay here until we have a chance to interrogate you," he told us. "A doctor will be in shortly to block your powers. I suggest you cooperate." He excused himself, telling the guards at the front door to keep an eye on us while he took care of his wound.

"At least they left us water." Tim sipped at one of the plastic water bottles they'd left for us in the fridge and offered me one. I took it, dizzy.

"If they block our powers, we'll be defenseless." I could already feel my vines drifting as the agents took them farther down the hall. A moment later, the plants were jostled one last time, then left alone.

I sighed. At least I could still sense them.

Lance perched himself on the table, brooding. "Pops was telling the truth."

"It kind of looks that way," Tim agreed.

"I wish it didn't." I hung my head between my knees. "I wish we could get some kind of message to Inese, but I don't think they're going to let us borrow their wireless."

Tim paused. "Hey . . . that's not a bad idea." His eyes lit up, and he pushed a bottle of water into Lance's hands. "Drink."

"What's not a bad idea?" Lance waved his hand at the water bottle. "I don't want anything they have to offer."

"Do you want a chance to escape?" Tim pushed the water bottle at Lance. "You need to rehydrate. We all do."

"How exactly do you expect us to get past armed guards? They're *agents*. We don't stand a chance." Lance scowled but drained the bottle in a few gulps, and then winced at what I presumed to be brain freeze.

Tim took a deep breath. "This room isn't monitored. No cameras or bugs. I think they just put us here as a temporary fix. There are two guards outside, both wearing EYEtoEYE tech. Their helmets are sensitive to techno sight. The locks on the doors are digital, and —"

The door swung open, and a woman entered in a Special Forces uniform without the visor, followed by a single guard. She sat a metal box on the table and clicked the locks, revealing a set of hypodermics in black foam. She turned toward us. "The more you relax, the easier it is for me to inject you." She held up one of the needles, as if to demonstrate. "It's a basic power block, so you will sense a loss of your powers, but that's all. Any questions?"

Tim raised his chin. "They've already given us the injection."

Lance and I stared at him.

The agent frowned. "I could have sworn Master Matoska said you needed the injection."

Tim licked his lips. "Someone came in shortly before you did. I mean — I'm sure he kept a log of it."

The agent eyed him warily. "What did he look like?"

Tim glanced at me, his breath shallow. His eyes darted across my face, but he wasn't looking at me. "Older guy . . . a bit bald on top. Had a funny looking mustache?"

She sighed. "I guess Doctor Ogden forgot to tell me." She removed a tablet from her pocket and scrolled through it, then nodded, her lips twisted in mild annoyance. "Yep. Forgot to tell me. I'm going to have to get onto him about that," she murmured. "Don't want to overdose you."

"Uh —" I raised my hand, hoping I could play along. "What would have happened if you gave us the second injection?"

She snapped the metal case shut. "Well, one injection inhibits the gene that allows powers to work. The second causes your brain to go haywire. It suppresses higher cognitive functions. You'd act a bit like a beast does."

I swallowed hard. "I see."

She nodded to us and gestured for the guard to step out with her. "I hope everything goes well for you," she said softly. The door clicked shut behind her.

Lance spun around and stared at Tim. "What just happened?"

"It worked!" Tim burst out laughing.

"What worked?" I asked.

Tim grinned. "I hacked into their network. Rewrote their system to think we'd already had the injection, then looked at their staff list to see who would have been most likely to give it to us. And they bought it!"

"You can do that remotely?" Lance asked. "No tablet?"

Tim nodded and flopped in the chair beside the table. "When Jenna mentioned borrowing their wireless, I started hacking their communication satellite."

"You sent for help?" *Tim . . . you're a genius.*

"If Inese is paying attention, she should have gotten a 'we're here' signal to track us. I'm trying to see if I can find Gwen now — but I'm not sure how to show you. I think I know where my tablet is."

"My vines are just a little way down the hall." I motioned in the direction I could sense them.

"Probably the same spot." Tim glanced at us. "We might be able to escape."

Lance nodded, fire lighting in his eyes, and he grabbed another water bottle. "Let's take a few more minutes to rest, and then we'll run."

"Right." I took a deep breath. Hopefully we'd have enough time to make our plans.

CHAPTER
EIGHTEEN

"I think that's her," Tim said.

The three of us crowded around Tim's tablet as Lance strapped his sword to his belt. I finished fastening the vine straps around my arms, and then peered at Tim's tablet.

Breaking out of our prison had been surprisingly easy. Tim overloaded the agents' headsets with a high pitched squeal, then digitally unlocked the door. We ran three doors down to where our weapons were, and with Tim's techno sight, we managed to get inside without a problem.

Now the tablet's screen was locked on a black and white security feed. An elderly woman sat at the end of a long table, her wrists strapped to a chair.

The Coalition's symbol came to mind. The lady being tortured; defiant to the end.

I swallowed a gulp, keeping clear of the metal door in case anyone came in. "We should try to help."

"What if it isn't Gwen?" Lance asked.

"She's being tortured."

"And her profile matches." Tim showed us a picture of Gwen on his tablet, then switched to the corridor view. Two guards ran toward our door, and they weren't wearing visors. Tim wouldn't be able to use techno sight to distract them, but Lance had his sword and I had my vines. So long as we acted quickly, we'd be all right.

As for Gwen, she was a few rooms past this one, so getting there would be relatively easy. Inside her room, though, was a lady in long robes. She kept her back to the camera as she paced behind her captive.

"Where do we go from here?" I pointed to the tablet.

Tim opened a map and ran his finger along our most likely path. There were only a couple other guards on the preferred route, and neither were Special Forces.

"Anyone else think this looks too easy?" Lance asked.

Tim lowered his tablet. "We're in an enemy facility, exhausted, and dehydrated. Once we get out, we have to hope Inese got our message. Otherwise we're stuck in the jungle with Special Forces on our heels."

"Still seem easy?" I raised an eyebrow at Lance.

"Point taken." Lance stepped against the wall, his sword at ready.

Tim waited until the guards were almost on us, then gave the signal. Lance charged out, flashing his sword to the only exposed part of their bodies. One guard blocked with her rifle, but I curled my vine around the second one's gun and sent it skittering down the hall.

Lance struck that guard with the pommel of his sword. The guard dropped, unconscious. Tim fired at the other. He hit him square in the chest.

A short, empty corridor opened on our right, and I ran. "Come on!"

Muffled sounds echoed from the far-off hallway, and the white walls blurred into streaks. My muscles burned, but with the adrenaline, I didn't care.

"Jenna!" Lance shouted.

My breath caught in my throat.

My speed—I'd left Lance and Tim behind.

At the far end of the corridor, Tim scrambled to aim his weapon. A lanky beast with overly long arms and legs sprinted around the corner. Tim shrieked, changing direction and firing without regard to anyone around him. One bullet hit the beastie in the arm, while the other ricocheted beside Lance. Lance ducked before striking a beast in its stomach.

Cold, paralyzing fear rushed through me. The halls were supposed to be empty!

Something slammed into me. I spun and smashed the butt of the spear into a soft, fleshy body. The creature snarled, righting itself.

No-no! I should've been helping them, not fighting alone! We were supposed to stick together!

I maneuvered the spear between the pacing beast and myself. Electricity crackled at the spear's tip. I didn't want to hurt the creature. It wasn't its fault it was instructed to attack me, but what choice did I have except to defend myself?

It circled me like a cat, then lunged. I swung the spear, faster with my power, then brought the electrified end along its back. It howled, and rather than attacking me again, it slunk away, hissing and showing its fangs. A bruised burn mark scored its lower back.

I stayed against the wall, keeping the wounded creature in the corner of my vision.

A moan twisted from behind the door of the interrogation room. I shivered. The beast crouched. An unrestrained scream blasted through the door. The beastie squealed and dashed down the hall, not bothering to stop at the skirmish ahead.

What in the Community *was* that? Nothing I'd ever heard sounded so painful.

I rattled the doorknob. No answer.

There was a keypad next to the door. I didn't know the code, but since it was digital, I positioned my spear at the keypad and then jammed its tip against the screen. Electricity popped. The keypad sparked and the lock clicked.

Success!

I pushed the door open.

Inside, a lady wearing a flowing, deep purple robe stood at the end of a long metal table. Her robes were fringed by golden swirls and thick, bold lining. Part of her white hair was rolled into an elaborate bun; the rest cascaded to her shoulders.

Except for the strange attire, she looked exactly like Lady Winters.

The lady's eyes narrowed and her face contorted, twisting into a mass of wrinkles. She wore just enough eyeliner to accentuate her fierce eyes, and her nails were painted a gold that matched her outfit. More than most leaders, she was dressed for appearance; a stark contrast to the Lady Winters I knew.

Beside her, an elderly woman with graying hair was bound to the chair. Her shoulders were slumped and her head lolled back.

Go away.

I jumped, then stared at the Lady Winters imposter. I hadn't *heard* anything, but it was clear that the woman standing with her manicured hand on the corner of Gwen's chair had spoken. She lifted her chin and scowled.

"Let her go." I tightened my grip on my spear.

The woman smirked and slid her nail along the edge of the chair. Something forced me — my mind — away.

I couldn't move. My arms were frozen in place.

If you won't leave, then let us see who you might be.

I sat in my house, watching the videos I'd seen of Lady Winters playing on my parents' television set. "In order to ensure that all Community citizens have jobs," she declared, her proper accent shining through each syllable, "each student shall take a qualifications test to determine their best placement in our workforce.

"On another note, it is my great pleasure to announce an upgrade to our laboratories, allowing for a more efficient means of studying the cause of theophrenia so that we might one day be free of the plague entirely."

My favorite speech. The one that meant I might not have to keep taking the stupid pill.

You didn't take the pill? You rebellious child.

I stood in the bathroom, confused, staring at my pill bottle. I'd missed yesterday's pill, but no one had noticed. No one had asked. I felt so . . . alive. I couldn't go back to taking it now.

"Jenna?" Mom called.

I stared at the door. What if Mom found out? She would insist that I go to counseling, or at least give me a lecture. I turned to the toilet, fumbling with the pill and the bottle.

"Jenna Nicole Nickleson, for the love of efficiency, you're going to be late!"

I capped the bottle. The Health Scan was almost a year away. I'd be fine.

I dropped the pill in the toilet.

Nickleson. Ah, yes. I remember that name. Any relation to Dr. Nickolai Nickleson?

The room wavered and I fell against the edge of the table, grabbing the chair to right myself. Lady Winters watched me, wrinkles tarnishing her coy smile. "I'll give you a chance, Nickleson."

I stared at her. Chance at what?

She'd seen my thoughts, my past . . .

Lady Winters smiled and brushed back a wisp of white hair. *Drop the spear. Close the door behind you. Take a seat.* She gestured to the chair in a slow, elegant motion.

I dropped the spear, took a seat. Listened.

"Do you know who your grandfather serves?"

The Coalition.

Lady Winters clasped her hands in front of her. "What about you, Nickleson? Whom do you serve?"

I . . . didn't know. I was from the Community . . .

A slow smile crawled across her cheeks. She gestured to the lady in the chair. "The true plague is disobedience. It makes our society inefficient. This woman is a traitor. She spreads the plague by her presence. She's a lost cause. Kill her."

I stood, vines uncoiling from my arms, and walked the length of the table. Power pulsed through my vines, urging me to take control. To let them flourish. To *use* them.

The traitor turned her head, her eyes half-shut.

"She's the true monster," Lady Winters murmured. "A beast is nothing more than a subhuman servant, and they serve us well. A rebel, however, is a threat to everything we hold dear."

I wrapped my vines around the woman's throat. Felt their pressure against her skin. Closed them tight. The woman coughed, gasping, but I didn't let go.

Funny thing, Nickleson, Lady Winters whispered in my head. *Do you ever wonder how a beast feels when it's given orders? Is this what you want?*

I stared at the dying woman, confused. What *did* I want?

A beast is such a mindless thing. You could be so much more.

Gwen sputtered and fell limp. Her head lolled. A chill clawed through my spine.

She was dead.

I'd killed her.

CHAPTER
NINETEEN

Lady Winters smiled. "If you leave the rebels, I can gift you with a scholarship to continue your biological studies. You could train with me. You are intrigued by how powers work, aren't you?"

I uncoiled my vines and pressed my fingers against the woman's throat. I didn't feel a pulse.

I'd just killed the woman I was trying to rescue.

I stumbled back, my knees giving way to shock. I shook my head. "I'm not training with you. I'm not training with anyone who can manipulate me like that. You tricked me."

"Do you know what happens to rebels?" The leader smoothed the purple silk of her robes.

"They die?" I asked, bitter.

Incorrect.

Fire wrapped around my brain and I clutched the base of my head. The pain . . . for a moment the pain subsided, a numbing throb in the back of my skull. I gasped for air and blinked tears from my eyes.

Lady Winters clucked her tongue. *Poor Miss Nickleson . . . Let me show you what happens to the people who rebel.*

A rocket slammed into the ground, blowing a beast to bits. Sun scorched the back of my neck, and the stench of burnt flesh tainted the air. A blast of heat rolled over me. I shielded my eyes while debris pelted me with dirt. Something smashed into my chest. I removed my hand from my shirt and found it hot and sticky. The pain threatened to destroy my vision —

The hot wind grew cold. Lady Winters dragged me inside a prison. The coolers morphed into a long row of liquid-filled tubes, and she forced a breathing apparatus over my mouth. I gagged, scraping my nails against her arms, but she shoved me inside without a second's hesitation. The door slid shut. I pounded my fists on the glass as water gurgled around my feet, but it wasn't water — it was a greenish liquid I couldn't identify, burning my chest, stinging my arms, numbing the skin where it came in contact.

No! Let me out! Let me out —

I fell against the doorway, my head throbbing. Lady Winters stood firmly in front of me, her hands behind her back. My breaths came ragged.

"Why are you doing this?" I snapped, panting as I tried to regain my breath. "Why create beasts?"

She grinned. Pain squeezed through my skull, wriggling through the nooks and crannies until I couldn't think. Couldn't feel anything but her words repeatedly punching my consciousness.

Why don't you ask your grandfather? she crooned. *Betrayal seems to run in the family.*

The pain stopped. My limbs shook, but all that remained was a dull throb and a rising hatred for the leader I'd trusted.

Carefully, gingerly, I knelt and picked up the spear.

I lunged onto the table and skidded along the metal surface. Fast. So, so *fast*. My thumb jabbed the electric button, and I shoved the spear into Lady Winters' shoulder. The spear resisted entry before plunging through her thick robes. She crumpled, trembling from the electricity.

Blood pounded in my wrists. I retracted my spear and hedged back, crouching on the edge of the table. "The Community is supposed to be safe. You were supposed to be part of that!" I swallowed gulps of air and thrust my spear at her again. Everything spun as the weapon sunk into her chest. Blood welled from the wound, soaking through her robes.

Her eyelids fluttered and she went limp.

Dead. She'd made me kill Gwen, and now I had killed her.

I removed my spear from Lady Winters' body and raised it over my head, ready to keep stabbing until there was no chance of life remaining in her useless corpse.

"Wait, Jenna! No!" A pair of hands caught my spear and a body thrust itself between me and Lady Winters. Tim stared at me, his eyes wide. "We're not beasts," he said quickly.

The lights were too bright; the smell of blood too strong.

I looked from Tim to the leader's lifeless body. I wanted to kill her. Make sure she was dead.

"Oh, Community . . ." I stumbled away from Tim, my spear loose in hand. I'd acted in self-defense; Lady Winters was in my mind. I swallowed a gulp. "Tim—"

"We need to get Gwen free." He gave me a worried glance, then moved past me and knelt beside the woman. Lance stood in the door, keeping a lookout. Tim untwisted the crude knots from around the chair. "See if she's awake."

"But she's dead. Lady Winters made me kill her."

"She's not dead," Tim assured me.

Gwen moaned, her arms slack as Tim removed the ropes. My eyes widened. "But how—" Tim wrapped his arm around her waist and placed her free arm over his shoulder, then helped her stand.

"Thank you," she murmured, coughing.

I glanced at Lady Winters' corpse. She was the only leader who'd ever been worth the speeches she gave. And by killing her, I'd firmly excluded myself from ever returning to the Community. My skin felt clammy and I tucked my vines around my arms, letting them offer what little comfort they could.

Telepath. Lady Winters was a telepath. Everything I saw . . . it was all in my head.

"Who are you?" Gwen asked, her voice hoarse.

"I'm Jenna, and this is Tim," I whispered. "We're with the Coalition."

The words tumbled out of my mouth, and I realized I'd chosen the rebels over the Community.

How quick that choice could be made.

She smiled weakly. "Pops' grandchild. We weren't so sure he would find you. But I'm glad he did." Her smile faltered and she sagged into Tim's arms. He winced—he wasn't as strong as Lance—but he managed to walk her to the door.

I started to follow, but a glint of light around Lady Winters' neck caught my attention from the emerald pendant she wore.

She didn't deserve the honor.

I reached my hands around her tangled hair and unfastened the necklace. It had brass loops and hooks along its edge, and a large, four-sided emerald at its center. A smaller emerald dangled from its oblong end. It felt important, antiquated. Something from before the plague.

I shivered as I withdrew the pendant from her neck. Something unsettled me about being near the dead leader, as if she was still here, still taunting me.

I stuffed the necklace into my pocket.

"Are you coming?" Lance helped Tim brace Gwen on his shoulder. "The hall won't stay clear for long—"

He froze, his eyes wide.

Master Matoska stood at the door behind me, a knife in his hand. He'd changed into a dark green tunic, and though he wasn't wearing the upper body armor, he looked every bit as deadly as before. Even more so, because the shirt revealed the toned muscle of a skilled fighter that the precisely-fitted armor did not.

"You rookies have more fight in you than I thought. This time I won't make the mistake of underestimating you," he said. "I told you I'd only give you one chance before I killed your friends."

Fear spiked through me.

There was a door at the back of the room, one I hadn't noticed before. That was where he'd come from. Behind him, an agent in black uniform sighted her rifle toward Lance, Tim, and Gwen.

I could buy them time, but I doubted that they'd leave without me.

Matoska glanced at Winters, then at my bloodied weapon. He sighed. "Let's get this over with."

Suddenly he barreled toward me and swung his knife overhead. I dodged, but right before he struck, he twisted around and wrangled the spear from my hands. I stumbled as he rammed the flat end against my collarbone.

I gasped for breath and leaned against the table. Lance drew his sword. Matoska rammed the spear forward, thumbed the button, and sent a spark of electricity down Lance's weapon.

Lance collapsed, his face torn in a grimace. Matoska raised the spear, aiming at Lance's throat. The room blurred in a burst of speed, and my shoulder collided with Matoska's upper body.

The spear struck the floor with a metallic screech.

Without warning, Matoska grabbed my arm and shoved me into the agent's hands. "Don't let her get away." He turned toward Lance, still holding my spear in hand.

Lance!

The agent thrust her knee into my back. I tried to catch my breath and reorient my senses, but it wouldn't happen. My fingers grappled with the cold tile.

I had to get up or Lance was going to die—

Thwap.

Matoska dropped the spear in mid-strike, a bolt sticking from his chest. A figure ducked behind the door; a blur of green jacket and dark red hair.

Jack!

Matoska jerked his head at the agent, his hand tight around the base of the arrow. He was bleeding badly. "Fall back," he instructed. The agent grabbed my arm, then hesitated. She dropped it. My arm fell slack against my side as the agent moved toward Lady Winters' corpse. Movement flashed in the corner of my eye. The dead leader's hand twitched, barely perceptible.

She was alive?

My head throbbed, but I pushed myself from the floor, staying close to the wall and out of harm's way. Matoska started toward his escape route, but he froze halfway to the door, his eyes distant, unseeing.

I blinked in surprise. Lady Winters stood in the entryway, the agent supporting her as she scowled at the scene before her. She eyed Matoska with a look of distaste and rubbed her wounded shoulder.

Matoska gritted his teeth as Jack notched another bolt. Then Matoska spun on his heels and launched himself at Jack, roaring as if he were no more than a beast.

What was Lady Winters' doing to him?

Jack fired the second shot and Matoska sunk to his knees. Blood seeped into his shirt, but he pushed himself to his feet, swaying before he lunged again. Jack took a half-step back, then tossed the empty crossbow aside and tackled Matoska. They both dropped to the floor. Matoska let out a strangled cry as the arrows plunged deeper into his chest.

Lady Winters cast a glance at me, smiled, and then closed the door. *Until we meet again, Nickleson.*

But she had been dead. How was she alive now?

A subtle movement drew my attention to where Matoska lay on the floor, barely able to lift himself. He gasped for breath. Jack grabbed the man's head and snapped his neck in a single, fluid motion. The leader slumped unceremoniously to the floor, blood smeared across him and Jack.

Jack motioned to me. "Come on, Jen. This place is going to be crawling with beasties, and we've still got a ladder to climb." He tossed me my spear and headed into the hallway.

I clutched the weapon, numb.

How was the Community going to explain Matoska's death?

The hall was eerily quiet, covered in drying spatters of blood. Tim and Lance carried Gwen between them. They avoided the remaining corpses. Bile rose in my throat. I clasped my hand around the pendant in my pocket, letting its ruts and grooves distract me. There was another little charm behind the main pendant, round and nubby to the touch.

Bring me the girl. Kill the others.

Lady Winters' voice laughed inside my head—a deep, maniacal laugh that stopped me in my tracks. Two Special Forces agents burst through a nearby door and raised their rifles. A large beast lumbered beside them.

I stared at the badges, rereading the letters underneath the red, rising sun half-cog.

COE.

Traitors. All my life, I thought the letters stood for the Community of E-Leadership. I thought they stood for safety, security, and efficiency. But that was a lie. They didn't serve the Community of E-Leadership, dutifully protecting the Community.

They served the Camaraderie of Evil.

A scrawny, agile beast slinked at the Special Forces' feet while another one paced behind them. One had scabby, blackened arms with smoke wafting around him. Another had green-tinted skin and a thin, slender appearance. Her hair draped in clumps that resembled moss, and numerous vines twined and twisted around her body.

I froze, stunned by the resemblance.

I was a plant elemental—and so was this beast.

CHAPTER
TWENTY

A gunshot exploded behind me and I shrieked, covering my head with my arms. I swung around the corner. "Get out of here!" Jack shouted. He barreled into one of the agents.

A gun fired, but I didn't see what it hit.

"Behind you!" Lance called.

A vine wrapped around my ankle and I crashed to the floor. My chin snapped against the tile. My vision went dark, hazy. I rolled over, growing my vines, but I couldn't see where to aim. A beast's vine cut through my leg's circulation. Through my fuzzy vision, a female beastie sailed over me, teeth bared. I scratched the floor with my fingers, scrabbling to establish some sort of hold, but there was nothing of the smooth tile to grab onto as the vine pulled me closer.

I thrust my spear at the plant beastie. It staggered, a long red smear marring its exposed chest. The plant vines loosened from my leg. I latched onto them with my mind. *Let me go.*

The beastie's vines unraveled. I kicked the last one free as Lance forced the plant beast back through the hall, strike after strike. Every few strokes, my head spun and he turned into a colorful blur. I blinked, trying to clear my head from the fall.

Thud-thump. Thud-thump.

"Run!" Jack raced for the door. Lance slashed at the fire beast and took off. The walls danced around me. My speed power was enough to follow Lance to the entrance, where a toughness beastie lumbered toward us, each foot hammering the floor.

Thud-thump. Thud-thump.

Jack slammed the door behind us. I struggled to stay upright. While Lance scaled the ladder, I pressed the palms of my hands against the pebbly concrete.

Thud-thump.

Boom!

The concrete walls shuddered and rubble clattered outside the maintenance shaft. Silence. Then there was a long, loud crack, and the beasties shrieked.

"Go!" Jack waved his whole arm for me to move.

I struggled up the ladder, using my speed to stay oriented. It was slow going, made slower because I didn't let go of my spear. I was only six rungs up when another explosion shook the building. Jack shouted into his radio, his words jumbled.

At the top of the ladder I tumbled off the platform ledge and collapsed on the roof. Its hot, black shingles stung my skin. The car hovered above the rising shimmer of heat. A giant, gaping hole in the roof spat dust.

Tim finished helping Gwen into the car and rushed to my side. He opened the back door. "Are you okay?" From the way Tim's eyes searched my face, his expression concerned, I didn't think he was asking about my physical wounds.

I shook my head. "I think it's going to be a long time before I'm okay." I scooted against Lance before Tim had a chance to respond. I appreciated his concern, but we had more important things to worry about at the moment—like getting out of here alive.

Lance repositioned his sword so I could sit. Tim frowned, then hopped in the front seat with Gwen. My eyes wouldn't focus, and when I tried closing them, the image of the plant beastie with all of its twisting vines and mossy hair implanted itself against my eyelids.

That would have been me. The plant beastie. When Pops told me, I didn't believe him.

But now I had proof.

Beside me, Tim's tablet lay in the empty seat. It played and replayed a black and white image of Lady Winters picking herself up during the middle of the battle, aided by the female agent. She walked past me without me ever seeing her. Not until she was in the door, anyway.

I win . . . Nickleson.

I shuddered and scooted closer to Lance. Jack hopped in the car beside me and slammed the door. The car lifted sharply, and the butterfly sensation in my stomach grew as the car became invisible, revealing the gravel and grass below. A silver canister shot from underneath the car and crashed into the facility's roof, exploding in a shower of flame and debris. I gripped the edge of my seat. Lance gagged. Tim whispered to the Community for safety, but the Community wasn't going to help us here.

The invisible car lifted us above the treetops and followed the road. An armored van sped along the path, gravel dust rolling behind it. I wondered if Lady Winters was in it, or if she'd stayed at the facility.

"I saw them load the artifact into the van," Inese explained.

In my haste to save Gwen and not get pummeled by beasties, I'd forgotten about the stone. What did it matter, anyway? My head hurt and my shoulders hurt and my neck hurt . . . I couldn't forget the feeling that I'd attacked Lady Winters like a beastie attacking its prey.

I stuck my hand into my pocket and rubbed my fingers along the antique pendant's surface. It felt old, hardly practical.

The car jolted and another missile sped across the sky before striking the road in front of the van. Rocks and gravel exploded. The van veered, flipping until it crashed into a thick of trees.

Inese landed the car and Jack launched himself onto the first guard that climbed from the van as the man tried to pull a gun from his belt's holster. A second man tried to flee, and I raised a jungle vine underneath his feet so he'd trip. He tumbled headfirst into a bush. I imagined roots rising from the ground and anchoring him to the jungle floor. He shrieked, firing at the roots until I caught his arms in a knot of leaves.

Lance rammed his sword through a guard's stomach and started toward the one I'd trapped in vines.

"Stop!" Jack shouted at the same time I did, but I imagined he had strategy in mind, not mercy. Lance caught his swing, then gave us a puzzled look.

Like Tim said, we couldn't act like beasts. If we did, we'd just prove that Lady Winters' version of the plague was real.

Jack pushed Lance aside and leaned over the guard. "What do you know about that stone?"

The guard cowered, wriggling his shoulders where he couldn't move his hands. "I don't know anything! Brainmaster ordered us to ship it away for safety!"

"We should kill him," Lance said quietly.

"He's just doing his duty," I snapped. "What if he really doesn't know?"

"In the Community, he'd already be in the coolers." Lance's voice was low, threatening.

I jutted my lower lip. "This isn't the Community."

Lance narrowed his eyes and looked away, but he didn't counter Jack's orders.

"Don't try anything stupid," Jack warned the huddled guard. The guard nodded, pressing against the overgrown roots to avoid Lance. I didn't blame him; Lance had murderous, unforgiving eyes.

Jack unhooked the latch on the back of the armored van, then clambered inside the inner compartment. He passed over the upturned crates—boxes with "Ammunition" stamped in red ink across their sides and another word in a foreign language underneath. He removed a bundle from the center crate and tore apart the bits of fabric that concealed it. Inside was an elaborate stone carved with dozens of markings. Those markings matched the art of the ruined temple.

Aside from the carvings, though, the only things of significance were four gold bands running around the stone's circumference: two on top, two on bottom.

"Doesn't look like much," Jack muttered. "But what do we know? Come on—let's get outta here."

We returned to the car and Inese got us airborne, invisible as always. "Destroy the van," Jack commanded. "That ammunition doesn't need to be used against our allies."

"Understood," Inese said. "Jenna?"

I released the plant's grip. Inese waited long enough for the guard to untangle himself before firing a warning shot overhead.

"Arming weapons," she said.

The armored van exploded in orange fire and debris. A dark cloud spilled into the air. The jungle blurred beneath us, leaving me to reconstruct everything that had just happened.

Lady Winters was a traitor and I'd let her get away. I couldn't let her escape again. I couldn't let her hurt anyone in the Coalition or the Community, not after Chill and Alec. Not after how she'd treated me. But what was I supposed to do? When I'd attacked her, I'd been in a complete rage. I'd seen that same look when Lance tried to kill the restrained guard. I hated it. I hated that look, and I hated that I'd been acting without any sense of self-restraint.

"I've gotta admit, I hadn't expected to kill Great White," Jack murmured.

"Great White?" Tim asked.

"Master Matoska," I explained. He didn't respond, and the rush of air conditioning took over the conversation. Far, far too silent. "What about Lady Winters?"

I preferred not to hear the silence.

Jack grunted. "Lady Winters . . . you mean Brainmaster? What about her?"

"We tried to kill her, but she got away when you went after Matoska."

"Wait—" Inese said. "You were up against Brainmaster?"

I explained what happened. How I'd fought Lady Winters first, and how Matoska caught us on our way out.

Jack whistled. "Congrats on injuring her. You want to kill the telepath before anyone else, since they change how you view the situation. She must've been waiting for the best chance to run. I didn't even see her."

Silence.

"Jack—how did you kill Great White?" Inese asked.

"Shot him with his own crossbow. Thought he was going to retreat, but he kept on attacking. Gotta admit, I thought he was smarter than that."

A chill ran through me. "He tried to leave, but he stopped when he saw Lady Winters in the doorway. He was . . . struggling."

No one said anything for a long moment.

"Brainmaster sacrificed him to save her own skin," Inese murmured. "I'm surprised she used one of the other council members. I thought they'd have rules against that."

Lance shifted restlessly. "How is she not dead? Jenna *killed* her."

"The Camaraderie's got more power than most," Inese explained. "Jim says it has to do with the pendants they wear. Even their new inductees show promise in a matter of days."

I clamped my hands tight on my knees, feeling the brass loops of the pendant jutting into my leg.

Jack grunted. "Not exactly promising for us. Anyways, always do a death-check if there's time. The Camaraderie's been known to have life-spirit agents waiting to knock you unconscious or heal their fallen comrades."

Lance snorted. "Next time I will."

We returned late to the airship and I staggered to my room. I didn't bother taking off my armbands, and I barely made it to my bed with all the exhaustion setting in. I stared at the lights, only to wake up minutes later with a splitting headache and something pricking my thigh. The loops and hooks of the emerald pendant dug through my clothing and into my already bruised skin. After I finally managed to unhook it, I flipped it in my hands.

On the back, scrawled in tiny letters I could barely read, was the inscription "Elizabeth" in flowery cursive. A tiny identity charm hung behind the pendant; a miniature flower comprised of five clear yellow gems for petals and a tiny green emerald for the pistil.

Odd. I'd never seen Lady Winters wear this charm before.

I twisted the charm from the necklace chain, then stared at the numerous little lights sparkling within the gems. I stashed it in my pocket, then sunk into my mattress.

I'd find out what all this was tomorrow.

CHAPTER
TWENTY-ONE

I pressed my ear to the door of my grandfather's office. The cold from the metal seeped into my skin, but I balanced myself, trying not to put too much weight against the wall. If it groaned, I'd give away my position. I had come upstairs to ask about the pendant and see if Pops could contact my parents, but apparently this wasn't the best time.

"This is the second time we've gone on a 'simple' mission that nearly got us killed. You sent Gwen after a *stone*?" Jack's enraged voice filtered through the cracks in the door's insulation.

"I sent Gwen on a mission of diplomacy," Pops retorted. "Whether the stone is helpful or not, we responded to an allied call for help."

"You wanted an artifact," Jack growled, followed by the loud clang of metal. I backed away from the door and edged nearer to the wall. If he stormed out, I wanted to at least *look* like I was passing by instead of standing there the whole time.

"I didn't send her for the artifact." Pops' voice was strained.

"Gwen was tortured! What did her message say? Did it warn you there might be danger?"

"There was no sign of immediate danger during her first week, though the villagers had suspicions that their temple was being scoped by mercenaries. Right before she lost contact, Gwen said three mercenaries had been spotted in the area. All elementals. Electricity, earth, and plant.

She didn't mention anything about Master Matoska. You think I would send her somewhere that isn't safe? I can retrieve my conversations, if you like."

There was a pause, and this time, Jack's voice was quiet. "Next time, if there's even the *hint* of danger, tell me. Or have Inese do whatever she does and give me a heads up."

A bit of metal clanged behind me and I jumped, but the hallway was clear.

Must've been the vents.

"I do my best," Pops said. "What about the kids? How'd they do on the field?"

"Well, Lance has a good hand with swords, and he's exactly the type of guy we need right now, but he's inexperienced and brash."

Pops snorted. "You're one to talk. What about Tim?"

"Besides being Community, he's a good kid with a good heart, and he managed to hack the Camaraderie's communications without them batting an eye. I didn't get a chance to see his shooting skills, but if you want to get Crush on the ground again, Tim should be able to run navigation without a problem."

Pops cleared his throat. "And my granddaughter?"

I pressed closer to the wall.

Jack grunted. "She needs Inese to teach her to gather intelligence without being caught."

"What do you mean?"

"Given that she's been listening for the past five minutes . . ."

Heat rushed to my cheeks as the door swung open. Jack smirked. "Come in, kid. Your ears must be burning." I stared at him, mortified, but he waved me in and pulled the door shut behind us.

Pops stroked his beard, evaluating me. "How long have you been out there?"

"Since you were arguing about the reason you sent Gwen to Guatemala," I said sheepishly.

Jack patted my shoulder. "See? What'd I tell ya? She has a knack for the sneaky spy stuff. All she needs now is some training."

Pops fixed him with a glare and sipped at his coffee. "I'm guessing you have questions about the mission?"

"Actually — my parents."

Pops motioned to a chair with his coffee mug and I sat, twining my fingers around the pendant's chain in my pocket. "I want them to know I'm alive, and what's going on in the world. The beasties, the powers. Everything."

"Jenna . . ." Pops sat the mug aside. "We can't afford to make outside contact."

"But—"

"Here's why: every communication we make runs the risk of being traced. When we contact each other, or other rebellions, those messages are encrypted. Your parents don't have access to the decryption technology."

I knew Mom might, but if she broke the code, she'd probably report our location to security. "How are they supposed to know I'm alive?"

Jack slapped me on the back. "For now, they won't. But if it makes you feel any better, we could ask Crush to check EYEnet and figure out what they've been told."

"I thought you couldn't access EYEnet."

Pops sighed and rested in his chair. "We can't scan or hack EYEnet directly. But we can access archival files that aren't directly connected to the network."

"The archive isn't as up-to-date," Jack said, "but it's not as risky, either."

"That's better than nothing," I agreed. But there had to be some way of contacting them. I glanced at Pops. "About yesterday; I didn't think there were supposed to be beasts."

"Neither did I. But you handled the situation well, from what I'm told. I'm proud of you."

"For what? Nearly killing a leader?"

Jack cracked his knuckles and grinned. "That *is* impressive. Not all of us can snap their necks and be done with it."

I stared at him. They were respected leaders. How could he be so callous?

Pops rubbed his forehead. "I was impressed that you stayed alive. Lady Winters is . . . difficult."

I wrung my hands and glanced at the two of them. Lady Winters had confirmed my relation to my grandfather, and I didn't see any reason for her to lie about that connection. "What did you do before you joined the Coalition? Why were you banished?"

Pops' hands closed tight and his beard twitched. For a moment I thought he wasn't going to tell me anything, but then his shoulders slouched and he cast his gaze on the torn photograph hanging on the wall. The family looked happy and proud, dressed in the simple garb of the Community. But the rip marred the image, and with the brown stain in the corner, the photograph took a different meaning.

"Perhaps we should talk about this later," Jack suggested. He crossed his arms over his chest and raised his chin. His eyes betrayed concern.

"No, I'll tell her. Can we have a bit of privacy?"

Jack blinked his surprise and quirked an eyebrow in my direction. "Let me know if you need anything." He shut the door behind him, and Pops cleared his desk of the keyboard and mouse pad.

I waited. The vents clacked overtime, trying to pump heat into the chilly room. The computer fan whirred, filling in the gaps of silence that the vents missed. Hints of my grandfather's cologne sifted through the air.

"Lady Winters said to ask you about creating beasts. She said 'betrayal runs in the family.' "

"Did she?" His eyes darkened. Goosebumps prickled my skin as he stood and limped to a metal file cabinet near the giant, arched window behind him. The cabinet drawer scrolled open, and he flipped through several manila folders before tossing one on his desk. "I did my dissertation on radiological genetics. People with powers give off trace amounts of radiation that correlates with the type of power we use. Individual powers give off a radio wave with a very specific frequency, which can be predicted by using DNA sequencing on a person's genetic sample. It's how the scanners work. The device reads the radio frequencies coming from a person's body."

"That's how it reads powers," I guessed. With all this stuff about radiation, I knew I should've taken a physics class alongside advanced biology.

"Right." He pushed the folder toward me. The whole document was a couple hundred pages of small, double-sided print. Diagrams, charts, and footnotes led to obscure, esoteric references. The document contained a list of powers and their related genetic sequences; written so strangely that it looked like a foreign language.

I had no clue how to read this, though I suspected it would've been a lot easier to sort through on a tablet. But maybe they didn't have tablets back then.

Pops drummed his fingers on the desk, waiting. Once I pushed the folder back, he looked at the thing as if it were diseased.

"How were you studying powers if powers were thought to be delusions caused by theophrenia?" I asked.

He sighed. "At the time, the Community was still in development in Eastern Europe and Russia. Our experience with theophrenia was limited, and memories of powers were still commonplace. The Camaraderie wasn't scanning for powers on a regular basis then. That came later."

"So you knew how powers worked."

"I had the general idea, yes. As theophrenia closed in, E-Leadership commandeered the hospital where I worked and repurposed it to house those who were infected. That's when they discovered my research."

"What does this have to do with creating beasts?"

"My knowledge of powers gave me an edge in administering the scan."

I frowned. "I thought only certain doctors were allowed to perform the scan."

"I was one of those doctors. They needed people with persuasion, and they needed beasts to fight their war."

"But if you knew —"

"I didn't, at first. The Camaraderie's agents came to me under the guise that I'd been infected. They explained that I could learn to control theophrenia's effects and use my resulting abilities and current knowledge to help others. Eventually I learned what was really going on, but I believed it was for the better of the Community. I continued my research on radiological genetics and linked it to the work I was doing in the hospital. I inadvertently drew the attention of Lord Black" — he spat the name — "who was impressed with my resume. He offered me a job improving the treatment."

I gaped at him. "Lord Black spoke with you?"

Pops refused my gaze. "The treatment, of course, is the process they use to turn people into beasts. I needed money for my family, so I accepted the job. One day, Lord Black introduced me to his young granddaughter, Miss Emily. She had a talent for persuasion, he said, and she was interested in working a job similar to mine. He asked me to train her."

My jaw dropped. "You taught Lady Black?" No wonder she was trying to use me as bait — and no wonder Pops knew about her powers.

"She excelled, and though I didn't know the details, she informed me that Lord Black was considering me for placement in the highest levels of E-Leadership."

Despite the cold, beads of sweat formed on my forehead and the back of my neck.

"Then one of my patients refused my persuasion. Instead of agreeing to join the commander's army, which would have transformed her into a beast, she asked for my help. It was as if she knew the fate I had planned for her. Her minor power was telepathy, and the emotion she conveyed —" He shook his head. "I couldn't do it anymore. I shut down the hospital. I persuaded the workers that there was a malfunction in the gas lines and that everyone should be released. The prisoners escaped, and so did I. I returned home, planning to tell your grandmother goodbye . . ." His voice cracked. He clenched his jaw and didn't say anything for a long, uncomfortable moment. Finally, his lip quivered and he spoke bitterly. "I found her dead."

All warmth drained from my body. "Dead?"

"Special Forces told your father that your grandmother had contracted the early stages of theophrenia, and that she'd been killed to protect the rest of the population. They said I'd created a more deadly, mutated version of the disease and set it loose near the facility where I worked." He clamped his jaw shut, not saying anything for a long, uncomfortable minute. "They leveled the facility and the nearby town, so the truth of the place could never be discovered. There was no warning. Everyone there was murdered, as were the prisoners I had released. The workers I'd convinced to evacuate were killed—all because I tried to help."

The town north of St. Petersburg, the one that was wiped out when a mutated form of theophrenia struck it, that was because of *him*?

Pops gritted his teeth, his lips twisted in firm determination. "Your father was told that I was a danger to the Community, and for the Camaraderie's sake, they told him that I'd died. But I never created this deadlier version of their plague. I developed a more humane 'treatment' that resulted in better control of their beasts and a faster transformation. When I couldn't stand it anymore, I tried to make amends. In the end, my actions killed more people than I saved."

"But if you have your research, there might be a way to change the beasts back," I pointed out.

"I lost all my beast research when I ran away," he said, his voice stiff. "Any chance we had at recovering that is gone. We don't have the manpower to get inside one of their laboratories and retrieve it. Without the equipment and skills necessary to continue the research, the mission and lives would be wasted."

"So what do you plan to do? Run around and steal artifacts? How's that any better than what the mercs do? If you really want to make a difference—"

"Jenna—" He rubbed his temples and looked at me from under his wrinkled hands. "You may not be able to understand this, but I'm responsible for every death that occurs on this team. I do everything in my power to ensure that a mission is set up properly, but a single, unknown element can cause an entire mission to fail."

"Like when I didn't leave the Community," I whispered.

He shook his head. "If I had a way to undo this, I would. But right now, we don't have that option."

"I'd still like to look at what research you have, if you don't mind." It might take me a while to understand, but I could at least try.

Pops motioned to the cabinet. "Go ahead. All I have is my notes on radiological genetics. But understand, the transformation is permanent. Once the memories have been erased and the body changed, the process cannot be reversed."

"I understand," I whispered. But maybe I could find something he missed.

Pops eyed me cautiously, then handed me the folder. He caught my eyes with his. "Be careful, Jenna. Not all monsters are beasts. Don't get caught up trying to fix what's broken beyond repair." He glanced at the torn photograph. "It's better to protect what you still have."

CHAPTER
TWENTY–TWO

It's better to protect what you still have.

I couldn't shake the feeling that Pops had been talking about his family and me.

I stopped by the kitchen for a snack, dropped off Pops' notes downstairs, and then headed to Jim's room to ask about the pendant. He acknowledged me by placing a bookmark in the pages of a yellowed magazine, then telekinetically setting the magazine on top of a towering stack.

"I heard the mission did not go as planned," he said softly.

"No, it didn't." I flopped into the comfy red chair. The details of the mission came gushing out, and I hadn't realized just how much I wanted to talk to someone. Jim was the perfect listener; he waited patiently through my rant. "I just don't understand how they could be so heartless," I protested once I'd complained about everything else. "Especially Lady Winters. She's the most efficient, Community-oriented person I know. But she's evil."

Jim nodded sympathetically. "Unlike the villains from my time, the Camaraderie does not wear masks. But they hide behind a facade none-the-less. Just another way for them to ensure cooperation from the general population."

"I guess. How long will it take them to replace Master Matoska? He didn't deal a whole lot with the Community, but he was still a leader."

"Depends on if they had anyone planned as a successor. Regardless, I imagine the Camaraderie will find someone soon."

I murmured agreement. I'd taken too many quizzes in history about the succession lines of international leaders to doubt him. I just wondered how many of the leaders actually died or retired the way the books had said.

I slipped my hand into my pocket and traced my fingers over the pendant. "Inese said that you think the leaders' pendants have special abilities."

Jim nodded. "They do. Before the Community, artifacts were enchanted to hold special properties. Rings, charms, necklaces . . . Anything which permits skin contact. Some of the more powerful artifacts were a set of five necklaces known as the Elizabeth pendants."

Elizabeth?

The pendant weighed heavy in my pocket, its hooks and loops pressing into my thigh. I traced the jewel. A few scratches nicked the emerald's surface, and the pebbly brass back felt warm to my touch. It seemed unlikely that something could be enchanted like the things in Jack's video games, but with everything I'd seen yesterday, it no longer seemed so implausible.

"What do the pendants do?"

"A friend of mine from the early days—Clara—said that when the five pendants were brought together in close proximity, time slowed for those nearby. The pendants could boost powers. Prior to leaving the Camaraderie, they were used on her. She could portal hundreds of miles without breaking a sweat, so long as she used a portal ring. The pendants are incredible tools, and we have tried several times to get our hands on them, without success. The Camaraderie started wearing them in public just to taunt us."

My hands were clammy as I removed the necklace from my pocket and let the pendant drop from my wrist. It dangled on its chain, glinting in the lamp's yellow light. Jim's eyes widened. He yanked out a splintery desk drawer, fiddled with its contents until he retrieved a magnifying glass, and then flipped the pendant between his fingers.

"How did you get this?"

"I took it from Lady Winters when I thought she was dead," I said quietly. "She betrayed the Community."

Jim stared at me a long moment. He clucked his tongue. "The Camaraderie will want this back. Tell Pops what you have found, and I will research this further." Half a dozen books lifted from the bookshelves and flew to his desk.

"Sure. By the way, would you happen to have an extra necklace chain?"

He frowned. "What for?"

Heat flooded my cheeks. I'd never been fond of identity charms, but I wanted to keep the one I'd found. I pulled the charm from my pocket and handed it to Jim.

"This was on Lady Winters' necklace. If I'm going to keep going on missions, I want a reminder that people like her exist."

Jim floated the charm from my hand and it hovered centimeters from his nose. "Beautiful craftsmanship," he murmured. "No sign of a tracker, so it should be safe. I wonder . . ." The charm settled inside his cupped palm. He closed his eyes, breathing softly.

Jenna? Can you hear me?

I nearly jumped out of my chair before I realized the voice was his. He opened his eyes and flipped the charm between his fingers. "Been a while since I used one of these."

"It's an artifact?"

He nodded and returned the charm. "Telepathy. I used to have a ring that functioned in the same manner. Skin contact. The charm should be safe, but be careful to test how strong the enchantment is before you use it."

I shuddered. After my experience with Lady Winters, I had no desire to experiment with telepathy. "I just want a reminder of the mission."

"As you wish." After a moment of sorting through the odds and ends in his desk, he offered me a ball chain strand. "Will this work?"

I scuffed my shoe against the fringes of the rug, embarrassed but pleased. The chain itself was old, but the tarnished metal diminished the glamour of the jeweled charm. A twinge of satisfaction snaked through me. I slid the charm over the chain, and then under my shirt.

"Thanks." I left Jim to his research as he murmured about why Lady Winters might need a telepathy artifact.

I frowned. Why *did* she need a telepathy charm?

Outside Jim's office, Pops' voice echoed from the command room. ". . . I'm not sure these stones are worth our time. We can keep this one safe because the locals asked us to, but I don't think we should try collecting the other stones."

I peered through the door. The giant windows at the far edge of the room streamed in the bright, sunny sky, and fluffy clouds blanketed the airship. Inside, Crush stood at the console. A map of the jungle covered the screen, split apart by the translations Tim recorded and a photograph of the stone artifact sitting on some kind of altar. Dust spots covered the image, as if the picture had been taken with a poorly lit flash.

"The Camaraderie's making such a big deal about these stones, they could be special," Crush said, gesturing to the photo. "Tim has data suggesting time travel, and the Maya were pretty protective of the thing. Not to mention—how often does the Camaraderie send Great White after a stone?"

Pops sighed. "I doubt the Camaraderie believes in a time traveling stone. The locals didn't see any sign of Master Matoska until Gwen showed up."

"Maybe not, but there *were* mercenaries in the area."

"Probably looking to make a fast buck." Pops rubbed his forehead, then waved Crush of the notion before he could protest. "How's Gwen doing?"

Crush's shoulders slouched and he closed the documents. "She's not tossing as much. Been trying to remove the damage Brainmaster did. Blasted telepath—if Gwen weren't a life-spirit user, she'd have broke."

The warm metal of the charm pressed against my collarbone, a firm reminder of Lady Winters' betrayal. She was the Head of Efficiency. *She should have been using her powers to find flaws in how people work, not to torture them.*

Crush froze in the middle of grabbing a glass of orange juice from the console. "Did you hear that?"

"Yes." Pops frowned and tapped his cane. "Almost like someone was broadcasting their dislike for Lady Winters." He glanced my direction and I ducked behind the door. I hadn't *meant* to use the charm. Was it really that easy?

Pops cleared his throat. "Jenna?"

I peeked in, my hands shaking. "I—Jim said I should tell you that I stole Brainmaster's pendant."

"Her pendant?" Crush asked.

"Jim called it an Elizabeth pendant."

Crush choked on a swig of his orange juice. He coughed and smacked himself in the chest. "*That* pendant?"

Pops' eyes grew wide and his mouth moved to form words, but he didn't say anything for a really, really long moment. Finally— "You stole an Elizabeth pendant." He didn't sound like he believed me.

I fidgeted. "Jim's looking into it."

He raised an eyebrow. "And you have telepathy, how?"

I pulled the charm out from under my shirt.

"Where did you get that?"

"Lady Winters."

He snorted and shook his head. "Jack's right. You should be training with Inese. But if Jim's correct and you stole one of the Elizabeth pendants, the Camaraderie won't be far behind."

"What's going on?" Inese stood behind me in the doorway. "I could've sworn I heard someone telepathically—"

Crush pointed at me. "Apparently Jenna stole an Elizabeth pendant *and* a telepathy artifact from Brainmaster, and Pops wants you to give her lessons."

Inese squinted at me. "In telepathy?"

"No—the 'sneaky spy stuff,' " Pops said.

Inese wiped her forehead as if she were relieved. "Ah, good. 'Cause I'm not a telepath. But why would Brainmaster want a telepathy charm? Not like it'd do her any good if she was shielded."

"No idea. Now, if you'll excuse me, I need to speak with Jim. Jenna—" He gave me a pointed look. "Be careful with that thing."

I winced. "I don't plan on using it."

"What you *plan* to do and what you *do* are two different things."

"Yeah," I mumbled, ducking my eyes from his scowl. *All I wanted was a stupid reminder.*

"And what you've *got* is trouble," Inese retorted. I stared at her. I hadn't said—

"Now stop worrying about the shiny. We've got work to do."

"Work to do?" I stared at Inese as she sized me up.

"Jack keeps telling me I should train you, and since Pops now agrees, you're in for a treat." Her eyes glinted mischievously, and she removed a set of pointed metal picks from her pocket.

"What are—"

"Lock picks. They won't work on electronic doors, but you may have some use for them. I've got a set of locks downstairs you can practice on."

While I *had* been planning on reading Pops' notes, instead I spent the next several hours trying to pick a set of mechanical locks in the engine room while *not* getting a head full of increasingly accented curses from Inese while she tried to fix the broken dryer.

CHAPTER
TWENTY-THREE

A couple days later, I ventured into the command room, planning on dragging Tim to sparring practice with me and Lance. He clicked away at the keyboard while Pops watched the screen. After a moment, he turned to Pops. "The signal's legit when compared to the records."

"Good. Patch the signal through." Pops glanced at me. "Could you alert the others? I'd like to talk with them. Seems we have a message from the Mexican Resistance."

"Uh—sure." I left the two of them to their own devices and headed downstairs. Warm light and a chorus of laughter spilled into the bronze corridor from Crush's room. I peeked inside. A couple photographs hung next to a large comic book poster. One photo had Chill and Alec standing beside Crush, each trying to give him a noogie while he laughed and evaded their attempts. Another was a snapshot of Alec flying through the air while Crush balanced on a teetering platform of rock and soil.

"Wasn't my fault!" Jack protested. He sat backward on a chair while Inese leaned in the crook of Crush's arms. "I was just trying to kill the beastie. You're the one who shot it onto the car." He tipped a bottle in their direction to emphasize his point.

"*That* dent was fun," Inese muttered. "You realize how long it took to remove it?"

"You had the dent fixed in five minutes." Jack popped his neck. "Now, you want fun messes, *who* got to clean up the paintball splatters in the gym? *Who's* still finding paint splatters under the rails?"

Inese chortled. "That's why we're sticking to the forest next time. Nothing like a bit of friendly competition."

"Last time you sat in a tree and picked us off one by one."

"If you'd learn to use your life power, you'd have known I was there."

"Actually," Crush interrupted, "paintballing might be a good team exercise for the new guys." He paused, distant, and the other two exchanged glances. He leaned closer to Inese. "Remember the time Alec realized Chill was going to freeze his tea solid, so he boiled it first?"

Inese wrapped her arm around him gently. "Yeah. He got himself a nice iced tea."

Jack smiled, but he didn't meet Crush's eyes. "To old friends," he said quietly. He raised his glass.

The others did the same. "And a better tomorrow," Inese said.

I held the door tight, my stomach in knots. Crush and Alec must've been close. If I'd gone with Pops when he first warned me, Chill and Alec would be alive.

I balanced on the balls of my feet to keep from making noise as I stepped away from the door. I didn't want them to know I'd heard.

Still . . .

I took a deep breath and knocked. The talking quieted.

"Pops wants to see you guys," I said quickly. "Something about a message from the Mexican Resistance."

Jack motioned his bottle to me. "We'll be there in a moment."

I nodded and hurried out. I felt guilty enough without eavesdropping on their private conversations.

Fifteen minutes later, the crew assembled in the command room. The large computer screen flickered, lighting dimly on a middle-aged man with stubble on his chin. He smirked, looking at us through the camera. "Looks like you've still got a decent sized team. Who's the new recruits?"

Jack grunted. "Nice to see you, too."

Pops stepped forward. "Captain, this is my granddaughter, Jenna, and her friends, Lance and Tim. Tim's the one who saw your message."

The man eyed Tim, then nodded. "You know—I've got a son about your age. Nice to meet you. Name's Cortez." He tipped his fingers to his head in an informal salute, then turned his attention back to Pops. "You really should've introduced me," he said, wagging his finger.

Pops raised his chin. "You didn't give me a chance."

"Ah, well—gotta speak faster. Anyhow, there's been a leak in the Camaraderie's intelligence. They're transporting some sort of *'piedra de los viajeros'* to a so-called 'abandoned' warehouse in southern Mexico. They're making a pretty big racket for a routine delivery."

"We've picked up an artifact by the same name from Guatemala," Pops said.

"Anything special?"

"Nothing more than local superstition."

The captain raised an eyebrow.

Several documents filled the screen, each more detailed than the original translation. "According to the translation," Tim explained, "there's five 'travelers' stones,' each in a temple around the world. I'm not sure *where* exactly, but each one is from a different ancient culture." He clasped his free hand around his identity charm. "Right now I think there's another stone in Japan."

"Any idea what they do?"

"My translation suggests some form of time travel," Tim said.

The captain grinned. "Makes sense why the Maya would be so protective. Might be a way to stop the Camaraderie from existing."

I crossed my arms. "Going back in time might stop the Camaraderie from existing, but that doesn't exactly have nice implications for us, either."

He chuckled. "Technicalities."

Crush peered around from one of the computers near the front windows. "There are signs of recent activity in the area, but otherwise, the place has been abandoned for some time now."

"What kind of activity?" Pops asked.

"Flight beasties." Captain Cortez ran his hand through his hair. "I'm guessing the Camaraderie's going for aerial surveillance. Nothing your invisible car can't handle."

So . . . a lithe beast with wings, flying circles around our car.

Joy.

"The Camaraderie has something worth guarding." Inese suggested.

Jack grunted. "Or it's a trap."

"What'd you do to get them all riled up?" the captain asked. "Seems they've been going at you non-stop lately. Not that it hasn't been useful for *us*, but—"

Jack jabbed a thumb at me. "*Someone* stole Brainmaster's pendant the last time we went on a mission."

"You're pulling my leg!" Captain Cortez burst out laughing. "I'll believe it when I see it."

Jim held up the pendant.

The captain quieted. He cast a glance at me, then at the pendant, and then softly murmured in Spanish. Multi-faceted reflections glinted across the pendant's surface. The antique looked even older than when I first held it.

"As farfetched as the idea sounds, there is no denying that there are unusual artifacts in this world." Jim twisted the chain around his fingers and drew the pendant into his hand. "Given our dwindling numbers, these 'time stones' may be the only thing we have preventing the Camaraderie from gaining unprecedented power. We cannot reverse the Camaraderie's influence. But if we could return to the source, back to a time when their influence could be prevented, should we not take that opportunity?"

"What if they don't do anything?" Inese asked.

Crush shrugged. "Then there's no loss. It shouldn't be too hard to snoop around an abandoned warehouse. Check it out, and if it's not worth it, leave. I say we give it a shot."

"Unless it's a trap." Jack crossed his arms over his jacket.

The captain nodded. "I've got a few teams in the area. We can provide backup if you investigate."

Pops looked around the room at his team and sighed. "In that case, Inese will take a team to Mexico three days from now — Jack as team leader and Jenna and Lance as support. That should be enough time to prepare."

"Why don't I go with them?" Crush suggested. "You know — stretch my legs, get some sun — maybe smell rusty old warehouse pipes and crates?"

"No." Pops shook his head. "I need you to continue training Tim on the navigational system, and Gwen could use the company."

Crush shrugged. "Fair enough, but I want to go on a mission sometime."

"Noted. Any questions?"

There were none, and Pops dismissed us while he continued working out the details with the captain. Tim dashed down the stairs without a second's hesitation, probably trying to avoid being invited to sparring practice again.

"So, what do you think about all this time stone stuff?" Lance asked me in the hallway.

"Sounds interesting," I admitted, "though I'm not sure I believe it."

"Well, you'd never see it in the Community. But hey—" He nudged my elbow. "It's a chance to see something *other* than a rusty old airship. Besides, we could wander around the jungle and see all the pretty flowers. Or we could keep sparring. Your choice."

I glared at him. "As long as we don't run into any more beasts or telepaths." I touched my fingers to where the charm lay on my chest, out of sight to keep him from asking about it.

Lance smiled and left the door to the training room cracked open.

He peeked out. "I'll see you later, all right? Don't forget—you're shooting with Inese after lunch."

"I won't." The charm pressed against my sternum.

Shooting practice—right. Telepathy couldn't harm anyone if the telepath was shot in the head. Somehow, it seemed less brutal than stabbing them.

CHAPTER
TWENTY-FOUR

"It's a damn stone and we're walking into a trap."

The sea blurred, hazy and silent underneath the invisible car. I toyed with Brainmaster's identity charm, trying to focus on the vines at my side rather than what would happen if the warehouse wasn't abandoned.

"*Or* we're getting an artifact that'll send us back through time," Inese countered. "Sounds better than investigating an abandoned warehouse for a new yard decoration, don'tcha think?"

Jack grunted. "I'd hardly call it new."

"We should've brought Tim along," Lance whispered. "He could've set them straight."

I sighed. "I don't think he knows any more than they do. Besides, we can't go back in time—it's not scientifically possible."

"Superpowers aren't scientifically possible, either," Lance said.

I glowered in his general direction. "Powers *do* have a logical explanation. At least, some do. Some are weird. Like laser eyes. How can a person shoot lasers from their eyes? Wouldn't that burn out their retinas?"

"You tell me. You're the one reading Pops' dissertation."

The sea gave way to tall trees and sprawling shrubs, and shortly after, we circled a large warehouse with gaping holes in its roof. Creatures flew over the building and its shabby fence. Like the other beasts we had seen, short hair covered their bodies. A thin membrane of skin extended from their wrists to their waist, resembling translucent, bat-like wings, which they occasionally flapped as they glided high above the grassy terrain. There was a feral crudeness to their hideous features. Untamed. Wild.

The car swerved, knocking me back in my seat as one of the beasties nearly hit the windshield. Lance gagged. For someone who liked adventure, he sure got motion sick.

"You should've hit it," Jack said.

Inese scoffed. "And reveal our position? I'd rather not deal with the mess."

"They used to be human," I muttered, annoyed at their insensitivity.

Inese landed the car near the door of the warehouse. Cracking paint peeled from the wall, but the door's silvery handle gleamed in the bright sun. A shadow passed overhead from a flying beast.

"Inese — can you make other people invisible?" I asked as I unfastened my seat belt.

"I'd have to leave the car unmanned."

Jack grunted. "Jen's got a point. We're gonna have to get in."

"I guess we *could* hold hands until we get inside." There was a hint of a smile in Inese's voice, and a moment later, the door latch opened. A flight beastie shrieked and dove overhead, landing on top of a not-so-defunct security camera that faced the other direction.

"Jenna — you there?"

A rough hand — invisible — smacked my shoulder, and then Jack pulled me from the car. We fumbled to add Lance to our invisible human chain, and someone, presumably Inese, guided us to the warehouse door. The parched grass flattened under our feet and Jack's outline faded into the wall. Flying beasts perched on top of light posts, silhouetted against the sky. Two beasties balanced on the barbed fence.

The door opened a crack, and then we were inside.

Lance shut the door behind us before anything decided to investigate. Inside, fluorescent lights with a green cast illuminated tall stacks of crates. Carts squeaked, wheeled away by the shadows of workers. I tried not to look at myself. We looked like chameleons, as if we'd faded into a world that wasn't ours. Jack tugged my hand, and Inese led us through the maze of boxes and into a side corridor. At the end of the hall, we went visible.

"Sorry, guys, that's as much as I can do for the moment." She rested her hands on her knees. "Want me to stick around?" She looked at Jack for an answer, but he directed his attention to a hulking beast that stood several meters ahead.

The beast locked its eyes on us and grunted. It charged. The floor shook under its massive body.

Jack yanked me and Inese into an elevator behind us. Lance raced inside and punched the "close" button. The beastie skidded to lumbering halt as the door slid shut, and I pressed against the other side of the circular shaft. Large impressions dented the door where the beast banged its fists and shoulders.

Lance jabbed his thumb against the down arrow. Jack poised himself to strike as Inese retrieved a pistol from its holster. I took several deep breaths, trying to hear anything outside the pounding in my ears.

Ding.

The elevator descended. It whirred with a harsh screech as the contorted metal scraped against the concrete. Lance nervously bounced on his heels, though he grinned from ear to ear. "I thought this place was supposed to be abandoned."

"You don't seem to mind," I snapped.

Ding.

Inese traced the welts in the metal and whistled. Jack eyed the LED display as we dropped farther into the basement. "Still think we're going after a yard decoration?" he asked.

Ding.

Inese raised her chin, cursed softly, and removed her second pistol.

Jack shifted. "Inese?"

Ding.

The elevator jolted to a stop and opened halfway. A sterile, gleaming white corridor loomed ahead, filled with a low, indistinguishable noise; something like walking into a busy swimming pool. A dozen voices overlapped and wallowed through the entrance.

"Told you it was a trap," Jack muttered.

Inese pulled out her radio and thumbed the call button. "We're going to need that backup."

"What is this place?" I asked. It smelled like a laboratory: chemicals and soap and the sting of unknown solutions.

"Your first beastie plant," Jack said, crouching on the balls of his feet.

I stared at him. "This is where they turn people into beasts?"

The sterile, bright coldness, the echoes . . . The hall was wide and clean, with rows of LEDs in the ceiling. I'd imagined something a little more dark and slimy.

"We need to find another exit." Inese unclipped the second pistol from her waist. At the end of the hall, an agile beast rounded the corner. Lance drew his sword and followed Inese into the hall, but Jack grabbed the collar of his shirt and yanked him back.

The beast's reflection weaved across the metal walls as it slunk toward us. Everything about it screamed of wrongness: the thin, wiry hair along its skin, the slight protrusion of its forehead. The golden cat eyes — slitted, calculating — and the way its claw-like nails clicked the tile.

The beastie balanced. Back. Forth. Shifting its weight on all fours despite the deformation of its skeleton. It hissed, showing fangs, and curled its tongue in warning like a cat. Then it sprung, its scrawny fingers curled into ferocious hooks. Jack swiped his claws along its side. The beastie hissed and scrabbled back, but Lance rushed forward and slashed his sword through its neck.

The beast crumpled on the slick tile.

"New plan," Jack said, wiping his claws on his pants. "We get out of here in one *human* piece."

Lance checked the doorways as we walked, and the echoes grew louder and more painful near the end of the corridor. I shivered, edging closer to the group. Voices rose and fell, merging in a horrible wail as we turned corner after corner in the winding maze.

"That sound . . ." I whispered. "What *is* that?"

Jack looked over his shoulder. "You don't think the transformation feels good, do ya?"

"You mean that's *them*?" My voice caught in my throat.

As we walked, we passed various doors with locked keypads. The sound ebbed and rose but never stopped. This is where they turned people into beasties. Not just one or two, but dozens or hundreds. Students. Rebels. All those voices . . .

No wonder Pops decided to leave.

I stopped short, my limbs frozen at my side. Community —

Pops did this.

The maze of silver walls and glaring LEDS . . . my skin was clammy; my heart thudded in my chest. He'd sentenced people to die like this. To become inhuman.

"You all right?" Lance asked.

I closed my eyes, dizzy. "I'm fine," I whispered, but my voice hitched without regard for my attempt to stay calm. Lance fell back to my side.

"We'll get out," he said.

I nodded, not trusting myself to speak.

We turned another corner and a door in the hall behind us slammed against its hinges. I recoiled, but the rest of my team didn't seem to notice.

"Guys?"

A scream erupted from the room. The hair rose on my neck. I ran forward and punched random numbers into the keypad. It buzzed and blinked red. I kicked the door. "Come on!" I snapped.

There had to be a way in!

I thrust my vine at the edge of the door, urging the tendrils between the door and the wall, but the door was sealed tight. I paused, staring at the keypad. If there was one thing I'd found could counter Tim at his enhanced ability to play video games, it was button mashing. If I randomly punched a bunch of numbers, would it alert security? Surely *one* of the combinations would work.

I yanked on my speed power and jabbed the buttons at random. Didn't matter what I hit—just so long as I kept pressing buttons.

Red.

Red.

Red.

Green.

The door lock released at the same time Jack got his hands on my shoulders. I curled my vines around my arms and thrust the door open.

Neither of us moved.

A naked young man, not much older than I, lay inside. His hair dripped with sweat and he stared at me, frightened. "Please help me," he whispered. "Please. I don't understand—"

I stepped toward him, but Jack yanked me back. "There's nothing you can do," he hissed, his breath hot in my ear.

The young man convulsed, his whole body shuddered, and then he screamed. Without the door to block the sound, the wail reverberated through my core. The young man trembled, clutching his legs to his chest. His eyes changed from blue to gold, the pupils stretching into something feline.

He scratched his fingers along the floor. His skin bled where his nails broke and changed and hardened. He tensed, curling into a ball. His muscles rippled like liquid under his skin, then bulged and solidified. Tears streamed down his face and he roared. He grew larger and menacing, his hair thinning and turning wiry. His forehead grew thick and prominent. He no longer looked like the crying young man from when I'd opened the door.

"Community . . ." I whimpered, my fingers clamped around Jack's wrist. The transformation lasted forever, though it must've been less than a minute. The young man—if he could even be called that now—collapsed, groaning and panting.

I choked on a disbelieving laugh. "This can't be real. It can't be."

The beastie woke and locked its eyes on me. It snarled, stumbling on new legs, and lunged. I slammed the door. In that same instant, Jack yanked me down the corridor and shoved me against the wall. The door burst open and a gunshot cracked; the hallway exploded with noise. Spots of fire danced in my eyes from Inese's pistol, and though Jack protected me with his body, I saw the beastie fall.

It twitched, failing to push itself up.

There was another gunshot, and this time the beastie didn't move.

I shook too hard to trust myself not to run. I couldn't look away. Only minutes ago he'd been a student like me. A student who might've taken his pills without question and not understood why he failed. A student who didn't know . . .

In progress. Transformation complete. Released. Deceased.

If I'd stayed in the Community, Lady Black would've done the same to me. She'd have made *me* go through that transformation.

And Lance.

And Tim.

Now it made sense why Jack hated them and why Pops had been so determined to get me out. Why Lady Winters' attack left me so cold and helpless.

How many other students were going through this process? Did I know them? How many more would be taken next fall?

Did Sam pass?

Inese put her hand on my shoulder. "Jenna?"

The Camaraderie wanted to strip me of my powers and make me fight and kill for them. They wanted to use me against Pops.

"Jen . . ." Lance wrapped his arm around me, pulling me away from the too-bright metal.

"I failed. I tried to save him and I failed."

Inese squeezed my shoulder. "This is one of the reasons we fight the Camaraderie."

I gritted my teeth and pushed her and Lance away. Fight the Camaraderie, sure. But what I really wanted was to know how to reverse the transformation. I'd read Pops' notes on shapeshifting, and though I didn't understand the mechanics, if the transformation was similar, surely it could be reversed. Just because I didn't understand something now, didn't mean it wasn't possible.

Then again, the same could be said of time travel.

I clenched my fists.

If I saw the Camaraderie members, I'd kill them for this. It didn't matter who they were, or if they were good Community leaders. I'd end this horrible practice.

Lance twisted his swords in nervous figure eights, then paused when he realized I was looking at him. "You ready?" he asked, his eyes curious. Concerned.

"Yes," I said. "Let's get out of here."

CHAPTER
TWENTY-FIVE

The winding corridor opened to rows upon rows of floor-to-ceiling tanks, each filled with thick, greenish fluid. Bubbles traveled up the tubes, passing over occupants who had been stripped of everything but a breath mask. A helpless, sickening sensation spread through me. I stared at the liquid, petrified.

Lady Winters dragged me into a tube and shoved me inside, the numbing liquid surrounding me, slick against my skin. Burning.

I needed to escape, to breathe, to run —

"Let's not open these doors, 'kay?" Jack said, jarring me from my nightmare. I glared at him, but for once, I didn't mind his sarcasm. Lady Winters had taken *joy* in giving me that memory. Her identity charm rustled against the fabric of my shirt.

"Isn't there some way we can help them?" I asked.

"By the time they're here, it's too late." Inese motioned to the tanks around us.

I closed my hands into fists. Lance pushed me forward, and as we passed the tanks, one of the occupants woke. Bubbles erupted around her mask. Her eyes bulged, terrified. She pounded her fists on the glass.

Lance stepped back, despite all his show for strength, but I saw my reflection. It placed me in that tube—in that thick, unknown liquid with its sense of helplessness . . .

I flinched and turned away. I was betraying the people who were imprisoned here, but every time I looked at them, *I* was the prisoner.

"Can't we do something? Anything?" I asked.

"Sorry, Jen." Jack sighed. "None of us know how to reverse it. Trust me, kiddo. I wish I did."

"What about shapeshifting, like what Lady Black has? What if that power could be used to reverse the process?"

"Even if the physical process was reversed, you couldn't get their minds back," Inese told me. She kept her eyes averted from the tubes, and I did my best not to see the faint green reflections flickering on the ceiling and floor.

We passed into another hallway with more rooms and muffled cries. The hallway forked, one path leading around a corner, and the other to a pair of guards standing in front of a security console. Behind them, a glowing blue force field held back prisoners.

Unchanged prisoners.

I pointed. "There!"

Inese raised her pistol defensively. "We've got to avoid the guards."

"But we have to rescue them!"

The guards heard me and reached for their guns. I clenched my fists, anger burning inside me. Those prisoners hadn't started the process. Those prisoners could still be saved.

I pushed my speed to move faster than the guards could cock their weapons, then extended my arms, uncurling the vines. I lashed out, knocking one man over before I heard the gunshot. Something erupted through my shoulder. I choked on a scream. My arm was on fire and spots danced in my eyes, playing havoc with the ceiling lights.

So many lights . . .

One guard fell to Inese's aim while Lance stabbed the guard I'd tripped. I clutched my shoulder, dazed. It felt like hours before Inese helped me sit. The bloody spot where the bullet grazed my shoulder wasn't deep, but it stung. I didn't see how anyone could handle being shot directly.

"At least it should be easy to clean." Jack unzipped a pouch from his belt and removed a small bottle of liquid and gauze. "Hold still," he instructed, biting off a strip of the bandage before pushing aside my torn shirtsleeve.

I ground my teeth, whimpering. Every time I took a breath the room spun, flashing between hot and cold. The room kept going dim, then bright again, though the lights never changed.

Then Jack poured liquid on the wound. It burned and I screamed, clamping my teeth on my wrist. My scream mixed with the screams of people turning into beasties, and for a moment I was in the tanks again, struggling for freedom.

Inese tightened her fingers around my good shoulder and pulled my arm from my teeth. Small teeth marks bruised the skin, marred by a spot of blood. "It'll be okay," she told me.

Jack gave me a hefty pat on the back. "That should do it."

I swallowed, trying not to move my shoulder. I didn't want the gauze rubbing the raw wound. Every slight movement, every little thought threatened to send me into unconsciousness.

"We'll have Gwen look at your shoulder when we get back," Jack said, helping me stand. The floor seemed far away. "How about we don't run at guards with guns unless I say so, hmm?"

I winced.

"Hey, guys? Stand clear of the field!"

I barely had time to register the new voice before electricity surged around us. The blue force field flared white. The console crackled. The lights flickered and dimmed, and then the shrill whir of the field emitters vanished. The glowing force field outside the room dissipated, and the lights returned to their peak.

Once the spots had cleared from my eyes, I saw that the speaker was maybe five years older than me, with dark brown, wavy hair and a nervous smile. She stood outside her prison while the other prisoners stared at the empty space where the force field used to be. They cautiously stepped over the threshold.

"Nicely done," Inese said.

The new girl let out a sigh of relief. "No problem. I'm just glad to be out of there."

I stared at her teeth. She had fangs. No claws, like Jack, but fangs.

Inese nodded. "I'm sure you are. Now let's get these people out." She glanced at me. "We might be able to do some good while we're here."

One of the prisoners shook Inese's hand fiercely. "Thank you, thank you, thank you," he said, then turned to Lance and did the same. I edged toward the stability of the wall, not wanting him to shake my wounded arm.

A woman ran to the new girl and hugged her. "How'd you do that?" she asked, wiping tears from her eyes.

"Do what?" The girl's English was heavily accented, similar to the captain we'd met over the view screen.

The woman raised her arms to where the force field used to be. "You knew exactly where to hit the field. Girl, you've got a gift."

The new girl blushed and ducked her eyes. "I've been able to do that ever since I was fourteen," she said, shuffling her feet. "A little bit of insight . . . electricity in the right spot, and there you've got it — disabled force field. I would've tried escaping earlier, but the injection didn't wear off until a couple hours ago and I wasn't sure I could get very far with the guards there." Her lacy black skirt swished around her ankles.

"Well, we appreciate it," the woman said, patting the girl's shoulder. "What's your name?"

"Val." She smiled. "Valerie Salazar."

Her entire ensemble was black and reminded me of a leader's outfit. A long-sleeved shirt billowed from her upper arms and a lacy skirt flowed to her ankles above short black boots. She wore thick dark makeup around her eyes. A thin, silver chain rested on her hips.

I touched the charm under my shirt.

I didn't trust her.

It wasn't the leader's clothing . . . half the people here were wearing something that belonged in one of Jack's old movies. They obviously weren't Community.

But something about Val . . .

"How'd you know you have powers?" I asked. "Are you one of the rebels?"

Val blinked, confused. "No, I help Mama at her shop. But why wouldn't I know about powers?"

"It isn't uncommon for the Camaraderie to keep a known presence in the territories," Inese explained. "They use both powers and beasts in public."

I stared at her. "They have beasts in public?"

Val nodded. "It's a pretty fitting punishment for a criminal. They don't act human, so they don't get to *be* human. They're lucky they lose their memories halfway through the transformation."

"Oh, really?" My hands quivered. "So having powers make these people criminals?"

"They don't *just* turn people with powers into beasties, and I didn't say *everyone* deserves it." She twisted her lips. "Why do you think I'm trying to escape?"

"Maybe you electrocuted someone, and the Camaraderie decided you'd be better off as a beastie," I snapped.

Her fingers clenched and electricity popped. "You're one to talk. You look Community — I'm guessing you didn't take your pills and they found out, didn't they?"

How in the Community did she know that? "I — "

Lance cleared his throat. "Uh — guys? Not that I want to interrupt, but this *is* a beastie plant. Shouldn't there be more beasts? More guards?"

Val shot me a glare, then jabbed her thumb at Lance. "He has a point."

Inese and Jack exchanged glances. "Listen up!" Jack called, loud enough that everyone could hear him. "Has anyone seen a fancy stone around here?"

The prisoners shook their heads.

"Figures. We're gonna try to get you out, but we can't guarantee your safety." He repeated what he said in rapid Spanish, to which several of the prisoners nodded.

"Let's get going," Inese said. The new girl filed behind Inese as I massaged my wounded shoulder. I still didn't trust her.

Jack took the lead. As we reached the end of the corridor, a cacophony of clanging doors sounded behind us. Jack rushed to the back. Val spun, electricity crackling around her as beasties flooded the hallway. The prisoners scattered.

"Get the prisoners to safety!" Inese shouted to me.

Me?

She fired at one of the beasts and it dropped, a bullet in its head. "Go!"

I stood, frozen, as Val reached her hand into the air. Lightning danced from the ceiling lights into the oncoming beasts. A loud *boom* shook the floor. Lightning shot in a chain from one beast to the next. Jack staggered back, away from the onslaught, then swiped at one that tried to get behind him.

"Go!" Lance snapped, dodging a ball of ice that cracked against the wall beside him. "We'll hold them off."

I nodded frantically, then waved for the prisoners to follow. My vines sprouted thorns along their length. I raced down the corridor, heart pounding as I kept my speed in check. Inese said we had backup coming. If I could get these guys upstairs —

There was a loud *buzz* behind us and a man cried out.

Half the prisoners who'd been following me skidded to a stop behind a force field. They helped the man stand as he gritted his teeth, his hands shaking from the run-in with the shimmering wall of light. The force field effectively split the hall in two, and the field emitters were buried within the wall. There was no way for me to reach them with my vines. No sign of any switches in the hall that might've accidentally triggered it. The field must've been activated remotely, and Val, our electricity girl, was nowhere in sight.

"Can any of you use electricity?" I asked.

The prisoner whose clothes were as plain as mine shook his head, so I doubted that he knew how to use his powers. Meanwhile, one of the other prisoners asked a question in Spanish to the people who weren't Community, then shook her head, too. "No electricity here, sorry."

"Jenna!"

Jack spun around the corner, pursued by a beast that sprang off the wall. He twisted, caught the beast by the scruff of the neck, then flung it into Lance's waiting sword. Lance felled the beast in a swift arc.

Jack gestured to the prisoners on his side of the field. "You guys with me. Jenna, see if there's a way that leads back around. These halls should reconnect somewhere ahead." He nodded sharply, his face twisted in a resolute grimace before running back into the fray.

"Connect *where*?" This whole facility was a twisted mess of chambers and tanks.

Lance bit his lip, one hand on his bloodied sword. "Jenna—"

Jack called for him to come.

"Be safe," Lance said, then hurried to their aid.

I stared at the spot where he'd been. I was wounded, stuck on the opposite side of a force field with five wide-eyed prisoners for backup and no idea how to get to the other side.

The other side . . .

"Wait, Lance! Lance—your portals!"

The hall remained empty and my chest tightened. He'd left me behind.

I motioned for the prisoners to follow and then led them along the winding hallway, searching for an exit that didn't seem to exist. Then, around the corner, a team of Special Forces agents leveled their rifles at us. Two knelt on the floor at the center of the hall, and the other two stood. Behind them was a woman in long, deep purple robes.

Lady Winters.

I could shoot her. I had a gun. Inese showed me how.

The shrill whir of a second force field erupted behind us and Lady Winters chuckled. She sipped a foul smelling coffee from a black mug with a symbol of the rising sun half-cog, then flicked her hand to her troops.

Miss Nickleson is mine. Kill the others.

CHAPTER
TWENTY–SIX

One by one, the shots went off.

I saw the bullet enter a man's skull. His eyes rolled back. The bullet, nothing more than crumpled metal, left the back of his head. Blood splashed against my cheek and dotted my vines, which wavered as if the liquid were nothing more than a pleasant mist.

Isn't it lovely how the brain slows one's perception of time? Lady Winters sent.

The image replayed itself over and over.

The prisoners were dead.

All those people I'd tried to protect and save . . .

Lady Winters laughed, a cackling perversion of reality. She raised a manicured hand to my forehead and her identity charm burned against my skin.

I believe you have something of mine, Miss Nickleson.

My brain roared with pain.

A reminder, the charm was a reminder . . .

I grappled at the smooth curve of a clear cylinder. Green bubbles erupted from my mask.

Let me out! I don't want to be a beastie! Please . . .

My eyes watered, tears mixing with the burning liquid. I hit my fists against the glass until my left arm was completely limp. I tried to scream, but my throat was raw. My arm floated dead, half-raised to the glass.

My mom stood outside the tank, blurred through the green liquid. Her eyes were wet—she'd been crying.

Mom, Mom, please . . .

My lips were paralyzed.

"Why did you betray the Community?" Mom's voice sounded distant, garbled. She pressed her hand to the glass. "Haven't we been good to you? Wasn't I a good mother? If you had just taken the pill, everything would be okay. Instead you listened to your no-good grandfather."

My heart lurched as she burst into tears. It didn't matter if I took the pill or not. I had powers. But maybe I was wrong. *Please, Community. Please let this be nothing more than theophrenic hallucinations . . .*

"He took you from us." Dad stood, somber, his hands clasped behind his back. He wore a simple blue banker's uniform, his dark hair neatly trimmed. "You shouldn't have trusted him, Jenny. Never should have trusted someone from outside of the Community."

Mom sniffled and turned her back.

Where are you going? Mom, Mom! No, don't go! Please don't go! Let me out of here—I won't let you down again, I won't—

The water drained, swirling and slapping the back of my neck. I collapsed to the metal grate. The door slid open. Lady Winters dragged me out, her nails digging into my wrist. I was too numb, too paralyzed to resist, and she pulled me effortlessly past the dead bodies of Jack and Inese and Lance.

Not Lance!

I'd led him to this . . .

You played him for a fool and killed him, Nickleson.

Lady Winters threw me into the room with the body of the man-turned-beastie. Sensation crawled through me like hundreds of pins and needles, as if everything had been asleep. I felt warm, uncomfortably hot under my skin.

That hissing sound . . .

Gas!

My head spun.

Rip and claw and tear . . . My muscles tensed, itching —

Tear the dead beastie, extend my vines and wrap them around its throat . . . Suffocate it — Make the room my own — tear it to shreds, tear the monster to shreds — Kill — kill the intruders with their swords and guns —

I gasped, heart pounding in my chest, and screamed. I couldn't stop screaming. My mind stung as if I'd run head-first into a concrete barrier. But I wasn't in the room with the gas and a beastie. I wasn't a beastie, either, but now I stared at the prisoners' sightless eyes. Their shocked, parted lips.

Have to move, have to move . . .

I struggled to stand, but my legs refused, and I flopped on the tile like a dying fish. Lady Winters knelt beside me. Her nails dug into my cheek and she twisted my head toward her. Her eyes were bright and fierce, and she looped her finger under the ball chain necklace around my neck. *This belongs to me, child.*

She lifted the charm from under my shirt.

The yellow, petal-shaped gems sparkled in the light, twisting this way and that. Her nails squeezed tighter. All the memories of Pops . . . him telling me what he'd done, our discussion about the beasts, the reading I'd done on his dissertation . . . they all came flooding through as though Lady Winters were flipping pages of a book.

Her eyes lit with excitement. *Do you take after your grandfather so clearly?* She jerked my head so that our noses almost touched, and I smelled the musky odor of her makeup. A presence forced itself into my mind and clawed at my brain, refusing to let go. *Let's see where your true talents lie, Miss Nickleson. You were a biology student, yes? Perhaps —*

"My lady —" A male voice cut through the choking suffocation of her thoughts. "Hostiles have infiltrated this facility. We need to get you out."

The presence retracted, slithering away until my whole body collapsed. I took a shuddering breath and clasped Lady Winters' charm in my hand. *Traitor,* I thought. *I can't believe I ever looked up to you.*

She smirked. *Bring the girl with us. She's an asset.*

"My lady, we don't have time —"

The man grappled at his head, screaming.

If you die, she retorted, *you aren't fast enough. Now move.*

He doubled over, gasping for breath while one of the other agents hoisted me over her shoulder. I tried to kick her, but my legs were too shaky to be anything more than an annoyance.

I clutched the charm in my fist, trying to build up the resolve to fight back. They needed me alive because I knew the rebels. Because they thought I might change sides.

Lady Winters turned sharply and raised an eyebrow. *You're better at using artifacts than I expected.*

An explosion tore through the corridor behind us. I ducked my head. Bits of concrete pelted my skin. Shadows wavered in the settling dust, followed by shouts as people in green camouflage forced their way past the broken rubble and the decimated force field.

I urged my vines to creep to the agent's neck, then flatten against her helmet. They slipped inside and she jerked, trying to throw me, but I gave the vines one sharp *flick* toward her ear. She yelped and I fell. Lady Winters ran, her robes trailing behind her.

She was in my sight, then gone. There . . . not there . . .

She was messing with my mind.

There.

I see you.

Lady Winters rounded the corner, well ahead of the agents who picked off the rebels behind us. I was no longer their priority. One of the rebels shouted in Spanish, then threw a canister that trailed smoke.

I pushed my speed as hard as I could, cutting across the corner as fire exploded behind me. Lady Winters spun on her heels, robes fluttering. She smirked.

I leapt, vines outspread —

She disappeared.

I crashed against the tile and pain flared in my shoulder. My head pounded from Lady Winters' earlier assault. Smoke trailed through the darkened corridor, stinging my nose. A good section of the lights were out. No sign of Lady Winters; just gunshots and shouting.

I pushed myself from the ground.

If you want to play with beast transformation, then perhaps we'll meet again on better terms. Lady Winters laughed. *Do keep up with your studies, my dear. I'm certain your work could match that of your grandfather's.*

I clenched my fists. Just ahead, a long section of corridor led to two elevators and a dead beast. At least now I knew where I was.

I pressed my hand against my shoulder, hoping the pressure would relieve the pain, then stumbled ahead, forcing myself to walk. I tucked the charm under my shirt. If Jim hadn't kept the pendant on the airship, Lady Winters would've taken that without a second's hesitation.

The minutes walking felt like hours before the winding corridor split into one that went back to my team. I followed it, gritting my teeth as the sounds of beasts grew louder.

Orange light flickered on the metallic wall and I slowed my walk. Something was wrong. Fire crackled where there hadn't been fire before. A beastie with flames dancing along its skull and hands stepped around the corner and trained its cat-eyes on me.

Notgood-notgood-notgood . . .

I wrapped my vines around its neck. The beastie struggled. Its flames seared the plant tips. The rotten stench of the withering vine assaulted my nose. I tackled the beast and knocked it off-balance. Its hot skin stung my knuckles and flames erupted around me. I stumbled away, swatting at the embers that were burning through my sleeves.

Fire flashed in the creature's hand, forming a glowing orange fireball. The beast reared, baring its teeth in the ghastly light. It punched the air with its clawed fingers. I dropped to my knees as the fireball soared overhead. Its heat burned my arms and my shirt smoldered. The chemical stench of burning hair stung my nose, and the heavy heat made it hard to breathe.

The beastie raised its hand, steam wafting from its body.

I was going to die.

I didn't want to die like this. I needed to stop Lady Winters.

I forced myself up, limping away as fast as I could. The pads of the beast's feet *whuffed* against the floor. A door clanged and a thick hand grabbed me by the throat, lifting me from the ground. I couldn't breathe —

The lumbering beastie's sweaty hand threatened to crush my windpipes. My vision blurred. My spine popped and I grabbed the beast's wrists to give myself air.

Its dull pupils glowed in the firelight.

Thunder cracked. My muscles surged. The beastie roared, swaggering on its heavy legs, and it dropped me. Then a bright bolt of lightning arced into the beast, blasting it over my head and against the wall. My head . . .

A loud thunderclap rumbled through the floor. I sat against the wall, my skin tingling. Everything was sparkling bright.

"Get down!"

I dropped, not caring to argue considering how close I was to the floor already. Another bolt smashed overhead, catching the fire beast at the end of the hall while a wave of fire blasted the room.

When I opened my eyes again, steam rose from the fire beastie's burnt flesh. Sections of the wall were scorched black, and the lights flickered. I didn't care to move, finding that it kept my shoulder at a nice, dull throb. Both beasts remained still, except for an occasional electrical twitch.

"I saved you," Val said proudly. Thanks to the spots in my vision, all I could see of her was her short height. "By the way, I never got your name." She extended her hand toward me. I took it.

"Jenna. My name's Jenna." My legs shook, and those spots in my eyes wouldn't go away.

Val nodded furtively. "Nice to meet you, Jenny." She pumped my hand. "Glad you're all right. The rest of your team's this way." She motioned for me to follow and her skirts swished as she ran around the corner.

"It's *Jenna*."

But she was already gone.

I couldn't complain too much. She *did* save my life.

Didn't mean I trusted her.

Bodies of both prisoners and beasts littered the sterile hallway. Men and women in camouflage hoisted the living over their shoulders and tended to the wounded while Val hopped over a set of bodies, oblivious to their plight.

I scowled, covering my nose from the stench of blood.

She was so insensitive.

Inese knelt by Jack and wrapped a bandage around his chest. She nodded to me as I neared. Her left eye was marred by a swollen purple bruise, but it looked like her armor took the rest of the damage. Jack, on the other hand, was covered in blood and I had no idea how much of it was his own.

Captain Cortez called out orders in Spanish. Like the others, he wore camo, but he carried twin swords at his side instead of a gun. Lance would be thrilled to meet someone else with his power.

My heart skipped a beat. I hadn't seen Lance since coming back. I frantically searched the bodies, then found him next to a water-soaked beast. His skin was pale, and my hands shook as I crouched next to him. "Lance?" I whispered.

His hair was plastered to his face, his shirt soaked through.

I'd dragged him into this mess. If he was dead, it'd be my fault. I reached my hand to his waterlogged sleeve, and relief flooded through me when he shifted at my touch.

Thank the Community.

I squeezed his hand and he rested his head against the wall. "We'll get out of here," I whispered, settling beside him.

Inese spoke with a pair of rebels who guarded the open corridor, and she passed Jack to one of the prisoners. The woman carried one prisoner over her shoulder and let Jack lean on the other, completely unhindered by either. A strength power, probably.

The other prisoners stayed clear of the bodies and followed the rebels the way they'd come. Inese came to me and Lance, followed by Val. "We need to get Lance and Jack medical attention. Go with the rebels and make sure those two are all right."

"What about you?" Val asked, swaying her hips. The tiny point of a fang gleamed white against her flushed lips.

"I've got to get the car." Inese turned to me. "The rebels should have a transport. We'll rendezvous at their camp."

"What about the stone?" I asked. "Isn't that why we came?"

She shook her head. "It's not here."

"You're sure?" Considering all the winding hallways this place had, that stupid stone could've easily been hidden in one of the chambers and we'd never know.

Inese patted me on the shoulder and went invisible, shimmering against the metal walls before vanishing entirely. "I'm sure. Now, we don't have a lot of time before the next wave of Special Forces shows up."

"But—"

"Go. That's an order."

I swallowed hard. Without Inese, I was the only remaining Coalition member able to help. The rebels were already gone with Jack. But what about Lance?

"I've got you, Handsome," Val said, cradling his head in her arms. "What's your name?"

My jaw dropped. Why, for the love of efficiency, was she flirting with him? He was wounded!

"Lance," he said, dumbfounded.

"I'm Val. We've got to get our handsome warrior someplace safe." She smiled and draped his arm over her shoulders. I tried to cut in, but Val shook her head. "You're in no condition for this after fighting those beasties; I can do it."

Lance gave me a slight smile. "I'll be all right."

My cheeks burned. Of course I could do it if she'd give me a moment's chance. Problem was, my throbbing shoulder disagreed.

I scowled, wishing there was some way I could be useful.

"Is there any place for us to go?" The woman who'd been thrilled about Val's lightning wrung her hands, glancing furtively at the reeking battleground around us. "I ain't going back to Mexico. Not with the order that put me here."

Val opened her mouth to speak, but Captain Cortez maneuvered his way back through the crowd as the last few rebels helped the injured. "There's a place with us, if you're interested. We tend to stay out of the Camaraderie's sight." He rested a hand on the looping hilt of his sword, a design that looked far more fancy than practical. "Can't say it's a peaceful life, but we can always use the help." The woman's eyes widened, but she nodded as he motioned us toward the exit.

"I remember how they brought us in," Val murmured to Lance. "They took us in a van and told us we needed to wait in the patients' room. But when they closed the door, I started feeling funny, and I realized they were gassing us!" She paused for emphasis, her dark brown eyes wide with fear. "I huddled down and covered my nose with my sleeve so I wouldn't breathe as much. That's how come I remember them taking us to the processing chambers — the room with the force field."

"Sounds . . . unpleasant," Lance said.

I clenched my fists. If everyone had been knocked out, there was no way she could've stayed awake.

The captain stopped by a room with the prisoners' personal belongings. A couple of the rebels escorting us had already incapacitated the guards inside. The prisoners grabbed their possessions: charm necklaces, a watch, wallets, phones. Val snatched a black leather briefcase from one of the lockers and pressed it to her chest.

That briefcase stood out like a file marked confidential. Why had she been sent here?

The rebels skirted us through the corridors, and when we came across a team of agents waiting in ambush, the captain proved uncanny with his swords. He snuck up behind them, dispatching all three of them before they realized he was there.

Farther ahead, gunfire and shouts and the purring roar of rotors emanated from the exit.

"Go!" The captain commanded, and the prisoners ran upstairs between bursts of gunfire to a large transport with its cargo hatch extended. Flight beasts tore after them. There was a scream and a deafening gunshot near my ear, but I didn't want to know how many didn't make it through the smoke and cover fire.

The flight beasties descended. I thrashed a vine in the air, trying to hold off the creatures while the captain maneuvered people into the transport. Val pushed Lance into their waiting hands, then dropped a number of beasties with lightning.

She seemed to be an expert; those beasts didn't stand a chance.

"Incoming!" a rebel shouted as a whole team of agents rounded the building. Their guns were on their backs, but one had ice crystallizing over his hand. Another lifted the visor on her helmet. Her eyes glowed red, menacing.

She stared right at me.

Someone shoved me out of the way. A laser burst hit the guy's arm instead of my chest. The agent blinked, cleared her eyes, then refocused.

A blast of ice raced up the side of the building, freezing a rebel in place before another agent shot him between the eyes.

The whole place became a panicked frenzy with people screaming and running. A rebel threw fire at the agents. A flight beast pinned another rebel to the ground and gouged out his eyes. It tore at the man's throat and swallowed, then snarled and soared into the frenzy.

I struggled into the transport ship's cargo bay and found myself smashed between writhing prisoners who were trying all at once to get away from the exit. The engines roared. I lost my balance as the ship lifted from the ground, the hatch closing behind us. The captain tore across the field, trying to keep up. At the last minute, he caught the edge of the ramp and hefted himself inside, then scooted among the escaped prisoners as one of the agents mounted a rocket on the ground and aimed for us.

Bits of dirt and flesh — Beasties being fired on by mechs —

Community, no . . .

A tiny silver canister appeared in mid-sky, soaring toward the man with the rocket launcher.

Inese!

My heart leapt to my throat as the ground exploded in a blast of fire. Dirt erupted from the ground and the hatch closed.

CHAPTER
TWENTY–SEVEN

I wasn't sure how long we flew toward the rebel camp; I slept. My shoulder throbbed in the brief moments I woke. The sterile facility smell from the prisoners assaulted my nose and suddenly I was back in the tanks with their stinging green liquid. The chambers, filled with their terrible, hissing gas —

A flowery perfume broke the illusion.

I opened my eyes. Val sat beside me, her briefcase tucked under her legs. She noticed me watching, then grinned. "We made it. We're alive."

"Not everyone," I murmured.

"*You're* alive, aren't you? Your team's alive, too. Take what good you get," she said matter-of-factly.

I narrowed my eyes. "We didn't destroy the plant."

She shrugged. "So?"

"They'll just keep making beasts."

"You're such a downer. Look at these people. You think they care that you didn't destroy the plant? They're just happy we rescued them."

Most of the prisoners were asleep, resting on each other or staring into the distance with vacant expressions.

I fingered Lady Winters' charm. "*I* care. It's wrong."

"Why?" She frowned, her eyes on the charm. I quickly closed my hand around it.

"It's wrong because having powers *isn't* wrong. The Camaraderie shouldn't keep our powers secret."

"I don't know . . . your Community seems pretty nice. Have you ever been to the territories? Some people use their powers in horrible ways, and they deserve to be turned into beasties. In the Community, the Camaraderie just roots out the troublemakers before they cause trouble."

I glared at her. "What trouble did you cause?"

"I stole candy from the governor's baby."

"You—what?" I raised an eyebrow. "They sent you to a transformation facility for that?" Why would she steal candy? Surely candy wasn't that expensive . . .

She smirked. "I didn't *really* steal candy. I just got on the wrong side of a governor that the Camaraderie endorsed."

"And you're defending the Camaraderie?"

"I'm just saying that beastie transformation isn't always a bad thing."

"You're wrong." I rubbed the smooth gems of the charm. I'd felt the transformation through Lady Winters' mind. It was terrible. "Criminal or not—no one deserves that fate."

"You have no idea what you're talking about," Val retorted. She scooted herself the other direction, which suited me just fine. We didn't need to talk.

The transport ship landed among tall, dense trees. A group of rebels passed out bologna sandwiches, and I laid in the brush beside Lance and Jack while we waited for Inese to arrive. Makeshift tents were spread across the clearing, filled with the rebels who'd been scouting the place before the incident and with the prisoners who needed treatment.

The plants around me felt *alive*; they contorted their vines to offer me comfort. I cozied into the brush, letting the foliage spread. Their roots offered a cradle against the hot, pressing night. Huge flowers above us scented the clearing like a tropical garden, and thin vines wrapped around my arms like a blanket.

It felt like the whole jungle was watching over me.

∿

Inese woke me later and coaxed me away from the plants. She offered me a granola bar and told me that Jack and Lance were already in the car, thanks to Captain Cortez and Val.

I stretched and yawned. The sky was turning a soft, velvet-pink, and birds chirped in the trees. My clothes felt damp from the early morning dew, but at least I'd gotten sleep. Evidently, so had Inese.

She led me past several tents and sleeping escapees. A few rebels tipped their camo hats as we passed, then returned to pacing the dirt trails between tents. The car sat on the other end of the makeshift camp, and Val bounced in the backseat.

I stopped in my tracks. "She's coming with us?"

"She asked if she could help, and well, we could use it." Inese patted my good shoulder. "Cortez said he wouldn't mind."

"I'll bet," I mumbled. "Probably doesn't want his troops getting electrocuted."

Inese raised a stern eyebrow and I fell silent.

Captain Cortez sat against the hood of the car. "Looks like you woke the sleepyhead." He grinned, planted one hand on the pommel of his sword, and offered her the other.

She winced as he shook her hand. "Thanks for the help," she said.

"No problem." He smiled and leaned against the car. "We struck a Camaraderie base and got a few rebels on our side. Not bad for a day's work. Looks like you got yourself a new team member, too."

"Given her powers, she could be useful."

He clapped Inese on the back. "Don't let me keep you. I know you've got people to tend, and we're busy with our own."

After Inese thanked him and started the car, I hopped inside—beside

Val, unfortunately—and the car went invisible.

"Wow," Val whispered. "An invisible plane-car!" She spewed a dozen questions as we flew, and Inese patiently answered each: How fast could the car go? Where'd we get it? Thanks so much for letting her come with us; she really hoped she could help. Was there something special she'd have to do to join? She couldn't wait to see the airship . . .

Val had as much energy as her electric powers implied.

Maybe I was mad because she electrocuted me with the beastie, but she was so dang *cheerful* that I couldn't get any of my own questions in.

Halfway through the trip, I finally managed to ask if Lance and Jack would be all right.

"Gwen should be able to heal them," Inese said.

"She's your doctor?" Val asked.

"Yes."

I glared in Val's direction, but she couldn't see me.

"Too bad Captain Cortez couldn't have taught Lance anything about his sword powers," I said, changing the subject. "I don't think any of the agents managed to touch him."

Inese chuckled. "He's an excellent fighter, but he doesn't have powers."

"He doesn't?"

"His swords are shielded," Val said happily. "I asked him while you were sleeping. They've been in the family for generations."

"His swords are . . . shielded?"

"Right. As long as he's touching them, telepaths can't manipulate his thoughts, beasties can't aim a fireball at him properly, and life-spirit people can't sense him. If he cuts someone with the sword, they experience a temporary power loss. It's really quite effective."

"So those swords were fancy for a reason."

Val giggled and playfully punched my bad shoulder—despite our invisibility. I gritted my teeth. "If you like sword fighting," she continued, "you should've seen the captain's son. He's training for the same. I saw him walking around camp, and he's *gorgeous*. Give Lance a few more years of practice . . ." She sighed happily.

I glared through the invisible window. "We've got more important things to worry about," I grumbled. "Like stopping beast creation."

Back at the airship, Crush showed Val her quarters while Inese took the rest of us to Gwen for medical treatment. The warmly-lit hall was a welcome change from the bright, antiseptic beast plant, though my leg muscles cramped from the long car ride.

"Here we are." Inese braced Jack against her shoulder and knocked. Lance leaned against the wall, grimacing where his wounded arm touched the bronze. In retrospect, I'd suffered the least damage: the gunshot wound and a few minor burns . . . and the dull, constant headache from Lady Winters' attack.

"Come in," Gwen said, her voice not much louder than a whisper. She scooted to the edge of her bed and clasped her hands in her lap. Jack grunted as Inese helped him lay down.

"Don't strain yourself," Inese warned Gwen. "I'll be back in a bit. I've got to check on our newest recruit." Gwen nodded, and Inese headed out.

"Can you help him?" I asked. Jack was in pretty bad shape, and the rebel medics hadn't had a chance to work on him before we left.

"I'll do what I can," Gwen said gently. "Normally we would use the sick bay, but this will have to make do until I can use the stairs safely." Her formal speech reminded me of the Community's elderly population. The familiarity was comforting. "Please pull up a chair."

I dragged a heavy wooden chair to the spot she'd indicated.

"Thank you, dear; he shouldn't be standing."

A tinge of satisfaction snaked through me as Lance sat. Val wasn't here to flirt with him.

"Beasties?" Gwen asked. I nodded, and she placed a hand on Jack's shoulder. "Let's start by mending the broken arm."

"Do you need anything from upstairs?" I asked.

"I'm good for now." She tucked the blankets around her charge and then placed her hand on the break in his arm.

The room went silent, save for Jack's pained breathing and the airship's hum.

An ancient alarm clock buzzed faintly, one of its LED numbers missing. The desk had a neat stack of papers beside a pencil holder with half-used pencils. Soft, faded cloth hung along the wall. A few pictures hung here and there, one in which Gwen and Jim laughed among people I didn't recognize. Judging by her accent, she was from the Community of North America. I wondered when she had joined the Coalition.

After a while, Gwen patted Jack's shoulder. "You need rest, but you'll live."

He shifted on his back and fell into a deeper slumber. It was a wonder he could sleep comfortably, knowing he might've died. But then, I'd fallen asleep in the middle of a jungle. Not the safest of places.

I rested my elbow on my knee as Gwen moved to treating Lance. *It'll be okay*, I wanted to tell him, but I couldn't. I didn't know how much this elderly woman could help us. According to Pops, she had life-spirit and telepathy. Her telepathy explained how I got my chance to attack Lady Winters the first time I confronted her. Pops guessed that she'd acted as a distraction, as a buffer to keep me from completely losing my mind.

Over the next half hour, the bruises cleared from Lance's face and the deep scratches turned to faint scars. Finally, Gwen leaned against the wall and rubbed her eyes.

Lance rotated his shoulder as if he'd never been wounded. "What'd'ya *do*?"

"My power is in healing: the ability to save or suspend lives." She rubbed her forehead gingerly, then looked at me. "It's your turn. I won't go deep in your thoughts; I just use telepathy to find the damage."

I swallowed hard, then felt something else — *be there*. She was present, searching across my mind, but she wasn't intrusive like Lady Winters. Each memory was tucked away, as if it'd come unbidden, and her presence was much friendlier. When she did find pain, the memory flashed to the surface and vanished as quickly.

"Sorry about attacking you," I whispered. "I . . . I wasn't acting like myself."

Don't worry about Brainmaster right now, she sent gently. *You were under her influence, and I have no memory of the attack. Help me decide what should be mended, instead of dwelling on what might not have happened.*

Her thoughts were strange—hard to distinguish but certainly not my own. I tried to focus on memories I didn't mind her seeing, drowsy as she soothed the grazed shoulder and eased the bruises. She healed the burns from both fire beastie and electricity.

Then the reflection in the tank surfaced, followed by the screams of humans turning into beasts and the horrible acrid gas. My arms tingled, changing, itching—

Gwen's presence vanished and I gasped for air.

I'm not in a tank; I'm not in a tank—

The burnt scabs on my skin stung, a small patch turning into a white blister, and my shoulder hurt again.

"You okay?" Lance reached for my shoulder, consoling, but quickly withdrew his hand when I jerked my arm.

That memory—

It never happened, so it wasn't a memory.

Gwen leaned against the headboard and sighed. "There are more than physical burns that must be taken care of. Brainmaster left behind a memory seed—a false memory planted to cause distress. They're used primarily to weaken their victims against further attacks. I'll see if I can soften the seed tomorrow, but I'll need a little more time to recuperate. For now, can the two of you get Jack to his bed?"

Lance nodded.

Gwen woke Jack with a gentle touch to the shoulder. "I'm fine," he muttered in a half-snore.

She smiled weakly. "Glad to see you're back to your usual self." She dismissed us, and Lance and I helped Jack into the hall.

"She gives us a lot when she heals us," Jack said, yawning in mid-sentence. "But she's got the benefit of being a telepath, so she knows when she's appreciated."

Once inside his room, he brushed a stack of comic books from his couch and tried to pick up a video game controller, but he fell asleep instead. His chest rose and fell softly, one hand draped off the couch with the controller in hand.

He hadn't even bothered to change clothes, but he looked like he was more comfortable now than before.

"She did say it'd be a while before he fully recovered," Lance noted.

"Come on," I tugged his elbow. "Tim's probably wondering what happened to us."

"Right," Lance said, and we headed upstairs.

CHAPTER
TWENTY-EIGHT

"**What do you mean,** *beastie plant*?" **Tim skidded to a halt in front of** Lance and I. "I thought it was supposed to be abandoned."

I gestured to the singed ends of my hair, the silvery burns across my arms and the blackened patches on my shirt. "Just be glad you weren't there." My head wasn't ready for anything above a whisper, and he was talking like Inese flew—fast.

Tim worried his charm between his fingers. "You actually saw a transformation?"

His muscles rippled like lava . . .

"Yeah."

Green liquid numbed my hands, numbing everything . . .

I winced. I needed to stay as far from that memory as possible.

"There were a lot of people inside these weird tanks and chambers," Lance said. "Jenna tried to rescue one, and he turned on us."

The young man cried for help . . .

I shook my head, trying to shake off the memory. Tim continued down the stairs, his sneakers clanging against the metal with each step.

Doors clanged open, followed by painful howls . . .

I grimaced, lightheaded, and hastily fished out the snack bar I'd picked up from the cafeteria a couple minutes ago. I peeled away the plastic wrapper, watching the glue unstick at the corners.

A s'mores mix. Granola and brown sugar and chocolate and teeny, icky marshmallows.

"There's got to be a reason." Tim hopped down the last step and onto the second deck. "The Community wouldn't make beasties if there wasn't."

"Like taking over the world? Get enough beasts on the field, and they could overwhelm their opponents," Lance said.

"Who are they going to overwhelm? I've read through the files on the Oriental Alliance, but we've only seen the small rebellions—"

Ripping and clawing and tearing . . .

I clutched the granola bar so tight that even its expired expiration date didn't save it from getting squashed.

Come on, guys. Can we please stop talking about this?

"What?" Lance asked. They both stared at me.

"I—Did I think out loud again?"I asked.

Tim nodded.

"Sorry," I muttered. They could hear my complaints but *not* the terrifying images left behind from the memory seed. "It's just . . . it's a little too soon to be reminded of the details. You know, the memory seed Gwen mentioned?"

"Right." Lance twisted his lips and glanced at Tim. "I'll fill you in on the details later."

"What details?" Val hopped up the stairs, practically bouncing with energy. She'd changed from her skirt into midnight purple sweatpants with dragons and skulls printed on the sides, far flashier than anything the rebels wore. Her hair was braided into numerous loops and black ribbons. She must get bored easily. Bored and cold. Couldn't fault her on the last one. The airship *did* get chilly.

Val paused, looking at us with her doe-eyes. A stab of jealousy surged through me as both Lance and Tim did a double-take.

"Um . . . Crush said there was a cafeteria upstairs?" She pointed at the next flight of stairs, then pushed her hair from her face. "He mentioned getting started on lunch soon and asked me to pull out the ingredients . . .

You must be Tim."

Tim clamped his hand around his light bulb charm. The other hand disappeared into his pocket. "Uh, yeah. Tim Zaytsev."

Val grinned, flashing her fangs. "I'm Val, the new girl." She twisted her hips playfully. "I came from the transformation facility."

"I'm the new — well — not so new . . . I work in the control room. Your teeth —"

"Had 'em since I was fourteen." She grinned wide, revealing pointed fangs. "I'm not a beastie, though, if that's what you're thinking."

He ducked his head, his cheeks crimson. "I didn't mean —"

"Lighten up!" She laughed and punched his shoulder and weaseled between him and Lance. "I'm not *that* easy to offend."

Tim stared at her. "I —"

"I think he's found a girl who actually notices him." Lance elbowed me in the ribs, but I peered around him at the newcomer.

"How can you be so chipper?" I snapped. "Our last mission was a trap. Several people died, and countless others were wounded while we were trying to find a *stone*. We need information on how the transformation process works. We get that, and then we can sabotage their facility or reverse the process altogether."

Val rolled her eyes. "No offense, but you might want to get better at fighting. Your plants were kind of useless. And . . . what stone?"

"That's not important," I fumed, balling my hands into fists. "Besides, I used speed, too!"

"You used your speed powers to release a beast," Lance said flatly. He crossed his arms over his chest.

"I was trying to save him!"

He held up his hands. "I know, but she has a point. You could use more practice. Maybe more shooting lessons, that way you can stay out of harm's way."

I glowered at him. "I'll be fine. Besides, the plan would be to *avoid* direct confrontation. If we did it right, Inese and Tim could go invisible inside the facility, and then Tim could hack into their records. They wouldn't even know we were there."

"They don't need to see you to know you're there," Val said, planting her hands on her hips. "Ever heard of telepaths? Life-spirit people? Air elementals?"

"They'd have to know where to look, first."

She harrumphed and refused to look at me, but I'd won that argument. "All we'd have to do is convince Pops to let us run a covert mission," I said. "We might have to wait for things to calm down, but that'll give us time to practice."

Then we could undermine everything Lady Winters stood for. We'd rescue the prisoners and sabotage their factories. No more beasts.

No more torture.

"What if I don't want to go?" Tim asked.

I blinked. "What?"

"I don't mind helping on the airship; I'm good with tech, but I'm not as coordinated as you guys."

"You do better than me."

Tim snorted. "Which isn't terribly well."

I winced. "The point is, you would go in invisible. That way there wouldn't *be* a confrontation."

"Inese can only help so many people at a time," Lance said. "She was exhausted after escorting us through a hallway. What happens if we get caught?"

"Clara happens," Tim said softly, "and I don't think any of us would be laughing."

Val gave him a confused look. "Clara?"

"A Camaraderie thief who defected," I explained. "She was caught and tortured, but all she did was laugh at them until they killed her."

"It's our symbol," Lance said.

Val made a little "oh" expression and shuffled her feet. "I see."

The silence stretched uncomfortably long.

"Um . . . would anyone mind showing me to the cafeteria? Crush wanted me to pull out a few supplies . . ."

Tim nodded and motioned her to follow.

Lance waited beside me as the two of them headed upstairs. "I don't like her," I said.

Lance frowned. "Why?"

She was obnoxious, annoying, flirtatious, and yet she had the verisimilitude of actually caring about people. Except that she didn't mind the existence of beasts.

"She's like a battle-hardened Sam," I said finally.

Lance shook his head. "Nah. Val's not Community. Sam is."

"I gathered that."

He glanced at me. "That's not a bad thing. The Community's too strict. Out here, we can think for ourselves. Val obviously does."

"You're on her side?"

A corner of his lip turned toward a frown. "You've been acting weird ever since we got back. Everything all right?"

I scowled. "I ran into Lady 'Brainmaster' when I was trying to lead the prisoners away. Her team killed the prisoners, but she went into my mind—made me think—" My voice caught in my throat at the memory of the transformation.

"Jen?"

"I'll tell you later, okay?" My fingers felt clammy, and my eyes locked on my bronze reflection in the wall.

Lance stood on the other side of the force field, then ran to help in the unseen battle. He didn't come back. He could have portaled us out of there, but he didn't come back.

"I'll talk to you later," I said quickly, then hurried down the stairs. I needed time alone, and once I recovered, I needed to talk to Pops to see if he had any other ideas. I didn't want to go back to the beastie plant, and I wasn't sure I *could*. All those tanks, those memories . . .

Please, Gwen. Please remove these memories.

CHAPTER
TWENTY-NINE

I stared at my grandfather's door for a long minute before twisting the knob and stepping inside. A computer screen lit Pops' face in a harsh blue glow and cast shadows across the thin wrinkles around his eyes. The daunting light leaked onto the metallic wall beside him and spilled across the torn family photo, leaving the rest of the room in shadow.

I swallowed hard. He used to turn people into beasts.

Pops motioned to the light switch, his eyes fixated on the computer. "Please, turn on the lights."

I flipped the switch. Bright light flooded the room.

"The Camaraderie is planning something," Pops murmured, his thumb on his lip as he scrolled down the screen.

I took my seat nervously. "They're probably trying to get their pendant back."

"Not just that." He folded his hands in his lap and swiveled his chair to face me. "The Cuban Resistance said they're pulling specific beasts from the transformation facilities. Not the usual fighters. Beasts with shapeshifting and radiation and laser eyes. We're not sure why."

Of course he would notice that. He'd been one of the doctors who transformed them.

I lowered my eyes to the symbol on the front of his desk. "You think they're planning something outside of their usual attacks?"

"Possibly."

"Do you think Lady Winters has something to do with it? I had a run-in with her at the beastie plant."

He glanced at me, concerned. "Inese told me you faced her again."

"Yeah, she—" I looked up from the symbol on the desk and the lights wavered. My legs felt numb and heavy. My skin burned—I stared at Pops from inside a tube. I screamed for him to let me out, but my tongue stuck in my mouth, thick and swollen. A tickling fire rushed through my arms and legs, and I collapsed to the ground, shaking and burning—

"Jenna!"

My grandfather's rough hands shook my good shoulder and his blurry fingers snapped centimeters from my nose. My knuckles had gone white from gripping the chair's cold metal frame.

"Jenna," Pops repeated, softly. He knelt beside me and lifted my chin so he could look me in my eyes. "What happened?"

"I don't know." I took a deep breath, grateful as Pops returned to my side with a cup of water. He waited until I could hold the cup steady, and after several gulps, I lowered the cup to my lap.

He asked me again what was wrong.

"I think Gwen called it a memory seed," I said. My blood pounded in my ears. "When I was at the beastie plant—"

Rows and rows of green tanks, each inhabited by the helpless—

"Brainmaster attacked my mind."

Pops lifted his head in recognition, but didn't interrupt.

"In my mind, she turned me into a beastie. She asked me what I thought of you. She—" Fear flooded through me. Saying this aloud was so much worse than keeping it in.

"I'm sorry." Pops wrapped his arms around me. His suit was stiff, his cologne strong, but it'd been so long since anyone hugged me, anyone I remotely considered part of my family, that I relaxed. Warmth spread through me and I let my body still.

Whatever he had done before, that was in the past. He was my grandfather. "Thank you," I whispered.

He nodded and withdrew from the embrace. "Talk to Gwen about removing those memories as soon as she's recovered enough." He stood, his knees popping. "Can I get you anything else?"

I nodded. "I want to sabotage the beast plants. I want to find information on the beasts so I can stop them from being made. I want to fix everyone who's been hurt."

Pops tucked his cane neatly under the drawer handles and sat, his face twisted as if he understood but didn't agree.

"I want to try a covert mission," I continued. "But I think—I think it would help if we knew how the Oriental Alliance fights. If they can stop these beasts, then we can use that to our advantage."

Pops' eyes held a telling sadness. "Jenna, the Camaraderie has us vastly overpowered. But if you want to see how the OA works, I'll have Inese make the arrangements. The more you know about this world, the better suited you'll be to take what life gives you. I know Gwen will remove the damage Lady Winters has done, but you might also speak with Jim. He's missed talking with you these past couple days."

"I'll do that."

"Good. Do you need me to escort you anywhere?"

I shook my head and tested my ability to stand. My knees felt weak, like they could buckle at any moment, but I steadied myself against the wall. "No, but thank you."

A smile tugged on Pops' lips. "Anytime."

Jim held a magazine in one hand, the cover of which had a thick yellow border and a woman wearing white makeup and red lipstick. Her black hair contrasted sharply with the rest of her face, and I'd never seen a leader's costume so unusual. Stacks and stacks of these magazines were piled in the corner of Jim's room, some older than he'd been alive.

Jim sat the magazine on his desk and eyed me through his reading glasses. "Are you all right?"

I sunk into the plush chair and explained what happened between me and Lady Winters. The memories. The accusations. The transformation I'd seen. I tucked my legs against my chest. "Half those prisoners were from the Community, and their only crime was having powers." I scowled. "Too bad the car doesn't have enough firepower to blow up the beastie plant. Then there would be no place to send them."

He chuckled sadly. "I know how you feel, but if we used the car to make a direct attack, then the car would be a target, and it is vital to our sabotage operations. We have lost too many of those who serve our goals to accomplish anything bigger."

I rested my chin on my knees. "Is that why everyone's so eager to take on Val?"

"She seems like a nice young lady. Very enthusiastic."

I scowled. "She's too chipper. She just seems . . ." I fiddled with Lady Winters' charm. I didn't trust Val. I *couldn't* trust her. "She was one of the prisoners, yet she doesn't fault beastie creation. How can we trust her?"

"Throughout the Coalition's history, we have worked with many people we did not immediately trust. During the early days of the Coalition, before we officially started calling ourselves that, one of our founding members was a black market hacker." He paused. "I hated his guts."

I blinked. Jim hated someone? That didn't seem like him at all.

"However," he continued, "this hacker was crucial to our success. Without him, the Coalition would never have secured this airship and made it out of the U.S. alive. I eventually came to terms with him, but it took time and a considerable amount of patience." He smiled and interlaced his fingers over his magazine. "Give Val a chance. There will always be people you don't like, but get to know her. You may find that she is as nervous as you were when you first joined. She has been exiled from her home, unable to return without being targeted by the Camaraderie. Similar to you."

I sighed. "I guess. I'd love to go home with Lance and Tim, and have

Mom chide me for bleaching my hair too long and for Dad to go on a walk with me and talk about daily life. I guess Val might feel the same."

Jim nestled his reading glasses onto the crook of his nose and smiled.

The smell of warm beef called me from the kitchen. Out of everyone here, Crush was the only one we all agreed could prepare food well. His concoctions outperformed Jack's frozen burritos, and the time Inese tried making scrambled eggs, she'd almost set off sprinklers I didn't know we had.

Since then, we'd been lucky to find scrambled eggs left warming in the skillet every morning, though Crush adamantly claimed he wasn't the one who cooked them. My guess was that he didn't want anyone taking dinner duty and leaving scorched pans in the sink for him to clean later.

But his cooking aside, I longed for Mom's shredded beef and cabbage dish she made before I left home. I still hadn't heard anything about my parents. I didn't know if they had the same jobs, or if the Community relocated them. Families were sometimes relocated if a relative was taken away, but I now doubted that was a good thing.

"This airship is so big!" Val's voice carried down the hall, interrupting my nostalgia. "Tim, I can't believe how lucky you are. You must be really smart to learn so quickly."

"Well . . . my power helps out a lot with that—"

I eased my way into the kitchen and took the long way to the stove. Crush had left the pan simmering, presumably with Tim keeping an eye on it. He was the only other person here with an ounce of cooking sense, though he usually didn't exercise it. The warm, spiced beef smelled delicious, and I was happy to find there were potatoes and green beans in it, too. I just didn't plan on checking the expiration dates of the empty cans littering the sink.

"What about you, Lance? What's *your* superpower? I know you've got a thing for swords. I'll bet you can get really good with them if you keep up your practice."

Lance beamed at Val's words, and I froze in the middle of heaping a nice ladle of stew into my bowl. Val traced her finger along his shirtsleeve, smiling eagerly into his eyes.

He coughed, then smiled back. "I can make portals."

Don't do it, I told myself. *Flinging the ladle at Val would waste perfectly good stew.*

Val grinned. "You saw my fangs," she said, turning to Tim. She made a little growling sound. He yipped and jumped away, delighted.

I dug through the drawers for a spoon. For some reason, finding a fork around here was getting a lot harder. Crush suggested they were somewhere under the piles of Jack's DVDs, but Jack blamed a so-called "Ghost Cook" and suggested that Crush had misplaced the garbage shoot for the dishwasher.

Either way, I wanted forks. It was difficult to eat waffles with a spoon.

Val raised her hand toward the ceiling and leaned into Lance. "I can also make electricity do what I want."

The lights flickered.

Great. She was using all our power reserves.

"That's awesome!" Lance said. "My other power is speed, but I'd go with electricity if I had the option. Imagine—electricity with a metal sword?"

Val giggled and hopped up on the table. "That would be cool."

"Yeah."

I didn't see what was so great about being an electric elemental—

I fumbled and dropped my spoon. All three of the them turned to stare as it clattered to the floor. My cheeks burned.

Val scooted to face me. "Your major power is plants, right?"

I nodded coldly and took my seat, then tried the stew. The once-delicious green beans tasted lumpy and hard to chew. The potatoes were too stiff; the beef . . . scarce.

Stupid Val.

She swung her legs and tossed her head from side to side. "I once heard of a guy with plant powers, but he was creepy; totally antisocial. He had plans to take over the world, or so the stories said. They called him Ivy Man."

"Ivy Man? What kind of name is that?"

Both of the guys moved closer, intrigued. "What'd he do?" Lance asked.

"He encased his victims in vines and messed with their minds to make them turn on each other." Val glanced at me. "Kind of like you, except without the telepathy."

My skin prickled from the warm metal of the charm, and I clenched my teeth. If I wasn't going to use the charm before, I definitely wasn't going to use it now.

And did Val just imply that I was antisocial?

"Your other power is speed, right?" She grinned.

I glowered at her. "Yes."

"Right. Being able to run from beasties is always a good thing."

I sat down my spoon, deciding against a second helping. "Yeah, plenty useful," I murmured, then took the bowl to the sink. I wasn't going to deal with another Sam.

Instead, I headed downstairs and stopped by Gwen's room to see if she'd recovered enough to try again with the memories, but she didn't answer her door.

I didn't want to disturb her, so I headed back to my room.

I'd try again tomorrow.

CHAPTER
THIRTY

The next morning, I woke to a knock at my door. I twisted deeper into my covers. *The woman inside the cylinder — my reflection — I* thrashed against the sheets, then shrieked as they tangled around me and I fell off the edge of the bed.

Thump. Right on my bad shoulder.

"You all right in there?" Inese called.

"No."

The lock chinked and the door creaked open, letting in a stream of light. I squeezed my eyes shut, but Inese wasn't done tormenting me. She flicked the light switch and motioned to the ceiling. "You might want to get those trimmed."

Vines crisscrossed the frosted glass cover with tiny leaves. A few had thorns, a product of last night's nightmares, and yet others concealed the porthole window with thick leaves. A homemade curtain of sorts.

"I like them."

Inese shrugged. "Your choice. Anyway, you wanted an introduction to the Oriental Alliance, right? I've made the arrangements. Crush and Tim found a reference to some kind of underwater ruins off the coast of Yonaguni, so Crush gave us those coordinates, too. Figured we could take a look around for any artifacts. We leave in a couple days." She looked me over. "You can swim, right?"

"Well, yeah."

"Good. That makes this easier. Since Jack needs to rest and Gwen is sick, I'm trying to avoid the more dangerous missions. No beasties, no guards, and nothing trying to kill us."

"Gwen is sick? But I thought she was a life-spirit elemental. Shouldn't she have recovered by now?"

"As of last night, her powers don't seem to be working. Healing you guys must have been more of a strain than we thought. Crush is making sure Gwen stays comfortable. If she's not up and moving before we leave, I'll buy medicine while we're out." Inese put a hand on her hip, one finger looped around a large key ring with lock picks. "I'll see you after breakfast."

She jingled her keys and left me to my sheets. I was pretty sure that was a reminder that I was supposed to be practicing my lock picking, but all the locks I'd seen outside this airship were keypads.

Lock picks didn't help.

"I can't wait!" Val announced. "I've never been to Japan. Of course, I've seen beaches and they're amazing, but those were in Mexico."

Tim smiled. "You've had an amazing life."

"No kidding," Lance agreed. "No Community? What was it like?"

I popped a piece of bread in the toaster and faced them. "You realize it'll be a day or two before we leave, right?"

Val shrugged. "That's okay." She turned to Lance. "I wouldn't have minded the Community; it's similar enough. You have more freedom in a territory, though—no curfews, for one thing, but there's beasties."

Tim leaned his head on his hand, gazing at Val.

Of course, *I* was just one of three girls on the ship. As soon as *she* came on board, they noticed someone aside from Inese.

I took my toast to the table. We obviously weren't ready to go on a regular mission anytime soon. If I could just relax —

"Glad you joined us, Jenny," Val piped cheerfully.

"It's *Jenna*," I snapped, taking a prompt bite of toast.

Stale, burnt . . . and *really* stale.

"Are you looking forward to the beach?"

I raised an eyebrow as I scraped off the blackened bits. "Beach?"

Well, Inese did mention searching through an underwater temple. I guess that implied there would also be a beach.

Tim nodded. "After Crush and I found the reference to the underwater temple, I figured it might have one of the stones that my translation mentions. And with Gwen sick and Jack recovering, Pops agreed that there wouldn't be any harm in looking."

"Inese said something about that." I took a bite of toast and frowned. Pops' dissertation said powers were caused by a genetic component. If the body was tired, they might not function properly. Reserve power would go to the immune system. Since Gwen's powers were life-spirit, she would have a natural connection to her own life. But if those senses were severed —

I remembered all those times I got sick from taking the pill and being injected with liquid adominogen. I hadn't even had that strong of a connection to my plants then, and I still went in shock.

Someone with life-spirit would have it much worse.

But how had her powers been blocked?

I twisted the charm between my fingers, careful not to let it show while I pondered.

Most likely, Gwen had strained herself when she stumbled into my memories of Lady Winters. But how those memories blocked her powers, I wasn't sure.

After breakfast, I left Tim and Lance with Val and found Crush alone in the command room. His legs stuck out from underneath a computer console. An orange glow reflected on the floor. I stood back until the torch shut off.

"Crush?"

Metal twanged against metal. He scooted himself out and lifted the mask from his face, then touched his forehead gingerly. "Yeah?"

"Have you found any information about my parents yet?"

"Right." He jammed his finger into the computer's power button and the screen booted from black to loading. "The most I've found so far is that you're one of the most wanted people in the Russian Community."

My palms sweated as I rubbed my arms, trying to dispel the cold. "What am I wanted for?"

"According to security, you contracted theophrenia, infected and blackmailed Tim into hacking EYEnet, and then evaded capture." He flipped through a lanyard of flash drives, selected one, and inserted it into the computer. "You're wanted for endangering public safety."

"So much for keeping the incident quiet," I muttered.

Crush shrugged and removed his torch from under the desk. "Sometimes it's better to come up with alternative explanations. They want to catch you, so they need a reason for you to still be around."

"They think I might go back to my parents?"

Crush clicked through the articles regarding my search warrant. "Pops tried to warn your father what was really going on shortly after you were born, but your father called security instead. They might think you'll do the same. But there's no word on your parents in the security logs, so evidently, they aren't trying to use them as direct bait."

"Are they safe?"

"Well, I don't know. They haven't reported to work since you disappeared."

My heart jumped. "Are they—"

"Don't worry yourself yet," he said. "Pops *did* warn your father a long time ago. I'm sure he's a smart man. They may have gone into hiding."

"Into hiding?" I swallowed hard. "Let me know what you find."

"Of course. And Jenna? I'm not sure I told you this, but thanks for going after Gwen. She appreciates what you did."

"Even though I attacked her?"

"She's not convinced you did. And even if you did, she might not be here now if you hadn't gone on the mission." He laid a hand on my shoulder and smiled. "Thank you."

I ducked my eyes, sheepish, though a hint of pride seeped through me.

Two days later, we reported to the hangar bay. Inese wore a v-neck shirt and jeans, her hair pulled back in a dark pony-tail, her sunglasses atop her head. Tim stopped short when he saw her. "Nice outfit," Lance whispered to Tim. He glanced back at me, smiling, and Tim's face turned red.

Val giggled. "*Boys.*" She grinned.

I rolled my eyes. Ever since she'd come on board, they hadn't spent nearly as much time trying to find a solution to our world problems. Instead, they'd been teasing Tim about girls, teasing me about how much time I spent studying, and teasing Lance about how much time he spent practicing, showing off his skills to Val.

As for practice, I'd walked in on one of the training sessions with her, and she was blasting little cardboard targets to smithereens.

I'd avoided the metal railing that day.

"Take it easy," Crush told Inese. "You guys deserve it."

"No problem. We're just visiting a military base and going to a beach. Piece of cake."

"Wish I could come with you, but with Gwen still out, I imagine I'm going to be running errands all over the ship."

Inese patted him on the back. "Don't let Jack con you into playing video games all night. He needs his sleep, whether he wants it or not."

Crush grinned wide, his eyes glinting under the florescent lights. "Have a little faith in me . . . I can handle a game or two. Anyway, have a good time." He waved and stepped aside.

Inese flipped her shades over her eyes. "All right, guys. You'll want these." She tossed us each a small, metallic bracelet with a little cylinder on it. Each bracelet had a different color. "Keep them on you at all times."

"Ooo, shiny!" Val strung her bracelet over her wrist, raising her arm and jingling it in the sunlight coming from the open hangar door. Tim gave a soft, sappy sigh.

I sighed and held the bracelet to the lights. The thin trinket looked flimsy; I expected it to snap when I tugged on the band. But despite its lack of substance, it hardly budged.

Inese wore one as well.

"What it's for?" I asked.

"It's how you keep from being shish-kebabbed, shot, zapped, and-or pummeled by friendly fire," Inese said cheerfully.

Val's smile faded. "Do what?"

"This little bracelet lets mechs know we're friendly, and therefore not to shoot us." Inese tugged at her bracelet, as if to demonstrate.

"This is safe?" I asked dubiously. It felt loose.

"Sure—long as you keep that bracelet on. I don't plan on taking you down where any of the beasties are, though you might see a few."

At least we'd get to learn more about the fabled OA.

"Get in," Inese said. "I'll explain as we fly."

Lance took the front seat with Inese and I took the back with Tim and Val.

"We've been sitting over South Africa," Inese said as we flew over patches of savannah and city that turned into sea. "They're the ones who fund us. In Egypt you'll start seeing some semblance of the Community, but it's mostly Camaraderie territory."

"Only downside is the beasties," Val said softly. Her words were directed at me, but we hadn't yet come to an agreement regarding transformation as a penal system.

I stuck to watching the rolling waves beneath us.

Even if I hadn't followed Pops, I'd have left home behind, and the outcome wouldn't have been nearly as pleasant. I closed my eyes, avoiding the memories of transformation.

The hours passed. The waves under us went to trees and then open fields — then movement. The car veered left, swooping low with a sharp drop in the pit of my stomach.

"What's going on?" I asked.

"I don't see anything," Tim complained.

"Neither do I," Lance said. "Wait — there!"

We'd entered India not too long ago, and just under the trees, several large, boxlike robots lumbered across the landscape with shining arms. They stood on heavy, gleaming legs, and they dwarfed the creatures that attacked them. A few of the machines had visible, glass pods inside their main frame, and the robot's arms were their guns, some blasting rounds of heavy fire and some shooting bolts of electricity, while yet others shot small, guided missiles that crashed into the ground and exploded into debris. Whatever was on the ground got blasted into the air.

I inhaled sharply. Mechs.

The car took a sudden dive, bringing us between an explosion and a tree. Beasties raced to attack. One leapt across the machine before latching onto the metal with its claws. Though the mechs were huge and destructive, the beasties didn't seem to care if they got underneath a missile when it exploded, tearing them apart.

I dug my fingernails into the palms of my hands. Those creatures had been human once. Now they were being sent uselessly to their deaths.

My arms felt cold and clammy.

Seeing anybody, even Val, would have been more comforting than watching the dark clouds obscuring the battle behind us.

CHAPTER
THIRTY-ONE

Once we reached Japan that night, Inese sat the car in the outer sector of a military complex. Thick barbed wire curled over the mossy, concrete walls, which were punctuated by small turrets. Large floodlights surrounded the landing pad; they towered above us, all stark steel and white burning lamps. Tiny insects flittered in the beams like dust against the black jungle.

"Welcome to the largest Japanese training facility for mechs," Inese announced, stepping from the now-visible car. "Got your bracelets on?"

I tugged at my bracelet and eyed the mech closest to us. Machine guns were attached to where its arms should've been, and thick, bulky legs held it aloft. I edged closer to Inese. No sense in getting trampled by allies.

She smirked, then motioned to a man clambering down a rung behind the glass pod at the center of the mech. He had short hair, and similar to the Mexican Resistance, he wore camo pants with a plain, long-sleeved shirt.

"*Konbanwa,*" he said.

Inese repeated the greeting and they launched into a messy dialogue of Japanese and English. The man paused and touched his headset—something about needing to speak with his superiors.

"I can sense it," Tim whispered.

I thought he meant the headset, but he stared at the empty mech. The mech's foot moved — seemingly of its own accord.

I backed toward the car as Inese clenched Tim's shoulder. "Let's not mess with that, okay?"

"But—"

She lifted her glasses and gave him a stern, disapproving glare.

Val placed a hand on his back, comforting, and he stepped away from the hulking machine. "All right," he grumbled.

Inese returned to her conversation, but the moment she wasn't looking, Val shot her a nasty glare. I paused. She'd seemed friendly a second ago.

I tugged at Lady Winters' charm. Val should realize that if Tim squished us like one of those characters in Jack's video games, I was not going to be happy camper. Or a living camper. I twisted my lips and clasped the charm tighter. Why couldn't I trust her?

Once Inese's conversation was complete, she instructed us to grab our luggage from the trunk. The mech's driver led us inside a nearby bunker with guest quarters. I settled into the top bunk and stared at the ceiling, the charm an uncomfortable reminder of why I was here.

Tomorrow, I hoped, would bring a way for us to end beast transformation.

The next morning, a lady in a pale green uniform brought us breakfast. Her brown hair was cut short at her chin, and she wore camo, the same as everyone else around here. She barely paused to look at us before setting a large bowl on the table beside the door. "Is there anything else you require?" she asked.

Inese finished holstering her gun on her hip. "You're taking us to Commander Kita after breakfast, right?"

"Correct." She dipped her head. "I will direct you to him when you are ready."

FLINT

"Good. That should be all." Inese smiled, and the woman smiled back.

I frowned, twisting the charm in my hand. I'd been playing with it all morning. There was something odd about the woman, but I couldn't place what. Something about her smile? Other than her, everyone and everything around here were what I expected from a military base—minus the fact that I hadn't thought mechs were still in use.

"I will wait outside until you need me," the woman said. She shut the door behind her and Tim peered around Inese.

"She wasn't . . . she was . . ." He scratched his head. "She was *tech*."

Lance looked up from polishing his sword. "What do you mean?"

"Well, she was . . . I could read her thoughts. She's a computer."

I stopped fidgeting with the charm and instantly thrust it under my shirt. Had I been using it again? Was that why she seemed so odd? "What do you mean, a *computer*? Are you trying to say she's a robot?"

Nuh-uh. We already had mechs and powers and subhuman monsters. I did *not* need another one of Jack's movie fantasies running around out here.

Val dipped her head down from the top bunk, her dark hair flopping upside-down around her ears. "That's exactly what he's saying. Haven't you heard of androids?"

"In *movies*."

Val giggled. "Art imitates life, silly. And vice versa. You don't see many humanoid robots outside the OA—they're really protective of their tech—but they exist. You know, I did a couple jobs for a guy who had a robot for a wife. Well, I always assumed she was a robot. She had an abundance of electricity around her. Kind of like the lady who brought us breakfast. Never asked the guy about her, though. Didn't want to embarrass him."

Tim glanced up at Val, his eyes wide. "You mean androids actually exist?"

She grinned. "Yup. You just met one."

"That's awesome!" He spun around to face Inese. "Do you think they'll talk about androids on the tour?"

252

Inese sorted out the bowls and began pouring a thin, steaming broth into each one. "Well, it wouldn't hurt to ask. We *did* stop here so you guys could get a feel for how the OA works. Now, who wants miso soup? It's got tofu. Better than that granola stuff we've been having in the morning."

"I do!" Val hopped off the bed and was second in line behind Lance.

I sighed. I couldn't complain about having something other than cereal, though I wasn't sure why we were having soup for breakfast.

I raised my hand in agreement and took a bowl.

After breakfast, the android led us to the main building—with Tim dancing back and forth between staring at the mechs and staring at her. She strode purposefully across the concrete courtyard, while the lumbering mechs made giant strides, each footstep causing a light tremor to rumble through the base. Cadets rushed underfoot, skillfully avoiding being squashed. They were braver than I'd be—I was staying as close as I could to Tim. I figured with his techno sight, he'd be a little quicker to notice if we were about to get stepped on.

The android lady stopped in front of a pair of sliding glass doors and waved her wrist over a keypad. The pad beeped and the door slid open with a *whoosh*.

"Hold out your bracelets," Inese said. "That way the sensor recognizes you're friendly."

"What happens if it doesn't recognize us?" Lance asked.

"If the base isn't on lockdown, you'll have at least half a dozen guards coming after you with rifles and their powers," Inese said, walking through the open doors. "If the base *is* on lockdown, I've heard that the OA has a fondness for lasers."

"Lasers?" His eyes widened.

"Yes," the android interjected softly. She pointed to several small holes in the ceiling above us. "They are highly effective at dismembering any number of targets who might be standing two meters from the doorframe."

Lance leaned toward Tim and whispered, "Is she serious?"

"I think so?" Tim swallowed nervously. "There really are lasers in the ceiling."

The android quirked a chipper smile. "Wonderful, yes? This way, please. Commander Kita's office is just down the hall."

Here I'd thought *Val* was too perky, and the android was thrilled about deadly lasers. I shivered. This reminded me a bit too much of Jack's video game antagonists.

She led us from the main entrance into the commons area. Computer terminals lined the silver-white walls, skirted by students in dark green uniforms and camouflage. Most looked Asian. At the end of the first wide hall, the android stopped beside a simple metal door with a security camera in the overhead panel. She knocked softly and clasped her hands behind her back, her head bowed.

A moment later, the door opened. A middle-aged man with a crisp white dress shirt under his dusky green uniform stepped out and closed the door behind him. Given his scars and crooked nose, he must have seen his fair share of battle.

The android lady bowed at the waist and then turned to us. "Allies, this is Commander Kita, your tour guide for the day."

Inese bowed respectfully. "Thank you for having us, Commander. This is Lance, Tim, Val, and Jenna."

The commander narrowed his eyes and looked us over. "You are interested in our tactics, yes?"

I nodded and glanced back at the others. "We wanted to see if you might have any advantages in fighting the Camaraderie."

Commander Kita smirked. "We do. Unlike the Community, we do not hide our powers. As soon as we know our abilities, we start training. The students here are some of our brightest techno sight users. They've come to our facility from across the Alliance."

"You start training as soon as you know your powers?" Val asked, surprised.

He nodded. "Yes. They do not come here until they have reached fifteen years of age, but we waste no time ensuring that they get basic training."

I blinked. "Fifteen? Isn't that kind of early to be at a military base?"

He gestured for us to follow him to the next room. "Hardly. Our soldiers start early so as to be better suited for missions once they are older. In addition, those who train studiously typically receive a high officer status. Puts them in line for a better mech when the time comes to go into battle."

"What about us?" Lance asked, eyeing a passing student who held a tablet in his hand. "Is there any chance we could train here?"

"Techno sight is a must," Kita explained, "since that is how we make the mechs move."

Lance pouted, but I shuddered. Fighting in close quarters was bad enough. Why would anyone *want* to go onto a battlefield?

"There are other training facilities, of course," Kita continued, "but ours is the biggest."

He stopped and opened a door into a small room with three rows of desks. Students, all of whom looked younger than fifteen, focused intently on the touch screen at the front of the room. Though I couldn't understand what their instructor said, I recognized what might have been advanced trigonometry equations on the board. The students had to be older than they looked, but that didn't erase the feeling of unease that settled in my chest.

"As you can see, they train in academics, not just powers. This way."

We followed Kita to another room that had gleaming metal walls which reminded me far too much of a beastie plant. This room had a pair of students standing on opposite ends, each wearing simple white tunics. Fire flamed in a young boy's hand. He punched it toward his opponent, who spread a wall of water before her. The two elements met in a hiss of steam.

"Does everyone with powers come to these compounds?" I asked. "Are any of them—" I took a deep breath. "Are any of them turned into beasts?"

"No. Beasts are subpar. An irresponsible waste of talent. We need everyone we have available to fight, whether they are here, managing the communications technology, on the field, or at their homes, fostering the next generation. Everyone has a place. So yes, they train at facilities like this one," Kita said.

"If you need everyone you can to fight," Tim asked, "do you send robots onto the battlefield? Wouldn't it be better than sending out an actual person?" He glanced at the android, then winced. "No offense."

"None taken." She shrugged, though I could have sworn her lower lip quivered with indignity. "I am not programmed to be offended by such questions."

Kita glowered at Tim. "You are the one with techno sight? We cannot send our androids onto the field because of people like you. I saw the report about how you tried to control one of our mechs."

Tim's cheeks went red. "I—"

"If we sent robots to fight, there is little doubt that the Camaraderie would recruit more of their tech masters to fight on the field rather than serve in hubs. As a result, our intelligence and soldiers would be compromised."

"What about shields?" Val asked. "Couldn't you just block their powers?"

The commander shook his head. "Calroe Industries charges ridiculous prices, and our agents have not been able to procure the details to making our own shields."

"So, you send people to fight instead," I said softly. "Is there anything you can do to sabotage the transformation facilities? Lower the number of beasts attacking you?"

"Sabotage? I see you take after your grandfather," he noted. "Our methods are a little more straightforward. As many of their beasts they send, we destroy. And when we get close to their cities or their strongholds, we destroy those, too."

I bristled. My skin prickled under the metal of my charm. The last person who said I took after my grandfather was Lady Winters, and she was as blunt. But Commander Kita didn't seem to notice my agitation, and he took us onto the perimeter of an outside training field. Two mechs fought ahead of us, both with hand-like mechanisms instead of guns for arms, and each tried to wrestle the other to the ground. Globs of mud spattered us as one mech slammed the other.

The once-forest grounds were battered with deep, muddy ruts. Very little grass remained, and the nearby trees were scorched and half dead.

I rubbed my arms, avoiding my powers near so much destruction.

Commander Kita smirked and locked his hands behind his back. "These mechs are useful against the Camaraderie's vehicles. They also eliminate pesky beasts."

I could only imagine a beast leaping onto the mech, only to have a giant metal hand send it flying into a tree. I didn't want to be on the receiving end of a beastie battle, but I didn't like picturing them killed so quickly. "You don't have to be so callous," I said, irritated.

Commander Kita raised an eyebrow. "They are weak, worthless vermin. They have no will of their own; a result of their previous human counterparts being raised as mindless drones."

"We're not mindless," I snapped. "And it's not the beasts' fault they were forced to undergo the transformation."

"Jenna . . ." Lance gave me a pleading look.

I didn't release the commander's gaze. "You should figure out how to reverse the process, not kill them left and right. Otherwise, the Camaraderie will just send more."

Seemed like the logical thing for *them* to do, anyway.

"You think I care how many they send? The Camaraderie is losing ground." He scowled down his nose. "As for you, I would expect you to be more respectful of your superiors, considering you are a guest."

I clenched my fists. "You blatantly disregard the fact that those beasts were human—so no, of course I don't respect you!"

A stark "v" formed between his eyebrows, and Inese cleared her throat, stepping between us. "Jenna, we're here to see how *they* handle the war."

"Agreed," Kita said sharply. He set his jaw. "We will continue."

I scoffed. I'd hoped that seeing the OA's training grounds would give me ideas on how to end beast creation, but I felt like I was right back where I started.

Tim and Lance shared a look. "Was she like this when she argued with Ivan?" Tim whispered.

Lance nodded. "Close."

I glared at him and remained silent as the tour resumed, guided by Val's "ooo"s and "ahh"s and excited gesturing at every little thing—including the fire alarms. Tim remained fascinated with the androids—which earned a few jealous pouts from Val—and with mechs, especially a large, four-legged mech designed to carry troops into and out of battle.

"Maybe someday you'll get to pilot one," Val said as we returned to the car. She shot a glance at the android, who smiled and waved.

Val scowled, but Tim grinned and looked at the facility behind us. "Piloting a mech? That'd be cool."

"Just remember that this place was made for war," Inese reminded them. "It isn't about having the coolest toy; it's about stopping the Camaraderie from overrunning their cities."

"The easiest way to prevent them from overrunning the cities would be to remove their army," I muttered. I'd *hoped* the OA might have a way stop the creation of beasts. Instead, all I'd learned was new ways to kill them.

CHAPTER
THIRTY-TWO

Inese chose a relatively open highway to lower the car onto, then she shifted the gears and actually *drove*. She opened the windows. Fresh, moist air rushed in. I grinned, enjoying the experience as we cruised along at a speed higher than normal in the Community.

The parking lot was surrounded by leafy bushes and a craggy cliff. Skinny trees periodically dotted the concrete barriers between the parking lot and the ocean. Though I'd seen the ocean from an aerial view, I'd never seen such a large body of water up close.

Once Inese had the car parked, I scooted from my seat to escape the faint traces of Val's perfume. Outside, the muddled din of vacationers mixed with ocean waves—

Voices overlapped, rising and falling . . .

I flinched and pushed that memory away as fast as it came.

"Now, the plan is to keep this mission simple," Inese announced. "At fifteen thirty I expect everyone to meet me for scuba diving lessons. There's an underwater ruin nearby that might have one of those time stones, and Pops figured we ought to take a look. I don't expect to find anything, but if you see anything unusual, let me know."

"So—" Val swayed on her heels. "This is a vacation?"

I glared at her. "Hardly. We have a distinct purpose to this trip."

"We're on a *beach*. What do you plan to do until fifteen thirty?"

Inese cleared her throat. "For one, we need to get you the proper attire to wear under your diving suit. Then you're free to relax."

"Shopping!" Val clapped her hands and cheered. Even Inese winced, rubbing her ear after the high-pitched squeal subsided.

"She's way too excited about this," Tim whispered. Lance nodded his agreement. Couldn't say I was surprised. Unless we were on the market for a new sword, I couldn't have dragged him shopping through a candy aisle.

"See? It's a vacation!" Val grinned. "Haven't you guys been shopping before? I guess you haven't, since you're wearing *those* old things, but come on, it's *fun!*" She grabbed Lance and Tim by their wrists and bounded after Inese.

I twisted my lips. Our clothing wasn't *that* bad.

Then again, Lance's borrowed shirt from Jack had a not Community-friendly message, Tim's attire had to be run through the washer several times before it was wearable again, and I was wearing a shirt that Gwen outgrew around 2030.

So maybe it was that bad.

Val, on the other hand, wore her flouncy black skirt along with a black head veil—supposedly to keep the sun out of her eyes—and yet she looked Community compared to the people on the beach. Most of the men had shorts and no shirt at all. The women followed the leaders' less-is-better theory, wearing nothing more than a bikini and thong. A few kids had one-piece suits, but those didn't come close to the full-body swimming gear I was accustomed to wearing during swim practice.

Inese led us inside a small apparel shop made from whitewashed planks of wood. While Lance and Tim hesitantly chose from a variety of swimming trunks, my options were limited to two-piece swimsuits with hardly any fabric, and one-piece swimsuits my grandmother wouldn't wear.

"How about this?" Inese tossed me a light blue bikini that had the most fabric of any of them. "Go try it on."

While I'd have preferred something less revealing, this particular piece was better than the neon orange one she showed me a few minutes ago. I reluctantly shuffled into the dressing room and tried on the stupid swimsuit. I felt naked, which wasn't far from the truth.

After several minutes of trying to think of an excuse to find something else, it was Tim's excited voice that made me wonder what Val chose.

"You look amazing!"

"Yeah," Lance agreed. "That looks really, *really* nice on you."

Lance? I propped the door open. "What are you going on a — What is *that*?"

Val had chosen a shiny silver material that hid almost nothing, held together by teeny straps of fabric that I wouldn't have trusted to tie my shoes.

Lance's eyes widened when he saw me. "Wow, Jenna — you look . . . very nice." He smiled and tilted his head.

Community help me . . .

I ducked behind the door and pressed my hands against the splintery wood to reassure myself. Everyone else wore the same type of swimsuit, and they couldn't all be leaders.

I took a deep breath and stepped outside. "This one will work."

Inese nodded, proud of herself, and I hurried to slip my shoes on while the others chatted about their choices. Up front, the cashier's desk peeked through spinning racks of various trinkets — necklaces with metal flip-flop charms and seashell bracelets and something called a toe ring.

Sure, the Community had simple ring bands to designate those who'd been given partners, but what was the point of a ring you couldn't see?

"Does this look all right?" Val asked, shuffling her feet and trying different poses. "I couldn't decide on the white one with sequins or the silver one."

"The silver one looks amazing on you," Tim said. He never took his eyes off her.

"It does look nice," Lance agreed. I snorted and glared at the brightly printed sign behind the counter. Just because Tim was girl-crazy didn't mean Lance had to be.

"What?" Lance looked perplexed. I tucked my hands under my armpits, not expecting him to understand.

Inese paid for our swimsuits and I woefully stashed my old clothes into my backpack. At least the outside breeze was enjoyable. It was warm and comforting after the chill indoor air conditioning, and a soft mist sprayed from the ocean. The hot sun burned my shoulders.

No one gave us a second glance, except to Val, who strutted to the shoreline and dragged Tim into the water. She laughed and giggled, tugging his arm and tripping over her own flip-flops.

"Come on, Jen. Let's go swimming." Lance smiled and held out his hand. Behind us, a couple girls pointed at him, whispering and giggling. One of them shouted something in Japanese and waved, but he didn't notice.

"That's okay, you go," I said.

Lance frowned, then tugged my elbow. "I thought you liked swimming." He ran a hand through his dark hair, and I paused. He was fit. If we were in the Community, he wouldn't have a single problem passing the physical for Special Forces. He just had the whole rebellion issue, which they would probably break.

I shuddered. "We should be rescuing people, not out here playing 'leader,' " I said. "Why is everyone so quick to call this a vacation?"

"Because Jack is still recovering. We'd be stuck on the airship if we weren't here." He held out his hand again. "You've got to relax. Otherwise you'll wear yourself out, like Gwen did. Besides, the diving instructor won't be ready for us until later. We have to be patient."

I sighed. He had a point.

"By the way . . ." Lance gestured to Lady Winters' charm. "I didn't think you were going to use that."

"I'm not! It's just a reminder that we have work to do."

He grinned. "Can I see it?"

I held the charm out, watching it glint in the watery sunlight. There was nothing of the swimsuit to hide it.

Lance's eyes went wide. "Fancy." He smirked, as if challenging me to complain about Val's leaderesque attire now. But then his expression softened. "It suits you. Even looks like a flower."

I'd noticed that. I fingered the stone petals and the little emerald gemstone at the center. "It's a bit gaudy, but at least it means something. Better than a mass-produced charm that anyone can wear."

He laughed. "Still your old self, I see."

I glared at him. "Oh, you think running from the Community changes any of that? I still plan to graduate college."

"Well, maybe one of the OA bases will take you in. I'm sure they have a use for a biologist." He nudged my shoulder playfully, but the thought soured my mood.

They had no use for me. All they did was kill beasts, not save them. No wonder Commander Rick fought the Oriental Alliance. I just wish he hadn't lied to us about already winning—or about the true nature of the Health Scan.

I grunted and slipped off my socks and shoes, then stashed my backpack with Inese's gear. She'd laid out a long blanket and blissfully relaxed with her usual sunglasses.

Unfortunately, this beach wasn't the smooth poolside that the Community covered in a soft rubber mat to keep people from slipping. The rocky sand was hot and I winced every time I stepped on a shell or piece of flotsam.

Once in the water, the pain subsided. The warm ocean lapped across my toes, then cooled when the tide returned to the ocean and wind ran across my feet. Too far away for me to hear, Val splashed Tim. He ducked, disappearing under the blue water then coming up, grinning hysterically.

I gritted my teeth. There were people *dying*. I laced my arm through Lance's. "You're right—this'll be relaxing," I said, more sarcastic than intended.

He frowned. "You've been acting funny ever since we got back. I know Gwen wasn't able to help you, but—"

Drowning in beastie tanks were a perfectly good reason to act funny. Having a strange new girl usurping best friends was also a good reason. So was not knowing where my parents were.

I stepped into the water. Sharp sand lodged between my toes.

"I'm fine."

Deep blue waves crested in the distance. Maybe I could talk to Lance out there, where no one would hear my fears of being turned into a beastie, where I might not imagine hearing Val and Tim's laughter. Where I didn't have to watch my back for fear of being electrocuted, shot, or roasted alive.

"Let's go farther out," I suggested. Seagulls circled above the fog-hidden island in the distance. "Race you?"

Lance grinned, his eyes sparkling with the reflections of the waves. "Sure."

A thrill of excitement ran through me. It'd been a while since we'd raced. I ducked my head underneath and the water washed around me. Without a full body swimsuit, my muscles tensed at the unexpected drop in temperature, but once I kicked my legs and propelled myself forward, the water warmed and the weightless sensation relaxed me.

I heaved my body upward, thrusting away the surrounding water in a splash. The overhead breeze was cold. Still, despite the distance of the plant life, it felt good to be in water again.

Lance sputtered, presumably at the sharp temperature drop in the wind, then shook his head to get his hair out of his eyes. "You could've warned me!"

I grinned. "Feels better once you get used to it." I sank underwater, just below the surface. Considering that we needed a physical fitness course every year, we'd both had plenty of chances to swim in team exercises and relays.

"Ready?" I asked, treading lightly. He nodded. "Three. Two. One . . . Go!"

I dove and pushed through the water. Bubbles rippled around my feet before I surfaced again, interchanging strokes so I could breathe. Lance was right behind me. I pulled at my speed power until I felt like I was punching the ocean with each stroke. I kept at it until my muscles began to tire, and then I slowed for Lance. I closed my eyes and enjoyed the freedom of the ocean, the cool air . . .

My connection to the plants distanced, like I'd taken the pill. Goosebumps formed along my arms and legs. The ocean stretched around me and the water deepened. Lance and the shore seemed too far away, and the tide was stronger now. I gulped, trying to keep calm, but the water dragged at my legs and tugged me under. I gasped and kicked, trying to keep myself above water, but it got into my mouth and stung my eyes.

Even as I spat it out, the water dragged me under again, rushing into my mouth and nose. It turned murky and green, numbing my skin where the swimsuit didn't cover it . . .

I shrieked, but my mouth filled with water. I couldn't breathe. My eyes burned and I struggled to see which way was up.

Not again – not again –

Sunlight!

Rapid bubbles formed around me as I propelled myself upward.

Air!

I gasped and spit what water had gotten into my lungs.

Where were the plants?

I reached out to them, but they were far below, and even if I combined my powers there was no way I could've reached them for help. I blinked, salty tears forming in my eyes.

Someone swam toward me.

I treaded water, feeling like lead weights were attached to my limbs.

Shivering, flighty, waiting for that tide to return.

I'd never been scared of swimming before. Why was so I scared of the water now?

The tiny shape broke into view — Lance. He wasn't far behind. Relief flooded through me and I steered clear of the stronger current, my heart pulsing in my ears. Lance went underwater, then came up again, his strokes as clear as I remembered.

We met past the dangerous tide and he squeezed my hand. "What happened?"

I shook my head, too numb to speak.

"Come on, Jen. Let's get back." He wrapped his arm around my waist and helped me swim. His bare skin felt smooth and I held my breath, surprised. It was warm, comforting to the touch.

We reached land and I flopped on the shore, wishing I hadn't exerted my already aching muscles. Even though Gwen helped heal my wounds, the gash in my shoulder had reopened and stung from the salt.

"Thanks. I wasn't expecting the current."

Lance nodded. "Neither was I."

We sat in silence, the now-cold wind drying us while sand clung to our skin. A towel would've been nice, but at least the sun kept us warm.

"There you are!" Val shouted.

I closed my eyes, wishing she could've stayed away for another five minutes.

"Tim and I are going to get lunch. Wanna come?" She jabbed her thumb at the crowd of sunbathers. "We found a hotdog stand a little way up the hill if you're interested."

Tim stood behind her, his arm entangled in hers. His short, sandy-blond hair was pointed in wet little spikes, and he grinned from ear to ear. "It smelled delicious," he added enthusiastically.

"Sure," Lance said.

I scowled, but regardless of who invited me, lunch *did* sound good.

"Come on!" Fingers linked with Tim's, Val ran up the hill in a funny half-skip with her white flip-flops slapping the sand.

Lance offered me his hand. "Want lunch?"

Following Val wasn't that great of an option, but my stomach rumbled. I sighed and accepted his hand. He pulled me to my feet, and we stopped by Inese for yen.

"Don't forget to meet me at fifteen thirty," she reminded us, pointing to a little white boat at a wooden dock. "And have fun." She tossed her blanket over her shoulder, grabbed our luggage, and then headed toward the shore.

Val led us to a vendor partially hidden by the crowd of vacationers.

At the front of a ten-minute line, the stall consisted of a ceramic container with a metal flap on the top. It opened in a whoosh of steam, where dozens of hotdogs bobbed up and down in boiling water. A man in shorts, a pink t-shirt and a yellow apron stood behind the kiosk. He tried to ask Val something, presumably what she wanted, but she shook her head.

"Do you speak English?" she asked.

"Oh! English . . ." He sounded disappointed, but he was articulate in his pronunciation. "What would you like?"

She grinned and batted her eyes at Tim. "The works."

I glowered at Val, but my attention soon went to the hotdog. Evidently, "the works" involved the vendor taking a minute to scoop relish into a seeded bun before adding shredded cheese, bacon, ketchup, and mustard. He topped that off with onion bits.

My mouth watered and Tim's jaw dropped. "Make that two," Val said, smiling.

Lance laughed. "I want one like that."

"Ketchup and relish," I said quickly, afraid I'd betray myself and say the same. No matter how good that hotdog looked, I was not following Val's lead.

Val shrugged and paid the vendor with Inese's money.

Afterward, we headed down the beach and watched seagulls searching for crumbs. Val found us a spot to sit and talk. I ate quietly, savoring the pickled relish and ketchup smell wafting from the steaming hotdog.

Though I'd had hotdogs before, this one had cheese inside and the meat was more flavorful than anything the Community served. But the hotdog's delicious, savory taste was ruined by Val's cheerful rendition of building sand castles with Tim while I nearly drowned. "How about you?" she asked, turning and flashing me a white, toothy grin.

"We went swimming." I jerked my thumb at Lance. "The water was nice."

"The current was strong, though." Lance glanced at me. His eyes showed concern, though he didn't say it. "I didn't know it was like that."

"Of course." Val nodded between a bite of the hotdog. A drip of relish and mustard fell into the sand, and a seagull hopped closer. "You have to watch for riptides. You don't want to be sucked under, after all. It wouldn't be good to escape a bunch of beasties, only to get lost in the sea."

She pouted, but underneath her innocence, there was a hint of a predatory smile.

"No, it wouldn't," I replied quickly. I pretended to ignore her in favor of watching a boat in the distance.

Lance elbowed me in the ribs and I jumped, surprised by the sudden skin-on-skin contact. "We should come here again."

Sure, once I'd gotten rid of that stupid memory seed that nearly caused me to drown. Once the Community was safe again.

I looked out at the shore. "Yeah . . ."

Across the beach, people laughed and joked around, tossing a colorful ball over their heads. The ball soared high, and one guy disappeared from the sand and reappeared midair, then slammed the ball toward his laughing companions.

He had teleportation. He could freely use his powers here.

I smiled and settled back on my beach towel. Other beachgoers ran and collected seashells or built sand castles. Though some had light tans or bright red, sunburnt skin, almost all of them looked happy; except the one crying kid being chased by a crab.

At least I hadn't stepped on anything with pinchers.

The voices around me turned to white noise, and I watched birds fan out and search for food. Despite Val's giggly chatter, I felt more at peace here than I'd ever felt in the Community.

If only the rest of the world was as relaxing as this. No beasties. No fear of powers.

Clear blue waves lapped on the shore, rising and falling to a soft tempo. They rolled and peaked, but there was no sign of the heavy current that pulled me under.

It was odd. Despite the calm of the surface, there was danger.

CHAPTER
THIRTY–THREE

Inese looked perfectly comfortable in her slick, blue-black wetsuit. She waved as we approached. "About time! Enjoy lunch?" Everyone nodded enthusiastically except me.

"When do we dive?" Val asked.

"As soon as we get you trained. Come on, I want you to meet your instructor." Inese led us up the dock. Considering how small the rusty boat looked from the beach, I was surprised at its actual size. It was a bit larger than a fishing boat, with three decks. A few passengers headed for the upper deck to sightsee and visit private rooms.

Tim twisted his light bulb charm between his fingers. "Is this safe?"

Val clapped him on the back. "Don't be a scaredy cat; of course it's safe! Just pay attention to the lesson."

Considering my experience with the tides earlier, I didn't blame Tim for being nervous. But I wanted to dive. According to my biology book, there were all kinds of unusual plant life underwater, and this time I'd have a rebreather.

The boat lurched as it disembarked, leaving the wooden dock behind. We followed Inese to Toru, a small man with unkempt black hair who spent the next two hours teaching us basic signs and breathing tips. I listened as he showed us how to secure our wetsuits and full-face masks so we could breathe safely. After the course, he had us try on the suits, which were uncomfortably warm in the hot sun.

"They'll feel better underwater, where it's colder," he assured us.

"Ready?" Inese asked through the mask's radio.

She dropped into the water, disappearing and then bobbing up again a couple meters away. Val followed, laughing mercilessly as she grabbed Tim's arm and pulled him in with her. He shrieked and crashed into the water. So not safe.

Lance and I did our best to follow Inese's example. Water burst around me in a muted *whumph*. Toru waved, and the five of us swam downward and deeper, practicing our new diving skills before we reached the ruins. Schools of fish darted around, a tiny rainbow of colors. Aquatic plant life grew on the side of rocks and in the sand below. Barnacles sat aimlessly on their rocky clutches and I drifted downward, where the colorful seaweed trailed in the deep ocean currents. The seaweed felt different than the plant life above water and took longer to mentally touch.

Too bad Mom and Dad couldn't see this. They'd love the view.

Since Inese had the watch, I wasn't sure how much time passed before I realized Tim and Val were nowhere in sight. I checked again, but there were only three of us now.

"Inese? Where are Tim and Val?"

A school of fish zipped by, but otherwise, we were alone.

"I don't see them," Lance said, drifting. "Inese?"

She must've called them privately, because after a moment she answered. "They should be all right. They went back to the boat."

She turned to face me and I saw my reflection in her mask. Her voice garbled. My heart pounded in my ears.

Green bubbles. My reflection, wide-eyed and helpless —

I gasped for breath as my mind tried to latch onto something, anything that would keep me out of Lady Winters' horrible imagination.

A lone fish swam by, and that fish turned into a beastie, forcing me into a tube, the little bubbles pricking my skin —

Lance passed into my vision, motioning to a crop of dull brown seaweed. "Do you like it? There's a lot of cool wildlife here." The stability of plant life seeped between the craggy rocks and into my powers, eliminating the terrible images.

"Yeah—yeah, I do." I gave him the okay sign and mentally thanked him for pulling me out of the nightmare.

"Thought you might. But why didn't they tell me they were heading back? These currents are rougher than I expected. And I can't move easily."

"Landlubber," Inese snorted.

But I was on Lance's side. My legs still hurt from the beastie plant mission, and my suit rubbed mercilessly against the blistered wound of my shoulder.

"Hey guys—come check this out!" Lance called a minute later.

As I neared his location, the murky water cleared. The silhouette of a large, rectangular structure rose from the ocean floor. We still had sunlight, but the colors had faded, lending shadows across the geometric rock.

The whole thing was massive. Steps descended along the perimeter, all perfectly angled. Each was vaguely reminiscent of the ruins we'd seen in Guatemala. As we floated closer, the rock rose on either side of us like a giant stone hall.

Inese paused to brush the mossy growth from the carvings along its face, and small fish darted from the seaweed and disappeared into the distant haze. She chuckled. "Looks like we get to go exploring."

"Is this all stone, or is there any way to get inside?" I asked.

"I could portal in." Sunlight rippled across the formation as Lance swam overhead. "We wouldn't be able to see where we were going, though." He held out his hands and a purple-pink oval swirled into existence in front of him, several meters out—

And closing.

Water surged through the swirling portal, dragging us along. Lance struggled against the current and I grabbed his hand as the ocean pushed us forward. But the short burst of momentum I got from my speed lasted only seconds. I heard my name shouted over the radio, and then water flushed us into darkness.

The portal shut down and we skidded to a slick stop against a stone block.

I gasped for air. "Where are we?"

All those things Toru told us would happen if our suits were damaged . . . My heart skipped a beat. If my suit was damaged, there was no way I could hold off another panic attack.

"I can't see anything." Lance's voice sounded ragged over the radio, but he was right. I couldn't even see my hands. It was like taking the pill, only this time I felt the plants high above the stone vault.

I took a deep breath—

What if I was using what little oxygen I had left? My chest constricted.

One breath at a time. I had to take one steady breath at a time; force myself not to hyperventilate . . .

A dive light lit Lance's feet and slowly passed over us.

"Turn on your lights. Let's see where we are," Inese said.

Lance pressed the button on his wrist's dive light, adding a second light. I did the same. Each beam crossed over the interior of the temple. The floor was covered in large, ancient stone blocks with pillars that rose to a high ceiling. The pillars were covered with Asian inscriptions and drawings, and the room was bigger than I'd expected. This place was *huge*.

"Well, there's why it's not filled with water. Not sure where it drains, though." Inese sounded nervous as she turned her light to a gilded grate that partially covered a large, square hole in the center of the floor. Water trickled into the cracks and disappeared into the hole as if it were a black oblivion.

I shuddered. "Don't step there," I noted. "Got it."

"Right," Lance said. "Is there air here?"

Inese unstrapped her mask and tugged it off, letting her hair fall free. She sniffed the air and made a face, her lips moving but making no sound. Both Lance and I removed our masks.

"It's a bit stale," she said. "Kind of smells like a fish tank—but yeah.

There's air."

The room stank, dank and forgotten, tempting me to put my mask back on. Conserving oxygen was more important, though, so I left it off. I took a deep breath. The air was thin here—my head quickly became woozy . . . I grabbed Lance's shoulder to keep steady, but he cringed and slipped on the slick stone.

Once we had righted ourselves, Inese motioned us to the corner of the vast chamber. Our flippers slapped the uneven rock. An echo rebounded from the walls. A large, Asian dragon had been carved from stone to hunch over a pedestal. Its jade eyes reflected our yellow lights. Each green eye glowed translucent under the light, whereas the gray rock was dull in comparison. It's long, snaking tail curled around the pedestal. The dragon had huge, clawed hands entrapping a bullet-shaped object underneath and, like the first time stone, this one had four gold bands defining it. Instead of Maya design, though, this one appeared entirely Asian in origin. Which particular mythology, I couldn't say. Washed-out paintings covered the interior of the temple, with little jade lion-dog guard statues resting at the feet of the paintings and colorful goldwork tapestries, and tiered rafters half-collapsed above us.

The dragon statue towered over everything, its face frozen in a fierce gaze. I held my breath. Outside, the ocean water murmured around us, currents rippling and sending tremors through the cavernous place.

Inese picked up the stone, then flipped it on its side. "Normally the Coalition doesn't go for tomb raiding, but I don't think anyone's going to miss it." She placed the stone in her bag. "All right, let's—"

The ground rumbled and knocked me against the wet floor. The statue trembled. Chunks and fragments of rock pattered at my feet.

"Of course, I could be wrong." Inese picked herself up and glanced at the crumbling ceiling.

Lance grabbed my hand. A crack snaked along the wall behind the statue. Rushing water spurted first, then poured inside. The ceiling groaned and cracked. I took a hesitant step back as pebbles clattered to the floor.

"Lance, get us out of here!" Inese fumbled with her mask and I did the same. She turned her light toward the dark grate. Water gushed in over the dragon statue, rushing through the grate, same as the rest of the temple. Lance opened a portal in front of us and a torrent of water flung us head over heels, waves trapping us against the wall. We'd be trapped here when the ceiling came crashing down. Lost forever —

The portal reappeared, halfway submerged under the rising water. "Go underneath!" Lance grabbed for my hand and missed. The radio garbled. The muffled din of water disappeared as I ducked under the surface, kicking my legs faster, using my speed until I made it through the portal's lower half. Lance grabbed my wrist, holding it tight, and we worked together to stay on the other side of the portal, clear of the shells and the sand and the unlucky schools of fish being sucked inside.

I choked, unable to breathe.

Stinging bubbles and cries for help . . .

The water moved too fast, too close to be one of the tanks.

Then suddenly, the flow of the water subsided. My legs felt like jelly, and I stopped struggling against the tide, instead hovering in the ocean and catching my breath.

"That was close." Lance turned his whole body to face his work. The portal was underwater now, just a wisp of purple matter before it disappeared. I pumped my hand in Lance's, thankful for his help.

"Good job," Inese said through the radio. "We've got the stone."

A strange reflection formed over her goggles — a pale, flickering glow.

"Guys —" Lance pointed to a bright form above the temple. It flickered, shimmered, then finally shifted so that it resembled the dragon statue. Translucent, bright blue light outlined its gaping, angry mouth and twitching whiskers.

The ghost-like creature was *huge*, even larger than its stone counterpart. I inhaled air; more than I should have. My head spun.

Community — what had we made angry?

CHAPTER
THIRTY–FOUR

Water tumbled around me as Lance created another portal below us. I fell, my sense of direction twisting up to down. Late afternoon sun blinded me. My back hit the ocean's surface. Bubbles swirled like the horrible beastie tanks. Water surged through the portal and I struggled to regain my orientation.

The boat was only a few strokes away—

Inese crashed into me, sending us both reeling into the ocean.

My side stung from the impact. Seconds later, Lance splashed beside me and the portal closed, ending the torrential downpour of seawater.

I reached the boat, numb, and my fingers slipped on the wet steel ladder. But the ladder had little rubber catches to keep me from sliding, and once on deck, I staggered to a wooden bench that was mounted on the side rail.

Inese and Lance went to find Toru while I tugged off my mask. I needed to breathe—to see straight.

No sign of the dragon-spirit-thing. Maybe it stayed at the temple.

"Well, hello again."

I started, gasping, then tried to calm myself. A man in a light t-shirt and shorts sat next to me, shaking his hand. He had reddish-brown, spiky hair and a goatee to match, and he looked familiar, though I couldn't place where I'd seen him before.

"Do I know you?" I asked.

He tossed two small objects at me, grinning. "Can't say you do. Not yet, anyway."

I caught whatever he'd tossed, and stared at him in disbelief.

Couldn't he see I was exhausted?

The man motioned to my hands. "What are the numbers?" His accent reminded me of Inese's — but different.

I unclenched my fingers to see what he'd thrown. The things were made of plastic, brightly colored and numbered on each side. One was a six-sided die with six little dots facing up. The other was rounded, with so many sides I couldn't tell what it was. "Nineteen and six," I said, puzzled.

The stranger nodded. "Reroll the six."

"What?"

"Do it." His smile never faded, and he waited expectantly for me to roll the die. I let it drop from my hand an onto the bench, where it landed on a five. The man whistled. "Well then, that's not so bad. Catonian relics can be such a pain to deal with." He plucked the strange die from my hand and pocketed them both, then gave an exaggerated half bow before he turned his back.

"Interesting game," he said. "Interesting game." And he wandered up the stairs as if nothing was odd at all. It was a good thing he wasn't born in the Community. Mental illnesses didn't get much slack for efficiency. It was one of the things I thought a biology career might help. If we could treat the illnesses —

"Vacation's over." Inese returned to my side, patting her hips for her pistols and grumbling when she realized they weren't there. "Find Tim and Val. Toru said they were resting upstairs. Tell them we're leaving, and alert any other passengers you see that there's a chance that dragon-ghost might come back."

Inese didn't wait for an answer; she disappeared downstairs.

Though I doubted anyone would believe me about the dragon, I ran up the stairs. I paused long enough to yank my flippers off after they nearly tripped me, and then I knocked on several cabin doors, rousing groggy passengers who'd been taking an afternoon nap. After telling a number of angry people they needed to evacuate, I knocked on a door that got no answer.

Inese *did* say they were resting.

I twisted the gold painted doorknob and it rattled. When I finally got the door open, a flurry of movement caught my attention—Tim yanking his black and green swimming trunks high above his waist line. His chest was bare, his shoulders marred by little red bite marks.

Bite marks?

He stared at me, horrified. "What are you doing here?" He grabbed the edge of a rumpled bedspread and quickly covered his upper body, hiding his tell-tale shoulders. The rest of the sheets were half-bunched on the floor.

"What—you were—"

"Who is it?" Val sang sweetly. She peered out from the bathroom door, adjusting her bikini strap back onto her shoulder. Tim spun around, then swallowed hard as he looked between the two of us.

I gawked at her. Tim was the most Community-oriented person I knew. Here we were, searching out time stones and being chased by a *dragon*, and they'd been having sex? He was in no position to have kids!

Val smirked. "Oh hi, Jenny. How was the water?"

If she called me *Jenny* one more time, after all she'd done, I'd—

She paused, looking me over. "You all right? You look like a drowned cat."

Not far from the truth, thanks. "You were supposed to be helping us!"

Val shrugged, adjusting the bikini so that Tim swallowed nervously and smiled. "You guys seemed to be handling the investigation well enough. Tim and I thought we'd take a break."

"A break? So you seduced him?"

She sighed. "Right . . . Community standards. Look, it's not my fault you can't focus on anything but business. You might try paying attention to Lance sometime; he's got the hots for you."

"There are more important things to worry about!" I lunged at Val, but Tim grabbed me around the stomach and I flailed, swatting his shoulders as he struggled to hold me back.

For being navigation, he had more strength in him than I'd expected. But I jabbed my elbow into his arm and he let go, shaking his hand as if I'd hit his funny bone.

I closed my hand into a fist and swung at Val, but she stepped out of the way, her bottom lip exposing the tips of her fangs.

"If you weren't so busy flirting, maybe we could actually do something productive!" I snapped.

"There's more to life than work. Can you blame us for wanting to relax? I mean, you've lived in the *Community* all your life. What a drag!"

I raged at her, wanting to shout but not able to form the words in my mouth.

"Jenna. Jenna!" Tim grappled with me, holding me back. "Don't hurt her —"

I thrust my knee into his stomach and he toppled. He'd only known her for a whopping week, and they'd abandoned us while we were getting pummeled.

I grasped the metal bed frame to right myself before launching myself at Val, putting all the speed I had behind me. The next thing I knew, the floor dropped and I crashed into the dresser. Someone screamed.

Val stepped back, nervous. "What's going on?"

My tailbone smarted. I rolled away from the heavy furniture, spots dancing in front of my eyes. My shoulder burned and I struggled up from the pitching floor. "If you weren't so busy seducing Tim, you'd know!"

The floor dropped again and I careened into Val. She pushed me off her and Tim grabbed the end of the bed. "There's a dragon ghost-thing attacking the boat," I said. Val's eyes widened and she sprinted out the door, followed by Tim.

Outside, the bright blue dragon weaved in and out of the water, sunlight rippling off its ghostly back. Thin lines rippled in the wake of its tail. A moment later, the dragon reared its lion-like head from the water and hissed, sending a cloud of freezing mist overhead.

The boat dipped and I crashed into the gilded handrails.

For the love of the Community . . .

I ran and kept running until I was at the bottom of the stairs. I slipped, but the man with the goatee and the dice caught me. "Watch out for snake eyes." He grinned.

I gaped at him, but once I had my footing, he headed back up the stairs.

How in the Community could he be so calm? All the other passengers were fleeing for the lifeboats. I shook my head, then yelped as the boat shifted again. I crouched, this time keeping my balance, then cast a glance up the stairs after the man.

I'd seen him before today, but *where?*

Before I made it to the stern, gunfire split through the creaking sounds of the hull. Inese backed away from the railing, sheltering her eyes with one hand while keeping her pistol steady with the other. Her bullets fell into the water, passing harmlessly through the bright dragon.

A glowing arc of light fell over us and the dragon's translucent tail crashed through the center of the boat. The hull shuttered and cracked. Splinters scattered. I fumbled. The rail caught me in the gut. For a moment I just stood there, trying to regain my breath.

"Jenna!"

Lance leaned on the wall next to the cabins, motioning me closer. I weaved toward him.

"What's going on?" I called.

"Bullets don't hurt it, and I don't have my sword," Lance shouted back.

"Bullets don't—and you want to *melee* that thing?"

"Works in Jack's video games." He grabbed my arm as the dragon roared, spraying us with an icy mist that stung my skin. I sheltered my face. The wetsuit protected most of my body, but my armbands would've been nice to have. Protection from falling overboard.

I tried reaching the seaweed below us, but it was too far away. Even speed wouldn't grow it fast enough if I fell.

Lance pulled me against him as a thundering wave crashed into us.

"Val! Get back!" Tim stood halfway between us and Val, watching the bikini-clad seductress raise her hands above her head. She stood at the edge of the deck, electricity crackling between her fingertips. The crackling arced between each hand, brighter and brighter until it formed a steady glow. I lowered my eyes, trying not to be blinded.

Lightning shot into the dragon, blazing white and purple.

It reared and shook its head, then turned a jade-colored eye on Val. Its tail whipped through the air and thrashed the rear of the boat. Inese and Toru slammed against the cabin wall on the other side of Lance, and Tim crashed into me.

Electricity sparked around the rail, dimming the boat's lights and collecting in Val's hands. She thrust her free hand outward, sending the lightning directly into the dragon's ghostly apparition.

The dragon roared and slammed its tail along the surface of the ocean, sending a torrent of water rushing against the tilting boat. Val's lightning persisted, the bright arcs lashing relentlessly.

The dragon moaned, twisted, and then vanished. Only a fading glow of light remained where it had been.

Val collapsed and slid down the floor's incline.

"Val!" Tim scrambled to right himself, kicking his foot off my stomach. I gulped for air, glad to have him off me. Lance offered me a hand. I pulled myself up and leaned on him, too shaky to have any real balance.

How did Val know electricity would hurt it?

Inese knelt beside Val and checked her pulse. Toru called for survivors.

"You all right?" Inese asked. Val coughed and nodded. She was drenched in salt water and, curled up, she didn't look nearly as annoying as she did when she bounced around, flirting with Tim.

She rubbed her eyes and peered over the sea. Broken scraps of wood and metal bobbed in the dark water. The surface glimmered in the orange sunset, broken by debris.

"Yeah, I'm fine," Val said. "Is the dragon gone?"

A pang tightened in my chest. She'd zapped me with lightening and seduced Tim. But this was the second time she'd saved my life.

"Come on. Let's get our stuff out before it gets waterlogged." Inese led us into the lower deck and stashed what we had in her bag—a lacy blouse and skirt for Val and Gwen's worn outfit, in my case.

Water poured into the boat through long, splintery cracks, and we sloshed through wide puddles on the wooden stairs. "Portal us close to shore," Inese told Lance. "Stay over the ocean, though; I don't want to mix the molecules of a bunch of vacationers."

Lance did what she asked. Cold, murky water lapped against my skin, but my wetsuit provided welcome relief. My muscles shook from the commotion as I swam back to shore. I clambered onto solid ground. Hot clumps of sand stuck to my hands and feet and nestled between my toes. My tongue felt thick in my mouth as I treaded the sandy hill, ignoring the stares of surprised sunbathers packing up for the day.

Behind them, the evening sky gave everything a red, shadowy cast, silhouetting the survivors as they dropped out of the portal into the ocean. Lance put his hand on my shoulder, steadied himself, and then nodded appreciatively.

Inese removed her sunglasses from her bag, and once the survivors were safe, we trudged up the hill through shadowy, colorless forms. My feet stung from the path with its sharp, hidden twigs, and I urged the nearby roots to wriggle under my feet for solace. I tried to pull the roots together for Lance as well, but I was too tired to make any progress.

Once we reached the parking lot, the burning heat trapped in the pavement felt better than the gravelly path. Inese led us through a long row of cars. Finally, we reached ours. Val slid into the backseat and coaxed Tim in beside her. Lance left me to take shotgun.

Inese cranked up the air conditioner. Cold air cycled out the hot humidity and the smell of the warm, leather seats. The cold gave me a headache from the moisture on my skin, but my upper shoulders throbbed from the beginnings of a sunburn.

"You did a great job," Tim whispered. "Saving us from that dragon." Val giggled softly. Too tired, I guessed, to be more enthusiastic than that. I squinted at the shadowy terrain, trying to focus on something other than Val and Tim's cutesy whispers. But everything was too dark to be of any use. The last of the sun died beyond the horizon and cloaked this half of the world in the shadow of night.

"We're here."

I awoke to a bright, mid-day sun blinding my eyes. I winced, stretching, but an invisible seat belt restrained me. It was the one comfort against the sense of waking up as nothing, with no body, sitting against some imaginary force like the dragon we'd just fought.

Inese flew the car into the airship and the hangar door closed on the puffy white clouds. We landed with sea legs jittery from flight, and I waited until everyone else dispersed before heading upstairs, grabbing what turned out to be an expired burrito, and then hiding in my room for the rest of the day.

I didn't want to hear everyone praising Val for the wonderful job she did, or how she'd rescued us all.

After dinner, I pulled Lance aside.

He yawned and stretched his arms. "Yeah?"

"Do you know what Tim and Val were doing while we were gone?"

"Does it matter?" He gave me a sleepy look and scratched his chin. He needed to shave. The pale brown stubble made his cheeks look rough. Even his untrimmed hair was starting to get shaggy, and it didn't help that he was wearing one of Jack's old, ragged t-shirts.

"Tim's our friend, and Val . . . seduced him." What if she'd seduced Lance, instead? She'd said that he —

I blinked. We were just friends. Lance knew that.

"Are you sure he didn't seduce her? Maybe he decided to make a move. I mean, she *is* attractive." Lance stifled another yawn.

He called Val attractive. He actually . . . My chest tightened.

Lance put his hand on my shoulder. "Come on, Jen, it's time for bed. What does it matter to you, anyway?" He looked at me with an expression I couldn't place.

I gulped. "It's just . . . he's *Tim* and he's always been focused on the Community and now he's just throwing that all away, for *her*. I'm worried for him."

Lance sighed. "Val saved our lives. She's saved yours twice."

"There's something wrong with her! Can't you see—" No, I didn't think he could. It was a gut instinct even I didn't understand. I sighed. "Never mind. Goodnight, Lance. I'll talk to you in the morning."

"Maybe you'll be in a better mood then." He rubbed his eyes and patted my shoulder, then shut the door behind him. I stared at that door for too long, stunned.

He didn't see the problem, and so far, the only thing Val had done was steal my friend and save my life. I gnawed at the edge of my lip. There was no one in the hall right now. Val was upstairs, trumpeting her victory with late night talk.

There had to be some reason I didn't trust her.

When no one was looking, I snuck into Val's room.

CHAPTER
THIRTY–FIVE

Val's silver bikini and thong lay crumpled on the corner of her desk, water dripping down the side. The airship's hum masked the door's creak as I closed and relocked it. I remembered what Jack said about not getting caught, and I wanted a fair warning if Val returned before I finished my search.

I tiptoed to the wooden desk and opened the first drawer. It rattled louder than I expected.

Nothing.

Each drawer was empty. Val hadn't even bothered to unpack her briefcase. I searched around for half a minute, checking the bathroom and the closet and any of the places the briefcase could've been hidden, then turned and found it stashed between the bed and the desk, almost out of sight. It slid out easily, and I noted which way the locks faced so I could slide it back correctly. Then I felt out the locks, checking each wheel for the hesitance that signified I'd found my number. The locks clicked open on my second try, each snap echoing in the bare room.

The first thing in the briefcase was another black outfit—a short, ruffled skirt and a halter top with lace for sleeves. I sat it aside. Beneath that lay a shiny silver and white jumpsuit cut low around the neck. Made of smooth, stretchy fabric, it resembled both Val's swimsuit and a leader's outfit. Though Val had the confidence and spunkiness of most leaders I knew from the Community, I doubted the likelihood she'd be one.

I scooted the clothes out of the way and found a glass vial filled with white, oblong pills.

Adominogen.

If a life-spirit person took even part of a pill . . .

I stashed the vial in my pocket. Though Val hadn't been here long, maybe she had drugged Gwen. I reached into the bottom layer of the briefcase and the doorknob rattled.

Val!

I thrust the outfits back into the briefcase and crammed it shut, hoping she wouldn't notice the lacy sleeve sticking out the edge. The door's lock clicked and I tossed the briefcase behind the desk. If she needed to use the restroom, it wouldn't be safe for me to hide there. I dove under the bed.

Val stepped in and paused, but I couldn't see above her ankles. My heart pumped and my hands shook. She had lightning, and if she didn't want me alive, I wouldn't be hard to kill.

"That's odd," she said. "I thought I put my clothes away better than that."

I flinched.

"Anyway, come in." Another set of feet followed, this time with Community pant legs. Val moved to sit, and something *thunked* the low mattress. "Close the door, Sexy."

"Are you sure?" It was Tim's voice and — *what* did she just call him? "I mean, Jenna seemed pretty mad when she found us."

No duh. They went off on personal leisure time while I was out getting chased by a dragon.

"Don't worry about Jenna; it's not like you like her."

Tim sat beside her. "Of course not. I love *you*."

I groaned inwardly at the sap dripping from Tim's voice, then glanced around the bottom of the bed. Considering Val zapped me along with the beastie, she probably zapped eavesdroppers, too. I tensed, not keen on experiencing that again.

"I like you, too, Tim. I enjoyed our little thing earlier. You were really hot, you know?"

"Really?" Tim sounded surprised. "You were pretty good, too."

Too. Much. Information. I wanted to plant my face in my hands, except there wasn't enough room between the bed and the floor.

"Jenny's too wound up. I mean . . . I think she's just jealous I got you first. Who wouldn't like you? You're a prodigy. You're smart, cute, and what you can do with technology is amazing. You only recently found out you have those powers?"

"Yeah—I did." Tim sounded more macho than usual.

"Impressive." She drew the word out, savoring each annoyingly placed syllable, then picked her feet off the floor and plopped on the bed. I could almost swear she aimed for my head. "I've always thought being able to use computers like you can would be awesome. You're really lucky."

"Really?"

"Really." Static electricity danced along the floor and I edged away from the metal bedposts. I couldn't see above her calves, but given that her gothic attire soon followed the electricity, I was glad I couldn't.

They continued chatting about technology and the Community and territories, and every so often Val made a jab at me as if she *knew* I was hiding under the bed, which was impossible—she would've called me out.

Unless her insight told her.

My heart sank. I couldn't stop them from seeing each other, and I couldn't very well convince Lance to open a portal outside the ship for Val to walk through. He'd just remind me that she'd saved my life. Other than those pills, I had no reason to suspect her for anything.

So . . . Lance was right. I was being cranky.

My legs cramped and my head throbbed from lack of sleep. When the bed shifted subtly above me I cringed. Tim's shirt joined Val's on the floor. I fiercely hoped this wasn't going anywhere private. They didn't know I was under the bed, so—

I wrinkled my nose and waited for the inevitable, but thankfully, they only murmured cutesy little whispers: Val had a "lovely" mole on the back of her neck and Tim had a soft spot for lily scented perfume.

Half an hour later, when I was certain they'd fallen asleep, I crawled out.

Hot spikes of pain shot up one leg while pins and needles shot down the other. I chewed at the inside of my cheek to keep from squawking, hopping on each foot and not daring to look back to see if they'd seen me.

I closed the door softly. The hallway lights were dim. No one was around to catch me sneaking. I stumbled into my room, exhausted, and fell asleep.

At zero three thirty, I woke to shuffling in the hallway. Soft, hurried voices . . . I fell against the light switch and flipped it on, then stuck my head outside. Except Val's open door, the hallway was empty.

Hadn't I closed that?

Maybe Tim had returned to his room, and that's what I'd heard. I leaned against the wall to keep my legs from protesting, then peeked inside. Val's room was bare. The sheets were messy, as if someone had slept there, but the silver swimsuit and the briefcase were gone.

Dazed, I stumbled to Tim's room and knocked. He didn't answer.

I opened the door. The sheets of his bed were tucked in, no sign of Tim. His desk drawers were devoid of clothes. His tablet was gone.

"Lance!" I shrieked, running to his room and pounding on the door. "Lance, get up!" I continued banging on the door until a groggy Lance showed his face.

"Val and Tim are gone . . . everything, their belongings . . . gone!"

Lance mumbled something about needing to save me from a dragon, his eyes half-closed.

Dragon? I stared at him. Val had known exactly how to defeat the dragon. What if she had been expecting it? Gwen *had* reported an electric elemental around the site of the Maya stone.

A cold chill ran through me.

"Wake Inese—I've got to see if Jim still has the stones." I raced up the stairs, leaving Lance standing in the doorway.

Please still be there . . .

Though Jim was tired, he didn't seem angry that I woke him. He opened the box where he was keeping the stones, then faltered.

"Are they still there?" I asked.

"Yes, but Brainmaster's pendant is not." He straightened his back and frowned. "Val must have taken it."

"Why would she want the pendant if she was here for the stones?"

"She might not have come for the stones. Check with Inese and see if you can get the car prepped for travel. I will alert Pops to the situation."

I nodded and dashed downstairs, where I found Inese giving Lance a perplexed look. He mumbled something about me and dragons and Val riding off on a pegasus.

"Val and Tim are gone, and so is the pendant," I babbled, not waiting for Lance to get his story straight.

Inese bolted from the door, still in pajamas. I used my speed to keep up as she dashed into the hangar bay. She swore the moment she entered. "Go wake Crush," she said fiercely. "They stole the car. I'll get Pops."

"Jim's already going to—"

She was already halfway up the first flight of stairs, and she continued cursing to Pops' room, her English accent coming on heavier than usual.

Crush, like everyone else, didn't want to wake. But he reached the navigation room in no time once he understood what was going on. Pops and Inese joined him, and Jim came shortly after.

I'd never seen the crew so alert.

"I can't track them," Crush said. "Tim must have disabled it."

"How did they know to do that?" Inese demanded. "Or fly the car, for that matter?" Her face twisted in anger, making me think twice about saying "I told you so" in regards to not trusting Val.

"Techno sight," Crush said. "Tim can adapt to almost any technology."

"Where's the tracking program?" Inese dropped a disk back into a cardboard box.

"One moment . . ." He punched a button at the top of the screen. "There's no way to tell where they went unless someone here has psychic tracking they want to tell me about."

"Tracking program!" Inese demanded. She brought the control panel onscreen, her lips twisted in a grimace.

"Still looking." Crush ducked under the console and accidentally smacked his head on the bottom of the desk. "Where'd that disk go?" he muttered, rubbing the sore spot. I pointed to the box of disks on the side wall, stunned by the flurry of movement. Crush didn't really stop well, and the disks went flying.

Lance stood half-dressed in the doorway, his eyes lit with anticipation. "Do we have anything we can follow them with?"

Inese shook her head. "Just the whirligig." She glanced at Crush. "Let me know if you find something."

"We'll find your car, don't worry." He held up a disk.

Inese nodded and then disappeared out the door.

The whirligig sat on the other side of the hangar, an egg-shaped pod ratcheted together with steel bolts and covered in brass plates. It stood on tiny round wheels and had a round, fan-like rotor above and on each side.

I'd forgotten that rusty contraption was here.

Inese propped the door open and scooted around a leather semicircle seat until she sat behind the control panel. The whirligig trembled and whirred. "Close the door," she said.

Lance fastened the steel latch as I took a seat.

The hangar opened and the whirligig lifted, crawling out as Inese guided it with a leather joystick and old fashioned knobs.

"Can it move any faster?" I asked.

"No. The car's our fastest method of transportation."

"We need to get Tim back. Val must've tricked him into stealing the car for her."

"Good luck. If Val's with the Camaraderie, Tim won't last long."

I swallowed hard. I should've stayed in Val's room longer. I could've stopped her from kidnapping him. But how? Without my armbands, I was powerless. At least Lance was a good fighter. Maybe if I confronted Val, I could use my speed to trip her and let Lance make the final strike. Maybe . . .

The sound of the ratcheting engine changed and I started awake.

Lance dozed on the other side of the cabin.

"Where are they?" I asked.

Inese snorted, only taking her eyes off the window to check the readings and dials on the control board. "I don't know. We won't find them tonight."

"We're letting her kidnap Tim? He's our friend!"

Inese gave me a cold, weary look. "We're not getting him back, Jenna. We'll be lucky if one of the undergrounds can tell us where the car is. But this thing demolishes fuel, and fact of the matter is, it's too slow. Val and Tim are long gone. Even if we did figure out which way they went, what are we going to do, shoot them?"

None of us had weapons, though Inese probably had something stashed under the seats. I leaned against the lumpy cushions, watching Lance occasionally wake, only to fall asleep again when he realized nothing had changed. He looked peaceful in his sleep, like he did in the Community when he didn't always carry his sword with him.

"In all honesty," Inese said softly, "I needed fresh air. We never had a chance of catching them in this thing."

"We have to rescue Tim somehow," I said, but Inese shook her head and continued flying.

CHAPTER
THIRTY-SIX

The next morning, I searched Val's room. It was as empty as last night, the bedding untouched. I tore off the sheets, looking for something—anything—that would tell me about Val.

I disassembled the desk. I removed its drawers and examined the chair, and even checked underneath it. But the desk—like the bathroom, closet and lights—had only the usual scratches and dents. I hoisted the chair by its legs, examining the skid pads, and then finally dropped to my knees and scooted underneath the bed frame, expecting to find a floor swept clean by my shirt.

Instead, I found Val's swimsuit with a soggy note attached.

> *Jenny—Here, you need this more than I do. I hope you took some*
> *tips while you were underneath the bed. Lance also likes lily*
> *scented perfume, he said so himself. You might get some.*
> *Makeup wouldn't hurt either. Enjoy. ;-)*
>
> *– Val*

Blood rushed to my cheeks and I jerked out from under the bed. My head bumped a small metallic object that was latched to the underside of the frame. The object was wedged firmly between the slats and the mattress. I cursed, mostly at Val, and after a minute of fiddling with the fussy thing, pried it out.

The object was flat and smooth on one side, with a set of serial numbers. The other side was rounded, with a small red LED in the center. It flashed a slow, steady pulse. I grasped it in my hand and headed to the command room.

"Inese?"

Pops stood beside her and Crush, monitoring the random pings while I handed Inese the device, now warm from where I'd held it. Her half-asleep daze transformed into shock.

"Where'd you find this?"

"Under Val's bed," I said. "What is it?"

Crush snatched the device from Inese's hand and darted to one of the porthole windows.

A portal whooshed open behind me, followed by a loud thunk. A man in bright yellow armor, something like a beefed-up construction zone outfit, slid down the side of the main computer station.

"Who put that there?" he grumbled, rubbing his bruised forehead.

Inese unhooked both pistols from her belt and aimed them at the portal.

I backed to the door. A buzzing noise filled the room and a dark swarm appeared through the portal. Large bumblebees landed on me and I swatted at them, trying to keep them from stinging my hands. A few landed on my face and my hair. I shrieked, flailing as their stingers bit me. I'd been stung by bees before, but these left spreading green and black bruises, painful to the touch.

I used my speed power to escape, then hurtled at the yellow-clad momentum guy, the one who'd left a dent in the side of the computer station. A bright fireball flashed over my shoulder and scorched the metal wall. Another man stepped through, his hands covered in flames. His eyes glinted in the firelight and the last man to come through the portal quickly disappeared behind it.

I spun around. I didn't have my armbands or the gun Inese gave me. I hadn't thought I'd need them.

Pops took aim at the fire elemental. "Stand down," he commanded.

"You're guilty of terrorizing the Community," Fire Guy said. "And you'll fetch a nice bounty from the Camaraderie."

Bounty?

The swarm of bees zoomed toward Pops. Crush crumpled, grasping the computer station and whimpering from the bright red welts that mingled with the spreading bruises on his hands and face. Inese dashed behind the computers, trading gunfire with the last man.

Crush needed to get to safety. I moved toward him, but fire crackled and the ceiling tiles cracked overhead. I covered my face as red-hot debris fell from the ceiling. An explosive force of flame threw me against the wall, heat burning my skin—

Seconds later I woke and gasped for air, tears running down my cheeks as the entire front of my body stung, painful to the touch.

The fire user didn't just throw little fireballs—he sent entire columns of blue flame at his opponents. One of our secondary computers was little more than a twisted heap of metal and plastic, and I had plenty of burns from the fallen debris.

But while I was out, someone had shot the man in the shoulder. He crept along the wall and raised his hand toward Pops.

Fire Guy was going to kill my grandfather.

I wanted so badly to wrap vines around Fire Guy's legs and trip him, crush him to the point that his windpipe was pulp. I wanted Inese's skill with guns, or for Lance to be here. But I didn't have any of those things.

I pushed myself to my hands and knees, wincing at the burns. My hand brushed a smoldering piece of debris, a jagged ceiling tile with a twisted metal edge. I stared at it, numb. It was like the pointed end of a spear. I didn't have my plants, but I had speed.

Inese moved toward Fire Guy and raised her gun for the kill shot. Behind her stood the yellow-clad intruder, his nose covered in blood. He ran at her, building momentum . . .

"Inese!" I shouted.

She spun, pony-tail flying as she jumped out of the way and went invisible.

Fire Guy paused near Pops' hideout. Blue fire laced across the palm of his hand, flickering and sending off tiny tendrils of gray smoke.

He turned his attention to my grandfather.

"Hey, you!" I threw a piece of ceiling tile at him, then *ran*.

The room blurred, but Fire Guy seemed unbelievably slow, his eyes trained on the debris I'd thrown. He didn't even register that I was coming at him, the uncomfortably warm piece of metal in my hand. I rammed it into his throat, but I wasn't prepared for the effect of speed. My fist punched his windpipe, and there was an awkward *crunch* before I dropped my power.

The fight resumed and he fell. His fire vanished. Pops stared at him, eyes wide, and then he looked at me with surprise.

"Fall back! Cripple their ship—" The construction guy vanished through the portal, and the others did as they'd been told.

Inese cursed and reappeared, this time beside the computer console. She slammed her hand on the keypad. "This is the Coalition. We need assistance. Anyone in the area, we need assistance—"

Something smashed into the hull of the ship.

Hot ceiling debris pattered around me and I crashed into the wall. There was another explosion, and everything went fuzzy.

※

A flashlight beam shined on my face, and a dark hand reached down and cleared rubble from my body. I stared at the ceiling, unable to move. "Over here," a voice said.

I tried to breathe and began panicking when I couldn't. I needed air—

"Easy . . . easy there. Keep still." The woman who spoke had dark brown skin and wore an olive green uniform, a cap pulled over her hair. I tried to ask what happened, but my lips were too swollen to speak.

Another shadow leaned over me, and I realized all the lights were off, even the computer's glow. If the airship was damaged, we couldn't go after Tim, car or not. "A Camaraderie bounty ship got wind of your location," the woman said, gently touching my shoulder. "They blew a hole in your cargo hold before we drove them off. We're making repairs now, and trying to find anyone who hasn't been accounted for."

"Did —" My voice caught in my throat. "Is everyone alive?"

The woman nodded. "Now that we found you, yes."

I rested my head against the debris. "Thank the Community." Every muscle hurt, and the knot in my neck sent pain through my spine. But everyone was alive. Inese was alive. Pops was alive.

Lance was alive.

"Go ahead and start the healing process," the woman said. The light shone in my eyes and I cringed, unable to block it. The beam silhouetted the shape behind it, but I recognized the jagged spikes of hair, the goatee on his chin. The guy from the boat. I stared at him, coughing and trying to shy away, but the ceiling tiles pinned me down. Pain seared through my upper body.

"You won't feel a thing," he said, and I drifted like I did in the invisible car. My heart pounded. I was terrified I'd lose grips with reality.

"Who are you?" I whispered.

He smiled, his straight teeth shining in the flashlight beam. "Just be glad you didn't die this time."

This time? Chills ran through my body. "What do you mean?"

The pain lifted. My whole body went numb, like in the beastie tanks. The man placed a hand on my shoulder — *through* my shoulder — and I shuddered at the coldness radiating from it.

"Who are you?" I screamed. The coldness spread, blackness radiating over my eyes.

I was hallucinating. I had to be. It was the only explanation.

You're delirious, he whispered, but his voice entered my thoughts, not my ears. There was the sound of dice hitting the floor, and I fainted.

I bolted awake, my body wrapped in bandages and a thick, oily substance. It wasn't the first time after the attack that I'd woken with that recollection, but I didn't remember anything more than that.

A man with short brown hair and brown skin, who wore an olive green uniform and a Red Cross patch, stood above me. "Glad to see you're awake."

The airship's hum echoed off the walls. Someone . . . Lance . . . told me that a South African scout team had helped us. That I was pulled out of the rubble by one of their medics.

Lance waited by my bed until I was fully awake. He soothed my terror every time I woke; every time I freaked out and thought I was hallucinating and had theophrenia. Beyond that, I didn't remember much except the spiky-haired man with his telepathic voice.

CHAPTER
THIRTY–SEVEN

There were three weeks after the attack where I had little memory, except that I'd been bed-ridden, delirious from the burns, and dreaming of beastie tanks or the strange man and his dice. Gwen was still weak from her temporary loss of powers, and though she'd been able to offer some assistance in healing us after the attack, she wasn't yet strong enough to remove Lady Winters' memory seed from my mind.

We hadn't heard anything from Tim or Val either.

I dropped my bowl into the sink. I'd promised Jack I would check on Gwen after breakfast and then I planned to continue my usual routine of power practice, video games, and self-imposed homework.

"We have a lead!" Inese stepped into the cafeteria, grinning. She clapped a hand on Crush's back. "The car is at the Cuban Camaraderie base. Looks like we're going on your joyride after all."

"Not the whirligig?" Crush smirked, earning a glare from her. He still had a few red pockmarks from the bee stings, but the greenish bruises had cleared.

"That thing isn't a joyride," she muttered.

I pushed my waffle aside. If the car was in Cuba, then . . . "Any word on Tim?"

Inese shook her head. "No, sorry. Anyway, Pops is taking us down for a briefing with the Cuban Resistance so we'll know how to coordinate."

Crush blinked. "We're coordinating?"

She plopped into the seat next to him. "I'm guessing their spies accidentally stumbled onto the car. Contacting us just gives them the extra firepower for whatever they've got planned." She didn't sound terribly fond of the idea, but as much as I wanted to question them why, I needed to check on Gwen.

I lingered a moment longer, then excused myself and found Gwen in her room, propped against a number of pillows with a thick, yellow paperback in her hands. She still had a rasping cough, and I doubted that healing us had helped.

"Feeling any better?" I asked.

Gwen glanced at me over her glasses and sat the book in her lap. "A bit. Jack sent you?"

I nodded, feeling bad that I hadn't come of my own accord.

She smiled wryly. "You can tell him I'm feeling better — and that he might let the soup warm for another minute before serving it. I'm not *that* old."

I chuckled. At least she wasn't offended. "Of course. I'll do that. Are your powers returning?"

She nodded. *To an extent.*

"That's good." I smiled.

During the times she was awake, she had told the others she couldn't feel her powers — no sense of life, no stray thoughts. It was a week after the attack before they returned.

"By the way, Inese said that the Cuban Resistance found the car. We're supposed to coordinate to get it back."

"The Cuban Resistance," she murmured. "I'm not surprised. Be careful, Jenna. We have few enough friends as it is."

I doubted Gwen realized it, but I had a momentary feeling of a ship crowded with energetic people. The picture on the wall, the one with Jim and Gwen, reminded me of how few remained.

The next day we gathered anything we might need — body armor, for those who had it, along with weapons — then met in the hangar. I brought my electric spear and vines.

"We need everyone on this mission," Pops told us, "though Gwen and Jim will stay. I'll come with you to the briefing, but then I must return."

"So — I'm actually going on a mission?" Crush asked, preemptively dressed in a dark gray and blue jumpsuit. "Stretch my legs, remember what the *ground* feels like, and fresh air . . ."

Inese chuckled, but Pops shook his head in resignation. "Yes, you can go. Jim will manage the ship. We need all the help we can get, especially since you know how to hack security systems. "

Crush cracked his knuckles and flexed his fingers. "Not a problem."

"Are you set?" The pilot's voice was thick with a Spanish accent. Jack agreed, and the pilot led us into a sleek, silver jet. We fastened our seat belts in seated rows with no windows. The jet's chilly air made me glad to have my jacket.

After the engines warmed, rumbling and shaking the whole contraption, the jet took off faster than the car. I enjoyed the rushing feeling in the pit of my stomach, but I soon realized we wouldn't be going invisible. Invisibility would've been nice. I could've ignored the talk about Val and Tim's betrayal and the speculation on how we'd get the car back.

Several hours later, we landed. A few clouds obscured the stars in the dark purple sky above us, and a wave of moist heat smashed into me.

"Come on." Our pilot ducked into a path hidden by guava, eucalyptus, allspice trees . . . and so many more I couldn't name. Another plane's blue and red lights blinked far overhead. Once we were hidden, the pilot motioned for us to stay put.

"I must hide the jet before it is spotted," he told us. "A woman will come and take you the rest of the way."

"We could guide ourselves," Jack muttered, earning a jab from Inese's elbow. The pilot disappeared. The forest came alive with chirruping and croaking that started slowly at first, then abruptly reached a crescendo.

It was loud enough to conceal the sound of our next guide, a woman with dark curls bouncing around her face. She wore a green uniform that looked stifling in this heat. I considered stripping off my own jacket, but I didn't want to bother removing my vines. Not when I was already trying to maneuver the spear through our clustered group.

The woman said something I couldn't understand, then added, "Come on! Go!" when only Inese and Jack followed.

Compared to the rest of the team, I had the most luck taking the hidden trail. I urged the vines to either side of the path, making it easier for everyone else, and soon found myself pushed to the front.

Shortly into the trek, our guide raised her fist and Inese halted. Lance nearly toppled into me. Meanwhile, our guide knelt to the jungle floor and brushed away dead leaves that concealed a concrete slab. She held her tablet next to it, typed in a code, and the concrete rose with a creak.

"Underground bunker," she explained.

She scooted her legs into the hole, then descended. Rusted metal rungs led into darkness, and I wasn't entirely sure I wanted to go into a hole where I didn't sense much in the way of plant life. It felt like a trap, especially after the "abandoned" warehouse didn't turn out so abandoned.

I climbed down and the muggy air closed in around me. It was slow going. I couldn't see anything, and I didn't want to step on Pops' hands or miss a rung. My foot slipped and I yipped, quickly snatching the upper bar. I narrowly missed Pops' head.

Lance looked down. "You okay?"

My foot touched solid metal. "I'm fine," I said, though I tightened my hands around the rungs to keep them from trembling. The top of Pops' salt and pepper hair, nearly white, was barely visible, while Lance's silhouette loomed above me.

I released my breath when my feet touched the floor, but the floor was slick and the room smelled damp, like a fish tank needing to be cleaned. A hand on my shoulder led me around the corner. Two streams of light flared on us, but Pops ushered me forward, past the blinding lights of the uniformed guards pointing assault rifles our direction. My fingers twitched from anxiety, but the guards probably felt safe.

Lucky them.

I glanced over my shoulder. "Where are we going?"

"The Cuban underground," Pops said. "It is quite literally beneath the surface. You'll see in a moment."

Our guide led us through a bulkhead door into a large cavern—a huge room filled with stalactites and stalagmites, pools of silently moving water, and the hum of dozens of computers. Everywhere the blue and white glow of computer screens cast heavy shadows. Men and women, some in uniform while others wore a t-shirt and camo pants, typed at the computers or delivered tablets between the stations. At the center of the spotlighted cave was a large oval console with a ring of screens glowing above, and data and schematics flowing down each. Every screen was different, and I suspected the security camera feeds were tapped from the Camaraderie's base. Most of the halls were identified, though there were entire sections of the map left blank.

"Wow," I whispered. Tim would have loved this. But he was probably dead, or worse, turned into a beast. I fingered Lady Winters' identity charm. We'd find Tim, and eventually, we'd find Lady Winters, too. And when we did, we wouldn't let her escape. She'd answer for her crimes against the Community, and we'd find some way to stop beast creation.

"Don't worry," Jack said, shoving me and Lance forward. After he got feeling better, he'd thrown us through more training to ensure we could each use our powers as effectively as possible. "You two have plenty of time to look around. Pops has some persuasion to do if we want to know what the Cubans got planned for us."

Pops set off behind a wall of natural stone, walking next to a broad-chested man with gold cords draped over each shoulder, while I spent the next half hour trailing Inese and Crush.

Once Pops returned, the resistance leader, a general, called out his people. Fifteen men and women took their places around the console and were joined by the Coalition. Most of the rebels looked fairly young — in their early twenties and thirties — compared to the general.

Half of the conversation was Spanish. The gist of it, when they spoke English, was that they would supply "guards" to act as distractions so we could get in and find the car. It was parked in one of the outdoor landing bays, so we would need to get past the real Special Forces agents.

The rebels had their own agenda, though, which sounded a lot like it involved explosives. Our job was to get where we needed before anyone was discovered.

"We infiltrate the base at ten hundred hours," the general said. "We should be able to slip in unnoticed while the COE works on this secret project of theirs." He turned to Jack. "You will need to be out before our people finish."

Pops raised his chin, and I wondered if it was the same project he'd been concerned about three weeks ago. Jack crossed his arms, examining the schematics of the base. "How long will we have?"

"Not sure," the general admitted. "That's the tricky part. All we know is that they're creating something secret enough that their own officers don't know the details."

"Your spies indicated an increase in the number of beasties present. Will we have to worry about them?" Inese asked.

One of the younger women spoke up. "That's the odd thing." Her English was a bit better than the others, so I understood what she said. "They've brought in more beasties, but they aren't roaming the facility or acting as guards. They've been put in a high clearance room. None of our operatives have been able to get past."

"Needless to say, you will need to be careful." The general touched his fingers to the console. An image of the car, partially obscured by an airship, popped onto the screen.

Crush rubbed his chin. "What type of beasties are they? At least we can know what we're up against."

"It varies," a different spy said. "Several of them have laser eyes, judging by the state of the COE's trucks. Others don't have any obvious traits, except shapeshifting and armored skin."

My imagination went to work picturing what a beastie that had lasers for eyes would look like, or one that could turn into other beasties, or was covered in metal plates like a knight from Jim's history book.

"Anything else? The more we know, the better off we'll be," Crush urged.

"Agreed," the general said. "So you should also know that once the all clear is given, we'll take out the facility — even if you're inside."

"Even if we're inside?" I protested. "What if there are other civilians or prisoners? They might not have a chance to escape."

I had no problems with destroying the beastie plants or even the base, but there had to be a way to protect the innocent.

The general shook his head. "We have a limited amount of time. There are rarely no casualties in war."

I started to protest, but both Pops and Jack shook their heads. I crossed my arms and scowled. If they were agreeing on something, they must have some reason.

"So we'll get out before the bombs start smoking," Jack said. He glanced at me, but I couldn't read his expression.

"Why is it important to blow up the base so quickly?" I asked. "Shouldn't we be trying to rescue any prisoners?"

The general raised his chin and tucked his hands behind his back, giving him an air of solemn importance. "This is our one chance to knock out the Camaraderie's entire council."

Pops stared at him. "The entirety of the Camaraderie's leadership is at this base?"

The general grinned. "*Sí.*"

CHAPTER
THIRTY–EIGHT

After the briefing, the Cubans escorted us down several narrow corridors that dropped bits of rock and water from the ceiling. A concrete platform overhung a rusted track, and thin green rope lights cast a dim glow over us, revealing worn pipes that showed through the cracks. The rails ran through a slightly wider corridor punctuated by faint, dim red bulbs.

"We'll take the carts to a storeroom inside the base. Our team will enter first, as part of their security force, and we'll do what we can to distract the actual guards from noticing your entry," our guide said.

Jack thumped me on the shoulder. "Better make sure yer vines are ready. If we're seen, there's gonna be fighting. They won't think we're prisoners."

"Not to mention their shoot first, ask questions later mentality," Crush said.

I grimaced and held my spear tighter. Lance nervously twisted his swords, and Inese double-checked the ammo in her pistols. Crush did the same. Jack watched us with his arms crossed over his jacket. His claws were nasty enough on their own, but he could swipe Lance's second sword if he needed one.

Several pebbles rattled atop the platform and a tram rumbled into the makeshift station. It screeched to a stop and slid a few centimeters past our concrete slab. A hand rested on my shoulder. Pops stood behind me, grim.

"Be safe," he said.

My mind added "be efficient." I licked my lips and nodded. I might not see him again. This was the first mission where we were *guaranteed* to run into danger.

"It is my duty," I whispered, so that only he could hear.

A smile tugged at the edge of his lips and he patted me on the shoulder. "No, it's not. That's the good thing about being free." He turned away, but I could've sworn his eyes were watering.

I let out a breath. I'd see him again. I'd made a promise.

"Enough mushy family stuff. Let's move." Jack grunted and hopped into one of the carts. The rest of us took turns stepping in. The cart was made from slats of rotted wood and a rusted metal frame, and it gave a rickety squeak when the tram pulled away from its platform.

Our guide waved, saying something that might have been "good luck," and the carts sped down the tracks, the closeness of jagged rocks and stalactites looming and flashing around us.

"Watch your heads!" one of the Cubans called cheerfully. He had a short face, and he sat with complete ease in his uniform. If I hadn't seen him joking with his friends earlier, I'd have thought he *was* a guard.

The tram cars clacked and dim red lights zipped by. The fast rumble and clanking chains formed a melodic symphony, a lilting harmony in the rambling track. I closed my eyes. The day had been long enough already.

"Together," Lance whispered, and I nodded.

All of us. We could do it. We could find the car and rescue Tim.

An hour later, the tram shuddered to a halt in front of another platform. The Cubans corralled us along a new corridor until we stopped at a single, bolt-locked door. One of the spies opened it and bright, blue light flooded in.

Community efficiency lights.

Inese linked our hands and turned us invisible. Though I couldn't see the tracks, the darkness resembled safety.

Here, everything was sterile, and a machine's steady hum filled the air. The room was so bright that even the shadows disappeared. I brushed my hand along my vines, bringing them close.

Safe. Secure. Efficient.

Cuba was only a territory, yet the Community's presence was strong.

The spies walked ahead, chatting with comfortable familiarity. Our team followed at a distance, ducking behind tall crates of supplies whenever Inese's invisibility faltered. We evaded a passing guard, then squatted behind a set of flats.

The spies showed their IDs to a guard, and the short-faced guy joked about the long night guarding nothing but food. The real guard laughed and the elevator dinged. I felt a tug on my hand and we moved into the elevator.

Confused by the long wait, one of the guards peered inside.

I pressed myself against the wall, urging my vines to stay as close as possible. The leaves tickled my skin. Short-Faced Guy shrugged and said he'd send down a mechanic to check the sensors. The real guard murmured his appreciation.

The elevator halted a couple levels up. Two of the seven spies stepped out, just enough for the rest of our invisible team to slip through unnoticed.

Beasties wandered the halls and I slowed long enough to stare at a female agile beast crouched on all fours. It sniffed the air. My skin felt sticky and hot, and I squeezed Jack's fingers tight.

So close to being turned into one of those things —

Jack tugged my hand and jarred me from my memory. I shivered, then hurried to keep up.

After five hallways, Inese lost invisibility.

"No visible security cameras," Jack muttered, looking to the ends of the empty corridor.

Inese rested her hands on her knees, breathing heavily. "Sorry, guys.

It's hard enough keeping myself invisible, let alone five."

I winced. Lance had been right. My idea of invisibly infiltrating a beast plant wouldn't have worked so well.

"Any idea where we're going?" Crush asked.

"Somewhere on this level. This is the ground floor, so it shouldn't be too hard to find the outer landing bay." Inese's voice echoed like the screams in the beastie plant.

Here, though, the place remained eerily silent.

Lance stopped. "Something's wrong. Didn't the spies say there'd be more people?"

"The place might be bugged," Inese warned him, holding a finger to her lips. "Be careful what you say. But yes, they did. Maybe their distraction's already started."

"Maybe the Camaraderie's working on that project," Crush suggested.

"If the Camaraderie has something secret going on, I doubt they'll let anyone else see it." Inese started around a corner and quickly drew back. "Guards!"

I backpedaled against the wall and Jack scraped the ends of his claws together. "Guess our luck ran out. All right then. Shoot to kill. Don't want them coming after us later."

Inese and Crush dashed around the corner and their gunfire exploded in the hall.

"Move!" Jack snapped. He disappeared into the fray. I clutched my spear to my chest and uncoiled the vines around my arms. They sprouted thorns. Three of the guards were already dead on the floor, but the ones at the command consoles wore non-combatant uniforms.

I froze. One of the men at the consoles was about Lance's age. He slumped over his computer, making screens pop up at random. It didn't seem fair that he hadn't had a chance to defend himself, though I didn't want my team hurt, either.

Farther back, the guards dropped to one knee and aimed their rifles at Jack and Inese. A bullet whizzed past my shoulder. I ducked away. I thrust my spear at the nearest guard, trying to distract him. He dodged, but I extended my vine around the guard's arm and threw him off-balance. He grabbed the vine in his hand, using his weight to yank me off my feet. My spear skittered across the floor. I crashed to the ground as a bullet shot dangerously close to my ribs and tore a hole through my jacket.

The guard spun from under me and smashed the barrel of his rifle against my head. Lights exploded in front of my eyes. I tried to command my vines with speed, but he rammed my back into the metal desk. My tears blurred the command room's lights into tiny blots, and the beginnings of a headache pounded in my skull. The guard rolled out of reach as I collapsed to the floor. He yanked a knife from his boot and raised it overhead. The headache flared. The knife came down.

My parents would never know what happened to me.

I wrapped my vine tight around his wrist. Sharp thorns sprouted into his arm. The guard screeched. I grabbed his knife from the ground with my other vine, adding my speed as its pommel hit him. He slumped, unconscious. I released his wrist and backed away, dizzy, but the desk behind me blocked my path. The warm barrel of a gun pressed against my skull.

The gun cocked.

A shiver ran down my spine. I didn't want to die—

A clawed hand ripped the gun from the guard and a flap of skin dangled from his mutilated wrist. The same clawed hand lifted the screaming guard from the floor and threw him over the console, and a moment later, I heard Inese's gunshot.

Jack lifted me, his hands leaving bloody streaks over mine. It wasn't my blood, yet I couldn't shake the feeling I'd been wounded. The lights swerved and the floor swayed under my feet. I clenched onto Jack's forearms, staring at murderous eyes.

Not murderous eyes. Resolute, gritty eyes. He was trying to keep me alive.

"You okay, Jen?" Jack asked.

I gulped. "Yeah."

"You're doing good," he said, and released me.

I stumbled and grabbed the console to steady myself. The ringing noise—I had no idea if it came from the gunfire or a concussion.

I tapped the console. "Would they have information here about how they make beasts?"

Jack shook his head. "Not right now, Jen. We take too much time here and we won't get out before this place blows."

I scowled. We had a chance to get information that might be helpful, but we weren't going to take it. The Cuban rebels were going to destroy the place and anyone innocent who was inside.

"Jack?" Crush pointed at the main console as Lance came up behind him, both swords covered in blood.

Lance tossed me the spear I'd dropped. I thanked him and took a deep breath, focusing on my vines. They shed their bloody thorns and curled around my arms.

"Security? Come in please," a voice called over the radio.

Jack cursed, then pressed a button on the console. "Yes, sir?" he asked, his voice cool, collected.

Lance offered me a hand, and together we crowded around the console as a clear, military voice cut through. "There are reports of gunfire from your sector. Is everything all right?"

"Yes." Jack's voice transformed from its gruff, usual state to something orderly and respectful, vaguely reminiscent of Community security. "Just a little miscommunication. We took care of it, sir. Reinforcements aren't necessary."

I winced. Jack's mockery felt painfully obvious.

"Miscommunication? With whom? We don't solve miscommunications by shooting our own people!" The intercom crackled and Jack stamped his foot. "What's your number, agent?"

Jack released the button. "Give me his tags!" He snapped his fingers at the young guard I'd seen earlier. Inese knelt beside the indicated guard and slipped the tags from his neck, then tossed them to Jack.

He flipped the chain in his hand, then pressed the button right as the officer called again. He read off a series of numbers and letters.

"Took long enough," the officer growled.

"Yeah, memory's not that great," Jack said, slipping into his gruff voice.

"Stay put. I'm sending forces to assess the situation."

Jack slammed a fist into the console. "Shoot the damn thing."

Inese happily obliged.

"What next?" Lance asked. He twirled his swords, nervous.

"More guards, that's what," Jack muttered.

A loud, far-off explosion rattled the walls and the screens jittered.

"There's our distraction." Inese hurried us down the next corridor and the next, but like the first ones, these were empty.

Then, in the corridor after that, a beastmaster stood behind several beasties, his arms folded behind his back. Heat flared through me. The beastmaster would get more reinforcements, more beasties, more creatures who'd once been power users like me. Beasties we'd have to kill.

I sped past those beasts faster than they could grab me. I didn't want to keep killing them. The beasts were innocent. But their master? He wasn't innocent.

He dodged around the corner. I skidded after him and plowed into a massive toughness beast. My vines thudded harmlessly against its thick chest.

The beastmaster stood behind them, a radio held to his lips. He smirked.

"Found them," he said.

CHAPTER
THIRTY-NINE

A lithe beast sunk its teeth into my shoulder. Its breath was hot and reeked of blood. I braced my spear between us and struggled, weaving my vines above me and trying to push it off.

The beast dug its nails into my arm. I laced my vines around the beastie's chest. The beast tried to scramble away, but I tightened the thorny vines until it squealed.

The young man cried for help, his muscles rippling under his skin . . .

Blood welled around the wounds in its bare flesh.

Crying, whimpering, his eyes changed from blue to gold . . .

No-no-no . . .

A large fist slammed the wall next to me.

I yipped, then used my speed to lunge underneath the lumbering beast. It raised its fist. The beastmaster grinned. He flicked his hands at a nearby beast with pale, hairless skin. I ran for the other, my spear raised to swat it aside.

The new beast caught the spear mid-swing. I tugged at the spear, but the beast didn't let go. I thumbed the switch. Electricity crackled around the tip in tiny purple arcs, and the beasts' eyes lit up with delight.

Delight?

I ducked, releasing the spear as the toughness beastie swung its fist at my head. The other beast grinned at me, one hand outstretched to the tip. A ball of lightning crackled in its hand, shimmering and reforming as if being sucked from the spear.

For the love of the Community . . .

The beastie barked happily, then sent the electric ball my direction. I used speed and scrambled behind the toughness beast, which howled as electricity arced through its body. It collapsed, skin smoking from the exit wounds of the lightning bolt.

The electric beast pouted and barked frustration, then thumbed the electric button again. I extended my vines, my heart pounding in my ears. Lighting could travel down tree trunks, so I expected it could travel through vines, too.

Thankfully, Inese raced around the corner before I had to prove my theory. Two gunshots, and the beastmaster crumpled. The electric beastie squealed and ran past me with my spear, terrified. Crush bolted into the room, his arms wrapped around a thin, water-soaked creature. They crashed into the wall. Crush stumbled back, shook his shoulders and arms, then let out a nervous breath. The front side of his gray jumpsuit was soaked.

The beast struggled to breathe with its neck snapped out of place. Inese put a bullet through its head. "Let's move," she snapped.

"Where's Lan—"

"Go!"

Three agents wearing black visors and black uniforms ran toward us. Each had a padded, bulletproof vest, a bandolier of heavy cartridges wrapped around their chests, and the rising sun half-cog embroidered in red across their left sleeve.

Crush grabbed my other arm and yanked me to my feet.

I shrieked as a bullet dinged the metal wall beside me. One of the agents grabbed a grenade from her side.

So much for going after my spear.

An explosion rattled the corridor behind us. Inese skidded and reversed directions, then turned us invisible.

"Where's Lance?" I shouted again, trying to follow her lead. My arm felt like it was about to be yanked from its socket.

"He's with Jack."

We raced around a corner, then another corridor, and then Crush thrust me into a side corridor and pushed me too hard against the wall. He clapped his sweaty hand over my mouth as Inese made us invisible once more.

"Any luck catching the rebels?" a woman asked from the intersection at the end of the hall. I craned my head to see the speaker, then blinked. The woman was Lady Black, but unlike the first time we'd met, where she swayed gracefully in a satin dress, she now wore a shining black outfit that hugged her skin and reflected the LEDs. Her hair flowed past her waist, jet-black and silky, while her arms were covered by shoulder-length gloves. At her side hung a long, twisting bullwhip.

Inese squeezed my shoulder. Commander Rick and an elderly male servant joined the lady's side. "None yet, my lady." The commander's voice was strong, likable. He looked the same as I'd always seen him: regal, with cropped, white hair and a neatly trimmed beard. He wore beige leather gloves, and the silver pistol he carried gleamed in the hall lights. "But today's work is complete."

"There is no need to concern yourself with the rebels now, my lady," said the servant. "The Legion Spore is well protected."

"Very well. Please return this to my grandfather's tomb." Lady Black placed a pendant, like the ones the international leaders wore but inset with amber, into a jeweled wooden box that had a small, broken segment at the top. Dried yellow glue peeled away from the spot.

Odd that something so important would be kept in a damaged case.

Lady Winters' charm pressed against my collarbone, and I shifted uncomfortably. If they knew we were here, why weren't they concerned? They were focused on their secret project, obviously, but hadn't they felt the explosions?

The servant snapped the box shut. "Of course, my lady." He smiled and strode past them, carrying the pendant to its destination.

Lady Black sighed. "How is our new recruit holding up?"

"She's cheerful," Commander Rick said shortly. "I am not so sure she can—"

Val came around the corner and Crush's hand tightened on my shoulder. Beside her was a faint, half-visible man with his sleeves rolled past his elbows and a work apron tied over his waist.

I gawked. I knew him. I'd seen him back at the Community's prison. He was the man with all the strange baubles and trinkets spilling from his coat. But the man at the prison had seemed older and wiser than this man here . . . more like the spiky-haired man on the boat. Yet this person still seemed like the man who'd healed me when the airship was attacked, the man with his strange telepathic voice and the sound of clacking dice. Never mind that *this* man had the transparent glow of the dragon spirit. Was he the same person I'd seen elsewhere?

Commander Rick gave the lady a telling scowl. "As I was saying . . ."

Lady Black smirked and tucked a wisp of hair behind her ear.

Rather than the black skirt and Gothic stuff Val had been so fond of, Val now wore Master Matoska's ruby pendant and her own, form-fitted metal armor that accentuated her every curve, revealing most anything that wasn't private. Worse, it sparked. Little bits of static electricity danced over her, glimmering next to Lady Black's outfit. Her hair, once held in thick, dark brown waves, now frizzed.

She was a master of electricity, the one who'd kidnapped Tim. Bile rose in the back of my throat. What had she done to him? Was he even alive?

I started toward them, but Inese's grip tightened on my shoulder.

The red-haired man smiled at me. *I don't believe we've met.*

Terror flooded through my veins. He knew we were here!

I won't tell. I'm curious to see what you do. Besides, I doubt they'd notice you. They're too busy working on our Legion Spore project.

Light projected through him, bluish white outlines that contoured around his figure like the dragon in Japan.

"Thanks for the help back there," Val told the spirit politely. "What was your name, again?" A spark of electricity trickled up her arms, and the spirit eyed her with an air of unspoken concern.

Benjamin, he told her. His thoughts echoed in my head. *Benjamin Calroe.*

Then, bored, he turned to Lady Black. *Are you satisfied with the Legion Spore? It's not a super soldier, by any means, but it is certainly more powerful.*

"Yes, Benjamin," she said as a pair of agents—the same ones who'd been chasing us—passed them. The agents gave her and the commander a nod and continued on their way. "Thank you for your help. Lord Black would have been pleased with your work."

Benjamin tilted his head, the corners of his lips twisting into a wry smile. *I'm sure he would. Let me know if there's anything else I can do.*

Lady Black smiled gently. "Thank you."

He vanished.

"How about you, what do you think?" Lady Black asked Val. She gestured for her to follow, and they continued down the corridor.

"It is a great honor for my family," Val said, her voice fading. "Thank you for letting me join the Camaraderie."

My stomach twisted, threatening to send me to my knees—though seeing the spirit might've had something to do with that. But before I could hear anything else, Crush grabbed my wrist and pulled me along the edge of the wall. My shoulder was numb from Inese's grip, but she didn't let go.

What could we do, really?

Commander Rick was an international military strategist, and though I hadn't studied the individual Camaraderie leaders, I knew Lady Black had a power similar to Lance with his swords when it came to her whip. And Val had her stupid electricity.

Once down the hall, Inese drew us to her side. "I've *seen* him before," she whispered. "The spirit. After the airship attack. And before . . . I know I've seen him."

I started to agree, but Crush stopped in front of a door that had "EXIT" written clearly in one of those red safety lights that the Community had everywhere.

"This isn't it," Inese said.

"What do you mean?" Crush's hand squeezed tight around mine. "This is the landing bay."

There was no indication of a landing bay. Just a single door and its safety light.

The corridor dissolved, revealing a white room with beasties pacing the walls. A huge toughness beast blocked the real exit. A beast with ice crystals dripping from its hands crouched in the corner. A female beastie with fire running along its arms waited patiently behind other beasts with elongated legs and sharpened teeth.

We lost invisibility and Inese cursed.

Behind the beasts, Lady Winters sipped from a mug of coffee. She reclined in a comfortable chair, her attention on the sandy-haired kid on the opposite side of the table. He twisted a light bulb charm between his fingers.

Tim.

Lady Winters had Tim.

CHAPTER FORTY

Beads of sweat formed on Tim's forehead and his whole body shook.
I clenched my fists. Lady Winters was doing the same thing to Tim that
she'd done to me and Gwen.

"Well?" Lady Winters curled her hands around a mug with the
rising sun cog symbol.

"I can't help them," he whispered.

I clasped her charm in my fingers, eyeing the pacing beasts beside
me. Their muscles twitched. The whole place was charged with thick,
palpable tension.

Lady Winters reclined in her chair. "Very well." She glanced at us,
then flicked her hand at the beastmaster. "Kill them. Let's see what this
boy thinks he can do. And bring me more coffee."

"This isn't necessary!" Tim protested.

"The coffee?" She smirked. "Of course it is."

There was a flash of movement beside me and I whipped the thorns
of my vines into an agile beast. It screeched and recoiled, then circled
me, its golden eyes catching the light.

"Nice beastie," I whispered, taking a step back. The beastie growled,
forcing me away from Inese and Crush and closer to the beasts near the
wall.

It was trying to separate us.

The beast lunged. I thrust my vines outward, but the beast crashed into me, kicking and screeching as I skinned my elbows on the floor. I smashed my elbow into the beastie's jaw. Its hind claws tore through my jacket and it snapped at my vines, jerking its head this way and that.

A shot exploded and the beast slumped over me, warm and sweaty. Inese held the other creatures at bay with the butt of her pistol while I untangled my vines from its corpse.

So . . . Lady Winters used telepathy to be heard over the beasties' snarls and shrieks of pain. *What can you bring to the Camaraderie of Evil, Timothy Zaytsev?*

Tim swallowed hard, his knuckles white on the table's edge.

Come on, Tim, I thought. *Help us!*

He glanced at me, his eyes wide. "I can hijack technology. I stole their anti-gravity craft."

"That is of use, yes," Lady Winters mused.

He couldn't have done it on his own. He wouldn't. Val must've used him. She must have manipulated him into stealing the car, just like Lady Winters was manipulating him now.

"Jenna, behind you!" Inese shouted.

I spun around. A fire beast cackled a weird half-laugh, half-bark. A ball of flame roared from its hand, twisting and turning. The fireball spiraled in golden orange streaks straight for my chest. I threw myself out of the way and Tim flung himself into the next chair as the fireball scorched the wall behind him. Lady Winters frowned, glancing to the beastmaster before taking another sip of coffee.

The beastmaster screamed and fell.

Several beasties lay dead, mostly due to Inese's gunfire, but others lay half dead with their arms and necks twisted at odd angles. Crush bowled into the fire beast, not stopping until they collided into the wall. The beastie's head smashed against the metal and Crush stumbled. He rubbed the smoldering hair on his arms.

Lady Winters cocked her head, smirking.

Crush bolted toward her.

She waggled a finger. "I don't think so."

Crush grasped his head and screamed. His feet twisted underneath him and Lady Winters stepped aside. He crashed into the table. Its metal legs screeched as his bones snapped, and the table crumpled against the wall and around his ribs.

Tim leapt to his feet. "Crush!"

Crush curled into a fetal position, his arms cradling his midsection. Blood trickled from his mouth as Lady Winters went to stand above him. "Inese—" he whispered.

Lady Winters smiled.

The ice beastie swung its hand in a wide arc. Hand-length crystals spewed across the room and imbedded into Inese's vest. She hit the floor. I clutched Lady Winters' charm in my fist and extended my vines, ready to kill the leader.

"Jenna, wait!" Inese tried to pick herself up, only to have the beastmaster clock her over the head with his fist.

"There, there," Lady Winters crooned. "Can't be helped. They simply can't stop themselves."

She chuckled, playing with the nail polish on her prissy fingers. Crush stared in horror at something only he could see. His body convulsed, then he didn't move.

His eyes were still open.

Tim rushed to Crush. "You killed him!"

"And?" Lady Winters looked down at Inese and myself, then back at Tim. "You have a lot to learn, child."

Tim's eyes burned with a hatred I'd never seen in him. If only looks could kill.

"I'm not a child," he whispered.

Lady Winters chuckled as Tim's knees buckled and he grabbed the edge of the table. "I see you won't be joining us."

Traitor. I lashed my vines around Lady Winters' neck and added my speed to their growth, letting the thorns grow deep. *Nothing about this is efficient.* Her eyes flew open and she closed her hands around the vines at her throat. She sputtered. Blood trickled down her neck, but I didn't expect her to be dead yet. She'd gotten away from me before. Not this time.

This time I'd check.

"Very efficient," she whispered. She coughed and held out a hand, telling the beastmaster to stop whatever he'd planned on doing.

I kept my vines tight. She'd die soon enough.

Kill. Rip and tear and suffocate. Maim and shred and kill . . .

I started and stepped back, unnerved.

Kill her like the beasts tried to kill me . . .

I gulped, my hands sweaty. I kept the vines in place, then removed Inese's gun from its holster.

"Stand down." I whispered, trembling. I held the gun to Lady Winters' head. A clean shot wasn't like the mangled marks of beasts. A clean shot would kill a telepath instantly.

Cold-blooded, but—

My vines were loose.

Lady Winters placed her hands on the puncture wounds and smiled.

The walls dissolved and she vanished. My pistol was gone. The room was sterile white, covered in Community sayings and posters. One poster read, "Thank you for taking your Health Scan." Another had a picture of the Community flag. Another had the Community's mantra:

> *The Community is safe.*
> *The Community is secure.*
> *The Community is efficient.*
> *This is our duty.*

"Excuse me, sir?"

I jumped as a young woman, about my age, raised her hand. She was dressed in a simple cotton gown, and she nervously sucked her lip. "Do I have theophrenia?"

I looked at my own clinically white lab coat. The nameplate on my chest read "Nikolai Nickleson."

I held a scanner.

Oh no. No-no-no-no—

This was the government facility I'd always heard about, the one where people went if they failed the Health Scan. Plastic lab trays sat across the shiny counter. One had a syringe, scalpel, and a small, locked box of shields. A bottle of adominogen sat beside that, the nasty white pills I'd tried to avoid.

Panic pushed its way through my stomach as I checked the scanner:

Identity: Siri Kerala
Infection: Positive
Suggested Course of Action: Recruitment
Field: Pyrotechnics

This couldn't be happening.

I rushed to the door. The handle didn't budge. I knocked rapidly, bruising my knuckles against the pebbled metal. "Is anyone out there?"

My voice came deep.

"Sir?" She treaded her fingers together. "Can you help me?"

A chill ran down my spine, and I spun around, facing the young woman on the medical table.

Maybe I could warn her.

"You'll be fine," I said instead. "We can administer a treatment that will enable you to live longer than if you are left untreated."

That wasn't what I meant to say!

Siri bit her lip and watched me with wide, scared eyes."What's the treatment?"

"It's experimental, but it has been effective on the field," I said.
Not true!

I clamped my hands on the scanner. My fingers trembled, what little control I had over my own body.

This was like a documentary. No matter how many times I watched it, the little boy always died of theophrenia because his mother didn't give him his pill. And if I didn't stop this memory, Siri would be turned into a fire beastie and killed by a mech, or a rebel or —

Or me.

All those beasts I'd wounded or killed . . .

Yes, Lady Winters crooned. *They had a chance to live a little longer, to make the Community safer, but you killed them.*

"Stop this!"

If only you would admit to their usefulness. You have the makings of an efficient leader, Jenny. Just like your grandfather. He was such a perfectionist. Too bad he didn't have the heart for his work.

I tucked the clipboard into the crook of my arm. "Commander Rick's mission would be impossible without the help of an army," I told Siri. "We need soldiers, and it is an honor to be recruited." I smiled. She'd need to see confidence, and maybe I wouldn't have to persuade her.

It was better that way.

Siri lowered her eyes. "You want me to be a soldier?"

"We can't administer the treatment you need in the Community. There's a chance that the disease will mutate. However, as a soldier, you might help the commander achieve world peace."

Part of me regretted suggesting this. The treatment wasn't pleasant. Not even a treatment, when it came down to it.

"Are there any other options?"

"No," I said, though that was a lie. The box and syringe and a minor surgery would return her safe to the Community. She'd be fine, a legitimately healthy citizen.

But those weren't my orders.

"Personally, I recommend joining Commander Rick's army. You could even work in pyrotechnics," I suggested, focusing on her willingness to join.

Her eyes brightened."Really? I've always wanted to play with fire. But it isn't safe," she added quickly.

I smiled, gently easing my charm over her, and then picked up the recruitment papers. "Sign these and we can begin."

She took the papers and pen, eagerly signing the condemning fields.

"Thank you, sir. The Community is safe." She handed them back.

"It is our duty." I took the papers and she scuttled outside, escorted by a waiting guard. He closed the door behind her.

I sighed. The treatment—the process—almost always resulted in a loss of personality. But if Miss Black's training went well, I might convince her grandfather that my powers were better suited elsewhere.

I paused at the mirror hanging on the wall. My reflection revealed a young man with dark brown hair and eyes.

This is your future, Jenny. To be a leader, just like him.

Fear clenched in my stomach and the reflection morphed into the face of Lady Winters, the reserved, efficient leader I'd always known, with her strict business suit and pale, wrinkled face. She looked calm and reserved compared to the harsh reality Brainmaster imposed.

"Interesting, child. You do fit the specifics," my mouth said, and the mirror image mouthed the same. I wore Lady Winters' flowing purple robes, my nails painted a rich gold. I'd never worn nail polish before. It felt heavy and fake.

The sterile room with the Community posters vanished, and screams, pain, terror . . . everything merged into a single condensed point at the back of my skull, the rich cacophony of pitiful creatures being created into something more efficient—

I gagged, reeling in the corner of a gigantic room. A large, metal structure was seamlessly welded at the room's center. Commander Rick walked along the perimeter, guiding beasts along the rails and into a towering structure of open-faced cages. A beastmaster tied their hands and feet to the chairs and the grid.

"Ready, Lady Nickleson?" Commander Rick asked.

I touched the pendant around my neck, rubbing my thumb along the grimy inscription on the back.

I strode past various beasties and humans who'd been tied into place.

"Yes," I said.

"Good. Let's get started."

The yowling mass of metal and flesh was larger than most airships. Benjamin, the enthusiastic spirit leading us through the procedure, held up the amber pendant. *Let's get everything connected,* he thought aloud. *Do you remember the arrangement?*

Lady Black took a moment to tie back her hair. "Yes, Benjamin. I remember." Her voice betrayed irritation.

Commander Rick awaited instruction, his pendant's chain already wrapped around his wrist. I did the same, though Lady Winters clenched the pendant in her fist. We formed a circle with Benjamin at its head, and behind us, the old servant waited with a keen eye. There was something in his mannerisms that made me think he looked at us like he was our leader, not the other way around.

No matter.

This particular procedure would hurt, but it'd make the Community safe. No more Oriental Alliance or Coalition of Freedom to keep us from world peace.

I felt a pang of regret. I'd miss the rebels, even if they wouldn't miss me.

Commander Rick? Benjamin waved his hand for the commander to begin.

Commander Rick placed his sapphire pendant into the circle.

Creation.

Lady Black hooked her diamond pendant to his.

Life.

Trying not to think of what it would happen to the beasties, I fastened the hooks of my ruby pendant onto the little brass loops. This pendant formed the base of the U shape.

Energy.

Lady Winters smirked and placed the emerald pendant on the opposite side of Lady Black's.

Growth.

You'll want to be ready, Benjamin warned her. *Otherwise these three won't be able to withstand the mental strain.*

Her grin widened and I glared at her.

She enjoyed pain too much.

Everyone? Benjamin asked.

"Yes," Lady Black said, but she averted her eyes from the monstrosity. The pendants would amplify her shapeshifting powers, and the beasties calmed with Commander Rick's efforts, but their whimpers filled the huge, four-story room.

"Affirmative," Commander Rick said.

Benjamin turned to me. *And you?*

I cringed. If there was one thing I'd learned about Benjamin, it was that he wanted to see if we could get this whole, crazy contraption to work. I took a deep breath. This wasn't one of the Camaraderie's brightest plans, but I could use my speed powers to increase the efficiency of the others' powers.

"Yes," I said.

The final pendant, binding, was next.

Good. Benjamin placed his pendant in the loop. Energy blasted from the pendants, hurling us against the wall. Waves of radiation obscured my vision of the construct, and the beasties and humans cried in pain.

I let go of the pendant, dropping to my knees and trying to block my ears. Cries—both human and beast—rushed through my head, consuming every feeling and thought. My legs and hands merged with the metal, pieced together from hundreds and thousands of parts. I struggled to move, but I was rooted to the steel beneath. Fire burned in my limbs and a thick skin enveloped me, draping bits of organs and flesh. I lost my sense of touch, but our smell was putrid with burnt flesh and we lost our sight, compiled into one piece, a giant creature with a single thought, a legion of spirits merged into one . . .

We are Legion.

"Brainmaster!" Lady Black snapped, and the cold seeped through my clothes where I lay on the concrete floor. My mouth tasted acidic, like bile, and I shook so hard that I couldn't unclench my fingers.

So much pain, we're in so much pain . . .

"Sorry, *my lady*." Lady Winters smirked. "This is my world now."

The room morphed again. I sat on the lawn outside my parents' house. A Community flag fluttered from a flagpole across the street.

The pain was gone.

I stood, my mouth dry and my lips cracked.

None of this was real.

Can't you see this is real? Brainmaster stood beside me, her hands tucked behind her back, her lips curved into a fierce smile. She wore a business suit and had her white hair wrapped in a tight bun. *I've seen your memories. You idolized me, and I know you have an interest in beasts. Why don't you finish your grandfather's job?*

Fear raced through me and she cackled, her eyes bright. *You will make an excellent leader, Lady Nickleson. Replace Master Matoska. Have your revenge on Val. She isn't truly one of us, but you could be. You would be better for the Community. Miss Salazar could not care less.*

I took a ragged breath. This felt real. But it couldn't be. Could it?

Everything seemed calm. The flag fluttered in the cool September breeze. A woodpecker called overhead and landed on the roof of my parents' house.

The Community was safe — there were no beasts there.

The Community was secure — everyone had a job and a place to live.

The Community was efficient — those who didn't benefit the Community were removed.

It was our duty to follow those ideals and to ensure that the Community continued for all future generations as peaceful as the last.

I rubbed my arms. Real or not . . . "Doesn't seem that peaceful," I said quietly. "Not if you have to kill people with powers to keep it that way."

If you had taken the pill, you wouldn't have panicked. But consider, Lady Nickleson, that you shall have a say in how the Community runs. A strand of white hair dangled across Lady Winters' wrinkled face and she offered me a coy smile. *You might convince us that there's a way to control the world without beasts — something Miss Salazar will never do.*

I clenched my fists. "What about that monster of yours?"

That "monster" is the key to our future. We need never worry about the Oriental Alliance destroying the Community. It's efficient, Lady Nickleson. All very efficient. She sighed contentedly.

I glanced at my surroundings. This was my parents' home. The mowed lawn. The sidewalk. The wooden fence that surrounded the garden.

Lady Winters couldn't have seen this before. She was in my mind. Telepathy and memory steal. According to Pops' dissertation, she could read me like an open book.

But how fast could she read?

"I don't want to be a monster," I said.

My dear, I have far greater plans for —

I took off running. The world blurred. If I was right, and this wasn't real, then as long as she was in my mind, she'd be distracted. That would give Inese a chance to recover and attack. Lance and Jack would have time to find us.

The fence zoomed toward me and I leapt. My speed propelled me the rest of the way over. I crashed on the other side. Chunks of grass and dirt spewed around me. I paused, reorienting myself.

The garden was here.

Most of my plants had died, but a few dark green potato plants and the leafy stems of celery remained. Not much to go on, but I urged them to grow around me, taking whatever nutrients they could and raising the plant leaves high.

They could only grow so tall, but anything would help.

I held my breath, peering through the thick maze of greenery. Maybe she couldn't find me here. Maybe —

Lady Winters tapped her foot behind me. *I'm in your mind, Nickleson. You can't hide.*

My breath caught in my throat.

She wore her purple robes now, her white hair cascading around her shoulders. Her forehead was a twisted set of angry wrinkles. Her eyes narrowed as she looked down her nose.

I propelled myself through the garden, wincing as leaves ripped from their stems and stalks were uprooted. The other side of the fence came fast, but I slowed enough to fumble with the gate's lock and set it loose.

Lady Winters moved toward me like a blurry dot. I flung the gate open and raced across the street. The concrete was a pebbled gray streak. Running, running —

Jim once told me that there was an old saying.

I spun around the corner, skidding. My sneakers burned rubber as I raced the length of suburbs.

He told me, *He who fights and runs away, lives to fight another day.*

A toughness beast loomed ahead of me, sluggish and lumbering. Lady Winters was too slow to make it act. It hardly raised a finger as I skirted around it.

As long as I was running, she couldn't touch me. But my sides ached and my lungs burned. My shirt clung to my back from humidity. I tried to keep running, but my legs cramped and I slowed to a jog, hoping that would keep me out of Lady Winters' reach.

She waited along the sidewalk's edge, patient.

I couldn't keep going, but I had to give my team a chance of attacking her. I tried. I tried to keep running. Then my legs gave out, and I collapsed in the middle of the street. The concrete was warm and gravelly against the palms of my hands. Sunlight peeked through the clouds.

The street melted away. I knelt at the base of the flagpole. Lady Winters stood several meters from me, her lips set in a permanent frown. *About time, Miss Nickleson.*

"Why can't you leave me alone?"

You're an asset, Miss Nickleson. She strode across the sidewalk until her silken robes were only a hairsbreadth away from my nose. Her perfume reeked like flowers long past their prime. *If you deny me, I will twist your thoughts until you heed only what I tell you. You will do my bidding, whether you like it or not. Now, will you come willingly, or must I make you my pet?*

I clutched her charm in my hand, too out of breath to try standing. I knew she wanted me to agree to her terms. That she wanted me to be her pawn in the Camaraderie. But whatever I chose, she would still play with my thoughts. If I gave in to her demands, I would exist only to serve her desire to rule everything.

I glared at her. "I'm not a leader, but I'm not going to follow you, either."

She crouched beside me, taking her charm in one hand and lifting my chin with the other. *Impressive, Nickleson. You know so little about artifacts, and yet you could do so well with the proper training. It's unfortunate that you've already made up your mind.*

I yanked my head away with what little energy I had left. Suddenly my feet were swept out from under me and I slammed against the flagpole. I gasped for air. The pale blue flag burst into flames, replaced by a flag with the Lady of the Cog.

The rising sun half-cog, but with the silhouette of a lady above it.

Your mind is mine, Nickleson. This can be easy or hard —

BOOM!

Fire wrapped around my brain and the memory morphed to her horrible creation; pain from so many others, no sense of myself. Everything was dark and blood-soaked, and the pain—

"That's enough," a voice said.

I stared at a haze of lights, my back against a cold metallic floor. I clasped my knees to my chest. My arms stung where my nails drew blood.

I craned my head. My neck was stiff from the unnatural position I'd been in for Community knew how long. Lady Winters' body lay crumpled on the floor, blood pooling from her forehead. Above me, Tim fired a second round into the lady's corpse.

The beastmaster's jaw dropped. The last ice beastie was nowhere in sight. Tim raised his gun as the beastmaster turned to run.

Another gunshot, and the beastmaster was dead.

CHAPTER
FORTY-ONE

"Tim?" My voice was hoarse, but I didn't remember screaming. Not in real life. "Thank you."

He nodded once, then lifted me to my feet. The door creaked behind us. Lance and Jack limped in, and Lance froze when he saw Tim in front of me.

The floor wobbled beneath me and my face felt sticky from tears. Tim squeezed my hand and pushed a tablet from Lady Winters' robes into my palms, then gently closed my fingers around it. He turned to the security camera at the ceiling's corner. The camera swiveled, a red light flickered on, and the camera returned to its original position.

"You killed Lady Winters," Tim said.

"But I—"

"The Community is safe."

Confusion flooded through me. "Tim—"

He returned to Lady Winters' body and took the pendant from around her neck, careful not to drop it in the blood. "It is my duty." He fastened the pendant around his neck, and all I could do was stand there. A door on the opposite wall beeped and slid open. Tim walked through, still holding Crush's gun. He stared at us, his expression unreadable.

But he had the pendant. If he stayed here—

"Traitor!" Lance snapped. He charged at the door.

"Lance, no!" I cried, but my voice choked in my throat.

Tim flicked his hand and the door slammed shut. Lance cursed, but his eyes widened when he saw me swaying on my feet. He grabbed my arms. "Jen—"

"Tim chose to stay," I whispered. "Why?"

Lance clenched his jaw. "Apparently, because he's a traitor."

I scowled. That didn't explain *why* he left. But, of course, Lance didn't know any more than I did.

"Come on, Inese." Jack shook her shoulder, felt her forehead, then wiped the icy slush off the back of her armor. Inese moaned and rolled over.

"Crush . . ."

"He's gone," Jack said.

Inese stared at Jack, her shoulders slumped. She forced herself to her feet. Jack hung back, his eyes trained on the floor as Inese lifted Crush into her lap and cradled his body in her arms. "Crush," she whispered, but the rest of her words were too soft to hear.

A tablet beeped.

"They're about to give the all clear," Inese whispered, cradling her partner.

Jack nodded. "Time to go. Lance and I found the car."

"I know." Inese nudged Crush's body onto her shoulder. Lance offered to give Inese a hand, but she jerked Crush's body away from him. For a moment I saw myself in her place, and I shook my head of the thought. It reminded me too much of Lady Winters' illusions, and besides, Lance would be carrying me, not the other way around.

Jack led us through the corridors to the real hangar bay. It wasn't far, and the only beast we saw fled.

The sight of the hangar brought memories of fighting beasties and watching Crush die. I squeezed my hands tight, digging my nails into the palm of my hands and checking to make sure I still had Tim's tablet.

It was like Chill dying all over again, but worse.

Lance glanced at me, worried, and I nodded weakly.

We would get through this. We had to.

A warm breeze swamped the hall. Outside, the mid-morning sky was accompanied by chirruping birds and the smell of freshly cut grass.

Lance breathed a sigh of relief. I propped myself against his good shoulder to keep myself steady. Our car was the only car among the transport ships. One of the airships looked particularly elegant in its design: slender, made for comfort and security. The Lady of the Cog was painted on its side, with "COE" painted underneath.

Commander Rick's airship. The one we'd seen before the Health Scan.

"A grenade would be nice," Jack muttered.

Inese's eyes flashed and her grip tightened around our dead teammate. She checked the sky with her pistol, and I half expected flying beasties to spring out and yell "surprise!"

None did.

As for the car, it didn't appear damaged, other than the lingering odor of Val's horrible perfume. It reminded me that Tim had chosen to stay, and I didn't understand why. Lady Winters was dead. She couldn't have been manipulating him now.

But I could almost hear the telepath's laughter echoing across some old, forgotten corridor. A chill ran down my spine. I glanced back at the facility, unnerved.

Inese started the car, and as we rose above the compound, Commander Rick rushed outside, his pistol aimed to the sky. Several beasties loped out behind him. They looked like the tame counterparts of the average beastie; their hair and fur were groomed and they wore simple, regal clothing that gave them an air of sophistication.

Commander Rick fired his pistol and a shot dinged the bumper, rocking us, but then we were invisible. He scowled. His beasties turned to watch a lone flight beast with curiosity, like guard dogs instead of how the other beasties I'd seen reminded me of wild cats.

The jungle rushed away. Behind us, a small section of the huge, white base exploded and caught fire. Flames enveloped the roof and turned the sky orange, but a huge, four-story section at the center of the complex — where the Camaraderie's secret project was housed — jutted out unharmed.

I leaned back in my seat, trying to watch the trees and not wonder which of Lady Winters' attacks were real.

I rested my head in Lance's lap and stared at the bright blue sky with its pale white clouds. Lance stroked the short strands of my hair, but I was too distracted to complain.

Tim was gone. He'd saved me, but taken the pendant.

I remembered his face, the determined grimace I'd never seen on him before today.

Lady Winters must've tortured him.

I took a deep breath, trying to hold back tears, and failed miserably.

We joined the airship halfway to South Africa. Our flight seemed rockier than usual, but no one mentioned that to Inese. She took Crush's body to the deep freeze in the storage room, the only place we could store it on the ship during transport, then disappeared into her quarters.

I paced in my room, noting the overgrown vines that climbed the walls and blocked the light. I didn't trust sleep. Shortly after stepping into a cold shower, I'd found myself in a beastie tank, bubbles rising around me. I couldn't relax. The images from Lady Winters' memories were too strong.

Jim's history book offered me some measure of distraction, but soon after I started reading, the words blurred together and formed the names of the Camaraderie's leadership, then shifted into images of jeweled pendants and shapeless monsters.

They'd called it a Legion Spore.

I could hardly remember the blast of energy that created it, but the awareness of what those pendants could do burned into my memory like the horrible screams of the woebegone creatures in the Legion Spore's formation.

I grabbed Tim's tablet. Maybe there was something in here about the beasts. I searched for any hint of beastie creation or why he'd left. One folder was marked "Legion Spore."

My mind flashed to the creatures in my memory, the feeling of becoming part of a legion . . .

> *The Legion Spore is an experimental project requiring beasts and power users to be merged with a computer AI to form a single entity of enormous capability and power.*

I stared at those words for a long time. The memory was real. The Camaraderie had created this monster.

I took the tablet to Pops.

"It has information from Tim," I said, handing him the tablet. "About their project."

Pops took the tablet and began the file transfer to a backup drive, but he didn't put the information on the mainframe for security reasons.

"Jack told me what happened. How are you doing?" he asked.

"I've been better."

Pops pressed his lips together and his beard twitched. He seemed so much older now. "I'm sorry." He handed back the tablet. "I can look at the information later."

I nodded. I wasn't giving that tablet up. Not yet.

"I had hoped to keep you out of our missions, but they may be much worse for you soon," he said.

"How much worse can this get? Tim just left us and Crush is dead."

I didn't tell him what Lady Winters had done. Something about the memories seemed too private, too uncomfortable to share. I rubbed her charm between my fingers, using it to distract myself.

I could get rid of the charm now that Lady Winters was dead. But I wanted to keep it as a reminder of what had transpired so that I wouldn't forget the evil she had created.

"The Camaraderie escaped, and the Cuban Resistance failed," Pops said softly.

"That's not much different than before," I said.

Pops glanced at the picture hanging on his wall. Dark brown hair, dark brown eyes. Same as Lady Winters' memory.

My face flushed with heat, and Lady Winters' identity charm pricked my fingers as I wrapped my hand around it.

Pops sighed. "You aren't the only one in your family to ask questions. Your father was worried about you. I'm afraid he asked too many questions of his own."

My attention snapped to him. "Are they —" I couldn't bring myself to ask if they were dead.

"Your father has been marked as a rebel. He's in hiding."

"What about Mom?"

"As far as I can tell, she's with him. He knows not to leave her alone in this." Pops returned his focus to the computer console. My heart skipped a beat and my voice caught in my throat.

"Will they — are they safe?"

Pops shook his head. "There is a considerable bounty on their heads. We're holding Crush's funeral tonight so we can find your parents as soon as possible. We should be there in two days."

I clutched the tablet in my hands, my knuckles white. "Thank you," I whispered, and I rushed out the door.

First Crush, then Tim . . . What if the Camaraderie took Mom and Dad, too?

I barged into Lance's room, grabbing him around the waist and squeezing as hard as I could. I needed someone I knew. An old friend. Someone who reminded me of home.

I woke up a half an hour later, clinging to him. I vaguely remembered him sitting me on the bed so he could get comfortable.

"You okay, Jen?" he asked.

I explained what Pops' told me while Lance tried to comfort me. He squeezed my shoulders reassuringly, but my ragged shoulder still hurt.

"Hey, at least your parents care enough to ask," he said.

"At least your grandfather didn't decide who got turned into beasties," I retorted.

"No, but my parents enforced it."

I shivered and snuggled against Lance, wanting to be as close to a familiar human being as possible, then tucked my legs beneath me. "Sorry," I whispered.

He patted my good shoulder. "I know."

❧

I forced myself to pore through files of autographed photographs on Tim's tablet, including the one of Lady Black posed like the Lady of the Cog, and was rewarded with an encrypted document listed under Tim's transcription folder as "Catonian Relics."

I'd heard that name from the man on the boat.

The document listed five places:

> Guatemala. Egypt. Japan. India. Peru. Beware the shifting guardian; the bearer of these five stones shall travel time on the solstice at the stone circle.

"The time stones," I whispered.

Lance looked over my shoulder at the tablet.

"Tim figured out where the last three time stones are," I said, bouncing on the bed.

He frowned. "It's probably a trap to get us captured."

"Tim could've captured us earlier. Why else would he give us a tablet that had the locations of the stones? What if they work?"

Lance just shook his head.

Too soon afterward, the airship landed in South Africa and Pops took us to the cemetery for Crush's funeral. The ceremony was candlelit. Small, rounded white tombstones lined the field as far as the eye could see. The closest ones were marked with the letters "COF," and far across the hill, hundreds of the same marble tombstones extended into the horizon. All white, all engraved with names, all engraved with "COF."

The Coalition's cemetery.

I hugged my arms to my chest. I hadn't noticed this when we were at Chill and Alec's funeral; I'd been too new.

Instead of a list of achievements, like in the Community, friends told stories, regrets, and moments of happiness. The service ended sooner than I expected, when a squad of South African soldiers fired a military salute in honor of Crush's memory. The soldiers left us to wander a room filled with memorial artifacts and stories about Crush's life: little video clips that showed him as who he'd been.

Looking at those, I realized that I'd barely known him.

Lance stood beside me, looking over the same clips and saying nothing. As I moved away from the table, he grabbed my hand. "Together," he whispered, "we'll stop this." He squeezed my hand and let it fall, then returned to the tables.

He'd changed so much.

He carried two swords at his side now, not just for show, but he was still the guy I had to wake in the morning. He might not have his career in security, but he wouldn't have been security.

He'd have been Special Forces, or a beast.

Jim stood by the door, aided by his walker. "Ashes to ashes, dust to dust," he said as I neared him. I closed my fingers around Tim's tablet. Though the phrase sounded like a common saying, I couldn't say I'd heard it before. He gave me a sad smile. "Are you all right?"

"None of the Community funerals are this depressing. They're based on efficiency, not emotion. Does the sadness ever go away?"

Jim shook his head. "No; it gets worse." He telekinetically hovered off the ground with his silver walker and floated through the door, ambling over the dirt until he stopped under a large Adansonia tree, what one of the soldiers called a baobab. The sky was dark, and the leaves rustled and blocked the stars overhead. The flickering made it seem like the leaves were mocking us, but little pinpoints of light shone through.

Down the hill, a shadowy figure knelt by a fresh grave.

I glanced away. Crush was gone, just like Chill. Just like Alec.

Jim pointed into the distance, away from where Inese was mourning. "The sadness remains, but you live, and you fight, and you hope that there is a better tomorrow just over the horizon. I have been hoping for a long time."

I twisted Lady Winters' charm between my fingers, watching the rosy light catch in the jewels' reflections. There needed to be a change in leadership. Or a change in history, if that was possible.

A cool breeze fluttered around us and large clouds obscured the distant horizon. "Soon, then," I told him. "Soon we'll have a better tomorrow."

I'd find a way to make the Community safe on my own terms. No more beasties. No more Lady Winters. No more stupid pills and Health Scans. I'd find a way to oust the Camaraderie, and once I'd found it, there would be no more need for secrets.

The Community would be safe.

Thank you for reading *Distant Horizon!*

Please consider leaving a review at your favorite online retailer. Honest reviews — negative and positive — are helpful for the authors, as they help readers find books they enjoy.

Thanks again!

Find out what Jenna does next in **Fractured Skies** . . .

and read what Tim has planned in **Glitch: Whispers in the Code** . . .

Acknowledgements

First, we would like to extend a thanks to our many beta-readers. *Distant Horizon* went through numerous revisions before we finally had the story we intended to tell. Thank you, all of you. A second round of thanks goes to Kell and Carissa, who read this story at least twice during the six years it took to write and polish this story. It wouldn't be the same without your input.

We would also like to thank Liz Ellis, our editor, who helped smooth out the rough spots.

Next, a thanks to our families, who have been supportive of us throughout college and into our married lives. Their support has helped us reach the point where we are today.

Also, a thanks to our writer friends, both online and off. They've been a real help in both supporting us and helping us hone the writing craft. This includes the Absolute Write community, who saw numerous versions of the first chapter and query letter — which eventually became the back cover blurb, as well as the Writers of Warrensburg.

Lastly, we'd like to thank *you*, the reader. We hope you enjoyed *Distant Horizon,* and our future books to come.

The Community is efficient,
Stephanie and Isaac Flint

About the Authors

Stephanie and Isaac Flint met at the University of Central Missouri, where they soon discovered a common interest in world-building and tabletop role-play games. *Distant Horizon* is their first joint world, the result of a role-play game Isaac ran in the summer of 2010. After graduating with a Bachelor of Science in Photography for Stephanie and a Bachelor of Arts in Psychology for Isaac, Stephanie and Isaac married in 2012. Together, they plot stories, torment each other's characters, and enjoy the occasional cosplay.

Want to read more by these authors?

Follow Tim's story in the *Glitch* saga . . .

Or try a different fantasy universe in *The Wishing Blade* series . . .

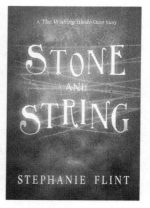